THE ENEMY WAS OUT THERE.
HE COULD FEEL IT . . .

Blake gripped the teak rail below the screen and waited, his heart a mallet against his ribs. He could almost feel some of the men near him, watching him, searching for their own fates in his eyes, from his reactions.

Andromeda hit the side of a cruising bank of solid water and split it apart like a battering-ram, the broken sea cascading along the forecastle and around A turret as if the ship had started to go under. Then, as her stem lifted again and the spray flew past the bridge like tattered sea-birds, Blake saw the other ship for the first time.

A vague, bulky shadow ringed with smoke and etched against a curtain of falling spray from the last salvo. The enemy.

He heard himself call, *"Open fire!"*

The rest was lost in the crash and recoil of the two forward turrets.

*Also by DOUGLAS REEMAN
from Jove*

DIVE IN THE SUN
THE GREATEST ENEMY
THE LAST RAIDER
PATH OF THE STORM
A PRAYER FOR THE SHIP
THE PRIDE AND THE ANGUISH
RENDEZVOUS—SOUTH ATLANTIC
TO RISKS UNKNOWN

DOUGLAS REEMAN

★★ A SHIP ★★
MUST DIE

A JOVE BOOK

First Jove edition published May 1981

First printing

Printed in the United States of America

Jove books are published by Jove Publications, Inc.,
200 Madison Avenue, New York, NY 10016

To Winifred
with love and with thanks

The author wishes to thank those officers
and men of the Royal Australian Navy and
the Royal New Zealand Navy who gave
their assistance

Contents

1

Help from on High

The New Year of 1944 was only two weeks old but already it looked as if it might be one of the hottest on record. The sun which blazed down across His Majesty's Australian Naval Dockyard at Williamstown was so fierce that it had stripped the sky of colour, and the crowded berths and wharves twisted and danced in an ever-changing mirage.

But it was Sunday, and the working parties about the dockyard were reduced to a minimum, leaving the ships to themselves, overlapping shapes of grey steel or vivid dazzle-paint.

The main berth was devoid of movement, the gantrys motionless like dozing storks, the massive wooden concourse all but covered with a litter of pipes, wire, anchor cable and debris of all sorts, a scrap-dealer's paradise. Ships being refitted, others being constructed to fill the unending gaps left after four years of war. Veterans too, their hulls showing hasty repairs, others still displaying their scars. Splinter holes and buckled plates, where weapons and men had once stood and faced their enemies.

But it was Sunday. War or not, the urgency could wait.

Halfway along the main berth was a cruiser. From her sharp stem to the motionless ensign which drooped from her quarterdeck staff she seemed to stand apart from the many vessels around her. Despite her seven thousand tons she had the grace of a destroyer, with her funnels trunked into a single structure to add to her air of power and speed.

At the foot of her brow, where a sentry stood almost asleep in a patch of shade, a lifebuoy hung on a small varnished stand with the ship's name, HMS *Andromeda,* for anyone who cared to read it.

She, of any ship in the Royal Navy, was a veteran in the clearest terms. She had steamed thousands of miles from one theatre to another. Norway, Dunkirk, the Atlantic and finally the Mediterranean, there was no sort of war she had not experienced. *Andromeda* had become famous, another of the

1

Navy's special legends which nobody could explain. Some ships were happy ones, others brought only trouble, even disaster to those who served them. Outsiders scoffed at the idea. How could a thing of steel effect people? But those who knew such ships were content to keep the secret to themselves.

Now, after two years of some of the hardest sea warfare in the Mediterranean, when *Andromeda* had rarely been absent from the nation's headlines, she had come far south, to this dockyard in Victoria, Australia.

The Pacific war was spreading in all directions, and with the United States Navy taking the lion's share of the operations, the Australians were in need of more ships to reinforce their scattered fleet and to replace the ones already lying on one seabed or another.

Soon now, HMS *Andromeda* would be paid-off, to recommission eventually into the Royal Australian Navy, perhaps even with a new name, one more in common with the men who would fill her messdecks and action stations.

The cruiser had been at sea for Christmas, an occasion of very mixed emotions as well as being a far cry from the previous ones she had seen.

For if *Andromeda* was special, so too were her people. Now, some had already left, to be sent home in the next convoy, others to work their passage on a newly repaired vessel needed elsewhere.

On this sweltering Sunday all the remaining members of the ship's company not required for duty were ashore. Again, it was an entirely new experience. No air attacks, no bitter cold or freezing nights, just sunshine and warmth of hospitality which left them breathless.

The ship was very still, with just the gentle murmur of fans and a faint throb of a generator deep in her bowels to show a sign of life.

Right aft in his day cabin, *Andromeda*'s captain sat alone at his desk, plucking his shirt away from his skin as he sipped at a glass of iced gin and considered his own feelings.

Captain Richard Blake was just thirty-three years old. Earlier in the war such swift promotions were compared with other, less demanding times, but now they hardly raised a comment. At the outbreak of war Blake had commanded a destroyer. It was a world he understood and enjoyed, in spite of all the hazards. He had imagined that nothing could ever replace a destroyer in his affection. Even as a small boy he

2

had read about them. The 'greyhounds of the ocean' as they were described by writers who had obviously never served in one.

As the war had increased momentum, and every belief he had gathered on his way up the ladder of promotion had been rewritten by the savagery of battle, Blake had seen his old world crumble. The enemy could not be stopped, or so it had seemed in those first months and years. Precious convoys had been decimated, while on land the British armies had been forced into retreat again and again.

At home, bewildered by the swiftness of apparent disaster, the civilian population had been made to endure air raids around the clock, rationing, shortages of just about everything, with only the tiny vapour trails above London or the Kentish fields to tell of the few who were winning in spite of the odds, or perhaps because of them.

Once more, Blake had been advanced in promotion, 'forced up under glass', as they had called it, and had joined *Andromeda* as her acting-commander. He had been with her ever since, and when her captain, Tom Fellowes, had been killed outright by a bomb splinter when they were escorting a convoy to Alexandria, Blake had been put temporarily in command.

The war had been going so badly throughout the Mediterranean that any change in a ship's pattern could spell disaster. Perhaps there had been somebody in Whitehall who understood about ships like *Andromeda*. Maybe he had served aboard her either in her three years of peace or since then in combat.

But Blake had stayed. Malta, North Africa, Tobruk and back again. E-boats, submarines, dive-bombers and powerful cruisers, they had survived it all together when many, many others had not.

They had fought duels with shore batteries, humped stores and fuel to beleaguered Malta and protected the army's flank whenever they could be of use.

Then, quite suddenly, the balance had hesitated. At a place called El Alamein the army started back along the coast road. And *Andromeda* had stayed with them, until last year when the Allies had taken that first, tentative stab at the enemy's own territory, the invasion of Sicily.

Looking around the quiet cabin it was hard to picture any of it, Blake thought. The clattering automatic fire, the Mediterranean sky pock-marked with drifting shell-bursts and ripped apart by tracer. Screaming dive-bombers, the bridge jerking and reeling to a near-miss, or too often a hit.

Blake could see their faces better than the actual events, or the order of each incident. Yells and cheers, curses and screams as the steel cracked into the cruiser's side. Grins on smoke-blackened faces when his promotion had been signalled and his steward had sewn an extra stripe on his faded reefer, bright gold against the three tarnished ones. Just for the hell of it. A thing for the moment. *Andromeda* was that kind of ship.

The deck trembled very slightly and Blake stood up and crossed to an open scuttle to watch a tug thrusting past.

Three months after Sicily had come the invasion of Italy, a far more ambitious and deadly affair. Costly too, in men and ships.

And then, after all the varied actions, the heart-breaks and the jubilant moments of survival had come that challenge which in hindsight might have been planned for the ship and for himself.

He felt his stomach muscles contract as he relived the moment. A great double column of landing craft, weaving and floundering about as only they could in anything but a flat calm. Each packed with troops, tanks and ammunition, heading for the beaches to join the fighting. Two elderly destroyers trying to maintain some sort of discipline, an even older anti-aircraft cruiser which had looked like a relic from Jutland. And at the head of the unruly flotilla had been *Andromeda*. It had been a Sunday then as now, he thought, his mouth suddenly dry.

Three ships had been sighted to the northeast, closing fast. They should not have been there. The approaches to Italy and Sicily were sealed and patrolled by a massive force of capital ships, cruisers, destroyers, everything you could think of.

The Italians had betrayed their German comrades and had thrown in their lot with the British and American forces. Their fleet, too, was in Allied hands, all their fine, beautifully de-signed cruisers were a menace no longer. At least so everyone had believed.

But the three approaching vessels were Italian cruisers, rac-ing at full speed towards the west to force the Gibraltar Straits and make for Biscay.

Andromeda had faced Italian warships many times, but the same vessels in German hands were something else entirely.

At the time Blake had had no idea of the enemy's intention. All he knew was that the slow-moving lines of landing-craft

4

were helpless, their hastily gathered escort no match at all for the powerful cruisers.

Plenty of other captains had made the same decision as Blake, most of them had not lived to recall it.

With her four six-inch turrets crooked to maximum elevation, a battle-ensign flying from each mast, *Andromeda* had increased speed and had curved away to place herself between the enemy and her vulnerable charges.

What had occurred next was a part of history. It could not have happened, but it did. No single ship, outgunned in strength and size, could take on three cruisers and survive. But she had. At the close of the day, one enemy vessel was on the bottom, the second stopped and unable to move. The third made off streaming smoke, to be sunk the following day by a submarine.

When the *Andromeda* had finally managed to reach Gibraltar there had not been a single cheer raised nor a siren blared to greet her. Down by the bows, riddled with holes from bow to stern, she was barely afloat. At her guns, cooks and stewards, writers and supply ratings had replaced the dead crews who had fallen during the fight. It was a sight too terrible for applause.

In 1936, when the ship's keel had first tasted salt water, they had built well. In a month the sights and horrors of battle were cleaned away, the hull patched, the blackened paintwork redone. In two months she was out of dock, and soon on her way to Australia.

There was a tap at the door and Moon, the captain's steward, peered in at him warily. Chief Petty Officer Moon was an odd-looking man. Gaunt and bony like a scarecrow, untidy ashore, but like a guardsman when he was tending to his duties.

In spite of his mournful face he had a well-hidden humour, and was a good judge of when to do things. Like the time he had sewn on that extra stripe which he had scrounged from somewhere, because he had known they were all at the limit of despair and exhaustion. And the time he had held a young signalman in his arms, had spoken about his early life as a steward in a clapped-out tramp steamer before the war. The youth had watched him entranced while he had slowly bled to death.

'Will you be goin' ashore today, sir?'

Blake shook his head. 'Doubt it. Into Melbourne tomorrow. Get things started.'

Moon nodded gloomily. 'It'll not be the same, sir.'

Blake looked away. *Not be the same*. Nor would it.

Two years in the same ship was a lifetime during a war. He glanced at a painting which hung on one bulkhead. It depicted Andromeda, the daughter of Cepheus, chained to a rock as a sacrifice to the sea monster. With her rescuer, Perseus, on his winged horse charging down to the attack.

Underneath was the ship's motto. *Auxilium ab Alto*. Help from on High.

A young hostilities-only sub-lieutenant, in peacetime a commercial artist, had given it to him as a present. The officer had been killed two days later off Benghazi. When you thought about it, the picture was all that he had had time to leave on earth.

Mood added, 'I'd like to stay with you, sir, when you gets another ship.'

Blake looked at him gravely. 'I don't think I could manage without you any more.'

The chief steward seemed satisfied. 'I've got your best whites ready for tomorrow, sir.' He held up a freshly ironed tunic. 'Can't' 'ave them Aussies thinkin' we don't know how to do things!'

Blake barely heard him. He was staring at the crimson ribbon which Moon had pinned on the white tunic. The ribbon with the tiny cross in the centre of it.

He still could not believe it. The Victoria Cross.

He saw himself in the mirror above Moon's special sideboard. The one where he hoarded his best glasses. He had even features, with brown hair bleached fair by many months of sea-going in the Med. A youthful face. *The boy captain*, one stupid journalist had labelled him.

But it was not the sort of face he would have expected to see on the holder of a VC. He did not know if it had changed him in any way, or might in the future.

Moon watched him and said quietly, 'You *earned* it, sir.' He looked round the cabin and added almost bitterly, 'So did *she*!'

Blake sat down again. Tomorrow he would take up the reins. See the admiral, meet his successor, explain about the ship, what she meant.

He raised his glass. 'Another, please.'

Moon padded to his sideboard. Captain Blake was the best he had ever served, although he had been a bit sceptical at the beginning. So young, so confident. Now Moon understood differently. He of everyone else aboard knew what the captain was like when he was hidden from the eyes of his men.

Blake tilted the glass. A proper pink gin this time. On his own he often forgot or neglected to prepare the drink properly. Always too busy. No time. He watched the sunlight reflected on the deckhead. No wonder Bligh's men mutinied at Tahiti, he thought drowsily. Melbourne must seem just as much of a miracle to his own men after what they had been made to endure.

His head lolled and Moon deftly removed the glass from his fingers.

Then, with the tunic and its crimson ribbon over his arm, he silently left the cabin.

Commander Victor Fairfax of the Royal Australian Navy opened the bedroom curtains very carefully and looked out at the brilliant moonlight. The house was in a quiet, tree-lined road on the outskirts of Melbourne, much like those on either side of it, but to its occupants so very different.

The night was quiet, the house on the opposite side of the road shining in the strange light like the face of a glacier.

Fairfax was thirty-one, a professional to his fingertips. He was naked, and gave a sensuous shiver as the air, cool and clean after the day's humidity, explored his body.

Tomorrow he would join his new ship, the British cruiser at Williamstown. It was always an exciting prospect, even the first times as a younger and less confident junior officer. But this would be different. He listened to his wife's gentle breathing in the bed behind him and felt his heart warm towards her. She was the real difference. They had been married for eight months after meeting in Sydney at a party on Garden Island. A whirlwind and passionate courtship, then marriage with all the trimmings, raised swords, the admiral, the whole lot.

The war had seemed a long way off then, despite the news from Europe and the Pacific.

She stirred and he knew she was awake, watching him in the filtered moonlight.

'What is it, Vic?'

He shrugged. 'I was thinking, Sarah, about tomorrow. *Today*, actually.'

'Come to bed. It'll be all right. We'll manage.'

Fairfax sat down on the bed and touched her bare shoulder, feeling his pain at leaving her, his need of her.

She rested her cheek on his hand. 'Who knows, you might be in Williamstown for months. New captain, new crew, it'll all take time.'

She reached out and ran her fingers lightly up his thigh, touching him, then holding him.

'You *need* the sea, Vic, as much as I need you.'

He climbed in beside her and without words they made love, slowly at first, and then with a mounting desperation which left them spent and breathless.

He lay with his yellow hair across his shoulder, his hand firmly against her spine.

She said huskily, 'What do you know about Blake?'

Fairfax smiled at the darkness. 'A VC, a hero to all accounts. God, his last action reads like something from a film.'

'That all you know?'

'He's young for his appointment. Bit of a loner, someone told me. He's married, but it's on the rocks.'

She snuggled against him, her hand exploring his body again.

'Well, watch your tongue, Vic. Don't put up a blue by asking him about his love life!'

'He'll be off soon, I expect. Back to the real war.'

'You said that as if you resented it.'

'I do a bit. You've seen Sydney. Full of Yanks, all covered with medals, and they've not heard a gun fired yet. If we're not careful we'll be pushed into the side-lines. I joined the Navy for this day and the one to come. Not to end up in a barracks teaching a lot of damn recruits!'

She said softly, 'This Blake. He's not another death-or-glory boy, is he?' She hugged him tightly. 'I don't want to lose you now!'

He grinned. 'Down to earth as usual. You're quite a girl, did anyone tell you that?'

Fairfax held her until she had fallen asleep again. He had almost blurted out his real worry to her. It was so easy with Sarah. They were like one person.

Captain Mark Sellars should have been taking over from Blake. He had seen it in orders. Sellars was a good skipper, probably the best man for the job when you considered that half the cruiser's new company would be as green as grass.

Now, Sellars had been appointed to another ship which was already serving in the Pacific. No new name had come out of the Navy Office's hat as far as he had heard. So who was getting the command?

He closed his eyes, but knew he would not relax until it was time to get up.

It would be interesting to meet a real hero, he thought. He was still smiling as he fell asleep.

It was a ten-mile drive from the dockyard to the Navy Office in Melbourne, and as he sat in a fast-moving staff car Blake tried to build up some enthusiasm for what he would have to do. Nobody stayed with any ship for ever. He had served in almost every sort of vessel in his service life, from being a humble and harassed midshipman in a battleship to a sloop, from her to a destroyer, and then on to a cruiser which had been commanded by an aristocrat who had spent more time with his polo ponies than with his responsibilities afloat.

Blake had learned something from each of them, what to remember and what to discard. The Navy was his world, and with Diana gone there would be nothing else.

The driver, an Australian seaman, said cheerfully, 'Bit different from home, I expect sir?'

Blake nodded. 'A bit.'

The Australian Navy was built on the RN's traditions and experience, but there it stopped. He could not imagine a British seaman chatting with a four-ringed captain at their first meeting. The man's casual acceptance was both warming and worrying. The open-handed, outspoken Aussies would have to learn that war was not always that casual. If you knew and understood them it was fair enough. But in Malaya and Singapore the Japanese army had *not* understood and had won every battle.

The car jerked to a halt in a patch of dusty shadow and the seaman said, 'Here we are. First right, second left.' He grinned. 'Sir.'

Blake walked into the shadowy interior and showed his identity card automatically to a man at a small desk. The man stared at him. 'Go right in. You're expected.'

Blake nodded. There was not much security down-under, he thought. But perhaps he had become too used to it.

He was shown into a cool office where two Wrens were typing busily and their officer was leafing through a folder on the opposite side of the room.

She looked at him impassively. 'Captain Blake.' Her glance moved to his decoration. 'This way, sir.' She was tall when she stood up, her face and hands very tanned, as if she were more used to the open air than an office.

A stoutly built captain, as old for his rank as Blake was youthful, ambled round a large desk and shook his hand.

'Sit down and take it easy.' He glanced at the impassive Wren officer. 'Okay, Claire, you can organize some tea when you get a moment.' The door closed.

The captain said, 'I'm Jack Quintin. I'm sorry to drag you here first, and I know you've an appointment with the First Naval Member of the Board in thirty minutes. However. . . .' He perched himself on the edge of the desk. 'My job is to liaise intelligence between the RAN and your people. I did most of my time with the RN, so I'm the obvious choice, I guess.' He grinned. 'I'd be on the beach with a pension otherwise!' It seemed to amuse him.

Blake said, 'I sent my report about the ship's present strength. There is a list of requirements for the dockyard manager, too. They only did a temporary job after the—' The words seemed to stick in his throat.

Captain Quintin eyed him gravely. 'We all heard. It must have been a terrible fight.' He pushed it from his mind and added, 'Fact is, you will not be leaving *Andromeda* just yet.'

Blake looked up quickly. 'What's wrong?'

'I don't really know. But a full refit will have to wait. Your ship is needed at sea. It's as simple as that.'

Simple? Blake stared at him. Over half the ship's company gone, much of the machinery in need of overhaul, even replacement.

He said, 'I understood that HMAS *Devonport* will be ready for any emergency while *Andromeda* is fitting out?'

Nothing he said seemed to make sense. He was staying in command, but why?

Quintin said, 'It's all top secret of course, but *Devonport*'s gone.'

Blake exclaimed, 'How?'

Quintin spread his hands. 'She was on the long patrol, the Cape Town to Melbourne convoy route. Pretty quiet these days, and anyway *Devonport* can, or could, take care of herself.'

Blake got a brief mental picture of the missing ship. A sizeable cruiser with the ability to patrol great areas of ocean without refuelling. Eight eight-inch guns, aircraft, a powerful force to be reckoned with.

The older man said, 'We received the usual signal, then

nothing. We've mounted a full search, escorts from an incoming convoy, aircraft, the Americans, everybody.' He banged one hand into the other. 'Damn all. Not even an empty raft.'

Blake wondered if he was thinking of another Australian cruiser, the famous *Sydney*. She had fought with a German raider in these very waters just over two years back and had sunk her. But *Sydney* had paid bitterly for her victory. The last that anybody had ever seen of her, including the many German survivors from the battle, she had been steaming away under a pall of smoke. Then she had vanished. Just a battered life-raft. It was as if she had never been. Oblivion.

She had been a modified version of the *Leander* class, like *Ajax* and *Achilles* which had won their fame against the *Graf Spee* at the River Plate. Blake felt the uneasiness stir his insides. *The same as Andromeda*.

'With the Americans building up pressure in the Pacific, and the war in your part of the world taking a turn for the better, we've been left very much alone. Bigger events elsewhere have tended to make us too smug maybe.' Quintin offered Blake a cigarette but then said, 'Of course, you're a pipe man.'

He became serious again. 'Fact is, we've lost trace of several ships in the past few months. Merchantmen sailing independently for the most part. You know the sort of thing.'

'You think the enemy's got another raider in these waters, is that it?'

'Could be.' Quintin looked at a large wall chart of the Pacific and Indian Oceans. 'The last operational raider which had any success out here was the *Michel*. She was sunk by a US sub about three months ago. But that was way up in Japanese waters.' He rubbed his chin. 'We've been in regular contact with the Admiralty in London and someone *very high up* made a signal to us just a few days after you berthed at Williamstown.'

Blake considered it. Even with her experienced and seasoned hands to back up a new company, *Andromeda* was unfit for immediate service. But against that he could appreciate Quintin's and the Australian Navy's point of view.

The next few months were very important for the Allies, even crucial. It was obvious an invasion would be launched against Occupied France while the armies continued to push up through Italy from the south.

Every man, ship, tank and gun would be vital. There would

be no second chance. It had to come off. If they missed it when the European weather improved they would have to wait another year. In Russia the German armies now on the defensive might regroup and push through yet again. In the snow and misery of the Russian front, despite the horrifying casualty lists, they had already achieved a brutal but significant record.

And in two world wars the Germans had learned to make good use of commerce raiders. There was no better way of disrupting the supply routes and making convoys take longer diversions to avoid attack. Equally important, the fact that a raider was known to be at large necessitated the deployment of large numbers of warships to seek out and destroy her.

If there was such a ship in these vast sea areas, the German command could not have picked a finer moment. Convoys round the Cape with men for the Pacific. Convoys from New Zealand and Australia with supplies for Britain. Hundreds of valuable ships, any one of which might be vital to some part of the war machine.

Quintin was saying, 'Anyway, the First Naval Member will put you in the picture. I thought you'd want me to soften the blow.' He smiled sadly. 'I knew your father. Liked him a lot. A fine seaman.'

The door opened and the Wren officer said calmly, 'Flags is here, sir. The admiral's ready for Captain Blake.'

Blake looked at her. 'Thanks.' To Quintin he said, 'I imagine it's going to be quite a day, one way or the other.' He thought of *Andromeda*'s motto. *Help from on High*. They were all going to need it.

As the door closed behind him the captain said, 'Well, Claire, what did you make of him?'

She brushed a strand of hair from her forehead. 'I think they expect too much. He looks like a man who has been through hell and back.' She grimaced. 'He's going to *love* our Commodore Stagg, I don't think!'

As she left him alone again, Captain Quintin gathered up his papers then let them fall on the desk unheeded.

He had been serving in a British light cruiser in that other, almost forgotten war. That was where he had met Blake's father. Christ, he thought, were we ever as young as that?

As soon as he returned on board, Blake went to his day cabin and opened his new orders.

Moon appeared and said, 'Commander Fairfax 'as arrived,

sir. 'E was down in the forrard magazine when you came off shore. Didn't get a chance to greet you, so to speak.'

Blake sat back in his chair, his mind still buzzing from his interview with the admiral in Melbourne.

Two cruisers were to be used to track down the raider if there was one reported, and be at first-degree readiness to carry out a search in whatever area it was known to be. Simple. A needle in a haystack would be gigantic by comparison.

To Moon he said, 'Ask him to come aft, then send for Number One.'

Lieutenant-Commander Francis Scovell was *Andromeda*'s first lieutenant. A tall, thin officer with a disdainful manner. Of all the cruiser's wardroom, he had been the one to miss the last savage battle. His reasons for being away at the time were not of his making, as he had been sent to North Africa in command of a small blockade-runner which *Andromeda* had caught close inshore during the night.

It just proved you could never be certain of anything. After she had convoyed the landing craft to Italy, *Andromeda* should have gone home for a refit anyway. Scovell was due a command, though God help anybody unfortunate enough to serve under him, Blake thought.

The three cruisers had changed everything. Now the ship was in Australia. The lieutenant who had temporarily taken over Scovell's duties had been killed, and the first lieutenant moved about the decks like a man with some unspeakable disease.

The door opened a few inches. It was Stock, the chief writer.

'Commander Fairfax is here, sir.'

Blake liked what he saw. A neat, athletic man with dark hair and a pleasant smile. Crow's-feet at the corners of his eyes as evidence of prolonged sea-duty and bright sunlight.

They shook hands and Fairfax sat down in the proffered chair.

Blake eyed him gravely. *In at the deep end.*

'*Andromeda* will remain in commission.' He saw the man's astonishment and added, 'What's your first name, by the way?'

'Victor, sir.'

'Well, Victor, in about two weeks we will proceed to sea to join company with one other cruiser. In that time we will take on the necessary complement of replacements, although thank God I still have most of the key ratings and the marines who man X and Y turrets in this ship. But the rest will have to be led, trained, driven, thumped if necessary into shape, all right?' He smiled at Fairfax's expression.

Fairfax nodded. 'If you say so, sir.'

Blake said, 'There will be a wardroom conference of course. Later, before dinner.' He cocked his head to listen to the drumming sound of rivet guns and drills. 'When this bloody row has piped down for another day!'

'A question, sir. Will you speak with the officers, or shall I?'

Blake smiled. 'You will. You're the commander. I've sent for Number One to put you in the general picture, although I gather you've been prowling round the ship already on your own. I like that.'

Fairfax stood up, trying to conceal his mixed emotions.

'I'll get on it right away.'

'Join me for a glass later, Victor. I've a ton of paper to go through. You've not asked me *why* there's such a flap on?'

'I can wait, sir.'

'Well, *they* think there's a raider hunting in this territory. We are going to find her. At least, that is the general idea.' As Fairfax turned towards the door Blake asked, 'What do you know of a commodore named Stagg?'

Fairfax swallowed. 'Very thorough, I believe, sir.'

'You don't like him?'

'I didn't say that, sir.' Fairfax was caught off guard by Blake's direct manner.

'It doesn't matter. We will be under his command.' He smiled briefly. 'Carry on, Commander. There's a lot to do.'

Outside the door Fairfax felt as if he was walking on thin ice. Blake was no fool, nor would he tolerate one.

He saw a thin lieutenant-commander hurrying to meet him. 'Number One?'

Scovell eyed him haughtily. 'Yes, sir.'

'Well, I want you to go over the watch and quarter bills with me. then we'll do a complete tour of all departments, right?'

Scovell drew himself up another inch. 'This is a pretty-well organized ship, sir.' When Fairfax remained silent he continued, 'We've seen a lot of action.'

Fairfax eyed him wryly, knowing they would not get along.

'Sure. But I understood that you missed the really big one, is that right?'

14

Moon, who was passing at the time, hid a grin. Poor old Jimmy the One had put his foot right in it. Serves the snotty bugger right, he thought.

Blake heard Moon whistling as he bustled about in his little pantry.

'It's only a reprieve, Moon. Don't get too excited.'

Moon peered through the hatch at him. 'We'll just 'ave to see about that, won't we, sir?'

2

The Return

Although *Andromeda*'s operational role remained a well-kept secret, the speed of her refit became something of a joke around the Williamstown dockyard.

Dockyard workers, ordnance artificers, engineers and mechanics swarmed over and through her hull like beavers, and Blake could imagine what it was costing in overtime. Other captains complained to the dockyard manager and his staff on the basis of *we were here first*, but without avail.

Ten days after Captain Quintin's bombshell, Blake took a breather to consider the ship's state. They had done well, and Fairfax's part had been invaluable. A second-in-command wore two hats. He had to take charge of routine affairs, from manning to discipline, and at the same time had to present the ship to her captain as a going concern, a team, a weapon which Blake could use with confidence under any given condition.

The new hands arrived and were soon sorted out, notwithstanding a few harsh words from the coxswain, Chief Petty Officer Couzins, to say nothing of Macallan, the dour master-at-arms, who referred to the Australian invasion as being like 'a home match at Glasgow'.

But the ship's company of some five hundred and fifty officers and men were already a mixture long before *Andromeda* had made her Australian landfall. There was the usual backbone of regulars in both wardroom and messdeck, but the rest were as varied as you might expect in any ship after four years of conflict.

The pilot and observer of the little seaplane were both temporary RNVR, while the taciturn navigating officer, Lieutenant Max Villar, was a South African who had served his time with the Union Castle Line before the war. Likewise, the paymaster commander, Nigel Cross, had been a chief purser with the old P & O, and Walker, the sub-lieutenant who ruled over the ship's motley collection of midshipmen, was a New Zealander.

Blake had a few who had been with *Andromeda* from the

beginning of those two harsh years in the Med. Bob Weir, the commander (E), who had managed to keep the shafts turning no matter what had been happening on the decks above his roaring world of machinery and noise. Lieutenant Gregory Palliser, the gunnery officer, had begun in charge of B turret and had been about the only man left in one piece after the last fight.

By and large they were a good company, and what Blake had seen of the newcomers he had also liked. There had been the usual banter between the Aussies and the Poms, but that would pass. It would have to if they wanted to stay afloat. Apart from Fairfax, there were a couple of Australian lieutenants, some petty officers and over two hundred and fifty ratings.

Quintin had left the ship and her frantic preparations well alone, and the admiral had contented himself with a mere handful of signals, when even his curiosity over their progress must have been at bursting point.

During the forenoon of the tenth day Blake was standing on the upper bridge with Fairfax and the engineer commander. It was like being on a sun-scorched steel island, beneath and around which half-naked figures bustled about with mysterious crates and sacks which were being checked aboard at each brow by the supply assistants like wary customs men. Above the cruiser the tall gantrys swung and plunged with their own offerings, while hourly the piles of equipment and stores on the berth alongside grew less and less.

Fairfax removed his cap and wiped his forehead.

'Pity if it's all a rumour, eh, sir? All this will have been an exercise of sweat and tears!'

Blake smiled. He had been thinking much the same. No news of the missing *Devonport*, but none of other losses either.

Weir said shortly, 'I'd best get below, sir. My second's a bright lad, but he's not the experience at handling dockyard mateys like meself!'

Weir was a remote man who strayed very little from his engines and boilers. He looked far older than his forty years and had the pallid features of a man just out of prison. Blake respected him greatly and trusted him absolutely. Equally, he understood his withdrawn manner, his inability to join the wardroom's occasional parties and sometimes juvenile celebrations.

Weir's whole family had been wiped out in the first big air raid on Liverpool. His wife, elderly mother and two children.

17

Perhaps, most of all, Weir's need of *Andromeda* was the greatest.

Blake watched him, knowing he should have had leave, even if he had nowhere to go. He had been at it too long, sparing himself nothing. The fact that the ship was still around them was a living proof.

'All right, Chief? Satisfied with her yet?'

Weir looked at him, his deepset eyes shadowed beneath the greasy oak leaves of his cap.

'I'm not sure, sir. It's too soon. She needs a break, like the rest of us.'

Fairfax grinned. He had never worked so hard in his life, but had loved it. The ship's past seemed to be everywhere, as if to defy a man who needed to stop and take a breath.

'Never mind, Chief. If this lot blows over you can leave the ship to us, eh, and be off home for a spot of leave!' He looked away, hating himself for the slip he had guarded against so carefully. 'I—I'm sorry, Chief.'

Weir glanced at him. 'I can see that.' Then he was gone.

Blake dragged out his pipe, recalling what Quintin had said about his being a pipe man. So they even had a dossier on him, down to the smallest detail.

He said, 'Don't take it to heart. You'll get used to it. There's barely a man aboard who's not lost a friend or a relative.' He jammed the unlit pipe between his teeth. 'This *bloody* war!'

Fairfax watched his profile and compared Blake's rare show of anger with his own feelings. This was what he had always wanted. He had already had two shore jobs, the last one in Sydney where he had met Sarah. But all the while he had dreamed about getting back to sea, getting into the war before it passed him by. It was what he had joined and trained for, and he had expected Blake to feel the same.

He knew something of Blake's background. He had entered the Royal Naval College at Dartmouth at the tender age of twelve, and came from a sea-going family which went back two hundred years. His father had been badly wounded, not during the last war, but during a riot when he had been serving in a gunboat on the China Station. Fairfax had also heard that the old man was unable to cope any more, his mind crumbled beyond repair.

Fairfax looked at him, wondering if he was anything like his father. A good face, firm chin, blue eyes which might have

18

seemed dreamy but for a slight hardness, as if he were finding it difficult to appear at ease.

Sarah would like him, he thought. Not in the least stuck-up like some of them.

Blake said, 'We'll take a stroll round the ship. See and be seen. I have an uneasy feeling that peace is about to be shattered.' He looked at his companion and shrugged. 'Just a hunch.'

Later, as he was finishing his lunch alone in his quarters, Blake thought about Fairfax. A bit too eager, not good at hiding his feelings . . . yet. But he liked him. When they were called to give battle Fairfax would be the man to take command if the worst happened. He grimaced at his grim mood and thought suddenly of Diana. What was she doing at this moment? He tried to accept it, show it no longer hurt. But he could not, and it did.

He heard the marine sentry in the outer flat moving his boots and knew a visitor was about to appear.

It was Villar, the navigating officer, a tanned, tough-looking lieutenant with an Afrikaans accent you could slice with a knife. He was wearing the sword-belt of OOD.

'Yes, Pilot?'

Villar said, 'Signal from Melbourne, sir. Commodore Stagg will arrive on board this afternoon at six bells.'

He watched curiously as Blake said, 'I was expecting something, but not this exactly.' He smiled. 'Tell the commander, would you, Pilot? Better pass the word to the marines, too. Farleigh will enjoy a visit. Bags of bull.'

Farleigh was *Andromeda*'s debonair captain of marines.

Blake added, 'But otherwise no change. We will work ship as usual.'

Villar marched out and Blake pushed his plate away, the meal only half eaten. It was always easy to make excuses. Too hot, too busy, or the war. But he knew better than that. He drank too much and ate too little. He would have to watch it.

He glanced at his locked desk and pictured his folio inside. Commodore Rodney Stagg, Distinguished Service Cross, one-time prisoner-of-war in Sumatra. It might be an interesting meeting.

His harassed writer came into the cabin. 'Beg pardon, sir, but the padre's here to see you.'

Blake sighed. The Reverend Wilfred Beveridge had already

been on to him about the Australian members of the company. There was some confusion about Beveridge's little forms on which he listed each man's religious details. They only showed Church of England or Roman Catholic, and the Australians who were not of the latter faith seemed to have no intention of having their names placed on the other one either. Poor old Beveridge. Known to the ship's company either affectionately or contemptuously as Horlicks, he was becoming a pain in the neck.

Blake recalled him during the battle, seeing his bared head with its sparse sprouting hair as he bobbed amongst the dead and dying. Terrified like the rest of them, but displaying the same determination he would no doubt show over C of E or RC.

'Ask him to come in, please.'

Blake glanced at the decanter on Moon's sideboard. Perhaps the interruption was just as well, with Stagg about to descend on them.

Timed to the minute, a large staff car rolled along the main berth, its driver avoiding the scattered remnants of dockyard waste with considerable skill.

At the top of the brow, Blake stood beside Fairfax, while nearby in a neat khaki line a marine guard waited to honour the visitor.

Blake watched the commodore as he climbed slowly from the car. A big man, even at a distance, his white drill uniform making him appear even more so.

Blake thought of his reply when Moon had told him he had laid out his new white drill for this occasion. He had declined, and was dressed now in shirt and shorts, his telescope tucked beneath one arm.

'No, leave the ice-cream suit for later, Moon. It's too damn dusty on deck.'

Perhaps as he had said it he had sensed embarrassment. So that was it. The crimson ribbon which was pinned to the white tunic was never worn on an open-necked shirt. Embarrassment that Commodore Stagg, his new chief, would have to salute him first as was customary to wearers of the VC? Or was it because he still felt uneasy at being given the decoration at all when so many had died for it?

Captain Farleigh gave a quiet cough and the line of marines stiffened as if a steel rod had been passed through it.

From the tannoy system a disinterested voice echoed around the ship. 'Attention on the upper deck!'

Farleigh made a minute adjustment to his white helmet and snapped, 'Carry on, Colour-Sar'nt!'

Sergeant Macleod brought his men to the shoulder arms position and stared threateningly at the head of the brow as Commodore Stagg, followed at a respectful distance by a lieutenant, strode up towards the side.

It was impressive, and apparently fairly unusual in the dockyard as several workmen paused to watch. The marines presented arms, the boatswain's mates' calls shrilled in salute and Blake stepped forward to greet his visitor.

Commodore Rodney Stagg was impressive. Broadshouldered, heavy-jawed, with dark brows which almost met above a pair of piercing eyes. The perfect white drill could not disguise his girth and the white collar made Stagg's sunburned jowl even more evident.

Stagg shook hands and nodded to Fairfax. 'You made it then, Commander.'

His accent was barely Australian, Blake thought, and it sounded slightly unreal, like an actor with an unrehearsed role.

To Blake he said, 'Busy ship.' He stuck out his jaw and gave a swift grin. 'Guessed I wouldn't catch you slacking, eh?'

Blake said, 'Would you care to step aft, sir? It's cooler.'

Stagg raised his voice and replied, 'The heat doesn't bother me. But I might stop your men from working if I remain here. And we don't want that, do we?' It was partly jovial, partly something else.

Blake led the way to the after companion while Fairfax ordered the side-party to fall out.

In the day cabin Stagg appeared too large to move about. His cap almost brushed against the deckhead fans as he prowled restlessly around the cabin, peering at framed photographs, the painting and just about everything else.

Moon appeared in the opposite door and took his cap from him. Surprisingly, Stagg had thick, iron-grey hair, all bunched to the top of his head like a copse.

'Would you like a gin, sir?'

Stagg grinned. He had strong teeth, again big and powerful. 'Why not?' He breathed deeply. 'God, the smell of a ship. It's worth ten of anything. A good ship, she's right.'

Moon asked dolefully, 'What will you take, sir?'

21

'Brandy an' ice.' He chuckled at some secret joke. 'Works wonders.'

Blake took his pink gin and regarded Stagg over his glass. 'Here's to us, sir.'

Stagg downed his drink with a nod. 'This raider.' He leaned forward in the chair, his gilt buttons tugging in protest. '*Our* raider. What d'you think about her, er, Richard?'

'I've studied the reports, sir, the past sinkings and cruises of other commerce raiders, but I don't see—'

Stagg waved his empty glass at Moon. 'Of course you don't see. This one's quite different. A wily bastard.' He rubbed his hands together noisily. 'I knew Pete Costello well, he commanded *Devonport*, by the way. Nice enough chap, but too careless, too *easy*.'

Blake's mind hung on the words *knew* and *commanded*. Stagg had obviously written off the other cruiser from the start.

'There are quite a few like that, these days.' Stagg's eyes momentarily lost their sharpness. 'It was all quite different before. In Malaya and Singapore when the war separated the so-called gentlemen from those with guts! Oh yes, it was all different. Nothing was too good for the servicemen when those soft bastards thought their precious skins were in danger, when before they wouldn't let a poor Aussie soldier or sailor into an hotel for a glass, did you know that?' He did not wait for reply. 'But people soon forget. Now the Yanks are in it, though not from choice,' he wagged his glass at Blake, 'as *I'm* always telling 'em. Jerry's taking a few reverses for a change, and even the bloody Russians have got their fingers out at last.'

Blake sat back carefully. Stagg's brisk, savage summings-up left no space for argument.

'Pete Costello must have been swanning along on that dreary patrol line, thinking of his pension, if I knew anything about him. Well, his widow will get it now!'

Blake said, 'I can see you really believe in this raider, sir.'

The eyes fixed and held him like twin gunsights. Searching for anything which might hint at disbelief or amusement.

Stagg nodded. 'I can go one better. I know who it is.'

He sat quite still watching Blake's reactions. 'Thought that would make you sit up, er, Richard.'

Blake tried to remember how many brandies Stagg had consumed. He seemed to drag at his glass as if his great frame needed it like energy.

He said, 'I think it's amazing, sir.'

22

Stagg stood up carefully as if to test the strength of the deck. 'Thought it would get you. Both the First Naval Member and the Chief of Staff think I'm halfway round the bend.' He patted his pockets. 'Must be off now. Just thought I'd meet you in person before we work together.'

Blake had a momentary impulse to ask him who the supposed raider was. But he suspected the visit had been more of an interview than anything, a test which had not quite finished.

Stagg said vaguely, 'Matter of fact, I was against your staying on in command. Like it or not, and I daresay you enjoy it, being a hero has its drawbacks. This ship has quite a reputation, even out here. Our superiors in all their wisdom want to hold on to the magic until this raider is run to ground. They probably imagine an ordinary, run-of-the-mill colonial is a bit slow on the uptake.' He searched Blake's face and then chuckled. 'Forget it. We'll get along. Just so long as we catch that bastard.'

Blake dropped his gaze. He had been so full of his own problems he had forgotten about Stagg. Taken prisoner when his command was set on fire and beached near the Sunda Strait. Immediately after the fall of Singapore, that was it. Blake had imagined Stagg's ship had been sunk by the Japs. So it must have been a German raider, one of the earlier ones which had worked out of Japanese waters before the hammer fell on Malaya.

Blake said quietly, 'You're obviously very certain about him.'

Stagg's eyes were distant. 'I'll not forget. Ever. He sunk my ship. Then handed me over to the Japs. No, I'll not forgive that one.' He gripped Blake's arm fiercely. 'All those days and weeks I sweated it out and thought about this chance. Now it's coming, and I intend to get my revenge on that murdering bastard!'

There was a timid tap at the door and the Australian lieutenant who had accompanied Stagg aboard said nervously, 'It's time to leave, sir. Your next appointment is in half an hour.'

Stagg said harshly, 'Wait in the car.' To Blake he added, 'He's scared stiff of me.' The grin came back suddenly. 'Can't think why, can you?'

Blake saw the commodore over the side and watched the car roll away in a cloud of dust.

Fairfax joined him by the guardrail and saluted. 'Signal, sir. We're to take on ammunition tomorrow.' He turned to follow Blake's gaze. 'All right, sir?'

'I'm not sure.' Blake walked aft again, his face deep in thought. *Nor, I suspect, was he.*

'I think we've just about earned a drink.' Blake plucked his shirt away from his ribs. It was like a wet rag. Something which Weir and the dockyard staff needed to be done had meant the ventilation fans were switched off. Just for half an hour, the taciturn engineer had assured him. But in minutes the motionless cruiser had become a sweltering oven.

Commander Fairfax, like Blake, looked damp and uncomfortable, and the pile of papers which were strewn between them on the cabin table stuck to his hands whenever he made to examine some particular item.

Three days since Stagg's brief visit, and now, to everyone's astonishment, the work had been all but completed. A holding job, as the dockyard manager had said. Nothing but a lengthy refit would put *Andromeda* properly to rights after her battering.

It was early evening, with many of the ship's company ashore. On the beaches or exploring the coastline, anywhere to get them away from the noisy discomfort of the dockyard.

Fairfax eyed Blake curiously. He knew how hard he had been working and could not understand how he kept going. Every day Blake had held an informal meeting with his heads of departments. Fairfax had never known anything like it. He had expected curt formality, perhaps even arrogance. Blake had earned his reputation, nobody would have been very surprised if he had been a bit rough on those slow to learn his ways. Perhaps that was what had made *Andromeda* into a legend? Or was it the other way round? he wondered.

He said, 'I could certainly use a glass, sir.'

Blake rang Moon's bell and forced his mind away from engine defects, shortages and mistakes. From the irritating fact that no new flying boat had been received to fill the space left by the old Walrus, which had been shot down by one of the enemy cruisers. People made fun of the old 'Shagbats' and asked how a designer who could create a creature as beautiful as the Spitfire could invent such an ungainly abortion. But the flying boat had useful eyes, and could endure the toughest landing before being winched aboard. Now, *Andromeda* had only her fragile Seafox, a seaplane which had been obsolete for a year. He had mentioned it to Stagg in one of his reports.

Stagg had sent the report back, his comment, *Make do*, scrawled across the page like a shout.

Moon padded across the cabin with a jug of ice which was already two-thirds water.

Fairfax asked quietly, 'D'you still believe in this raider, sir?'

'We've heard nothing. Not a single report of a sinking which was not verified. Submarine, collision, bombing, nothing out of the ordinary.' After four years it was easy to see each casualty as a cross or a tin flag on a chart. Not as agony, as flesh and blood.

Fairfax took his drink gratefully from Moon's tray. 'The commodore's always been a bit wild.' When Blake said nothing he added, 'He had a bad time from the Japs before he escaped. The German captain who sunk his command probably had no choice but to hand him over to his little yellow allies. Quite likely he had enough on his own plate at the time to care about a few prisoners.'

Blake had thought about it a lot. He had used the time when he should have been resting to sort through every intelligence folio which Captain Quintin's department could lay hands on.

The German officer in question was a remarkable man. *Kapitän zur See* Kurt Rietz, holder of the prized *Ritterkreuz*, had already commanded two commerce raiders and had successfully sunk or captured over one hundred thousand tons of Allied ships. His daring and infuriating sorties against solitary ships or small groups of unescorted vessels had given the Admiralty headaches from the Atlantic to the Tasman Sea.

He was also an enigma, with just the bare details of his background in Quintin's files on which to build a picture of him. There was always the risk of admiration creeping in to weaken a man's vigilance. Like an old-time pirate, Rietz's deeds were too often remembered for their impudence rather than their cost.

Rietz had once run down on an old cargo liner which had almost turned the tables on him. An impostor, like his own ship, she had shown her true colours as an armed merchant cruiser, and had given the German such a raking that it had taken all of Rietz's skill to creep back to Germany without foundering on the way.

But in all the reports, the eye-witness statements from released prisoners and survivors, there had been no mention of a single atrocity beyond the demands of combat.

25

Blake turned his mind back to Fairfax's comment. He obviously disliked Stagg. It would probably come out later on. Right now there was too much to do for idle speculation, raider or not.

A midshipman, his round face peeling painfully from sunburn, tapped at the lobby door and then stepped carefully over the coaming.

'Yes, Mr Thorne?'

Blake was once more grateful for his knack of remembering names. The cruiser carried eight midshipmen, 'snotties', most of whom had joined the ship after the last battle. To most of them, newly appointed to their first ship, *Andromeda* must have seemed awesome with her scars still plain to see. The gunroom had lost three of its members in the fighting. Thorne had replaced one of them.

'The first lieutenant's respects, sir, and there is a visitor from the Navy Office.'

Fairfax stood up violently, buttoning his crumpled shirt.

'Hell, at *this* time of the day!'

Blake smiled. He had noticed that about Fairfax. Any sort of intrusion, anything which he thought might be seen as a diplomatic breach of some kind, he was quick to intervene. It was as if he were defending his whole country from criticism.

'Send him in.'

The youth stared round the day cabin, his eyes recording everything for later, or for a letter home. The captain's quarters would seem palatial after the gunroom.

'It's a *her*, sir. Second Officer Grenfell.'

Fairfax relaxed slightly. 'Quintin's aide, sir. You met her, I expect?'

Blake stared at his reflection in the mirror and pushed his hair roughly from his forehead. He recalled the Wren officer vaguely. Cool and in control.

She stepped into the cabin and looked at him calmly.

'Captain Quintin sent me, sir.'

Moon bustled forward with a chair, but when he hovered over her with his tray, she shook her head.

'No thanks. Too early for me.'

Blake sat down and cleared his throat. It had sounded like a rebuke.

She said, 'I apologize for coming down like this, sir.' She flipped open her shoulder bag and took out a narrow envelope. 'For your intelligence pack.' She looked round the cabin for

26

the first time. 'Hard to believe there was a battle here.'

Fairfax opened his mouth but shut it as Blake replied, 'There were fifty men lying around here actually. The sickbay was too full to take any more. But it was too late for most of them.' He felt unusually irritated. With her casual appraisal, with his own hasty reaction.

In a calmer tone he asked, 'Shall I read this despatch now, or will you tell me what's in it?'

She looked at him directly. She had nice even features with steady grey-blue eyes. Beneath her tricorn hat her fair hair jutted forward like two pale wings. It was like seeing someone watching you from behind a mask, he thought.

She shrugged. 'Nothing definite, sir. But reports are coming in about a possible incident. A ship called the *Bikanir,* two and a half days out of Cape Town, on passage for Adelaide. An American patrol picked up a garbled distress signal and part of the ship's position.' She touched her upper lip with her fingers, it was moist with perspiration.

Fairfax exclaimed, 'This might be the one, sir.'

The girl said, 'Commodore Stagg is sailing in *Fremantle* this evening. You'll be sent a rendezvous in due course.'

Blake ripped open the envelope and read quickly through the neatly typed paragraphs.

The *Bikanir* was carrying chemicals for industrial use. She was in no state to cross swords with a raider.

His eyes fastened on Quintin's scribbled comments beneath the final paragraph.

Andromeda would be required to proceed to sea without further delay.

Blake could feel the girl watching him. He thought suddenly of Diana, her laughing mouth, her various ways of driving a man wild.

He said, 'Ask the Chief if he can spare a minute, Victor. Better tell Number One to be prepared to recall the libertymen. Just in case.'

It was very quiet after Fairfax had gone, and Moon in his pantry seemed to be holding his breath.

There was a sudden whirr and cool air spilled into the cabin from the fan ducts.

He leaned back in his chair. 'I needed that!'

She said, 'I wish you luck, sir. You and your ship.'

Blake got to his feet. He had wanted her to leave, but her casual simplicity made him want her to stay.

27

She said, 'Must be strange out here for you. After the Mediterranean, and England.'

He nodded, feeling dirty and uncouth before this tall, unsmiling Wren.

'Like being a tourist.'

She adjusted her hat and closed her shoulder bag with a snap.

'I'll be off then.'

Blake made to accompany her to the companion ladder but she said, 'I know the way, but thanks.' She looked round at the painted steel, the lights which glowed from a circular hatch to the deck below. As if she were searching for something. A reason, or an explanation.

Fairfax came back and watched the girl's legs until they had vanished through the hatch to the quarterdeck.

'Bitch!' He swallowed awkwardly. 'Sorry, sir, but she's got one hell of a nerve coming here like the Queen of Sheba or something!'

Blake smiled. 'I suppose you know her, too?'

Fairfax sighed. 'After a fashion. She stays her distance. Hands off.' He hurried on, 'Not that it matters to me, of course. I knew her brother quite well. But he's dead now. Bought it off Libya eighteen months back.'

'I see.'

Blake saw Weir's freshly laundered overalls approaching the door. They were already black with grease to mark the extent of his tour around the engine and boiler rooms.

'Be ready to move, Chief. Early tomorrow is my guess. What's still missing will have to wait.' He thought of Stagg's *make do*. 'If there is a raider, we'll have to keep our wits about us. We've two cruisers for the job, but one hell of a lot of ocean to cover.'

Weir placed a newspaper over one of the chairs and sat down gingerly.

'It wouldn't be the Navy if we weren't expected to do the bloody impossible.' He caught sight of Moon through the hatch and nodded. 'Thank you, a dram would suit fine.'

Blake watched him affectionately. He would never really know Weir. Not in a thousand years. But they suited each other well. More to the point, they both suited the ship.

Fairfax saw their quick exchange of glances. He felt excluded, cheated in some way.

Blake said, 'You can go ashore if you like, Victor. I can

28

ring your home number if a flap starts.'

Fairfax picked up his cap. 'No, sir, I'll stay. I've things to do.' He put his glass on the table and left.

Blake shrugged. 'What did I say?'

Weir showed his teeth. They were uneven and spiky, like a terrier's.

'Give him a chance. He feels out of it. He'll fit in. Eventually.' He tossed back the whisky. 'Hell, I've even learned to put up with Number One after all this time!'

Still at her berth, her shadow leaning over with the dying sunlight, *Andromeda* was content to wait. For her next chance. Her return to the killing ground.

3

Evidence

The ss *Argyll Clansman*, twenty days out of Sydney on passage to Cape Town, faced another bright morning and an empty sea. The water was calm with just a deep swell like heavy breathing to change the hues of its dark blue water. In spite of her clean lines, the ship was pushing up a great moustache of foam at her bows, with the wake streaming away from her powerful screws like something attached to her hull. For the *Argyll Clansman* was a fairly new refrigeration ship, and her holds were packed from keel to deck beams with frozen carcasses, which with luck would be broken into rations for the people in Britain.

The first mate stood on the starboard bridge wing, puffing at his pipe, his nose twitching to the aromas of frying bacon which drifted from the galley funnel. It was still very early, but the boatswain was moving around the hold covers with a party of seamen, getting some of the work done in time to beat the scalding heat of the day.

God, he thought grimly, we'll feel the difference in England. It was winter there, and a bad one too, from all accounts.

The quartermaster said softly, 'Old Man's comin' up, sir.'

The mate turned as the master stepped on to the freshly scrubbed gratings, his binoculars slung around his neck. That was unusual.

'All quiet, Mister?'

The mate nodded. 'Making good twelve knots, sir. We'll be at anchor on time.'

The master grunted. 'I'll not be sorry to see Table Mountain again, believe me.'

A seaman brought mugs of tea to the bridge, and from the radio room came the usual stammer of morse and static.

The master said, 'No more news of the *Bikanir*, I suppose?'

The mate smiled. The Old Man would have been the first to be told. They had had an Australian sloop as escort, but after the garbled distress signal from the *Bikanir* she had gone

30

off somewhere. Just like the Navy. Always dashing about the ruddy ocean and making a show. He sensed the deck's steady tremble under his shoes. The ship felt safe, confident. But with a raider about you could not take anything for granted.

'Smoke, sir. Port bow.' The masthead lookout was wide awake.

Master and mate bustled across the wheelhouse and out on to the opposite wing.

The master said, 'Ship, right enough.' He lowered his glasses, his face worried. 'What was *Bikanir*'s position again?'

The mate said, 'Longitude thirty east. That was all they could pick up. Two and a half days out, that'd be about right.'

The master glanced up at the lookout and down at the maindeck where others had stopped work to peer at the distant smoke. It stood against the sky, unmoving, like a black feather.

'Keep a good watch out.'

Then with the mate behind him he strode into the chartroom.

They stared at the stained chart, the fragile line of their long haul from Sydney to this last pencilled cross of their dawn position.

'We're four hundred and twenty miles nor' nor'-east of the Prince Edward Islands.' The master rubbed his chin. 'Can't be that raider. Couldn't possibly have got down here in half a bloody day.' He looked at the mate. 'Could it?'

The mate shook his head. 'No chance. Even if there is a raider, it's unlikely she's going to hang about and be sunk by the boys in blue. Anyway, she couldn't get down here, as you say.' The Old Man was rattled. Been at it too long. Convoys to America, convoys to Russia, sunk three times already. It was more than enough for a man of sixty-four who should have been at home in his garden.

'Masthead lookout reports that the ship is stopped, sir, and apparently on fire.'

The two officers looked at each other. Just a few days more and safety before the other passage to Britain. There would be U-boats and bombers in plenty for the last part. But in convoy you were with friends, not bloody well alone.

'What d'you think, sir?'

The master's eyes vanished into deep crinkles of flesh. 'Think? Alter course, Mister, but tell Sparks to prepare a signal, just in case. Have the guns manned, and pass the word to all hands.'

He picked up a handset and cranked a handle. 'Chief? This

is the captain. Get ready to shift yourself. There's a ship on fire. Might be a victim of an attack. I'll see what I can do.'

Later, as the sun made the ship's bow-wave gleam like yellow foam, a light stabbed through the smoke.

The first mate read slowly, 'Radio's gone, fire in forrard hold. They need medical help.'

The old captain watched the distance falling away. On the poop his ancient four-inch was already manned, and the one below the bridge was trained across the bulwark, its crew standing up to watch as the other vessel took shape through the smoke.

The second mate, whose jaws were still working on the remains of his disturbed breakfast, asked, 'What ship?'

The master replied, '*Mont Everest*, she's outward bound from—'

The second mate jumped forward. 'Not on your bloody life, sir! I know that French ship well, this one's too big, anyway—' He got no further.

The master yelled, 'Hard a-starboard, full ahead both engines!'

The first mate stood mesmerized until the old man punched his arm and shouted, 'Tell Sparks! Send our position! *Now*, for Christ's sake!'

Telegraphs clanged, and as the quartermaster spun the spokes of the big wheel someone shouted, 'She's hoisted her colours, sir! Christ, it's a Jerry!'

The smoke was thinning away even as the other ship's length began to shorten and she turned slowly towards the *Argyll Clansman*.

The master's lips moved in time with the stabbing light and the fresh hoist of flags at the other ship's yards.

Stop instantly. Do not use your radio.

Through the door he heard the urgent tap of a morse key, the sudden commotion on the deck below.

'Shall I call the engineroom, sir?' The young second mate watched his superior despairingly.

'No. Tell the guns to open fire. Hit that bastard now!'

Two long orange tongues stabbed through the thinning smoke and the enemy's shells hit the ship's side like a fall of rock. A great blast of searing heat burst through the bridge, and where there had been order and determination seconds earlier there was a raging inferno. A few screaming shapes, their bodies in flames, ran through the chaos until they were sucked back again, licked away like so many ashes.

More shells crashed alongside, and the master felt the pressure of the broken screen biting into his chest and knew she had started to turn turtle. Men were shouting and dying, and he heard the old poop gun fire just one shot before it was smashed to fragments by another violent explosion.

There was blood all over the screen's broken glass, and he knew it was his own, although he could feel nothing.

They would not get their meat after all, he thought vaguely. No rations.

Scalding steam shot up the side of the bridge as the sea burst into the boiler room, in the bright sunlight it looked like a fountain.

Then, like his ship, the old man died.

Fairfax stepped into Blake's day cabin, his cap tucked beneath one arm, as he said, 'Ready to proceed, sir.' He could not contain his eagerness, the excitement of the ship coming to life around him. He should be used to it, able to ignore the routine business of getting under way after all this time. Sarah had pulled his leg on that score often enough.

'Like a kid with a toy,' she had said.

Blake smiled. 'Good.' He looked round the cabin. He would not see it again until they anchored somewhere. The sea cabin on the bridge was his place, his command post. From where he could reach the fore-bridge in seconds rather than minutes. 'Has the pilot come aboard?'

Fairfax grimaced. 'Sorry, sir, I should have told you. Yes, he's on the bridge now.' He ticked off the items in his mind as he added, 'Postman's aboard, two libertymen still adrift, but the provost-marshal has got them, er, "in his care".'

'Very well. Tell the shore party to remove the last brow. I'll come up.' He patted his pockets. *A pipe man*. Tobacco and matches, his wallet wrapped in an oilskin folder.

A last look at the cabin and to the sleeping quarters beyond where Moon was busily folding up sheets for the laundry.

The ship gave a tremble. The creature reawakening.

He climbed to the deck above and walked slowly along the port side, past X and Y turrets, the tier of boats, the catapult with its Seafox perched upon it like a delicate bird, the great trunked funnel, smaller guns which had dirtied many a sky with patterns of smoke and tracer. Here was the bridge, dotted at various levels with white caps, intent faces, flags to be

33

lowered or hoisted, gunnery controls, radar, everything which *Andromeda* required to find her way, to seek an enemy, to kill. For if Weir's roaring domain below the waterline was her heart, then the bridge must surely be her brain.

Blake felt the sun, hot already, through his shirt. He put on his sun-glasses as he ran up the next ladder, conscious of the men watching him, the faces he knew so well, many he did not know at all . . . yet.

He had learned several years back that if he was worried about a ship's company it was certain *they* were more worried about the man who commanded them.

He reached the upper bridge and glanced around at the figures who filled it. Villar, the navigating officer, standing high on the compass platform taking a test fix on some object in the dockyard. Boatswain's mates, messengers, a newcomer too, Lieutenant Trevett of the Royal Australian Navy, who was assisting Villar for the moment. Harry Buck, the chief yeoman of signals, portly and red like a toby jug, a marine bugler, two signalmen, each man an essential part, fitting in or feeling his way.

The harbour pilot touched his cap. 'Fine day, Cap'n.' He gestured towards a tug. 'There's another waiting downstream.' He grinned hugely. 'Not do at all to see a Pom cruiser on the mud, eh?'

Fairfax gritted his teeth. 'Hell, another comedian.'

A seaman at a voice-pipe called, 'Brow's ashore, sir.'

Blake climbed up on to the fore-gratings and glanced briefly at the scrubbed wooden chair which was bolted there. How many days and nights had he sat there, trying to sleep, trying to stay awake? Out here, in the sunlight, it seemed like a dream. A nightmare.

'Single up to headrope and backspring.'

He ignored the repeated order and the sudden movement on the quarterdeck. To onlookers on the shore and elsewhere it would seem like a shambles. Men cutting away whippings and fighting with coils of greasy, treacherous mooring wire. On the forecastle, the first lieutenant, characteristically hands on hips, stood right in the bows, in the eyes of the ship. Near him a signalman waited to haul down the jack the moment the ship got under way.

'All gone aft, sir.'

Blake crossed the bridge and leaned over the warm screen.

The tug was ready to pull the stern out. There was no wind to help.

'Stand by.'

He heard the shrill clamour of telegraphs and pictured Couzins, the coxswain, in the dark cool of the wheelhouse with his quartermasters. Unyielding, like the armour-plate which protected the helm, as he had been during every such moment and in action more times than Blake could remember.

A boatswain's mate called nervously, 'Beg pardon, sir, but the W/T office has an urgent signal.'

He was speaking to Fairfax but Blake snapped, 'Read it out, man!'

'Slow ahead starboard.' The bridge quivered and then almost imperceptibly *Andromeda* nudged forward, Scovell's forecastle party hurrying to slacken off the big spring as it took the strain. 'Stop starboard.'

The harbour pilot was waving a small flag at the tug master. Froth surged at the tug's counter and a wire hawser appeared dripping between the two ships as she gently but firmly pulled the cruiser's elegant stern away from the piles.

Through it all the boatswain's mate's voice intruded like a bandsaw.

'Signal intercepted from ss *Argyll Clansman,* sir. *Position latitude 41 degrees south, longitude 38 east. Am being attacked by German raider.'*

Blake watched the shadowed arrowhead of water expanding steadily between the ship's side and the berth's stout piles, the sunlight flooding down to fill it.

'Let go forrard.'

His mind was like ice. *Frozen.* So that he could see and do all these things and still hang on to the seaman's words.

The man said huskily, 'No further transmission, sir.'

'All clear forrard, sir!'

Fairfax said quickly, 'Tell the W/T office to let me know if anything else comes.'

He turned and looked up to where Blake stood high on the gratings, his cap tilted over his dark glasses to hold back the fierce glare.

The ship, lean and beautiful, stood out at forty-five degrees from the berth and the line of bowing gantrys. Perfect.

If Blake felt any emotion or surprise at the signal he had not allowed it to interfere with his ship-handling. Even the harbour pilot was watching him with something like awe.

'Slow astern together. Wheel amidships.'

Blake looked at the funnel with its growing plume of pale smoke. Then down towards the decks again, the white caps of the seamen flowing along either side as if independent of their owners as they hurried to secure the wires and fenders, the strops and lashings, until the next time.

Somewhere a ship had been killed. That last pathetic signal still hung over the bridge like an epitaph.

'Stop together. Cast off from the tug, if you please. Tell her "thank you", Yeoman.'

Villar was crouching over his gyro-compass, his eyes slitted in the sunlight.

Blake said, 'Starboard twenty, slow ahead port.'

He waited for the bows to swing again, saw the land sliding away as if it and not the ship were moving.

'Midships. Slow ahead together.' He glanced impassively at the harbour pilot. 'All yours.'

Blake realized he was staring at the Australian lieutenant and that the man was obviously expecting a reprimand or worse.

Blake asked, 'Trevett, isn't it? Well, I'd like you to help the navigating officer to maintain a special chart from now on. Positions, possible sightings, distances, anything which might help us to get the *feel* of the raider's movements.'

He swung round and added sharply, 'Tell the engineroom, less revs at present.' He saw the harbour pilot's shoulders relax slightly and added, 'She may be a cruiser, but she reacts like a destroyer.'

The man grinned thankfully. 'You can say that again, Cap'n. She's quite a handful.'

Blake raised his glasses and trained them on the shore. On the last jetty he saw a parked car. In the back he recognized the shape of Captain Quintin, but beside it he saw the Wren officer, leaning against the door, her arms folded as she watched the cruiser turning slowly clear of the other shipping and towards the Bay.

Fairfax asked, 'Shall I fall out harbour stations, sir?'

'Yes. We will exercise action stations the moment we have dropped the pilot.' He saw the surprise on Fairfax's tanned features. 'Everything. I want the new hands especially to get their confidence, their bearings.' He gave a sad smile and touched Fairfax's arm. 'We're back in the war, as of now.'

36

● ● ●

Blake felt a hand on his shoulder and in seconds was awake. For á moment longer he looked around the small sea cabin, getting his bearings, putting his mind in order once again. How different from those other times, he thought wearily, and it was still impossible to accept the vastness of this ocean, the emptiness.

In the Mediterranean there had rarely been an hour, let alone a day, without an aircraft sighting, a bombing attack, a rescue attempt for some poor, battered merchantman.

He turned and looked at Moon's face, pale in the small light above the bunk. A cup of tea vibrated gently in his hand.

Moon said, 'Dawn comin' up, sir. Very quiet. As per usual, as they say, sir.'

The door closed silently behind him, but not before Blake heard the shipboard sounds which were part of his life. Shoes shuffling on deck and at gun sponsons, lookouts feeling the morning chill and their own frailty after hours of watchkeeping.

Blake put his feet on the scrap of carpet and felt *Andromeda*'s heartbeat pulsing up through each deck and flat, magazine and cabin. She was making nearly twenty knots, which after her short refit was asking a lot. If Weir was worried he was careful not to show it. He knew what was required and would speak out if he thought necessary.

Ten days out of Williamstown. He sipped the scalding tea and thought about it. Just three days after the *Argyll Clansman* made her frantic call for help there had been another. An old Greek freighter named *Kios,* which but for the needs of war would have been in the breaker's yard long since. She had lost her screw and had forgotten all the rules about security. She had been alone, stopped and helpless. There was not much her skipper could have done but fill the air with his calls for aid.

Then the signal had changed. Blake had been in the W/T office with Fairfax while Lougher, the Australian chief petty officer telegraphist, had tried to hold the feeble contact to the end. It was much like the last one, Blake thought. The *Kios*'s position, she was being attacked, then nothing. He tried not to think about the old freighter's final moments, the terrible realization that the oncoming ship was not help but an assassin. He concentrated instead on the bare facts. That the Greek's position was nine hundred miles east of the *Argyll Clansman*'s. *Nine hundred miles in three days.* That would put the raider's speed at some fourteen knots. But what was the point of it? The German had no way of knowing if assistance was already on its way to the Greek, so why the uneconomical dash, the waste and wear which would be alien to any commerce raider?

He put down the cup and stood up, immediately aware of the ship's regular rise and plunge as she maintained her course and speed. He could even picture her like the old photograph in his cabin down aft. Seven thousand tons, evenly proportioned. Her four twin turrets pointing ahead and astern, the other, smaller guns positioned around her superstructure like guardians. The big, stream-lined funnel above a central boiler room, the bridge, everything which made a ship, a cruiser. And her people, all five hundred and fifty of them, officers, seamen, stokers, marines, scattered throughout *Andromeda*'s hull, some, like himself, just being awakened, although very few would be greeted with a cup of tea.

What were they thinking about? he wondered. Of distant homes, loved ones, lost ones. Some longed to return to their wives and their girlfriends, others dreaded the prospect.

He put on his cap, slung his glasses around his neck and stepped out of the cabin.

Vague figures loomed past him or stood respectfully aside as if to become invisible.

The morning watch had settled down, the keen air over the bridge soon took care of sleep, dreams of bunks or snug hammocks.

Scovell had the watch and was lounging in one corner of the bridge, while his young assistant, Sub-Lieutenant Walker, a New Zealander, stood apart by the ready-use chart table.

'Morning, Number One.' Blake crossed to his chair and climbed into it. The smooth wooden arms felt cold. In a matter of hours they would be like furnace bars.

Scovell moved towards him, his hair ruffling in the air which hissed over the forward screen.

Blake peered ahead, then down at A and B turrets, the six-inch guns overlapping in pairs. It was still very dark beyond the slender barrels, but he could see the white painted anchor cables on the forecastle, the blob of a seaman walking aft with a bucket.

Scovell said, 'Nothing to report, sir.'

Blake nodded and put his unlit pipe between his teeth. By *nothing to report*, the first lieutenant meant there was nothing which *he* could not handle. Scovell was excellent at his job but difficult to work with. Intolerant over carelessness and even small breaches of discipline, and yet willing to spend hours with a junior watchkeeper until he was satisfied with his performance. The perfect first lieutenant. On paper, that is.

'How are they all settling down together, Number One?'

Scovell levelled his glasses above the screen and then let them fall to his chest again.

'All right, sir. I've a few defaulters, but the commander will deal with them.' He sounded bored with it. 'A fight or two, some disagreements over messing, the usual hard-cases finding out they're not so tough as they imagined.'

A voice said quietly, 'Radar wants permisson to shut down, sir.'

Scovell swung on the man. 'What the *hell*? *Again?*'

To Blake he added in a controlled tone, 'May I go and see the senior operator, sir? He's reliable.' He gave a rare smile. 'Which is more than can be said for the equipment!'

Blake replied, 'Carry on. I'll be here until we exercise action at six bells.'

He could almost feel the resentment behind him. But he had kept it up every day since leaving harbour. Action stations, fire drill, damage control, man overboard, the whole book. They could moan as much as they liked, but he knew that they were no way near ready to meet an enemy on level footing yet.

He leaned back in the chair, feeling the gentle pressure of one arm against his ribs and then the other as the ship swayed slightly from side to side. He saw spray flying like spindrift from the sharp stem and imagined the water parting across her bows as she sliced forward.

A good ship, everyone said. And a lucky one. So, resentment or not, he would see that where possible luck would continue.

He heard the sub-lieutenant's shoes moving on the gratings and said, 'Come here, Sub.'

Walker moved up beside him. A slim, dark-haired youth of nineteen, he would be a good example for the unruly midshipmen under his care, Blake thought.

Walker came from Wellington, the "windy city", he called it.

'Well, Sub, what do you make of all this?'

Walker shifted his feet. It was the first time he had ever been alone with the captain.

He said quietly, 'I think we'll catch the raider, sir. Trouble is. . . . ' He fell silent as Blake turned to look at him.

Blake said, 'No, go on. Tell me.'

'I think we need a carrier, sir. It's too big an area for us and *Fremantle*. The German might be anywhere, go anywhere.'

Blake nodded. 'True. But to have any success a raider has to cross and re-cross our main trade routes. In the past, the raiders have cut the sea into a grid, each square a rendezvous for meeting a supply vessel or for marking down a convoy for shadowing or attack. The grid is used by their people in Berlin too, rather like pushing model ships about a big chart in the War Room.'

Rather like us, he thought with sudden bitterness. Moved and used.

'Anyway, Sub, every carrier is pure gold at the moment. Cruisers are the best bet, with the range and the hitting power. What we need now is a bit of real luck. Then we shall see.'

Walker, who had been in the ship for seven months, and had survived the last battle without a scratch, said, 'I'd not want to leave this ship. If she were mine.'

Blake looked at him, moved by his sincerity. 'I know. I was of two minds in Williamstown. If you must leave a special ship it's best to break quickly and cleanly. But when my chance came to stay with her I didn't hesitate.' He knew Walker was staring at him but added simply, 'When you get a command, you'll know. You may serve in a dozen ships, but there's always *one* which stands out.' He reached out and touched the quivering steel.

'Able Seaman Evans requests permission to be relieved on the wheel, sir.'

'Very well.' Walker did not want to break the spell while the watch continued around them.

He said, 'My dad was in the last war, sir. At Gallipoli. He often talks about it, puts on his medals on Anzac Day.' He smiled affectionately. 'I'll bet he'd like to be here right now.'

Blake looked away, thinking of his own father. His mother had died shortly after that same war, in the terrible influenza epidemic which had swept the country like a plague. A nation worn down by sacrifice, bad food and despair.

He could see his father as he had once been. A quiet, grave-eyed man. A fine seaman, as Quintin had described him. Now he was just a husk, a mindless being for most of the time, nodding in his chair or pottering in a garden he no longer recognized. There were worse ways of dying than in a fighting ship, Blake thought. His father had been dying for years.

Scovell came back into the bridge muttering to himself.

Blake faced the sea again, excluding the watch, keeping within himself.

He heard Scovell say, 'God Almighty, you're a degree off course, Sub! Wandering all over the ocean like a drunken duck! What did they teach you in your Maori encampment or wherever you come from, eh?'

Walker replied brightly, 'Lots of things, sir! How to do a war-dance....'

'All right, Sub,' Scovell interrupted heavily, 'I can manage without the humour at this hour, thank you!'

Blake smiled. Walker would do all right. More to the point, Scovell was man enough to know it.

As sunlight spilled over the horizon and brought life and colour to the ship and the sea around her, the gongs jangled like mad things and the tannoy bellowed, 'Hands to exercise action!'

The bridge shook with feet stampeding up ladders and through doors. Hatches clanged shut, clips rammed home, while voice-pipes and telephones kept up their insane chorus.

'A and B turrets closed up, sir!'

'Damage control parties closed up, sir!'

'Short-range weapons closed up, sir!'

From end to end, from range-finder to the depths of the deepest magazine, until Fairfax reported smartly, 'Ship at action stations, sir.'

Blake glanced at his watch. Better. A *little* better anyway.

'Very well. Fall out. Port watch to defence stations. But pass the word to all lookouts. The radar's playing up again, so no slacking on reports.'

Eagerly the watch below scurried from their action stations, and with his usual dignity the marine bugler stepped up to his microphone, puffed out his cheeks and blew.

Hands to breakfast and clean.

Blake slid from his chair. Another day.

Walker stood up sharply from a voice-pipe. 'Sir! Masthead reports wreckage in the water, dead ahead!'

Blake jumped back to his chair and stabbed his thumb on the red button below the screen. Action stations shrilled through his command once again, and startled or bewildered, men cannoned into each other in confusion. Some climbing down ladders to get their breakfast were met head on by others rushing to obey the call.

Blake raised his glasses and watched the dark, bobbing fragments spreading out to meet the onrushing cruiser.

Then he said, 'Slow ahead both engines.'

He heard Fairfax breathing deeply beside him, like a man who has been running.

Scovell said, 'Both engines slow ahead, sir. Seven-zero revolutions.'

Blake lowered his glasses and looked at Fairfax. 'Tell the doc to take charge down there. We shall lower two boats, one port, one starboard.'

Fairfax hurried away, glad to be doing something. Relieved that he did not have to watch the pathetic, grisly remains which parted across the bows and drifted slowly down either beam.

A life-boat, its gunwale shot away almost to the waterline. Two corpses lolling inside, covered with oil, through which their blood shone like dried paint.

Bodies in life-jackets, pieces of men.

Blake heard someone vomiting helplessly below the bridge. Another was whimpering like a child, repeating himself over and over again, *'Oh God, Oh God'* until Buck, the chief yeoman, said savagely, 'Keep quiet, that man!'

Blake said, 'Check with Asdic, Number One. I'm going to stop.'

He heard the hum of machinery and knew that the derrick used to raise and lower the seaplane was being prepared to hoist a boat from its tier.

'Nothing to report, sir.'

'Very well. Stop engines.' He did not wait for the telegraphs. 'Send the boats away. Doc will know what to do.' He banged his fist on the warm metal. 'He should, by now.'

He saw Walker staring past him, his face pale despite his tan.

Blake said, 'We might find something.'

Nobody spoke as the first boat, a whaler, shoved off from the side and pulled slowly towards the blackened remnants of a ship and her crew.

Blake saw the plump shape of Surgeon Lieutenant-Commander Edgar Bruce squatting beside the boat's coxswain and guessed that his assistant, Lieutenant Renyard, would be in the other one. Renyard had only joined the ship at Gibraltar. Straight out of medical school. God, he would come face to face with war this morning, Blake thought.

He heard Buck mutter, 'Lucky there was no sharks about. Otherwise there'd be nothing left.'

Blake watched the padre's gaunt figure half running along the port side, peering towards the nearest boat, his wispy hair upright in the breeze, a prayer-book gripped in his hands like a talisman. Poor old Horlicks. Too late again.

'Starboard whaler's signalling, sir!'

Buck trained his long telescope on the boat's bowman who was semaphoring with his arms. The boat had stopped amongst some drifting woodwork and a solitary broken spar.

'One survivor!'

Blake swallowed hard. A survivor. From that filthy, obscene flotsam. It did not seem possible.

He raised his binoculars and levelled them with difficulty as *Andromeda* rocked more steeply in the swell. As if she hated being stopped amongst this horror, like a thoroughbred will rear at the smell of blood.

'Recall that boat, Number One. Tell the chief boatswain's mate to have his party ready to winch the survivor aboard.'

In the glasses he saw the young surgeon lieutenant doubled over the gunwale, a handkerchief jammed in his mouth. It was that bad.

Some of the oarsmen were looking near to breaking point, too.

The other boat reported it had found nothing, and with the oars rising and falling like wings she turned and headed back towards the dangling tackle.

'Boats hoisted inboard and secured, sir.' Scovell's face was like stone.

'Very well. Resume course and speed. Fall out action stations.'

He tried not to think of the men in the shattered life-boat. One had been staring up at the cruiser, his eyes black holes, but seemingly more intense. The sea-birds had done that to him.

There would not be so much eagerness for breakfast now, he thought.

The deck began to tremble again as Scovell reported flatly, 'Both engines half ahead, revolutions one-one-zero. Course two-eight-five, sir.'

Fairfax appeared on the bridge, his face set in a mask.

'They've taken him to the sick-bay, sir.'

Blake slid from his chair. 'I'll go and have a word with doc.' He looked at him gravely. 'So Stagg was right, after all.'

4

Rendezvous

Blake crossed the *Andromeda*'s upper bridge and paused to watch the remainder of the sunset. It was very red, spilling over the horizon like blood, losing its colour in the regular procession of deep troughs to rise again as it reached out to touch the ship's guns and upper works.

The cruiser was steaming at reduced speed and rolling uncomfortably in a quarter sea. Even on the high bridge it felt stuffy, humid. Blake did not need to consult the glass again to know there was a storm about.

He could taste the remains of Moon's last pot of coffee, and could picture the chief steward's disapproval when he discovered the untouched meal in his sea cabin.

Blake felt restless, unbearably so, like some form of illness. When he left the bridge to find solitude in the tiny cabin he needed to be back here. Like a cat which always seemed to be on the wrong side of every door.

His men could sense it, he thought. They kept their distance, showed extra interest in their duties, as they were doing now.

He gripped the chair on the fore-gratings and felt his ship lift and then slide deeply into another trough. Above the radar and range-finder the signal halliards clattered noisily, and the whole structure seemed to be groaning and protesting at the motion. Weir had asked permission to reduce speed. Blake never questioned his judgement. In real need the chief engineer would pull out all the stops, warning markers or not.

It had been three days since they had run down on the drifting flotsam and human remains. Perhaps that was the cause of his restlessness, his despair. Three days while they had waited for the sole survivor to die.

It would have been kinder to let him slip away. Of all the members of the *Kios*'s crew, the survivor had been a steward. A small, terrified Greek who had defied even the strongest drugs as he had relived the agony and the finality of his ship's destruction.

44

Had he been an ordinary seaman he might have been able to gasp out some tiny piece of information, a description of hull design or a hint of the raider's age, but as a steward he had had no understanding of such things.

The *Andromeda* had produced yet another unlikely asset in the shape of Paymaster Sub-Lieutenant Cyril Pim. He was a thin, bespectacled young man whose pallid skin defied the sun, and out of uniform would never have passed for a veteran of the Mediterranean war, let alone a naval officer.

But before joining the Navy as an hostilities-only volunteer, Pim had been learning Greek to help him in his job as a trainee travel agent.

For three terrible days he had not left the sick-bay, but had stayed beside the cot, listening to the dying steward, concealing his horror at the man's frightful burns, his stench and his pathetic belief that somehow, if he kept awake, he would live.

Blake climbed on to his chair and placed his cap below the screen. There had been no more attacks reported . . . yet. This time tomorrow they would rendezvous with Stagg in HMAS *Fremantle*. A pencilled cross on the ocean. Two ships meeting to discuss what they should do next. For all they had achieved so far they could have stayed in harbour.

Stagg would be fed up too, he thought. *Andromeda*'s slowing down would not help.

He let the wind ruffle his hair and clear his mind. He thought about the raider, tried to see her as the poor rambling steward had described her as he had carried some wine to the bridge for his captain.

Big, he had said. How big? The steward had mentioned a ship he had once served in on the South American trade routes. Blake, with Fairfax and Villar, who had done his time in the Union Castle Line, had gone through the manuals and recognition books until they had found the vessel described. If the raider was anything like her it would put her in the eight thousand tons class. It seemed likely. Big enough to cruise over long distances, agile enough to escape if the chase got too hot.

The *Kios*'s master had apparently escaped from Greece when the Germans had marched in to crush the last resistance and drive their British allies into the sea. Perhaps that alone had made him make the last gesture, the final spark of defiance when the enemy had run up her true colours.

The radio message, the desperate call for help, had cost

him his ship and all but one of his company.

The steward had died that morning and had been buried at sea. Pim had read something in Greek, his voice hoarse and faltering, while the cruiser stopped her engines and a marine bugler paid a last farewell. So now there was nobody left from the old ship which had lost her propeller and thought that the rules of the sea had not changed.

Lieutenant Palliser had the watch, and Blake could hear him muttering sharply to one of the lookouts. Palliser, the gunnery officer, had never suffered fools gladly, and after the last Mediterranean battle he had an even harder job controlling his temper.

Once, after a particularly frustrating gunnery exercise, and in front of Fairfax, he had exploded, 'All I can say is, sir, that if we run up against the enemy we'll have to attack stern first! The marines in X and Y are ten times as good as the forrard turrets!'

The two forward turrets, each containing a pair of six-inch guns, were manned almost entirely by Australian seamen. Perhaps Palliser could recall too clearly when he had been a quarters officer in one of them, blazing at the enemy cruisers while the ship seemed to be falling apart around him.

A torch showed itself briefly on the gratings and Fairfax stepped up beside the chair.

'Just finished my rounds, sir.' He watched Blake's profile. 'All quiet.'

Blake nodded. *How different we are.* Fairfax had a wife in Australia. He would probably have to meet her when they returned there. He knew he would feel it all over again. The hurt. The envy. Fairfax had her to think about, someone to wait for him.

He thought of Diana, how she had looked. *I'm leaving you, Richard. You go back to your ship. I've had enough.* Beautiful, demanding, tantalizing. And yet he felt now as if he had not known her at all.

Blake said, 'When we make the rendezvous, the commodore will most likely begin another search. We've most of the information about previous raiders, their grid system and so forth.'

Fairfax replied, 'He'll expect something dramatic.'

Blake twisted round in his chair to survey the bridge. The light had almost gone but he knew the yards and feet of this steel island better than anything.

46

He saw Palliser's buttocks protruding from beneath the canopy which covered the chart table. Lieutenant Blair, the Australian who had Palliser's old station in B turret, was assisting with the watch. It was unfortunate that their gunnery held them apart, but to change them round on the watchkeeping rota would be equally unwise now. A challenge to one, a slur to the other.

Lookouts, each with his powerful glasses moving through a prescribed arc, boatswain's mates and messengers at voice-pipes, one with a headset and earphones, like a man from Mars.

Blake turned back to the sea. They were all out of earshot.

He asked, 'What is this thing you've got against the commodore?'

Fairfax sounded surprised. 'He didn't tell you, sir?'

'I'm asking.'

Fairfax shrugged. 'It was after Singapore. Like a bloody rout, a stampede. Nobody knew where or if the Japs could be held. As it is, they're too close to Aussie for comfort. Anyway, I was a two and a half at the time. Straight from a command course and into the thick of it. I had a fleet minesweeper and two MLs.' He smiled sadly. 'Not exactly an armada. My orders were to probe along the escape routes from Singapore. Thousands of blokes had tried to escape before the sell-out. Sorry, sir, I mean, the surrender. Yachts, old tug boats, even a ferry steamer. It was close on six hundred miles from Singapore Island to Java. Some of the poor devils made it, but most of them were spotted by Jap aircraft and chased by destroyers.'

Blake listened, conscious of the ship noises, the hissing plunge of the stem through each trough. But even more aware of Fairfax's quiet voice as he relived the memory, the scar of Singapore.

'I was supposed to hide during daylight amongst the islands, camouflage nets and fronds from the trees, real boy scout stuff. Any people who had escaped, or got that far only to have their boats shot from under them, I was ordered to collect and carry to safety.' He lifted his chin slightly. 'We did it, too, soldiers, nurses, kids even. God, it was too painful to see their faces when we dropped anchor and found them.'

Blake waited, knowing it was coming, knowing they should not be talking like this.

'Stagg drove a destroyer in those days, sir. He was all blood-and-guts even then, a man's man, a winner. Well, his ship ran into a German raider, I don't suppose either of them expected it. The destroyer caught fire and the German took her company prisoner. It was either that or leave them to the sharks.' He turned away. 'Then something happened. The Jerry landed his prisoners to be handed over to the Japs. But we happened along at that moment and the German made off. I was already loaded to the scuppers with refugees, and then a Jap plane flew over and bombed one of my MLs. I had to pick up what was left of her people. I couldn't cram another soul aboard, let alone Stagg's ship's company. I tried to explain, but it was useless. I even offered to return when I had off-loaded my passengers, but he wouldn't listen.'

'And he was taken prisoner again?'

'Yes. It was all a bit vague, we had other things to think about at the time. But the Japs killed most of Stagg's people, and they made him suffer, tortured him and his officers. But especially him. Somehow he escaped. Went native, and was eventually picked up in a drifting prahu with two of his men. They were dead. But he's never forgotten. He blamed me for leaving him to the Japs, and the German, Rietz, for beating him in the first place. It's an obsession with him, but his record and reputation were enough to put him where he is now.'

Blake said, 'Thank you for telling me. In your place I would have done the same.' *Probably in Stagg's place, too.* 'In this sort of game we've got to know each other. Not just the enemy.'

Palliser stepped out of the gloom. 'W/T office have decoded a signal, sir. *Fremantle* is in contact with a German ship. Pilot is in the chartroom now working out the details.'

Blake slid from the chair. 'Right.' To Fairfax he added, 'This might be an end to it.'

Later, as they grouped round the vibrating chart table watching Villar's strong fingers working with parallel rulers and dividers, Blake said quietly, 'Must be a different ship. Unless. . . .' He watched Villar make another rapid calculation and then draw a pencilled line on the chart.

Villar looked up, his eyes glinting in the reflected lights. 'She's heading our way, sir, with *Fremantle* in pursuit.' He tapped his teeth with a pencil. 'Weather's worsening to the nor'-west of us and the glass is still falling. We might make first contact ourselves if we can increase speed.'

Blake felt the familiar pain against his ribs, the excitement which always lay hidden but ready to move him.

'I'd like to speak with the Chief. Let me have another look at your calculations, Pilot, then we'll alter course to intercept.

A lot will depend on the weather. A full-blown storm would make things difficult.'

He looked up from the chart and saw Fairfax watching him.

The commander said softly, 'All the same, sir, with *Fremantle* in pursuit the German isn't going to hang about. He'll be making good all the speed he can, probably hoping the weather will close down and separate them.'

They both looked at the pencilled lines on the chart.

Then Fairfax said, 'Whereas, *we* will be ready and waiting.'

The navigator's yeoman held out a telephone. 'Engineroom, sir.'

Blake put the instrument to his ear, picturing Weir down there with his roaring machinery and jungle heat.

'Chief? Captain. I think we have a German raider. Can you give me full revs when I call for them?'

'Aye, sir. Just give me another thirty minutes.'

Blake handed the telephone to the young seaman who was like Villar's shadow.

A vast ocean, and two ships heading towards an unplanned rendezvous. *Fremantle* with her eight-inch guns and two aircraft would be a formidable opponent, and after *Devonport*'s loss Stagg would have no use for carelessness.

Thinking aloud he said, 'I'd like to see our airman. We may be able to fly off the Seafox at first light.'

Villar grimaced. 'Pity we don't still have the old Shagbat, sir. I'd not fancy ditching in our little kite, not if the sea gets any worse!'

Moon's doleful face peered around the chartroom door.

'Coffee an' sandwiches, sir.'

Their eyes met. All those other times. The racket of gunfire, the dazzling panorama of burning ships and exploding ammunition. Moon had always been there. Now as then, he would know his mood. The sandwiches would seem like something special. Tea at the Ritz.

'Thank you. I'll come now.'

He looked at the two officers. One Australian, one South African. Chalk and cheese, yet they seemed to sum up what it was all about.

'Call me if you hear anything. Alter course when you're ready.'

He still hesitated, wanting to stay but knowing they could cope. Knowing too they would see his presence as lack of trust. Later that could prove fatal.

As soon as Blake had left Villar snapped to his yeoman,

'Go and get some coffee. Nice and strong, eh, Shiner?'

Alone and separated by the chart table, Villar said calmly, 'How do you feel about the ship, sir?' His voice seemed to hang on the last word as if he disliked calling anyone sir.

Fairfax replied, 'I think I can manage, Pilot!'

Villar spread his hands. 'Sorry, sir, I'm a bit tactless sometimes.'

'You'd never guess.'

Villar grinned unabashed. 'The skipper's nearly over the edge, you know that, don't you?'

Fairfax was about to shut him up here and now when he recalled his own words about Stagg.

He said evenly, 'I know what he's been through, if that's what you mean.'

Villar sighed. 'His wife went off with another chap. Just before we left for the Med. I've met her. Right tear-away, if you ask me.' He saw the warning in Fairfax's eyes and added briskly, 'The captain's worth fifty of her sort. He held this ship together when everyone said we were finished.' For the first time his voice shook with something like emotion. 'He drove us, he carried us, he *led* us.' His mouth curled in contempt. 'Those war correspondents, what did they know? The boy captain, they called him! Boy? *He's a bloody man!*' Just as quickly his voice dropped. 'But he's going to need you, make no mistake. He's like the ship, you can't go on driving, driving, driving without something giving way.'

His yeoman re-entered with a jug of coffee and Villar said offhandedly, 'Just thought I'd mention it.' He grinned. 'Sir.'

Fairfax left the chartroom and paused in the passageway, his hand resting on a clip as the ship plunged and swayed through the outer darkness.

God, they were right about this ship, he thought. A legend. No wonder it was hard for outsiders to understand.

He saw the small door with the word Captain above it and shook his head. *Andromeda* could give, but she demanded much from those who served her.

Blake wrapped a towel around his neck and trained his binoculars over the screen. The sea's face had changed yet again, and with dawn so close it gave an impression of endless movement and power. The *Leander* class cruisers had sacrificed only one thing in their design to appear so graceful. They were notoriously 'wet' ships, and as Blake lowered his glasses to

50

dab his eyes with the already sodden towel he saw the sea boiling up through the hawse-pipes and along the forecastle like a tide-race.

Villar called, 'Steady on new course, sir. Ship's head is three-three-zero.'

Blake waited for Fairfax to join him by the salt-smeared screen. Although the ship was and had been at action stations for a full hour, Fairfax had remained on the bridge. If they were called to fight, the commander's place was well away from the bridge and its open vulnerability. As *Andromeda*'s last captain had once told Blake, there was no point in putting both eggs in one basket. Fairfax would be with damage control, keeping the ship afloat and working, no matter what.

Blake said, 'Soon now.' He peered up at the sky. Instead of blue dawn there was scudding cloud, low and hostile.

Fairfax asked, 'Will we use the plane, sir?'

Blake nodded. 'Otherwise we could lose the German completely.'

He had a mad picture of *Andromeda* opening fire on Stagg's *Fremantle* while the enemy slipped past them both. He thought too of his talk with Lieutenant Jeremy Masters, the Seafox's pilot. A temporary RNVR officer, Masters was the one real odd-ball in *Andromeda*'s wardroom. He was never happier than when he was risking his neck, and as far as Blake could gather he had spent most of his life doing just that. He had flown in pre-war air races in his own plane and had raced cars at Brooklands. He had an outsized private income, but for all that was easy-going and well liked by his men, who nicknamed him Bertie Wooster. His young observer, Lieutenant Jimmy Duncan, another reservist, was his exact opposite. Serious, over-conscientious, and if he had a sense of humour at all nobody had discovered it in the past two years. He and Masters got along like a house on fire.

Blake had explained the difficulty of pinning down a single ship in such an expanse of ocean, and bearing in mind that the fragile Seafox had a maximum endurance of four and a half hours and a range of only four hundred miles and a bit, it did not leave much room for error.

Masters had listened with his face set in its usual attentive and blank mask.

Then he had said cheerfully, 'Piece of cake, sir. No bother.'

Feeble light played across the bridge, the intent faces, the eyes of men screwed up against the spray and wind. The spray drifted over the screens like bits of glass and felt much the same.

Blake said, 'Slow ahead both engines.' He stood upright, steadying himself against the rough motion as he peered aft at the whipping ensign and the tongue of smoke above the trunked funnel. 'Port ten.'

He felt the ship rising to respond to the alteration of speed and rudder, saw the sea's roughness ease away as the cruiser continued in a slow turn to make some sort of barrier to leeward.

There was a coughing roar from aft and he knew that Masters was ready, crouching at his controls while the catapult was swung outboard to meet the wind's challenge.

'Midships. Steady.'

'Steady, sir. Course two-nine-zero.'

'Very good. Yeoman, make the signal!'

The muffled toby jug marched to the screen and triggered an Aldis towards the pulsating seaplane. With a snarling roar it shot along the catapult, dipped, faltered like a stricken bird and then swung crazily round towards the bows. At one time it was so close to the leaping water that it looked as if the sea would snatch it down.

Blake let out his breath slowly. He saw Masters give a brief wave from his cockpit and the vague outline of his observer in his enclosed canopy before the aircraft climbed steeply and headed away from the ship.

'Resume course, Pilot. Increase to one-one-zero revolutions.' To Fairfax he said, 'I think that mad airman does that to give us all heart attacks!'

Fairfax had to raise his voice as the cruiser began to turn again, the sea crashing over the port side in a solid, creamy bank of foam.

'Told me he was in the last Paris race before the war, sir, but had to ditch in the Channel. Quite a character!'

Blake nodded. 'Tell the W/T office to keep a close check on his timing. I don't want to have to start searching for *him* just now!'

He glanced at the men behind him as Fairfax hurried away. Settling down again after Masters' spectacular departure. That was a sailor's life. Boredom, moments of interest, survival or oblivion.

The metallic voice from the rear of the bridge made everyone start.

'Ship bearing Red one-oh. Range oh-nine-two.'

Above them the range-finder and control tower seemed to come to life.

'A, B, X, Y turrets to follow director!'

Below the bridge the two forward turrets purred evenly to port, their slim barrels rising and depressing very slightly as the hidden crews tested their controls. It made the guns appear to be sniffing for their enemy, their kill.

Blake bit his lip. The other ship was less than five miles away. With better visibility they would have picked it up much earlier.

He said, 'Stand by, all guns.' He tried to ignore the regular patter of orders and bearings which murmured from speakers and voice-pipes like an insane chorus.

Scovell, the first lieutenant, had put on a steel helmet and was staring at the sea, his eyes reddened with salt. The helmet made him look different, like a yeoman soldier at Agincourt.

'All guns with semi-armour-piercing *load ... load ... load!*'

Blake snapped, 'Starboard ten!'

He looked aft to watch the two turrets swing their muzzles into view as the marines in X and Y followed the director's orders.

'Midships. *Steady.*'

He heard Villar correcting his calculations, as would the plot operators and the transmitting station behind their toughened armour-plate. Just the slight alteration of course would give all the main armament a chance. He thought of the missing *Devonport.* Had she been too confident, as Stagg had suggested?

Scovell said, 'We'll never be able to speak with the Seafox in this murk, sir. That R/T set has never been any good after the bouncing around it got off Tobruk.'

Blake said, 'Masters will fly back when he's ready.' He glanced at the fat yeoman of signals. 'Tell your people to keep their eyes peeled.'

The toby jug nodded. 'Will do, sir.'

They were a team, thinking as one at times like these.

'Ship bears Red two-five. Range oh-eight-five.'

Blake strained his eyes through his glasses but could see little but churning water and strange, distorted levels of light. There was no sign of the little seaplane. If he had held back from launching it, Masters would be safe on board right now. As it was. . . .

He blinked and held his breath. There it was again. Flash . . . flash . . . flash, vague orange distortions through the spray and feeble dawn light.

Gunfire. *Fremantle* must be close by. He sensed the two forward turrets moving occasionally, the muzzles feeling the range, the elevation and deflection as the unseen ship came steadily towards them.

Blake rubbed his chin. It would be light enough to see everything in a matter of minutes. He felt strangely lightheaded without knowing why. It had to be the ocean, the size of it. To die out here, and it could happen at any moment, did not make any sort of sense.

He snapped, 'Hoist battle ensigns.'

Someone gave a cheer as the first big flag broke from the upper yard, the white bunting with its vivid red cross very clear against the dull clouds.

Blake listened to the growl and crash of gunfire. Heavy weapons, they had to be *Fremantle*'s eight-inch armament.

He stood pressed against the wet steel and stared hard through the screen.

Soon now. Just once more. Like all the other times. No better, no worse.

He heard Palliser's voice again, distorted but intent, over the gunnery speaker.

'Stand by, all guns!'

The boom of explosions seemed to come from the sea itself, and rolled along the hull to be lost astern in the racing screws. Weir and his men would feel it more than most, some would be remembering, staring through the pounding machinery at the curved sides. Waiting for the tearing impact, the sea smashing in to become scalding steam in seconds.

Scovell shouted, 'Signal from *Fremantle*, sir. *Am engaging German raider.*'

Blake tightened the towel round his neck. Stagg was getting his revenge all right. It sounded like a major bombardment.

'Target on same bearing, sir. Range oh-seven-five.'

Blake gripped the teak rail below the screen and waited, his heart a mallet against his ribs. He could almost feel some of the men near him, watching him, searching for their own fates in his eyes, from his reactions.

Andromeda hit the side of a cruising bank of solid water and split it apart like a battering-ram, the broken sea cascading along the forecastle and around A turret as if the ship had started to go under. Then, as her stem lifted again and the spray flew past the bridge like tattered sea-birds, Blake saw the other ship for the first time.

A vague, bulky shadow ringed with smoke and etched against a curtain of falling spray from the last salvo. The enemy.

He heard himself call, *'Open fire!'*

The rest was lost in the crash and recoil of the two forward turrets.

Lieutenant Jeremy Masters eased the stick of the Seafox and guided it skilfully through a broken patch of cloud. To anyone without his experience the panorama above and below the racing propeller would seem impossibly wild. Jagged clouds rushing to meet them, bouncing the plane about like a leaf in a November wind, then great sections of empty sea, broken and violent, in every direction. Above the upper wing Masters could see occasional fragments of deeper, clearer blue. Like most of these storms, it would soon pass and the heat would envelop them once more.

Masters turned the aircraft in an easy banking dive, his eyes barely blinking as he concentrated on a thinning bank of cloud. Behind him he could imagine his observer, Jimmy Duncan, watching the cloud, waiting for the first break and a sight of the enemy. Stolid, dependable Duncan. It was good to know he was back there, even if the plane's only defence was an ancient Lewis gun.

The cloud whipped through the prop and between the wings and suddenly there it was. The ship, steaming diagonally below and slightly to port, smoke pouring from her funnel as if to show her determination to shake off the pursuit.

The seaplane bucked wildly as a great salvo ploughed into the sea and exploded in a towering wall of spray and smoke. Masters saw the other ship's wake start to twist as her captain manoeuvred to avoid the next fall of shot.

Masters jammed some glasses to his goggles with his free hand and fought against the Seafox's tossing motion while he searched for the warship.

Through his earphones he heard Duncan yell, 'There she is! Starboard bow!'

Masters eased the rudder and thought about the plane's safety as he headed for some cloud-cover.

He shouted, 'No sense in hanging about, Jimmy! They've got her cold!'

Duncan agreed. 'That's *Fremantle* right enough! Going like the clappers!'

It was useless to try and contact *Andromeda* by R/T. The Seafox was soon to be scrapped and replaced. The radio, like the rest of the little seaplane, had seen better days. But she had done well, Masters thought. He thought too of *Andromeda*'s Walrus flying-boat which with its crew lay scattered somewhere across the bed of the Mediterranean. Masters had been a friend of all of them, and had felt a lump in his throat as the slow old Walrus, spotting for *Andromeda*'s gunnery officer right up to the end of the fight with the three cruisers, had wandered just too close to the enemy's flak.

He shouted, 'I'm going round again! Hold on for tracer!'

Not that Duncan needed telling. He followed everything Masters told or showed him. He was more like a gun-dog than a companion at times.

Why was he going round again? Masters concentrated on the thinning cloud, hunched forward in his harness like all the other times.

There was something wrong, but what?

Here we go. Nice and easy. Level off. *Now*.

The ship swung into view again, smoke belching from her fore-deck and blotting out her squat bridge completely. A big merchantman, freighter of sorts, and fairly high in the water. Masters saw the sea curling along her hull, the patches of rust, the dents in her plates. A real old lady.

He could even see the bright dab of red at her masthead with the black cross and swastika. Against the *Fremantle*'s massive salvoes it seemed somehow pathetic.

But somebody was wide awake down there. Masters began to weave the seaplane from side to side as bright balls of tracer drifted towards the port wings with deceptive gentleness.

Duncan swore into his mouthpiece and sent a single line of tracer spitting over the side of the cockpit with his Lewis, which almost immediately jammed.

Masters said between his teeth, 'Serve you right, Jimmy, you bloodthirsty bastard!'

Spray shot up the side of the German and one of the lifeboats was blasted from its davits with part of the deck as well. Inside the enemy's hull the real effect would be felt. A massive

56

explosion and white-hot splinters ripping through in a lethal hail.

Duncan yelled, 'Look at that!'

That was the arrival of *Andromeda*'s first sighting shots. Tall waterspouts shooting from the sea in pairs. Palliser was red-hot all right. His first salvo was within half a cable. The twin explosions would be shaking the damaged ship like a terrier with a hare. The German would surrender right now if he had any sense.

Duncan shouted hoarsely, 'Christ, Skipper! There are men coming on deck!'

Masters gritted his teeth and put the Seafox into a steep dive. 'Hold tight, the Buffs!'

Through the racing prop he saw the ship reaching out on either side like a massive breakwater. Smoke belched over the cockpit and he thought he could smell burning paint, charred woodwork. But he could not drag his eyes from the mass of stampeding figures which were pouring up from the hatches, running about in confusion which even distance could not hide.

The enemy's tracer had stopped, and Masters saw the Seafox's shadow flit over the ship's scarred deck like a crucifix, the way that some of the figures had paused to stare up at him, and then to his astonishment to wave and cheer.

Duncan sobbed, 'God, they're *our* men! It must be a prison ship!'

Masters veered away, skimming so close to the sea that he seemed to be lower than the enemy's bulwark.

Of course, that was it. A supply ship for the raider, her holds packed with the crews of captured prizes.

'Call up *Andromeda*! Keep sending and I'll try to reach her right away!'

Beyond the cloud and drifting banks of spray, as her upper works and battle ensigns took shape in the strengthening light, *Andromeda*'s gunnery officer held his breath and waited for the target to settle in his prismatic sights.

'Shoot!'

It was a full broadside, eight shells, each weighing a hundred pounds, smashing across the enemy's hull in a perfect straddle.

Masters eased the throttle and pushed his goggles up to his forehead. He knew that Duncan had given up trying to use the

R/T and was triggering off his urgent signal with an Aldis lamp.

Cease firing. . . . Cease firing.

He watched the first sunlight breaking through the clouds and a lengthening pall of smoke. It was like seeing two sunrises at once, Masters thought. Except that one was the reflected inferno he was leaving behind. A ship blasted into a fiery ball by that last deadly salvo.

5

The Enemy

Moon, his small silver tray beneath one arm, stood in silence until Blake had re-read his typed report and signed it. After the violent motion on the fringe of a tropical storm, and the swift encounter with the German ship, *Andromeda* seemed unnaturally quiet. As if she were resting, deciding what to do next.

Through one of the cabin's polished scuttles Moon could see the shoreline rising and falling gently as the cruiser swung to her cable.

Like most sailors, Moon rarely considered the miles steamed, the oil consumed, the food eaten to get his ship from one dot on a chart to another. They had come from the Mediterranean, they had survived the worst fighting Moon had ever seen. To Australia then, for what reason their lordships probably knew best, and they would not consult him anyway. And now, across the undulating swell of blue water was Port Elizabeth, South Africa. He watched the distant houses, very white in the noon sunlight, a strip of pale beach, the land mass beyond, dull greens and browns. It even looked hot from here, he thought.

Blake sat back and stretched his arms. He had read his report and still barely recognized it. All he could see in his mind was the tiny seaplane rising and dipping through the wind, a lamp blinking frantically even as *Andromeda*'s broadside fell on the target like an avalanche.

With *Fremantle* steaming in a protective circle, Blake had stopped his ship in the great oil slick and the too-familiar work of clearing up the mess had begun. The black, choking survivors had mostly been their own kind, crewmen from the *Bikanir,* the first reported victim to fall to the raider's guns. Except that she was not the first after all. A Dutch freighter called the *Evertsen*, given up as a storm loss some weeks earlier, had also been captured and then sunk. Some of her people were dragged gasping and groaning up *Andromeda*'s side or into the boats which moved through the mass of bobbing remnants like undertakers' men.

There was a tap at the door and Fairfax stepped into the cabin.

'The last of the wounded have been taken ashore, sir. Captain Farleigh's marines have the Germans under guard, the uninjured ones, that is.'

Blake nodded. With the ship swaying gently at anchor, the inviting coastline of Port Elizabeth lying abeam, it was hard to hold the recent events in perspective.

He knew that the same sense of bewilderment was effecting most of his ship's company. The seasoned, battle-hardened ones would be taking it philosophically. *Trust the top-brass to foul it up.* What was the point of cracking an egg with a sledge-hammer, especially as some of their own blokes had bought it in the process? Others, especially the new hands, might see it as a kind of victory anyway. She was a German ship, a supply vessel for the raider, and they and not *Fremantle* had put her down.

There had been a report of another ship in difficulties to the eastward, but too far for the raider to have reached in the time available. But Stagg had made a brief signal instructing *Andromeda* to take the survivors and the few German prisoners to Port Elizabeth where they would await escort and interrogation by the proper authorities.

Only one German officer, a lieutenant, had survived the bombardment, and he, needless to say, had divulged little when Blake had questioned him. His ship, the *Bremse*, had been a supply vessel but had been about to try and penetrate the blockade and get back to Germany or Occupied France.

Any further information had gone to the bottom with the ship's confidential books and codes when the German captain had first sighted the *Fremantle*.

The raider had kept all his officer prisoners with him, but the boatswain of the Dutch *Evertsen* had been able to supply some valuable information. He spoke German well and had heard his guards discussing their chances of getting home again.

The man who commanded the raider *was* Kurt Rietz, so Stagg had been right about that. But at no time had he heard them speak of the Australian cruiser *Devonport*, which was strange, as she must surely have been quite a victory for the Germans.

Blake stood up. 'I'd better come on deck. Have the awnings

and booms rigged and all boats lowered.'

Even as he said it he thought of the unreality which surrounded them. Lying at anchor, so that the wounded and shocked survivors had to be ferried ashore, and likewise any replacement stores and fresh water had to do the same trip. Security or red tape, Blake did not know.

On the quarterdeck it was oppressively hot, the shore shimmering in a haze like an unfocused gunsight.

The Germans, in borrowed clothing or wrapped in towels, stood like beaten animals, dull eyes fixed on the shore, while they waited to be taken to a prison camp.

Blake nodded to the marine guard and glanced along the strained faces. Mostly older men, ex-merchant sailors, others too old for active service in destroyers or U-boats.

Fairfax said quietly, 'They don't look much, sir.'

Blake had seen plenty of German prisoners and felt the usual uneasiness. It was better to keep the war impersonal, the enemy at a distance. Brought face to face they were too familiar.

He said, 'The intelligence people will get nothing out of them. They'll know nothing. They carried the supplies, kept out of trouble, and that's all. I'll lay odds there's another supply ship already out here or on the way right now.'

A German petty officer barked, *'Besatzung stillgestanden!'* and the dismal collection of survivors shuffled to attention. The man saluted Blake, his eyes feverishly bright as he stared at a point above Blake's shoulder.

Captain Farleigh stepped smartly forward. 'Boat's alongside, sir.' He pointed at the prisoners. 'For them.'

'Very well.'

Blake turned away and looked along the length of his command. Men were busy swaying out the booms and the aircraft's crane was lowering the power boats alongside. Blake thought of Masters' return in the Seafox. That he had survived was a miracle, but the seaplane stood demurely on the catapult with its attendant mechanics as proof of his skill.

Blake recalled with stark clarity the pilot's bitterness and anger as he had clambered up to the bridge.

'What the hell are we? Bloody butchers? That was no raider. One popgun and a couple of m.g.s! Christ Almighty, Stagg must be raving mad!'

When he entered the bridge Masters had been outwardly calm again, but his words lingered in Blake's mind. Stagg had over-reacted, had seen only what he had wanted to see. The grim fact remained, however, that *Andromeda*'s guns had made the kill.

Blake ran his glance over the bridge. It looked remote from the quarterdeck, and yet he could see himself up there still. He knew what was partly wrong with himself. He was too protective about his ship, her name. Men died in war, it was a simple fact. With luck you came through. Usually more were killed because of stupid orders and impossible missions than by the enemy's skill. On either side.

But *Andromeda* meant something. She had survived so much, too much to be wasted on a stupid blunder. Think of it how you liked, Stagg had been too hasty. He had known *Andromeda* was on her way, and when the weather had finally improved he would have been able to use his two aircraft to seek out the *Bremse* whether Blake had made contact or not.

The fact that Fairfax had carefully avoided the subject of Stagg's strategy was almost worse. Like adding 'I told you so' to all the other doubts and anxieties.

He tried to relax, muscle by muscle, the sweat running down his spine like hot rain.

He was going round the bend. And why not? It happened to others.

Lieutenant Friar, the new torpedo officer, saluted and reported, 'Launch approaching, sir.' He was OOD but kept his eyes averted from Blake's, like the German petty officer, like most of them since the *Bremse* had exploded.

The approaching launch swept round in an impressive arc towards the lowered accommodation ladder, her bowman ready with his boat-hook, as smart as if he was at a peacetime review.

The heavier boat containing the German prisoners chugged past, the dull-eyed survivors staring at the glittering launch without recognition or interest.

Blake sighed. God knows, he thought, they've made enough misery in the world, brought on a war that seems unending, and yet they deserved some pity. As far as everyone else was concerned, except possibly for their close relatives, they had already been written off. Numbers, *things* to be shunted from camp to camp, fed and guarded, and that was all.

Lieutenant Friar lowered his telescope. 'There's a captain aboard, sir.'

Fairfax snapped, 'Man the side there!'

Marines moved into position, the OOD and quartermaster

stepped smartly to the head of the ladder.

Blake straightened his cap, tradition took over. It was useful at times like these.

The boatswains' calls twittered in salute, and then, with his hand to the peak of his cap, Captain Quintin stepped on to the brass plate on *Andromeda*'s quarterdeck.

He shook hands with Blake and nodded to Fairfax.

'I flew,' he said simply.

Several heads turned as the Wren officer called Claire Grenfell followed him on to the deck, her eyes and expression completely masked by dark sun-glasses.

Quintin ran one finger round his collar. 'What about a drink?' He waited for the girl to join him and added, 'Now what's this about you blowing up Germans? I want it all. Forget the report you've got ready for our superiors. I want the professional view.' He fell in step beside Blake. 'Whether it hurts or not.'

On the evening of the same day that the *Andromeda* anchored off Port Elizabeth, the German raider, *Salamander*, lay hove to some one hundred and eighty miles south-west of Madagascar. Although the Indian Ocean was restless with a deep, unending swell, the raider appeared to be motionless, standing against the sunset like an iron fortress.

Also stopped, and less than a cable away, the Swedish merchantman, *Patricia*, looked clean and remote by comparison.

Between the two vessels a motor launch plunged and bucked across the water towards her parent ship, empty but for some seamen and the Swedish captain.

High on the raider's square, business-like bridge her commanding officer, Kurt Rietz, studied the returning launch through his powerful Zeiss binoculars. It had been easy, almost too easy, he thought as he focused his glasses on the Swedish master. But there had been a rain squall, unusual for the time of year, which had deluged across the blue water, shutting off the horizon like a steel fence. When it had passed on just as swiftly, leaving the upper deck and life-boats steaming in the sunshine as if about to burst into flames, the Swede had been there. To turn away would have roused suspicion. The German's mouth lifted in a wry smile. Even neutrals raised hue and cry once they were at a safe distance.

Rietz turned on his heel and re-entered the wheelhouse.

Everything except the bridge equipment, compass and electrical gear looked worn and uncared for. Even the brass plate above the chartroom door which stated that the *Salamander* of eight thousand tons, built originally for general cargo and passengers on the South America run, and launched in 1936 at Hamburg, was green with salt.

Rietz was well aware of his ship's shabby appearance and he disliked it. But a raider was like no other sea creature. She had to live from her wits and her ability to survive against odds. To succeed she must use only what was necessary. Paint by the drumload to change her appearance and alter her identity. Like now, with the name *John A. Williams* painted in great white letters on her hull below the Stars and Stripes of America. Wood and canvas, wires and cordage, so that a false funnel could be hoisted to be a twin with her single one. Rietz had expected the false funnel to fall. It had been a hasty piece of work, and some new system would have to be introduced. He would pass the word around his command, as he always did. A bottle of schnapps or captured Scotch for the best idea.

It usually worked and saved hours of fruitless discussion. In a ship of this size there were plenty of original ideas lying dormant amongst her three hundred and fifty officers and seamen.

Rietz walked to the bridge screen to see if the launch was alongside. He hated hanging about. It was far too risky. He had been successful because of his ingenuity and his persistence, and, although he would dismiss it, his courage most of all. But he never took risks.

Looking down from his high perch there was little to show the raider's power. Her eight big five-point-nine guns were either concealed behind steel shutters cut in her hull or beneath false deck-houses, as were her two new Arado seaplanes and their catapult. Torpedo tubes, mines and six other cannon completed her armament, and her maximum speed of eighteen knots made her hard to catch.

Storch, his first lieutenant, strode into the bridge and saluted smartly.

'The prisoner is aboard, sir!'

Rietz was staring at the motionless ship. He never got used to it. A fight he understood, pitting his wits against the enemy he sometimes enjoyed.

He said, 'Bring him.'

Rietz was forty years old but appeared younger. He was

slightly built with dark, glossy hair and brown eyes. He looked more French than German, a composed, thoughtful man with little to show of the hunter, the corsair.

The Swedish captain stepped into the wheelhouse and opened his mouth to protest.

Rietz held up one hand. *'Please, Kapitän.* We are wasting time. My boarding party signalled to me what you are carrying, where from and where bound. Coal from the north of England, on passage for Port Said, yes?'

Even as he said it Rietz could sense the man's despair. All those hundreds of miles. In or out of convoy, hazardous enough at the best of times. Then taking the long route around the Cape rather than risk being stopped at Gibraltar or sunk in convoy through the Mediterranean. So near and yet so far. It was over. The *Patricia*'s cargo of coal would have been used by the Tommies.

The Swedish captain said huskily, 'I am a neutral. Sink her and I lose my livelihood.'

Rietz shrugged and pointed down at his own ship. 'This is my livelihood, *Kapitän.'*

A lookout called, 'The rest of the prisoners are being brought across, sir!'

Rietz looked at Storch. 'Make them comfortable. We will release them later. But now. . . .' He turned to the Swedish officer. 'We cannot risk your keeping silent.'

Storch said, 'Torpedo, sir?'

Rietz smiled gently. 'I have to tell you too often, Rudi. Waste nothing. Signal the boarding party to set charges. The coal will do the rest.'

A petty officer touched the Swede's arm, impatient to get it over with, but Rietz shook his head.

'Stay if you wish, *Kapitän.'* To Storch he murmured, 'No word from *Bremse.* The British cruiser must have caught her.'

Storch nodded. He was just twenty-six, and was still very conscious of his scarred face and the black glove which covered a disfigured left hand. He had been the navigating officer of a destroyer in the Baltic which had been attacked by Russian dive-bombers. Badly injured and scarred though he was, he was still a first class navigator and had been sent as such to the *Salamander.* He had felt it badly, like some sort of stigma, a temporary appointment for an expendable officer and ship.

Rietz had changed all that, and when the senior lieutenant had been sent back to Germany in command of a captured whaling ship, Storch had been promoted to his position. He no longer felt anything but pride in the ship and his work, and he would have died willingly for his commander.

Half an hour later, as froth mounted once more from the raider's screws, the abandoned *Patricia* lifted slightly, as if she was shuddering. The demolition charges barely made more than an echo against the raider's bilges, but as she gathered way, with the sunset just able to paint her poop and frothing wake in bronze, the victim leaned over and began to settle down. When the coal shifted to crash through the protective barriers and machinery broke loose in the hull, her end came more quickly.

The Swedish captain watched in silence. If he had not depended on the neutrality of his flag and he had urged his radio officer to wireless their position, the end would have been the same. He turned wretchedly and saw the German captain lighting a cigar. But at least he would have had the satisfaction of helping to finish the raider's career, he thought.

Storch heard the door slam as the latest captive was escorted below.

'What would you have done in his place, sir?'

Rietz blew out a stream of smoke. It was one of his last. Perhaps they would have brought some from the Swedish ship.

He replied, 'Ask me again. When it happens, eh?' He walked to the chartroom. 'Now we must move ourselves.'

He switched on the deckhead lights above the specially built plot and chart tables. Opposite, pinned to the bulkhead, was the front page of a Sydney newspaper.

Captain Richard Blake, VC, *arrives in Aussie! Hero of the* Andromeda *a welcome visitor!*

Rietz smiled grimly. So much for security.

The German secret agent who had put the newspaper in with the last pack of despatches had marked one line in pencil. *Why is he here? What is his mission?*

Aloud Rietz said, 'I expect *we* knew that before he did!'

He peered at Blake's picture and added, 'At least we shall recognize him when we meet!' He bent over the chart and added curtly, 'To work. We will assume the *Patricia*'s appearance tonight. Put both watches to painting and remarking the hull.' He took down the bulky recognition manual. 'Swedish flag, so I hope we've plenty of yellow paint.'

Night closed in around the darkened ship, while far astern

there was nothing left to betray that the raider or her victim had ever existed.

Captain Jack Quintin dabbed his mouth with a napkin and nodded approvingly to Moon.

To Blake he said, 'Damn good lunch.' He glanced around the cabin. 'You could have given me baked beans and I'd not have complained. Just to be aboard a ship again.' He shook his head. 'But I'm interrupting. You were saying?'

Blake waited for Moon to remove his plate. He had barely noticed what he had been eating nor that he had been speaking with hardly a break since Quintin and his Wren had stepped aboard.

She was sitting at the opposite end of the table, her hair shining in the sunlight from an open scuttle, so that her expression was in shadow. She had said very little, and then mostly to her boss, to clarify some point or other, which she immediately noted on a pad which had lain beside her throughout the meal.

It had been more like an interrogation than a casual encounter, Blake thought. Perhaps that was how they did things. He knew little about intelligence work, other than the people in the field. The hard men, the cloak-and-dagger brigade whom he had dropped on enemy coastlines to recover weeks later, tired, ragged but grimly pleased with themselves.

Blake said, 'That's about it, sir. I spoke with the prisoners and the survivors from the *Bikanir* and the *Evertsen*. I've a team aboard who plot the findings on a special chart and vet all the W/T signals we can pick up.' He shrugged. 'As for the *Bremse*, well, we may never know about her. She was probably going to another rendezvous even without knowing it until she got her secret signal with the co-ordinates of the next grid position.'

The girl said suddenly, 'If the *Bremse* had been less heavily attacked. . . .'

Blake met her gaze calmly. 'I know. I acted on the assumption she was the raider. I was wrong.'

Quintin held up his hand. 'Easy now, Claire. It's not that simple. Commodore Stagg gave the instruction.'

Blake kept his eyes on the girl, wondering if she was trying to antagonize him or if she and Quintin were acting as a trained team.

He said, 'But you are right, of course. Unfortunately, in

67

war there's never enough time, no margin for a perfect decision. If we had captured the German supply ship intact we might have discovered something more, codes or not.'

Quintin relaxed slightly. 'Anyway, Stagg was probably thinking about *Devonport*'s loss.'

Blake placed his hands on his knees below the table. *Here we go.* What it's all been building up to.

He said, 'That's just it. But for *Devonport*, I think I could almost accept the "official" view.'

The girl wrote something in her pad and Blake felt the same surge of unreasonable anger.

'I know we're in a critical phase of the war. I *know* that. They've been telling us long enough.' He expected Quintin to interrupt but he was sitting very still, an unlit cigarette in his hand, as if afraid to divert Blake's train of thought. 'Convoys round the Cape and between the major theatres of war have always been a headache. Long-range U-boats in the Atlantic, supplied by their milch-cows, pocket-battleships and minelaying aircraft, they've all made their mark, and deeply. But the cheapest weapon is still the commerce raider, and at this moment, when so much depends on preparing for the invasion of Europe to coincide with a massive offence by the US forces in the Pacific against the Japs, it could be the most dangerous.'

Quintin pouted his lower lip. 'So far I agree. Since the *Kios* sinking was reported there's been practically no independent movement. Convoys are being marshalled at Cape Town and at the Australian end of the line. Every cargo is precious these days, especially manpower and military equipment. So until we can find that raider, things will tend to slow down, become delayed, when we need every operation on topline.'

Blake felt for his pipe. It was still filled and unlit from the last time.

He said, 'According to my calculations, and *if Devonport* was sunk in the manner everyone believes, the raider has destroyed her and four other ships in a matter of weeks.'

Quintin seemed disappointed. 'Well, I *know* that.'

Blake drew a rectangle on the tablecloth with his pipe stem. 'Think about it, sir, just for a minute. It means that the raider has covered an area of some two and a half thousand miles west of the Cape and as far south as the forty-fifth parallel.'

He saw the girl's pencil had stopped moving, that she was watching him intently. Quintin too was staring at the pipe stem as if he expected to see it change into something else.

Blake continued quietly, 'It would seem that she was tearing about the ocean at full throttle, sinking ships which she just "happened" to come across.' He looked at Quintin for several seconds. 'And there's another thing. Why did the German captain take such good care of the Dutch crew and that of the *Bikanir*, yet slaughter those from the *Kios*?'

He recalled the young paymaster sub-lieutenant who had interpreted for the dying Greek steward. His face as he had translated each painful whisper.

Blake added, 'He apparently machine-gunned men in the water and left the others to die, exposure or sharks, it made no difference to him.'

Then and only then did he see the girl's hand move. She touched her shirt beneath her breast, and when he looked at her she lowered her gaze.

He said, 'We can't even *guess* what happened to the survivors of the *Argyll Clansman*.'

In the sudden stillness he was conscious of the ship around them, the gentle sluice of the current beneath the open scuttle, a far-off voice on the tannoy called, 'Out pipes. Both watches of the hands, fall in.' It was as if the ship was ignoring them.

Then Quintin said abruptly, 'The Germans aren't saints. We know that. Their record is bloody enough already.'

The girl said quietly, 'I understand, sir.'

Then she looked up, and Blake was astonished to see that her eyes were blurred, with emotion or shock, he did not know.

She continued, 'You think there are two different men, two separate raiders.'

Quintin stared from her to Blake. 'Now wait a minute! I've heard about everything now!'

Blake nodded. 'That's what I think. Two of them. Crossing and recrossing the area with arranged supply points whenever and wherever they are needed. It could tie down dozens of warships, hold up convoy sailings, make a mess of everything.'

Very deliberately Quintin lit his cigarette and watched the smoke until it was whipped up by the fans.

'But surely, with all our resources, our intelligence agencies and past experience something would have leaked out?'

Blake shrugged again. 'I don't see why. At the start of the war the *Graf Spee* was already in the South Atlantic but nobody was ready for her. In France the Maginot Line was not long enough to keep the Germans out but nothing had been done about it. In Singapore the big guns were facing the wrong way long before the Japs invaded, but did anyone do anything about that?'

Quintin shook his head. 'All right, enough said. Point taken.' He stood up. 'I'd like to use your radio.'

Blake looked for Moon's shadow beyond the pantry. It had been there for most of the time. Like a protective scarecrow.

'Take Captain Quintin to the W/T office, will you?'

Alone together in the spacious cabin, the girl said suddenly, 'That was something. You really came out with it.' She had her head on one side, watching his face, her composure apparently recovered. 'Do you believe it?'

He smiled bitterly. 'Will it make any difference?'

Then he said, 'Yes, I do, as it happens. The German character has given us our one clue. A tiny lead at present, but it's something. Two raiders, twins if you like, and that is what *I* would arrange, working an area like this one. It would make the needle and haystack problem simple by comparison. Provided, of course, you only *believe* in one vessel.' He broke off, suddenly tired of it, surprised he had let it burst out when he had probably jumped the gun.

He asked, 'Whereabouts do you live? In Melbourne?'

She smiled. 'Change of subject? Fine. No, my people live further out. Small town. You'd call it a village, I expect.'

Blake studied her. She had a nice smile, warm, but sparing, like her words.

Then she said, 'When you were in the Mediterranean, did you ever come across the destroyer *Paradox*?'

She had pushed her chair away from the table and had turned from him, her legs crossed.

The question had been just that bit too casual, and yet too rehearsed.

'Yes.'

He put his pipe on the table and walked to the open scuttle. The sea had been as blue as this one, he thought vaguely. Two lines of merchantmen plodding hopefully towards Alexandria. A week earlier there had been three lines.

He said quietly, 'I remember her well. She was a wing escort that morning. We'd had a terrible battering, and even *Andromeda*'s anti-aircraft defences were almost worn out!'

There it was again. Why had he said 'even'? That special pride.

'They came over in waves. German, Italian, the sky was full of them. We lost four merchantmen and an escort in an

70

hour. It was sheer bloody murder. But we kept going. Like we always did. Bash on regardless. Don't look back.'

He gripped the warm brass rim of the scuttle to steady himself. But instead of Port Elizabeth's placid shoreline he saw the lines of ships, the waterspouts of a hundred bombs falling around them, the insane clatter...clatter...clatter of the pom-poms and Oerlikons, the whoosh and crash of direct hits. And through it, drifting, ablaze from end to end, the wing escort *Paradox* had passed between the two slow-moving columns.

Some madman had been still firing a solitary machine-gun at the circling dive-bombers, the tracer spurting straight up, as if the last living soul in that inferno had already lost consciousness.

He said abruptly, 'We could not stop. If it had been any ship, the same thing would have happened. God, I remember the *Paradox* well enough. Her skipper was an old friend, as a matter of fact. From way back. You know how it is in the—'

He broke off as he turned and looked at her. She was wiping her eyes with the back of her hand, but not quickly enough to hide her tears.

He exclaimed, 'I'm sorry. Your brother was lost in her. I should have stopped. Commander Fairfax told me about him. I should have put two and two together.'

She sniffed and stood up from the table. 'It's all right. I don't usually behave like some stupid galah. It's me.' She shook her head, the hair bouncing across her cheeks in confusion. 'No, it's *you*. You're not what I expected. Perhaps when Dave was lost I needed someone to hate, to blame. When your arrival was announced, the vc, the real-life hero, I wanted to hurt you.' She looked at the deck. 'I feel such a fool now.'

'If there's anything I can do?'

She swallowed hard and groped in her bag for her compact. 'There is. If you come back to Williamstown, and I think you will, I'd like you to meet my mum and dad. Tell them all about it, if you can bear it. Just like you told me.' She looked away. 'They've nothing much else left now. Will you do it?'

He nodded. 'If I can.'

Quintin stepped through the door rubbing his hands. 'By God, I'll bet that signal has got 'em all jumping about! But they'll not like any of it. They've got the east and westbound convoys held up for want of additional fire-power, and your little bombshell will go down like mustard and jam!' He looked

71

from one to the other. 'Something wrong?'

She met his gaze calmly. 'No, sir.' She picked up her notebook. 'Anything to add?'

Quintin was watching Blake. 'Nothing much. Stagg's bit of excitement was a dud. The ship had merely lost her radio. Everything else is buttoned up, and all unescorted ships at sea will be notified about the raider's movements as soon as we know anything.' He looked at his watch. 'Would you call away my launch, please? I'd best get ashore and get things moving. I'll bet there's a hornets' nest waiting for me there right enough!'

The girl held out her hand. 'Good-bye, Captain.'

It was all she said, but her eyes and her handshake were like a truce.

Quintin nodded. 'It's been a pleasure.'

Blake saw his unexpected visitors over the side and watched the fast-moving launch until it had reached the harbour.

He was making a fool of himself. His sense of loss, his battered reserves after the demands of the Mediterranean had left him unsure and vulnerable.

But even that brief contact had given him a kind of strength, or was he still seeking a replacement for Diana's deception?

Lieutenant Friar saluted. 'Will there be shore leave, sir?'

Blake turned on his heel, his eyes blinded by the fierce sunlight.

Lieutenant Masters, the Seafox pilot, strolled up to the puzzled Friar and murmured, 'What's the matter, old son? You look like a chap who's lost a shilling and found a sixpence!'

Friar shook his head. 'The skipper. He walked right past me!'

Masters patted his shoulder. 'If I'd had popsie like that for lunch, skipper or not, I'd feel just the same!'

Unaware of the OOD's confusion, Blake re-entered his cabin and tossed his cap on a chair.

'Any brandy left, Moon?'

Moon gave a toothy grin. ''Course, sir.' He produced one of his best glasses and eyed it critically. 'A celebration, perhaps, sir?'

Blake sat down and thrust out his legs. *I needed someone to hate*, she had said.

He took the glass from Moon and replied, 'Perhaps.'

Moon bustled away. There had been a moment at lunch

when he had nearly accidentally but on purpose spilled a dish of tinned peas over the Aussie Wren officer. Now, he was not so sure. She might be just the job.

6

A Small World

Commander Victor Fairfax raised his hand to tap on the captain's door and then paused with it in mid-air. The door was partly open, and through it he saw Moon, assisted by a worried looking messman, bustling about with what he recognized as unusual agitation.

Fairfax stepped over the coaming, his eyes immediately noting the half-packed grip which lay on a chair, the newly-pressed suit of white drill draped across another.

Moon muttered, 'Never 'eard of such things. No respect. No bloody respect.' He saw Fairfax and added hurriedly, 'Captain's takin' a shower, sir.'

To Fairfax it sounded like, so go away. He smiled. 'He sent for me.'

'Well, then.' Moon snatched a shirt from the messman and said savagely, 'Not that way, you bloody 'alf-wit!' He took a grip on himself and explained to Fairfax, 'There's a flap on, sir.'

'So I see.'

A curtain jerked aside and Blake, his hair plastered down on his forehead, his bare feet making a trail across the carpet, hurried to his desk.

He nodded to Fairfax and waved him to a chair. 'Just had a signal from Quintin, Victor. He's flying back to Australia, starting tonight.' He was speaking in quick jerks as he sorted through his papers, discarding some and throwing others to Moon to be packed. 'I'm ordered to go with him. Bit of a rush job. We'll fly to Fremantle via Colombo with a couple of island stops to refuel.'

He paused and thrust the damp hair from his face. It made him look very young and strangely vulnerable.

Fairfax said, 'Must be important, sir. What about us?'

Blake eyed him steadily, as if unable to decide on something. 'I've left written orders for you. Finish taking on fuel without delay. No shore leave. Any problems, you can make a direct signal to our people at Simonstown.'

Fairfax was on his feet without realizing it. 'And then?'

Blake smiled gravely. '*Then,* you will weigh and proceed to Williamstown as ordered. You should meet the westbound convoy when you are three days from your e.t.a. You shouldn't have any trouble.' He tried to sound encouraging. 'Good experience for you.'

Fairfax looked away. 'Sure thing. Yes.'

He did not know what he felt. In the twinkling of an eye everything had changed. He had been writing to Sarah, although he would be home before it was even posted. But he often wrote to her in this fashion. Like a diary, a personal link. Now, he was too surprised to think clearly. He was in command of the *Andromeda*. Not only that, he was expected to put to sea in the morning and take her safely across the vast desert of the Indian Ocean to the port from which it had all begun.

He said, 'I'll do my best, sir.'

Blake slipped into his newly-pressed trousers and said quietly, 'You'll do better than that. You know the score. It can happen any time. It was how I got command of her. My skipper was killed and I took over. This is no different.' He forced a grin. 'Anyway, I'll be waiting for you on the pier, so don't scratch the paint!'

Lieutenant Palliser stood in the doorway. 'Your boat's alongside, sir.'

'Thank you, Guns. I'll be up in a jiffy.'

Fairfax said, 'It's a strange feeling. Not what I expected at all.'

Blake barely heard him. From the moment Quintin's personal signal had been brought to him he had been torn apart by his emotions. Once more, he was leaving *Andromeda*. Once again they would be reunited. It seemed to get harder instead of the other way round.

He glanced at Fairfax as if to reassure himself. A sound, unshakeable officer. He had proved that elsewhere, and aboard this ship too when they had destroyed the *Bremse*. The ship's company had not showed any views about him. As yet he was a stranger to the seasoned men and to the newcomers as well. Anyway, the commander, 'the bloke' as he was nicknamed, was always doomed to play second fiddle to the captain.

Fairfax saw Moon strapping up the grip and peering round to see if he had forgotten anything. God, he thought, Moon's going to miss him like hell. *And so shall I.*

75

They climbed to the quarterdeck where the side-party was grouped above the accommodation ladder. Like white spectres in the dying light.

Blake shook Fairfax's hand. 'Take care of her. *Good* care. And don't push the Chief. Just tell him what you need.' The handshake lingered. 'He's good. They all are.'

Then with a nod to Moon he hurried down the ladder to the swaying launch.

'*Bear off forrard!*'

The boat sighed away from the cruiser's hull and Blake was on his way.

Quintin's signals to the Admiralty and the Navy Office in Melbourne must have been something, he thought. Perhaps they would take his idea seriously. Or they might just as easily send him back to the UK to keep him out of trouble.

A big staff car was waiting for him, and as a seaman put his bag in front with the driver he realized that his travelling companions were already inside.

Quintin, smoking as usual, said brightly, 'That was fast!'

The car jerked into gear and he added, 'Be a long flight. The Americans have a Catalina laid on. It was going our way and better than waiting for something larger. It will take us as far as Fremantle. The RAN will fly us to Melbourne from there, right?'

Blake looked at the girl. She was pressed in one corner, her face towards the road as it flashed past the window. She looked tense. Worried even.

Blake asked, 'Is this the same way you came here?'

She looked at him. 'No. We flew in a big transport.' She shuddered. 'That was bad enough.'

Quintin said, 'Just take that pill I gave you, Claire. You'll be okay.'

So she hated flying. Blake was suddenly glad he was going with them. It might help on the long journey. The Catalina flying-boat was the best of its kind but had not been designed for luxury trips.

An hour later they were embarked in the broad-winged flying-boat and taxiing heavily across some choppy water while the aircraft's pilot tested his throttles and exchanged meaningless chatter with his crew and the shore control.

Bump, bump, bump, it was like an MTB as it gathered way, the sea surging back, hardening and roaring along either side until it felt that it would shake itself apart.

76

Then, with a shudder, they were off the surface, the engines' sound smoothing and easing while the pilot took the Catalina in a shallow climb away from the lights on the shore.

Blake felt the girl's fingers gripping his wrist, but when he looked at her through the gloom she shook her head desperately.

'Don't talk, *please*.'

Blake understood. In a few minutes she would either be sick or get over it. Until the next time.

An American, festooned with straps and map cases, stumbled aft towards them. 'Okay back there? Great! There'll be coffee and some chow shortly when my buddy stirs himself!' He clung to the plane and peered through one of the big perspex bubbles on the side. 'Here we go, folks!'

Blake smiled to himself. A young, unknown American. Flying above the Indian Ocean and thousands of miles from home. And enjoying every second of it.

He felt the fingers relax slightly on his arm and was vaguely disappointed when she took her hand away.

She said huskily, 'That was close.'

Opposite them, wedged amongst canvas bags and mysterious parcels, Quintin watched them thoughtfully. They looked just right together, he thought wearily. Pity it couldn't work out.

The engines droned and buzzed, until instead of an irritation they became a kind of balm. Robbing them of thought and objectivity. Nothing existed beyond the curved sides of the hull.

Blake saw Quintin's head droop as he dozed off. When he turned to speak with the girl she had leaned away from him, her pale hair pillowed on a rolled blanket.

Blake sighed. It was no way to travel.

Blake tried to stretch his arms. He peered at his watch, feeling every bone and muscle uniting in protest. Over ten hours they had been flying. A strange, unreal limbo of throbbing engines and pitching movement. Now, the light through the perspex was searing, and far below the ocean was deep, deep blue, broken here and there by tiny white cat's paws. Blake guessed that each patch of foam was miles apart. It was like a great mill-pond.

Quintin groaned. 'Another three hours of this, goddammit! I'm as stiff as a board!'

The young American came aft again, the daylight had revealed him to be a sailor.

'More coffee just a-comin', folks!' He looked maddeningly fresh and relaxed by comparison.

Blake glanced at the girl. She was wiping her face with a small cloth and trying to comb her hair at the same time.

Without turning she said, 'What wouldn't I give for a swim.'

The sailor turned to reply but one of his companions shouted. ''Nother plane up thar, Billy!'

The sailor hung over one of the Catalina's machine-guns. 'Navy plane. Must be nearer than we thought.' He slapped his friend's back. 'Nice cool Coke, eh? Then the sack for a coupl'a hours before—'

The pilot's voice cut through the intercom. *'Jesus! It's a kraut!'*

Blake was aware of several things at once. The young sailor staring at him with disbelief, Quintin reaching for his cap as if he was about to leave and the plane sliding to one side, the port wing tilting towards the blue water.

Blake threw himself from his small seat and clung to some cargo straps as he peered through the glittering perspex. The Catalina twisted violently, and he heard the pilot shouting over the intercom which he had failed to switch off, 'Christ Jesus! It's too damn fast!'

Then Blake heard it, the sound too familiar ever to be forgotten. *Brrrrrrrrr! Brrrrrrrrr!* Then the aircraft seemed to leap bodily from its course, reeling sickeningly to the sudden clatter of gunfire.

The hull cracked and bucked, and Blake was almost blinded by smoky sunlight which suddenly probed through the dim interior like a great fork. Holes appeared everywhere and he could smell burning.

Above it all he heard the pilot yelling, 'I'm going down, for God's sake! *Mayday . . . Mayday . . . Mayday!*'

Blake saw the young sailor on his knees, trying to pull his companion from the machine-gun. But there was blood all round him, painted across the metal as if by a madman's brush.

More violent cracks and bangs, and Blake shouted, 'We'll ditch!' He reached down and gripped the girl's wrists. 'Come on. Let me look at your life-jacket.'

She stared at him, her lips parted, her eyes suddenly terrified.

He added, 'Keep hold of me!'

He winced as more metal slammed through the Catalina, and he heard a man screaming like a tortured animal in a trap.

A shadow blotted out the sunlight, and for an instant Blake imagined they were about to hit the water. Then he heard the roar of an engine and saw the brief flash of wings as the other aircraft rushed past.

It all registered in his brain in a single, despairing second. The black cross on the wing, the spitting tongues of two powerful cannon, the twin floats beneath a German seaplane. It could have come from nothing else but a ship. *The raider*.

The sailor was yelling, 'Keep calm, folks! Sit down and put your heads on your knees!' He looked scared out of his wits and his determination to appear otherwise made him even more so. 'Nobody move until we land!'

Air swept through the Catalina and the engines were rising to a maniac scream as the pilot fought to level off and prepare to alight on the sea below.

The girl gripped Blake's arm with such strength that it was almost numbed.

She whispered desperately, 'Oh, God, I'm frightened!' She sounded as if she were speaking to someone else.

Brrrrrrrrr! Brrrrrrrrr!

Someone yelled, 'Leave us alone, you bastards! We're ditching!'

Blake put his arm around her shoulders to turn her face away. As the plane swayed over the dead machine-gunner had fallen backwards at their feet. His face and throat had been blasted away and his flying-suit was still smoking from the tracer.

Then all at once the sea was there. The plane hit violently, lifted free and smashed down once more, swinging round with the port wing-tip dragging under the surface like a giant scoop. Water surged through the hull and burst over the crouching occupants like waves on a rock. A necklace of blue sparks danced and crackled over the smashed radio, and then the Catalina gave one more terrible jerk before it heeled over, the engines still labouring and roaring like maddened beasts.

Blake gasped, *'Now!* We're getting out!'

The sailor reeled through the surging water towards him. 'The skipper's not given the order!'

Blake eyed him grimly. 'He's most likely dead, my lad! He'd have cut the engines otherwise. So it's up to us!'

The youth nodded, glad of something to do. 'I'll get the

rafts ready! You open the hatch!'

More bangs and grinding noises, and Blake guessed the flying-boat was breaking up.

He yelled, 'Have you got a gun?'

The youth nodded, staring at him.

Blake snapped, 'Bring it then.'

Sunlight tipped through the hatch and then the sea was washing around them, throwing them about like sodden dolls as they fought towards the exit. Two or three other figures were struggling through the hull, one of whom had obviously been wounded in the legs.

After being shut up in the small interior everything seemed larger and more violent than before. The great surging wash alongside, sweeping over the tilting wing, cruelly beautiful in the harsh sunlight. The insane roar of engines, the feeling of being unable to breathe or to think.

A second dinghy-like raft bobbed into view on its lanyard and the sailor gasped, 'Get in, miss!' He reached to help the girl over the side and then cowered down as the enemy plane came back, its guns stammering as before, flashing across the water to tip the floundering Catalina like a steel saw.

A man shrieked and fell headlong into the sea, the water frothing pink as he vanished beneath the surface.

Quintin groaned, 'The bugger caught my leg!'

Blake saw the blood running down Quintin's thigh even as he rolled heavily into the rubber dinghy and lay staring wide-eyed at the sky.

The sailor was shouting to his remaining companions and then with a cry cut the dinghy free.

The Catalina seemed to veer away in seconds, and Blake saw the other Americans framed against the starboard wing, struggling with their dinghy even as the German seaplane roared overhead in a tight turn. Sickened, he watched the feathers of spray darting around the last survivors until the men had vanished and with something like a sigh the broken Catalina lifted its tail and began to sink.

Blake gasped, '*Down!* Down, all of you!'

He could feel the tiny boat falling and lifting beneath his spread-eagled body, the very power of the great ocean just an eighth of an inch from him. He was more aware of the girl, pressed against him, her face hidden in his shoulder, her breathing more like gasps of pain.

The sailor whispered, 'Here he comes!' He made a last

effort. 'Bin nice knowing you folks!'

Quintin groaned, 'Murdering bastard!'

The shadow moved swiftly overhead and Blake waited for the final, terrible impact.

The seaplane's engine buzzed on and on, and at last he made himself accept it. It was going away. The pilot was satisfied.

Carefully, Blake lifted his head above the yellow side. He could barely focus his eyes through the glare. But there was no aircraft. Even the Catalina had completely disappeared.

The sailor swallowed hard and said, 'There's someone swimming over there! That'll be Nicko.' He started to struggle out of his flying suit. 'He's got a busted leg and lost a lot of blood!'

Blake seized his wrist. 'Get down!' He spoke so fiercely that the youth stared at him in surprise. Blake said, 'It's too far.'

The youth shrugged his hand away. 'Nicko's a pal. I'm not leaving him!'

Blake raised his arm and pointed, hating what he was doing, wishing they had laid in the dinghy for a few more minutes.

There were perhaps two sharks, but when they hit the wounded man it sounded like a dozen even at fifty yards. It seemed to go on and on, the sea bursting apart with spray and blue-grey shapes.

The sailor sank down and vomited.

Blake rested one hand on his shoulder and said quietly, 'In a minute or two we'll decide what to do.'

He looked at the girl, her slim figure rising and falling against the blue water as she leaned on the wet rubber. She was watching his face, his eyes, his mouth, as if to find some comfort there, or perhaps to read her own fate.

Blake said, 'It's the smallest command I've ever had, but I'll do my best.'

He recalled Fairfax's remark and his own retort. *You'll do better.*

He looked past the girl and above Quintin's limp figure and studied the empty sea. If the German had killed each one of them with a revolver he could have done no better.

With a sigh he looked at the sailor. 'What's your name?'

The youth was shaking badly. 'They call me Billy,' he hesitated, 'sir.'

Blake kept a firm grip on his shoulder. With Quintin

wounded he was going to need his help very much.

'Well, Billy, you help Miss Grenfell—'

She seemed to come out of her despair and interrupted, 'Claire. Call me Claire.' She touched the sailor's sleeve. 'Give me a hand to make Captain Quintin comfortable, will you?'

Blake turned away and began to search for an emergency ration pack.

A tiny yellow dot on the ocean, that was what they had all become. The Catalina, with its pilot and all but one of its crew, was gone for ever. They had paid the price of over-confidence, had seen only what they had wanted to see.

The German seaplane was miles away by now. Stowed in some secret hangar, its crew drinking coffee and schnapps while they described how they had shot down an enemy flying-boat.

He heard Quintin groan and when he looked over he saw the girl's hands, bloodied to her wrists, as she tried to clean the wound before covering it with a makeshift dressing.

Quintin stared at her glassily. 'God, Claire, lucky my wife can't see us like this, eh?' He gritted his teeth against the pain. 'She'd never believe it!'

The girl made to trail her hands in the sea alongside but Blake took them in his own and wiped them carefully with part of his shirt. He did not say anything, and he could tell from her sudden tension that she understood.

Not far from the boat was a dorsal fin. It would remain there until the end.

Blake clung to the dinghy's life-line and knelt beside Quintin's crumpled figure.

'How does it feel?'

Blake had to concentrate even on the way he spoke. The endless, sickening swoops of the little dinghy were unbearable. They must be a thousand times worse for Quintin.

And this was the second day. It was unbelievable. That they had survived, and that nobody had found them. All the previous night, as they had huddled together and endeavoured to sleep, Blake had thought about their position. He had tried not to think of the dawn, to hope too much. He knew from experience that the sea had endless patience when it came to the torture of its victims.

Quintin peered up at him, his eyes sunken with pain and fatigue.

'Only hurts when I laugh.' He opened his eyes wider, taking advantage of Blake's body which was between him and the blazing sunlight. 'Is our bush-ranger still with us?'

Blake looked over the side and found the dorsal fin without difficulty. 'Yes.'

His back, naked to the glare, felt as if he was being flayed alive. But Quintin's wound needed fresh dressings, and as the girl had said, 'Wrens' shirts make the best bandages.'

He could see her now. Turning away from them in their tiny, pitching refuge while she had stripped off her shirt and handed it to the American, Billy.

She was wearing Blake's drill tunic now, Victoria Cross ribbon and all.

Blake tightened his grip on the life-line to contain his anxiety, his bitterness. But for his insistence about a second German raider, Quintin and the girl would have waited for the usual air transport. It was that simple, brutally so. He had brought them to this. Billy had said there were eight in the Catalina's crew altogether. It was too high a price to pay for his own stubbornness.

Quintin wheezed, 'Where the hell d'you reckon we are?'

Blake made himself look at the sea. The horizon was blurred but the water glittered like sheet metal.

'Can't tell. Not less than two hundred miles south-east of Madagascar, I'd say.'

It might as well be a million, he thought. If only they had some rations, a sail, anything to give some hope. But as Billy had explained, the Catalina had been due for overhaul and someone had got a bit slack with the life-saving gear. They had two cans of fresh water, some boiled sweets and what had been chocolate but had since melted into a thick paste.

Quintin said, 'What about our lad Billy?' He tried to turn his head but the move was too painful.

The American sailor knelt over him. 'Right here, sir. I've got a line out. Might get a fish.'

Quintin stared at him glassily. 'Good boy. So long as you don't haul that bloody shark inboard!' He closed his eyes. 'You're all right, Billy. Like my own lad.'

Blake heard the girl say, 'He's drowsed off again. Best thing for him.'

He scrambled across to her side. Her hair was sticking to her forehead and there was dried blood on her hands from the last change of dressings.

She looked away. 'Don't stare. I know I'm a mess.'

Blake said, 'I know it sounds crazy. I think you look lovely. Even in all this.' He added vehemently, 'If it hadn't been for me. . . .'

She faced him and he saw a new flush on her face where the sun had made its mark.

'Don't start that again. *Please*. It wasn't your fault. How could it be?' Her strength seemed to ebb away. 'Anyway, what's the use? We're going to die. I can accept it. It's just that I don't want to be the last. I couldn't take it.'

Blake lifted her hand and held it in his, the dinghy, the misery of pain and helplessness momentarily receding as he looked at it.

Once, when he had been in a destroyer at the outbreak of war, he had seen a boatload of dead men. Drifting aimlessly in the Atlantic with all the time in the world. As the destroyer had manoeuvred carefully alongside and the sailors had lined the deck to watch the silent boatmen with sympathy or horror, Blake had found himself wondering about the last one of those human scarecrows to die. Watched by his sightless companions of how many voyages or how many runs ashore in unknown ports?

He said, 'I shall be here.'

He reached out and shook the American's shoulder. 'Wake up, Billy. Save sleep for tonight. Talk, sing, do what you like, but don't give in.'

The youth turned and stared at him. 'I don't want to die, sir. Not here. Like this.'

He looked so despairing that the reality of their danger seemed to close in even more.

Blake tried to smile. His lips felt as if they were cracked and raw, and it was an effort to speak and make any sense.

He said, 'Time for the water ration, Billy.'

The girl crawled past him and helped the youth to open the second container. It was lasting no time at all. Blake watched her as she dabbed some water along Quintin's lips, the way the American was gazing at her. Gaining strength from her example.

Blake shaded his eyes and looked at the horizon. If only the night would come. It was not a release. Just a reprieve.

Tomorrow would finish them. Their strength would give out, then their will to fight back. He could see it in his mind, stark and clear, as if he were there, as if it had already happened.

She moved beside him again and held out the metal cup. He sipped it carefully but it was gone almost before he could feel it.

She said, 'Talk to me.' Her hand shook as she replaced the water container and cup. 'I can't cope. Not any more.'

He waited for her to lean against him. Even the sunburn on his shoulders did not seem so bad now.

He replied, 'You cope better than any of us.'

'Tell me about yourself.'

Blake thought about Diana. When would she hear what had happened? Would she care? he wondered.

He said, 'I live with my father. On the Surrey-Hampshire border. It's an old house. Too big now, but there are some people billeted in the village who look after it and take care of the grounds. Most of them are dug up anyway. *Dig for Victory*. You know.'

He realized that his head had fallen forward, as if a string had been cut. Curiously, it frightened him more than the acceptance of dying.

She took a strip of her own shirt and laid it across his shoulders. Her touch felt cool and clean. The illusion of defeat. Of giving in.

Blake continued with sudden determination, 'My father's not well. He was badly injured years ago in China. But I miss him. Seeing him sitting in his garden or pottering round the glasshouses.'

She said, 'He sounds right.' She leaned closer, as if to exclude the others. 'What'll you do when the war's over?'

He looked at her and saw the pleading in her eyes.

He replied, 'Well, I've been promoted ahead of my proper seniority so many times I'll probably be busted down to ordinary seaman when this lot's over!' He shook his head. 'I don't know. I really don't.'

His head was throbbing badly, so that his brain felt as if it was bursting from his skull.

She was looking down at the crimson ribbon on the breast of her tunic.

'What about her? Your wife?'

He tried to chuckle but it wouldn't come. 'I forgot. You intelligence people know everything!'

She gripped his arm. 'Oh, God, here it comes again!'

The shark glided closer, one eye blank and staring, before it dipped down and under the dinghy.

The American said, 'Let me take a shot at it, sir.'

Blake shook his head. 'Might overturn us.' He was rationing his words. Like fresh, precious, cool water.

Maybe there was a search going on for them right now. He recalled what Quintin had said about the convoys, the need to prevent individual vessels from sailing without escort. That ruled out the chance of being sighted by any ship. He peered up at the empty sky, his eyes stinging from the glare.

And the rubber dinghy was drifting well away from land, and further still from the direct air routes. A tiny yellow dot. Their world. It made everything else seem futile and unimportant.

Her head lolled against his chest and he ran his fingers through her hair, feeling its softness through the blown salt.

He had not spoken to anyone about his father for a long time. The Mediterranean had kept him too busy. Too dedicated.

Sometimes his aunt, who looked after the old man in return for living in part of the house, sent him a letter with one of her own. Blake had often wondered what his father had been thinking about as he had carefully scrawled each line to a son he never seemed to recognize. They must have meant a lot to him to take such trouble. The letters were like those from a small child, important only to the writer, but otherwise meaningless.

Blake peered down at her face. She was sleeping but he had not the heart to wake her.

The little dinghy drifted on. Billy, the young American, lay crouched against the side, his makeshift fishing-line tied to his wrist, while Quintin endured his own suffering in silence. He was probably thinking about his wife in Melbourne and his son who was so like Billy and whom he would never see again.

Blake watched the sea and the occasional movement of the shark. Through his dulled and aching mind the realization seemed to force its way like a probe. He had brought them to this. Now, buried in his own self-pity and fear, he was letting go, allowing them to die without raising a finger.

Quintin was badly injured, and anyway had been too long on the beach to understand. The girl and the young American had never been made to survive against odds. It was his job and his alone.

Blake threw back his head, his lips cracking as he shouted hoarsely, 'A hero, are you? Then bloody well act like one!'

He felt her jerk awake against his shoulder and knew the others were staring at him apprehensively.

He said, 'Sorry.' He tried to lick his lips. 'How many seabirds can you think of, Billy?'

The youth blinked. 'Er, I—I'm not sure, that is....'

The girl clutched Blake's arm. 'Let me. Skua, osprey, gannet....'

Quintin struggled up on his elbow. 'I can do better than that....'

The little yellow dot was still there when sunset mercifully came to hide it.

7

To Die with Dignity

Using the young American sailor's shoulder as a support, Blake rose unsteadily to his feet and stared around. It was barely dawn, but it was already bright enough to reveal a clear sky, which within hours would be a furnace once more.

Blake swayed awkwardly as the dinghy's rubber bottom buckled under his feet. It reminded him of a circus, when he had been a small boy. The painted clown, struggling with such seriousness to remain upright while his friends tried to pull a sheet from under him.

It has been a bad night, made worse by the American youth's obvious suffering. Blake suspected he had been wiping his face with sea water and had been tempted to swallow some to ease his thirst.

All the previous afternoon Blake had kept them at it, asking mindless questions, awarding marks, telling jokes. Anything to keep them from falling into what they probably imagined was a harmless sleep.

It was strange, he thought vaguely. From the air, or from the deck of any size of ship, the sea would be like a mill-pond. Here, in it rather than on it, it seemed to have energy just for them, the need to disturb and tease away their attempts to rest.

If only it would rain. Any bloody thing.

He looked down at the others, feeling their despair like something physical.

She asked huskily, 'Still nothing?'

He watched her tongue move painfully across her lips, the way her borrowed tunic had fallen open to her waist without her noticing or caring.

He heard a voice answer, 'Empty. Might see something when the sun gets higher.' It did not sound like him. A hoarse, rusty murmur.

Quintin did not open his eyes. 'I'll be home later then.'

He spoke so clearly that Blake guessed he was either dreaming or quietly going out of his mind.

Blake sat down carefully. 'Get the water, Billy. One now and another—'

The girl looked at her bare legs as if seeing them for the first time. 'It's the last! There'll *be* no more after this.'

The American cradled the container between his knees as if it was pure gold. 'I was saying to my pal. A nice cool Coke. That's when it happened.' He doubled over, his voice choking in sobs. 'The bastards! They didn't need to kill all of them!'

His voice trailed away, the strength leaving him as quickly as it had shown itself.

Blake leaned against the dinghy and said wearily, 'You have mine, Claire, I'm not thirsty.'

She held the cup to his mouth, her hand remarkably firm. 'Don't pull rank. It's forbidden here.' She watched him as he sipped the water. 'Anyway. You promised. We'll keep together.'

He studied her, as if to implant each part of her in his memory. 'You're quite a girl, Claire. Did you know that?'

She turned away and passed the cup to be refilled for Quintin. It took two of them to help him, as any extra effort brought the pain from his wound like a hot iron.

She said quietly, 'You're not so bad yourself, *sir*.'

The sun surged over the horizon, reaching out in either direction, laying bare its emptiness. The first breath of sunlight brought vapour from the swaying dinghy and their bodies and made the surrounding water twist in haze.

Billy croaked, 'Shark's still here. 'N'other one back there, too.'

Blake watched him narrowly but the youth did not seem to notice that his pistol holster had been removed during the night. Blake knew what could happen even seconds before a man died. To be armed and not be allowed to fire at that stalking shadow would be enough to turn anyone's mind.

It was unnerving how long periods of time seemed to vanish, while other moments which you imagined had been hours were really a second's thought or memory.

Blake cradled the girl's shoulders in his arm and tried to keep their combined shadow across Quintin's reddened face. It was beginning. The slowing down, like an engine which has had its fuel line cut.

He could no longer gauge the dinghy's motion properly and was being flung about like a drunken libertyman. The girl was very still, and when he looked down he saw her bare skin through the gap in the white tunic. It looked smooth and soft, and her breathing seemed regular again, as if she too realized there was no more room for pretence or hope.

Blake closed his eyes and tried to concentrate on pictures. His father in his worn panama hat peering at his tomatoes. *Andromeda*'s gangway at Alexandria when he had returned aboard with his advanced promotion confirmed. The tanned, grinning faces of his men, the unrehearsed cheer, sharing it with him as they had shared all the other part of it. In his reeling mind the gangway changed abruptly to that of his first appointment as midshipman. The towering side of a battleship, a horsy-looking lieutenant glaring at him and rasping, 'Blake, is it, sir? Damme, Mr Blake, *you'll* never be an admiral, that's the only thing you can be certain of!'

He felt himself grinning at the stupid recollection and then blinked his eyes open as Billy rolled over, struggling to rise to his knees as he gasped, *'Jesus!'* He almost fell again. *'Help me!'* He stared wildly at Blake and the girl. 'Don't you *hear*?'

Blake tried to swallow but his throat was like dust. He gripped the life-line and pulled himself round. Billy had gone raving mad. He would have to do something.

Then he heard it. A low, humming throb at first, then as his senses returned he recognized what had brought the American out of his torpor.

The girl had her hand to her mouth. 'He's coming back!'

Blake looked at her, unable to speak. To think they had expected to die, been prepared as well as anybody could. But with dignity, if there was such a thing.

His eyes watered with sudden fury. The engine was that of a small aircraft.

It could only be a seaplane right out here. Stagg's *Fremantle* was hundreds of miles away and the westbound convoy barely clear of Australian waters. It could be nothing else but the raider. He had been wrong even about that. There was no mercy here, not even indifference. The aircraft was coming back to make sure, as it had with the Catalina.

Frantically Blake groped for the American's pistol. Just a few shots from the plane would destroy the dinghy. There would be nothing between them and the sharks.

She saw his anguish and said haltingly, 'Don't leave me to die like that.' She put her hand on the pistol. 'Use it, *Please*!'

Quintin muttered thickly, 'Might miss us. Fly right past.'

Blake shaded his eyes and peered at the blue water. It rose

and fell in great layers, like a moving range of hills. From a small vessel the raft might be invisible, but from the air. . . . His heart stood still as sunlight lanced across the aircraft's cockpit and changed its propeller into a solid silver disc.

He felt the girl gripping his arm.

'Hold me!'

Louder and louder, until the engine's roar seemed to stun them, smother them.

Blake tried to form his words carefully. Each syllable was agony.

'It's all right, Claire.' He put his arm round her, steadying her as she turned towards the rising sound. '*Look!*' He pointed at the opposite horizon, his arm waving about as he tried to hold it towards the tiny smudge of smoke, motionless in the sunlight. 'It's ours. It's *Andromeda*.' He felt her disbelief through her rigid shoulders and added quietly, 'God knows how she did it, but she found us.'

The Seafox swept overhead and seconds later a Very light exploded in a vivid green pear-drop high in the sky.

Blake thought he saw Lieutenant Masters waving down to the little yellow dinghy, but his eyes were too misty to be certain of anything.

Commander Victor Fairfax gripped the arms of the captain's chair and leaned forward to peer through the salt-smeared screen.

Lifting, then slicing down as the sea parted across her sharp stem, *Andromeda* seemed to be enjoying the unexpected freedom of speed.

Behind and below him the ship was going about its affairs, to outward appearance everything as usual. It was eight o'clock in the evening and the starboard watch had just closed up at defence stations. On the messdecks they would be clearing up for rounds, listening to the radio, writing letters or just passing the time.

Lieutenant-Commander Scovell stepped up on to the gratings, his face expressionless as he said, 'First watchmen closed up, sir.' He turned as two sheets of spray as high as B turret burst on either side of the forecastle.

Fairfax knew the first lieutenant disliked him for some reason, and guessed he was watching his every move.

He asked, 'Did you pass the word to the lookouts?'

'Yes, sir.' Scovell glanced at the sky. It was less glaring

91

already. Soon there would be a cool breeze, darkness, while the ship continued to hurl herself through the sea. Scovell added, 'Nothing from W/T yet.'

He moved away to supervise his watch, leaving Fairfax with his thoughts and his anxieties.

Fairfax made to lift his binoculars but let them fall to his chest. What was the point? The bridge was shuddering and jerking like mad, and he heard Villar cursing quietly as some of his instruments rolled off the chart table.

Fairfax stared wretchedly at the horizon. It was beautiful now that the real heat had gone for the day. The horizon was shark blue, like a darker barrier to the rest of the ocean. Above, the sky was tinged with orange where it met the sea's edge. It should have been one of the best evenings in his life.

He tried to think back clearly, see what he had done, calmly, like a spectator. *Andromeda* had been under way, standing clear of the mainland with a solitary patrol boat to see her clear, when they had received the signal about the missing aircraft. Signals had crackled through the atmosphere, some sort of a search had been ordered, but Fairfax knew from his orders and intelligence pack that there were few big aircraft spare for proper coverage. The eastbound convoy around the Cape would soon be due and the westbound one would need air cover too if the raider was still on the rampage.

Andromeda was ordered back to her temporary home at Williamstown. She had no part in the missing aircraft and would be needed for another patrol as soon as she was in position.

Quite suddenly Fairfax had made up his mind, although looking back it seemed as if it had been done for him. He had sent for Scovell and the engineer commander and had told them what he knew.

'I intend to alter course and look for that Catalina. It may be afloat and only damaged. They'll need help. There's nobody else.'

Scovell had said in his precise manner, 'Local patrols will be alerted. A flying-boat on the surface, even allowing for drift, should be visible.'

It had sounded like a challenge. As if Scovell was stating his own position before things went wrong.

Fairfax pounded his hand on the rail below the screen. Well, things had gone wrong all right. At maximum revolutions the ship had swung round and headed north-east away from her proper course. For two days they had kept it up with only rare reductions of speed while Weir and his men had checked or repaired some new strain or fault in their machinery.

Weir had been just as Blake had said. Like a rock. He had never complained, and when he had last spoken with him on the telephone Weir had said curtly, 'It's not a matter of choice, sir. You did the right thing, in my view.'

Fairfax removed his cap and ran his fingers through his hair. Weir's view would not be the one laid out on the court martial table.

He thought of Sarah, how she would take it. Fair enough at first. But later, would she see his ruined career in the same light? If it had not been Blake, *Andromeda* would have maintained her proper course and speed. Fairfax knew it and everyone aboard would be thinking it.

Shoes scraped on the gratings and he saw Villar watching the sea as it swept down the port side like a white-topped sluice.

'What do *you* think, Pilot?' Fairfax knew he should not involve the navigating officer but could not just sit there. Waiting, having the anxiety gnawing at his insides like hooks.

Villar regarded him calmly. 'When I was with the Union Castle we lost a hand overboard. One of the ship's orchestra, as a matter of fact. Blew all his cash playing poker and got himself pissed.' The South African looked at him without any pity in his eyes. 'Trouble was, he wasn't missed until the next morning. One of the first class passengers wanted the idiot to play for his birthday!'

Fairfax turned away. Villar was a hard man. An excellent navigator, and he guessed he would be good to be with in a tight corner. But you would never know him.

Villar added, 'The Old Man turned the ship round for that drunken bum. Found him, too.' He shook his head. 'Bloody fine, eh?'

Fairfax said quietly, 'You are telling me there's a chance?'

'There's always a chance, sir.' Villar paused as he made to leave the gratings. 'They'll say you did right. You see, sir.'

Fairfax turned in the chair and beckoned to Sub-Lieutenant Walker.

'Get Lieutenant Masters up here, will you, Sub?'

He returned to his thoughts. The Catalina must have crashed. He was wasting time as well as risking his own neck.

Villar came back, his face grim. 'Signal from W/T office,

sir. To *Fremantle* repeated *Andromeda*.' He peered at a signal pad. '*Most immediate. Unidentified vessel reported in position latitude thirty-six degrees south longitude sixty east. Sighted by whaling supply vessel* Tarquin. *No further information*.'

Fairfax slid from his chair, his mind cringing. 'Take over, Number One.' Then he led the way to the chartroom where Villar's yeoman was already plotting the latest sighting on his chart.

'Where's *Fremantle*?'

Villar's brass dividers measured off the vast span of ocean, each metallic click like derision. 'Too far, sir. Whereas we....' The dividers moved remorselessly to the pencilled line of *Andromeda*'s original course.

Fairfax gripped his hands tightly behind his back. But for leaving to search for a crashed aircraft, *Andromeda* would have been within half a day's steaming of the other ship's alleged position.

As if to rub salt in the wound Villar added, 'Very close to where the Dutchman *Evertsen* was sunk.'

Masters lurched through the door. 'Ouch, sorry, sir, but the old girl's rolling a bit.'

Fairfax asked, 'Is your plane ready to fly off?'

Masters nodded. 'Yes, sir. When?'

Fairfax was staring at the little pencilled crosses on the chart. Ignominy for trying to save life, whereas he would be well praised if he came on the raider. He looked at the widening triangle between *Andromeda* and her recommended course. Even now, if Weir could coax some more knots out of his over-worked screws, they might be able to track the enemy, especially if another report came through.

It seemed as if everything was going wrong. Whatever they tried to do the enemy knew in advance, or so it appeared. It was like hunting a blind man in a pitch-dark room.

Villar said softly, 'Shall I lay off a course to intercept, sir?'

They were all looking at Fairfax. Masters, unusually tense, Villar, dark and watchful, and the young seaman named Wright who was the navigator's yeoman.

Fairfax did not reply directly. To Masters he said, 'Do you think the Catalina would break up?'

Masters looked at the chart. 'No. The weather reports were good. Those milk-run pilots know their job and the planes are tough. If they had time to put down without crashing it must have been urgent. Fire maybe, in which case they would take

94

to the life-rafts.' His eyes were still on the chart, the vast span of the Indian Ocean. 'I know the captain could take care of himself. I'm not sure about the others.'

Scovell ducked through the door, his gaze moving curiously across the little group at the table.

'Sir? Chief's on the phone.'

Fairfax nodded. 'I'll come.'

On the open bridge it felt clean after the oppressive atmosphere of the chartroom. He picked up the handset.

'Chief? Commander here.'

'I'd like to know if I can send some of my key ratings off watch. They've been working full-time for hours, and if we keep up these revs I'm going to need every experienced man I've got.'

'Is it that bad?'

'It's not critical, sir, but I've never had her going at this speed for so long.'

Over the telephone Weir's Scots accent sounded more pronounced.

'Give me revolutions for twenty knots, Chief. Will that help?'

'Aye. For the moment.' The slightest hesitation, as if Weir hated to link his engineroom with the affairs of the bridge. 'Is there no news?'

'None.'

Fairfax replaced the handset and walked to the side of the bridge.

To Scovell he said, 'We will reduce to twenty knots. Pilot, lay off a course to intercept that unidentified ship and check it by the hour. Get your assistant up here to help you.' He turned towards Masters. 'I shall want you airborne as soon as it is light enough for you to make a recce.'

Masters said, 'Fine.'

Villar snapped to his yeoman, 'Shiner, fetch Lieutenant Trevett, chop, chop! Can't have all these Aussies sitting on their backsides, now can we?'

Scovell stood his ground. 'So you're not going after the raider yet, sir?'

'Is that what you would have done, Number One?'

Scovell shrugged. 'I'm not in command, sir.'

Fairfax felt the eyes watching from around the bridge. What did they feel? Contempt, amusement, anger, indifference? Whatever it was, it all seemed to flow straight from Scovell.

Fairfax said quietly, 'No, you are not, Number One. But I think you just answered my question anyway. Well, don't worry too much. You will be whiter than white, whatever happens!'

He swung back towards the chair, conscious of Scovell's look of shocked surprise and his own petty victory.

A shadow moved up from the interior companion ladder. It was Moon, his jacket pale against the grey steel. He held out a small tray and uncovered a pot of coffee. He did it with a kind of shabby flourish, as if he was trying to convey something.

He said, 'Made it meself, sir. From me special store. Just like the cap'n 'as.'

Fairfax took the cup in his hand, suddenly grateful for Moon's private gesture.

'Thanks. That was a nice thought.'

Moon blinked through the screen, his eyes watering in the breeze coming back from the bows.

Fairfax said softly, 'It's all right. We're still looking. I'm not turning back.'

Moon dusted an invisible speck from his napkin. 'Course not, sir. Told 'em you wouldn't. Not your style, that's what I told 'em, sir.'

Fairfax let out a long breath. It had been a close thing. But for Moon? He shook his head. Now he might never know.

Surgeon Lieutenant-Commander Edgar Bruce grunted with exasperation as he peered at Blake's blistered shoulders.

'Easy, sir, you can't expect to carry on as if nothing had happened.'

Blake, naked but for a clean towel, sat in his day cabin, trying not to listen to the ship's movements around him, to accept what had so recently been an impossible dream. *Andromeda* had steamed in a slow circle around their rubber dinghy, and as a motor boat had been lowered and sent to collect the four survivors, Blake had seen his men lining the guard-rails or standing up in the gun sponsons to wave and cheer.

It must have been a strange sight, he thought. Captain Quintin being carried across the quarterdeck by the sickberth attendants, the young American sailor, chin in the air with recovered pride although he had been almost blinded with emotion, and the girl, bare-legged, bloodied and yet so beautiful in the soiled drill tunic.

He glanced at Fairfax who had stayed with him since he had been hoisted aboard. If anything, Fairfax looked as if he had suffered with them, and even his great grin of welcome did not completely erase the strain from his face.

Blake said, 'See that the American lad is well looked after. Let Masters have a chat with him, show him the recognition cards. I think the plane was an Arado 196, but Masters may be able to glean something I've missed.'

He turned and winced as the surgeon dabbed something on his back. 'What did you make of Quintin, Doc?'

Bruce smiled. 'He's too old for this sort of lark, sir, but as tough as they come. He'll not be up and about for quite a bit. But for the dressings he'd have lost a leg, no doubt about that.' He stood back and wiped his hands. 'There, sir, best I can do if you're determined not to take it easy.'

Blake saw Moon hovering by the door. His face seemed to be all teeth and his eyes were lost in slits of obvious pleasure.

Blake said, 'A shave and a clean shirt will do for the present, Doc.' He hesitated. 'How's Second Officer Grenfell?' Could it all change so swiftly? With death within reach he had called her Claire. This seemed like a betrayal.

'I've put her out, sir. She'll sleep like a top until tomorrow. I've got her in my cabin. I feel more at home in the sick-bay. I hardly ever left the blessed place when we were in the Med.'

'She's going to be all right?'

Blake knew Fairfax was watching him with sudden interest but he did not care.

'I've examined her thoroughly. Nothing broken. Outwardly she's as good as new.' Bruce shrugged. 'Later . . . well, we'll have to see.'

Blake looked away, picturing the girl lying naked on Bruce's table.

He said, 'I'll be returning to the bridge, Doc. Keep me posted.'

As the surgeon left Blake asked, 'Any further sighting reports on the unidentified ship?' He knew it was troubling Fairfax more than he had admitted.

Fairfax said, 'No, sir. I guess the whaling supply vessel made off at full speed, just to be on the safe side. D'you think there'll be trouble about it when we get in?'

'We'll worry about *that* later.'

Blake stood up and felt the deck reel under him. It had been like that since he had been hauled from the dinghy. Survivors rescued from life-boats after weeks, even days on the open sea could rarely walk properly for a long time after being picked up.

'We know more than we did, Victor. The raider carries at least one seaplane. That gives her captain a far greater area to cast his net. Also, it can warn him about any threatening warships in his vicinity.' He looked at his hands. 'We also know that the man who commands the raider has no feeling for human life. The seaplane was merely an instrument. The German captain knew what he was doing.'

Fairfax watched him, moved and troubled by his words.

'Can I ask? D'you still believe there are two raiders?'

Blake eyed him gravely. 'I'm not sure. I'm certain of one thing only. We're going to finish him or them!'

He beckoned to Moon. 'You do the shaving. I'll probably cut my throat, I'm shaking so badly!'

As Fairfax moved to the door he called after him, 'There's not much I can say. Thank you sounds too feeble for what you did, for what it might have cost you. Whoever eventually gets command of *Andromeda* will be damn lucky to have you, too.' He tried to grin. 'I shall bloody well tell him so!'

Fairfax walked from the cabin, nodding to the marine sentry outside the door.

He heard the murmur of voices from the wardroom, the clatter of plates as the stewards prepared to serve the officers' lunch.

The motion felt easier as the ship headed towards her proper station, and Fairfax recalled the relief in Weir's voice when he had ordered a return to cruising speed.

He walked briskly along the upper deck, past a small working party who were lashing the yellow dinghy to the boat tier like a trophy.

Fairfax thought of the girl's face as she had been helped aboard, the way Blake had spoken of her.

He would tell Sarah about it. She would have had them hitched in no time if Blake had been unmarried.

The tannoy squeaked and then intoned, 'Cooks to the galley! Senior hands of messes to muster for rum!'

He climbed swiftly to the upper bridge, past the lookouts

and signalmen and the massive bulk of Toby Jug with his old-fashioned brass telescope.

Lieutenant Palliser had the watch and threw up a real gunnery salute as Fairfax climbed into the bridge.

'New course is one-four-zero, sir.' He could not contain a smile. 'No further reports from W/T.'

Fairfax nodded and smiled at the other watchkeepers. They seemed different. They *were* different.

He stepped up to the fore-gratings and stood beside the empty, freshly scrubbed chair.

Andromeda had decided. He was accepted.

8
Convoy

Kapitän zur See Kurt Rietz steadied his powerful Zeiss glasses on the slow-moving dot in the sky and then lowered them carefully to his chest again. He could feel the tension around him like steel mesh, the whispered commands and repeated acknowledgements from telephones and voice-pipes adding to the sense of apprehension.

Rietz was used to tension. It rarely left him. It was part of his being. He could barely remember feeling free, able to relax and chatter about unimportant trivialities.

Under her assumed colours and Swedish markings the raider was moving at a reduced cruising speed, her wake cutting a frothing track through the glittering blue water astern.

They had sighted the aircraft two hours ago, a black dot which changed shape and burst into brilliant light as it altered course across the sun towards them.

Unhurriedly, the raider's company had gone to quarters. It was always expected, like the dawn, and now it was here. The aircraft was a naval flying-boat, one of the old British Walrus type, so there was no room for doubt. There was a warship somewhere beneath the horizon. One of the hunters. The old enemy.

Rietz heard his first lieutenant's breathing beside him and said, 'It was as well we sighted the aircraft in time to alter course, Rudi. A few more minutes and they would have realized we were not on the Swede's proper course.'

Storch followed the distant plane, his eyes intent. 'Even so, sir, the warship will not be deceived.' He stared at his captain. 'Surely?'

A seaman with a handset banged his heels together. 'Main armament closed up, sir! All shutters sealed, aircraft secured!'

Rietz nodded. 'Good.' To his subordinate he continued, 'The *real Patricia* will not be reported missing as yet, Rudi. We wear her colours and we are *approximately* on her original course.' He gave a wry smile. 'Give or take a hundred miles or so. But with these German raiders about who could blame me for taking avoiding action, eh?' It seemed to amuse him.

The gunnery speaker rapped out from the rear of the bridge. 'Ship bearing Green four-five, sir! Range fifteen miles!'

A dozen sets of binoculars swung over the screen and from the lookout stations. Above their heads the disguised range-finder turned easily on its oiled bearings, making a lie of the scarred paintwork and rust streaks around it.

Rietz kept his face empty of expression as he steadied his glasses on the first sighting of the newcomer. The merest flaw on the horizon, a hint of smoke which might have been sea-mist parting before a powerful fighting ship at full speed.

He went over everything he had gleaned from the *Patricia*'s papers which his resourceful boarding officer had brought aboard after firing the demolition charges.

Bound for Port Said. A neutral on her lawful occasions.

He shifted his glasses to watch the flying-boat, awkward in the sunlight with its 'pusher' engine balanced on the upper wing.

He said, 'Tell all hands not to stand with their glasses on that aircraft, Rudi.' He controlled the sudden edge in his tone. Any sign of anxiety now would be asking for trouble. 'Put some men to work on the forecastle. That plane will come nearer soon. My guess is that the pilot went back to signal a report to his captain. That gentleman will need some more evidence before he closes the range.'

Rietz thought of his two previous voyages. One hundred thousand tons of enemy shipping put down. A tremendous effort for Germany, for all those at home who had only the carefully vetted bulletins to carry them through the days and the long, shattering nights as the bombers came and went.

This voyage was even more important. For the first time since the army had marched into Poland in 1939 Germany was on the defensive. In Italy, in Russia, even in the Atlantic.

He thought of the admiral in Kiel, grave-eyed as he stared through the rain-soaked windows above the dockyard. Germany had to have more time. For the new weapons, for the army's next push eastward when the Russian steam-roller was slowed down. There was talk of great new rockets to be fired on to London and the Channel ports, and an all-electric submarine which would be immune from any kind of detection. *Time, time, time.*

Storch called from the bridge wing. 'Aircraft closing to port, sir!'

In a wide arc, its engine throbbing noisily, the Walrus tilted towards the raider. Rietz made himself look along his command. Obedient to his order a few seamen were working around the anchor cables, another was squirting a hose over the side, possibly his own crude gesture to the enemy.

He snapped, 'Be ready to reply to the challenge, Rudi. But tell Fackler to make his number *slowly*. This is a Swedish ship, remember? Not a damned battle-cruiser!'

It brought a few nervous laughs, as he knew it would.

The Walrus rattled down the raider's side, and then an Aldis light stabbed from the cockpit. *What ship? Where bound? Number? Cargo?*

Rietz watched the signals petty officer, the way he was cradling his lamp on his elbow. It was convincing, and he had no doubt that the Walrus crew had their glasses on them right now.

The light flashed again and Petty Officer Fackler said, 'Requests we alter course two points to starboard, sir.'

Rietz nodded. 'Alter course, Rudi. Steer zero-two-zero. Warn the engineroom to stand by for immediate increase of speed.'

He removed his cap and waved it above his head towards the aircraft. It was already heading away, and when he lifted his glasses again he saw that the oncoming ship had gained identity within minutes.

'Gone to make his report.'

He patted his pockets, suddenly in need of a cigar. He must clear his mind, be ready to act without hesitation. The warship would be suspicious, her gunnery officer impatient to hurl his first salvo into them.

The speaker intoned. 'The ship is a cruiser, sir.' The smallest hesitation; and Rietz could imagine his own spotting crew whipping through their recognition cards as they had done so often.

'She's the Australian cruiser *Fremantle*, sir.'

Rietz let the details about the cruiser wash over him. He knew as much about the enemy build-up in the Indian Ocean as anyone. He had to admit that German intelligence were good. It was almost unnerving the way they seemed to know every ship movement, each rendezvous point as quickly as the enemy did.

So *Fremantle* was here already. Eight-inch guns. A good turn of speed. If it came to a fight it would have to be close action. Torpedoes, then rapid fire with every weapon which would bear. He pictured his gun crews sweating down there between decks, waiting behind the steel shutters, ready to swing out the powerful muzzles and blaze away.

A long ocean roller lifted under the *Salamander*'s keel and tilted her over. Rietz heard the clatter of machine-gun belts below the bridge and knew the ship was riding too high in the water. It was to be hoped the *Fremantle* did not notice. He needed more fuel and stores. A fresh rendezvous with another supply ship was vital now that *Bremse* had gone. He had received a signal about her, vague but definite. It must have been the spare mines she had been carrying. At least it would have been quick, he thought grimly.

He heard some of the watchkeepers murmuring between themselves and walked out into the sunlight again to study the oncoming cruiser.

He saw the smoke fanning from her two funnels, the sea sweeping back from her stem in a great moustache of white foam. She was capable of thirty-two knots, according to Storch's copy of *Jane's Fighting Ships*.

A powerful light blinked across the water like a diamond.

'Heave to!' Petty Officer Fackler peered at his captain uncertainly.

'Stop engines.'

Rietz glanced at Storch, wondering if he still remembered what they had been discussing only an hour or so ago. On the face of it he knew the young lieutenant was right. The second raider, the *Wölfchen*, had achieved real success in a matter of weeks. The big Australian cruiser *Devonport* must have seemed like a disaster to the enemy. Not a single spar or stick had been found. Rietz had wondered more than once what had happened to the survivors, if there were any. He thought of the other kills made by the second raider, the *Argyll Clansman* and the crippled *Kios*, and set them against the face he remembered of the man who commanded *Salamander*'s twin. It seemed unlikely.

He had served with the other captain early in the war, in the sunny days when they had swept through the Baltic, the North Sea and deep into the South Atlantic. *Fregattenkapitän* Konrad Vogel, so beloved then by the war correspondents, with his flashing smile and jaunty beard, the tiger of the convoy routes.

Perhaps he was the right man for this kind of work. Maybe

103

the early days of respect for an enemy on the high seas were a hindrance.

Storch had been hinting as much, although Rietz knew he was speaking out for his captain's sake. He hated Vogel's triumphs, his conceit, his cruelty.

The strange thing was that the enemy still did not realize there were two raiders working in the same ocean. It had been worked out to perfection in Kiel by the Grand Admiral himself. A new system of grids and rendezvous points. Fewer signals to avoid detection, greater care to move well clear of each other, but not too much to avoid suspicion. Whereas *Salamander* had made the long and precarious voyage from Germany, up and through the Denmark Strait and then southwards through the Atlantic, Vogel's *Wölfchen* had already been in Japan, fitting out under German supervision, when the plan had been decided.

He thrust Vogel from his mind as he studied the Australian cruiser. She was steering diagonally towards the drifting raider, her three turrets angled round and no doubt loaded with armour-piercing shells.

Storch said between his teeth, 'The officer you captured, sir, he may be watching you.' He sounded anxious.

Rietz shook his head. 'I had a beard then.'

He tried to remember the man whose broad pendant now flew above the oncoming warship. Commodore Rodney Stagg. But he could recall only his size, his uncontrollable anger.

He thought instead of the other man who was hunting him. Captain Blake of the light-cruiser *Andromeda*. Against the pair of them he and Vogel were well matched, when you considered it.

A lookout called, 'She's preparing to lower a boat, sir!'

Rietz examined his feelings. Why did he feel nothing? This was the moment. Once aboard, the enemy would know. Even alongside it would be too close for deception.

He said quietly, 'All guns stand by. Release the shutters over the torpedo tubes.'

Storch plucked at the front of his shirt, his eyes on the cruiser as if mesmerized.

He said, 'Not long now, sir.'

Rietz glanced at him. Poor Storch, he had not had much of a life. He had been about to marry a girl in Hamburg, but she had died in an air raid.

Feet clattered through from the chartroom and Schoningen,

104

the navigating officer, hurried towards him.

'Sir! We have intercepted a signal to *Fremantle* and *Andromeda*. Unidentified ship reported. We also picked up something about an enemy aircraft down in the sea.' He seemed to realize the nearness of the big cruiser and added in a strained voice, 'Instructions, sir?'

Rietz turned swiftly as the first lieutenant exclaimed, 'They are hoisting their boat and the Walrus is preparing to come down alongside the ship!'

'All guns standing by, sir! Torpedo tubes *ready*!'

Rietz said softly, 'Fingers crossed, everybody!'

The light began to blink again, and only the squeak of the signalmen's pencils broke the silence.

'*From* HMAS Fremantle *to* Patricia. *Proceed to Port Said as instructed. You will meet with northbound convoy and escort. You will remain with same until otherwise ordered.*'

In a strangled voice Storch said, 'She's almost stopped! My God, we could sink her right now, sir!'

Rietz thrust his hands into his pockets. Throughout his command his men would be thinking like Storch. Their executioner was almost motionless as she prepared to recover the Walrus from the water. There would never be another chance like it. *Fremantle* looked as big as a block of flats and she must be held in a dozen sets of gunsights like a giant in a net.

He said calmly, 'Reply, *thank you for your help*.' He looked at Storch's confused features. 'If we are near a convoy, why not do as the commodore suggests?'

A messenger called, 'The *Fremantle*'s radio is transmitting, sir!'

Rietz looked at Storch again. 'See? We are expected.'

He turned to watch the Walrus rising up on its crane to the cruiser's deck and noticed that the ship was already getting under way, curving away even as he watched.

Storch exclaimed hoarsely, 'The convoy, sir? The *whole convoy*?'

Rietz reached out and gratefully accepted a cigar from Petty Officer Fackler.

'You were just telling me to watch out for the *Wölfchen*'s successes against our modest victories, eh?' He turned to the voice-pipes. 'Resume course and speed. Revolutions for fourteen knots.'

Storch said, 'I am sorry, sir.'

Rietz shrugged. 'We need supplies. We have too many

mouths to feed, so many leagues to steam. I did not choose the killing ground, Rudi.' His eyes hardened as he watched the cruiser turning end on and increasing speed towards the horizon. '*He* did.'

'Convoy in sight, sir!' The petty officer stepped aside as Rietz levered himself from the throbbing plot table and turned towards the wheelhouse.

It was the first time they had broken their admiral's rules. Usually, the code would be flashed to both raiders together. To assume an already planned disguise, so that they would appear identical in the reports from survivors, if there were any.

But with two cruisers verified in this vicinity it would have been foolish to ignore the advantages gained by the Swedish disguise, the fact she was known to be heading for Port Said. Only when the owners or agents sent a signal with instructions for her master would the alarm be raised. Unless Rietz could force the Swedish master to send a false signal. He decided against it immediately. There was always the chance the Swede had had time to plan for such a moment. In any case, losing his ship was enough humiliation for any man, Rietz thought.

He walked out into the sunlight and raised his glasses.

Storch said, 'Seven vessels, sir, and two escorts. Small local convoy. Probably from Zanzibar. No other warships reported.' He clenched his jaw as he levelled his own glasses over the screen. 'Not much of an escort. The gunnery officer tells me the destroyer is an old one from the Great War and the other is a corvette.'

Rietz considered it. A small convoy in two unmatched lines steaming across blue, untroubled waters. The *Fremantle* would have signalled the escort commander. It would all be a matter of timing.

'Increase to fifteen knots, Rudi. Tell the gunnery officer I wish to engage from either beam simultaneously. The destroyer first. Torpedoes, full salvo. We will engage *her* to starboard.'

He pictured their position on his big chart table, the officers and men grouped around it as they always did. They were known as the 'Family' by the rest of the ship's company, exclusive in their special place abaft the bridge, free from the boring weariness of painting and re-painting or creating new disguises.

106

Fremantle would be many miles away by now. It was to be hoped that the commodore had not fallen on another supply ship. It was unlikely, but the men who commanded the raiders' suppliers had a lot to worry about. Rather like running a grocer's shop in the middle of an air bombardment.

Where was *Andromeda*? he wondered. Intelligence had reported her clear of Port Elizabeth, so she was probably well to the south of their own position. One great ocean. Curiously enough, he did not think about Vogel's *Wölfchen* at all.

'Guns standing by, sir!'

'Good.'

Rietz watched the two lines of ships, the sudden stab of a signal lamp from the out-dated destroyer. The signalman was sending in careful, precise English, just for the Swedish master's benefit. *Patricia* was to take station at the rear of the port column to make the lines even. Just as Rietz had anticipated. A tidy arrangement for the escort commander.

'Acknowledge the signal.'

Rietz glanced at the bridge team, the way some of them had their German naval caps stuck behind voice-pipes or lockers so that they could put them on when action was joined. It would not help much if you were killed.

It was a very slow convoy, and in the ocean's comparative calm the lean-hulled destroyer was rolling sickeningly as she sought to keep station on her charges. Two sizeable freighters, a coaster with a top-heavy deck cargo and what appeared to be a small tanker. The other three were masked by their consorts. The stubby corvette was the problem. She was at least two miles ahead of the convoy. With her tiny armament she presented no menace, but her radio was something else entirely. But it was a convoy, and to destroy it within days of entering harbour would create pandemonium and give Vogel a chance to avoid detection until he had refuelled.

Rietz watched the destroyer narrowly. She was on the starboard bow now, her signal lamp flashing at another ship in the convoy which had probably edged out of her proper station.

'Alter course, Rudi. Steer for the port line, astern of that freighter.'

He walked to the rear of the bridge, still able to ignore the snap of orders, the muted stammer of morse from the radio room.

He picked up the red handset and waited for the engineroom to answer.

'Leichner? This is the captain. Full speed in about ten minutes. Everything, do you understand?'

'Yes, Captain.' The line went dead.

Rietz moved to the bridge windows and peered down at the forward well-deck where some seamen were dragging themselves below the bulwark, heavy machine-guns and ammunition making their progress slow and painful. Somewhere deep in the hull a bell set up a short clamour, and Rietz could picture the torpedo tubes training on the bearings being passed down from the gunnery team.

The destroyer was almost abeam, rolling from side to side, hating the slow progress, when built originally for speed and agility. Rietz studied her calmly. It was rare to be so close to an enemy. She was barely half a cable away. He glanced at his watch. They were probably having their midday meal. Cursing at the motion, the way all sailors did.

The speaker intoned, 'Aftermost guns will now bear, sir. Ready to fire.'

Rietz made himself wait, counting the seconds to control his heart beats. Surely someone would notice how high his ship was in the water? The *Salamander* was the largest vessel in the convoy. Perhaps her neutral markings had stripped away her possible menace.

'Stand by!'

A seaman strolled with elaborate nonchalance to the foot of the foremast, and Rietz knew he was carrying the German ensign inside a roll of canvas.

He glanced over at Storch, who was watching like an athlete under the starter's pistol.

Rietz nodded. 'Now.'

Bells jangled throughout the ship, and Rietz felt the deck shudder as the massive steel shutters fell open along either side of the hull and the big five-point-nine guns swung outboard.

The bridge began to quiver as the chief engineer obeyed the telegraphs, and within ten seconds of the order three torpedoes leapt from their tubes, splashed gracelessly into the water and then speeded towards the destroyer, vicious and eager in their proper element.

'*Open fire!*'

Men were yelling and cursing, their cries suddenly lost and puny as the great guns crashed inboard on their springs, the smoke billowing over the rusty plates in a solid bank. Machine-guns hammered through the drifting fog, the tracer vivid and deadly as it swept across the destroyer and the ship immediately ahead of her.

From the guns on the port side long orange tongues stabbed towards the nearest freighter as *Salamander*'s helm went over and she turned diagonally between the two lines of ships.

Rietz blinked as a towering column, then another, burst up the side of the destroyer, followed instantly by a violent explosion and a jet of escaping steam. The third torpedo had missed its target, but the others were more than enough. The escort was swinging round, one funnel toppling overboard like cardboard while smoke and then searing flames burst through the fractured deck. Rietz saw figures running towards the gun positions, then being plucked aside as the tracer licked over them and scythed back again for anyone who had survived.

Another explosion crashed against the raider's bilge and Rietz saw the destroyer begin to capsize, her screws still racing as she was blasted apart by her magazines.

Rietz moved his glasses to the other ships, his mouth bone-dry as he heard the old destroyer go into a plunge, her end made even more desperate by the hissing steam, the rumble of water pouring into her hull as the screws continued to drive her down.

He heard his gunnery officer, Busch, rapping out bearings and targets as the individual weapons sought out the careering merchantmen. Two of the ships in convoy seemed to have collided and were soon ablaze as the starboard battery's shells slammed into them, hurling sparks and fragments high above their mastheads.

Someone was attempting to send a distress signal, but the transmission ended as more shells transformed the tanker into a blazing inferno, spilling burning fuel amongst the other vessels and screaming swimmers to add to the horror.

The *Salamander* seemed to be hemmed in by blazing ships and blinded with smoke. The first anxiety had given way to a desperate madness, so that men yelled and cheered through the haze and din like souls in torment.

One ship, a medium sized tramp steamer, apparently undamaged, had almost stopped.

Rietz shouted, 'Signal her captain to await our boarding party! Do not transmit! Do not scuttle!'

A lookout, his face bleeding from a piece of wreckage blasted from one of the convoy, pointed wildy.

'Sir! The enemy!'

Rietz ran to the forepart of the bridge, his ears cringing to the crash and recoil of his guns.

The lookout was dazed, almost incoherent. *The enemy.* To a raider, *everyone* was that.

He heard Storch yell, 'That ship has acknowledged, sir! She's stopped lowering her boats!'

Rietz could only stare through the smoke, past the chaos his guns had caused in so short a time, towards the small grey shape which was moving end on towards him. It was the corvette, made even smaller from this angle, her solitary gun already flashing from her forecastle as she pounded towards the stricken convoy.

Rietz felt the hull lurch under him, heard a chorus of cries as a shell exploded somewhere between decks.

Storch said incredulously, 'By God, he's attacking!'

'Starboard guns, change target! Warship bearing Green one-five!' Obediently the smoke-stained muzzles trained round even further until they were locked on the tiny, defiant warship. '*Fire!*'

Salamander gave another jerk as a shell from the corvette exploded close to her waterline. Splinters clanged and whined through the hull, and Rietz heard someone shouting for stretcher-bearers.

The corvette seemed to stop dead, as if she had hit a submerged reef. Then, as another salvo tore the sea apart in spray and flames she started to settle down by the bow, the gun abandoned as the sea surged aft towards the bridge.

Rietz called, 'Cease firing! Away all boats. Lieutenant Ruesch with boarders to that ship which is unharmed. The rest pick up survivors.'

He gritted his teeth as the corvette dived and then seemed to break surface again like a sounding whale. But it was only her stern, blasted away by depth charges which had exploded as she had plunged to the bottom. Someone had failed to set some of the charges to 'safe'. In the swiftness and ferocity of the attack it was not surprising.

Rietz watched the widening pattern of oil, the bobbing pieces of flotsam and finally the dead fish, killed by the depth charges. He turned away as the other fragments appeared amongst the floating fish.

'See what you can do, Rudi. We will keep under way until we know what is happening.'

Men stumbled past him, eyes glazed as they left their weapons to lower boats, to receive any survivors brought aboard.

But all Rietz could see was the little corvette hurrying towards him, her battle ensigns hoisted as she faced impossible odds. Foolishness? Supreme courage? They often went hand in hand.

Rietz ran his gaze over the listing and burning victims of his attack. Both escorts gone, the oil tanker and the biggest freighter also sunk. The others, apart from the solitary freighter which awaited the boarding party like a guilty spectator, were either sinking or beyond aid.

'Order them to abandon and take to their boats. As soon as they are alongside we will sink the ships by gunfire.'

Moving now very slowly the raider edged past the smoking ships, her shadow covering the drifting corpses and flotsam like a cloak.

Storch hurried back to the bridge, his eyes on the life-boats which were already being urged towards the *Salamander*'s side.

He said, 'That last shell from the corvette penetrated the medical store and killed the doctor, sir. Who will take care of the wounded from these ships?'

Rietz eyed him dully. 'And the Swedish ship carried no doctor either.'

He raised his glasses to examine the nearest life-boats. The anxious faces, the wounded lying amongst their comrades, here and there a gesture of defiance towards the German motor boat which carried them like a sheepdog. More mouths to feed. Men to guard, but as Storch had already commented, no doctor to care for the injured and dying.

He said, 'Tell Lieutenant Ullmann to take charge below, then report all damage and casualties. I cannot leave a single survivor behind, Rudi. To do so might endanger this ship, our people. We must manage. We *shall* manage.'

Petty Officer Fackler called, 'Lieutenant Ruesch has signalled that he is in command of the prize, sir.' He flinched as a man shrieked in sudden agony, the sound hanging over the bridge like something obscene.

Rietz said, 'Signal him to get under way and follow us. I will send him further orders for a rendezvous when he has listed the ship's cargo.'

'Gunnery officer requests permission to open fire, sir.'

Rietz climbed on to a grating and looked down as the first life-boat came alongside. 'Stop engines.' He watched the shocked and dazed men scrambling up ladders to the entry ports. 'Will this impress Berlin and Vogel?' He turned and looked at Storch.

Storch replied, 'It is what we came to do, sir. And it will be remembered.'

Rietz crossed the wheelhouse to the opposite wing, needing to be alone with his thoughts before, like the engines, he was set in motion once more.

Remembered? He thought of the little corvette, knowing it was how he would like to be remembered when his time came.

The first gun crashed out, the explosion swift and echoing as it found an easy target on the nearest abandoned ship.

Perhaps he was no different from Vogel after all. His pride had been his weakness, the need to prove he was better than Vogel before Storch and his men had drawn him away from his usual caution.

He heard a step behind him and he knew his moment of peace was over.

Orders, requests, the need to plan. As Storch had said so clearly, it was what they had come to do.

9

News from Home

The room which had been given over to the investigation into the German raider's movements and intentions was cool when compared with the dusty humidity which seemed to enclose the rest of Melbourne. Even the sounds of traffic and everyday noises were dull and vague, so that Blake had to force his mind to concentrate on what a lieutenant-commander from the intelligence department was saying.

Smashing through the sea or enduring the violent roar of gunfire had no place here, he thought. The Catalina flying-boat, the young American called Billy, the girl with her tanned body showing through the borrowed tunic, none seemed to belong to the officer's even tones, the occasional rustle of his notes or a quiet question from one of the other people present.

Blake glanced at Commodore Rodney Stagg. In spite of the room's size and the fact that he was seated, Stagg seemed to dominate it with his presence.

They had met only briefly when Blake had been driven straight from Williamstown within an hour of docking. He had said little, curt to a point of rudeness. Blake had sensed his anger, apprehension too.

He wished Quintin had been here, but was equally thankful he was not. Any sudden strain or excitement might have irreparably damaged his amazing recovery.

Blake looked around the room. A beautiful model of a ship of the line carved out of bone fragments by French prisoners of war maybe a hundred and fifty years ago. On the opposite wall a fine painting of Cook's ships lying in Kealakekua Bay. Blake jerked his head up as the drowsiness swept over him again.

The officer was saying, 'In spite of intensive interrogation of the *Bremse*'s survivors and the released prisoners after their landing at Port Elizabeth by *Andromeda*,' he paused as several faces turned towards Blake, then continued, 'no further information of use to our operations against the raider was discovered.' He flipped over a page of his notes. 'This latest attack on an escorted convoy can only add to our difficulties.'

Blake recalled his own feelings when he had received the signal about the complete destruction of a northbound convoy. To date no survivors had been picked up, and in spite of intensive patrols over the area no further evidence had been found.

The officer from intelligence added dryly, 'The Swedish government has already made strong representations to London and to the Royal Australian Navy. One of their ships, the *Patricia*, was ordered to join the convoy by the *Fremantle*. Left alone, *they* argue, she would be afloat and at her destination, Port Said.'

Commodore Stagg rose to his feet and stared at the lieutenant-commander as if he would strike him.

'That's great, coming from you! Sitting nice and snug in your plush office while the men doing the job are getting their backsides shot off!'

The younger officer said patiently, 'I am only repeating the collated information, sir. Captain Quintin might have done it better, but I have my work to do, too. The Americans are preparing a new offensive against Japanese-held islands, they cannot spare any carriers for a full-scale ocean search. Likewise, the Royal Navy are under pressure in the Atlantic, to say nothing of the proposed invasion in Europe.'

Stagg's face glowed as if his white tunic collar was growing too tight.

'I'm not talking about the Americans or the British, dammit! I'm speaking about us, *right here*!'

Blake saw the discomfort moving round the room. He was still not sure if Stagg was respected or feared.

Stagg rasped, 'I was given the job of finding and destroying the raider. I know the man himself, how he works. He's trying to get you all in a panic. From the look of it, he's succeeding without too much sweat! No raider can survive without supply ships. We've done for one, and I'll make damn sure we scupper the rest!'

A small rear-admiral who was representing the First Naval Member, whose face looked like tooled leather, said mildly, 'But all told, Commodore Stagg, the enemy have destroyed or captured *fifteen ships* including, for good measure, the cruiser *Devonport*, which, I might add, was larger than your own flagship, and a couple of escorts! I hardly think you can expect a fanfare of optimism for your efforts so far?'

The little admiral was mildly spoken but each word hit Stagg like a sledge-hammer.

He said thickly, 'I need time, sir. I've ordered an increase in vigilance, more patrols, and with luck some air cover over part of the shipping lanes. But I can't be expected to carry everyone. It's a tough job, but one I'm equal to.' He unexpectedly sat down and stared grimly at the floor.

The rear-admiral looked directly at Blake. 'Captain Blake. We have all seen your reports, which in view of your recent misfortune were clear and helpful. However . . .' the word hung in the air like a threat. 'Captain Quintin has already informed me of your *personal* opinion about the raider.' He leaned back, a small sunburned hand tapping gently on the table. 'Perhaps you would enlighten the rest of my department?'

A door opened quietly, and from a corner of his eye Blake saw the girl slip into the room and sit in a vacant chair. She was watching him between two officers, but was wearing dark glasses, as she had since the Catalina had crashed. *Andromeda*'s surgeon had kept her heavily sedated, 'guarded' would have been a better description, Blake thought. He had barely spoken to her as the ship had hurried back to Williamstown, with the air filled with news about the massacred convoy and the elusive raider.

He stood up and looked at the faces around him. All but Stagg and the girl were total strangers. They were looking at him in that same unreal fashion. He could almost feel the crimson ribbon on his breast like a burn.

Blake said, 'Like everyone else, I have been keeping a close check on the raider's movements. I have not met the German referred to by Commodore Stagg, but naturally I have read all I could discover about the man.' He looked round very slowly. 'The *man*.' He knew he had their attention and said, 'A professional naval officer, gentlemen. Someone fighting for his country, not necessarily his beliefs. Like we do.' He saw one of the heads nod, another officer exchange a quick glance with his companion. 'As I see it, he is trying to inflame us, to make us so desperate to destroy him that we will make mistakes, miss opportunities. We know from one source and his past record that this Captain Rietz is conscious of his duty to others. I will not dwell on it, but it is there. It is also totally at odds with the butcher, with the man who machine-guns helpless people in the water, who leaves them to suffer and die without hope or mercy.'

He glanced at the girl and saw she was clasping her hands

tightly together. Even the neat white uniform and the dark glasses could not hide her emotion, or what her memory must be at this moment.

He thought suddenly of Fairfax as he had seen him when he had left the ship that morning.

'Why not let it drop, sir? If you're wrong they'll crucify you later on for wasting time and delaying convoys. Even if you're right, we could be too late, the bastard may have gone elsewhere?'

Blake had been touched by Fairfax's simple loyalty. He was the one who should have kept quiet, just as he should have left them to die when the plane had been shot down.

Blake said quietly, 'I believe there are *two* raiders. I think they are working together and in conjunction with their high command in Germany.'

The little admiral showed no change of expression, but some of the others stirred in their chairs, as if uncomfortable with the change of direction.

Blake guessed they had been expecting an encouraging and rousing speech. A promise of victory, a link with some of the portraits around the room, Cook, Nelson or Bouganville.

He said, 'Our present search system is in my opinion inadequate. The enemy has always had a good understanding of our codes and movements, there are spies in every major seaport, and plenty of so-called neutrals ready and willing to sell information to the right buyer.'

The admiral asked, 'Have you *proof*?'

'Not yet, sir. But the German's quick change of location, his apparent disregard for fuel economy are firm indications that there is more than one raider at large. As I have already said, I think there are two different kinds of man we are up against.'

Stagg got to his feet, his face composed, even calm.

To the rear-admiral he said, 'I have naturally heard of Captain Blake's suggestions, sir. As he has admitted to us here, they are only suggestions and without proof. Of course the German hurries about, disregarding his fuel bills and the strain on his machinery.' He looked round the room, his face suddenly transformed by a great grin. 'I'd sure as hell do the same in his shoes! And *of course* he changes his methods. Germans write beautiful music, or so I'm told.' The grin vanished. 'They also butcher women and children. I don't go along with Captain Blake's ideas, not one bit, gentlemen!' He stooped slightly and added, 'Captain Blake has been in the thick of the naval war. We know that. And we have seen his record, the decoration of the Victoria Cross which anyone will envy if he's telling the truth.'

For the first time he looked at Blake, his eyes steady and relaxed. 'I'd not like to think that Captain Blake is under the impression that just one raider is too small a reward for his services. I'd hate even more to believe that the *second* invisible German is being put on record just in case we can't deliver the goods!'

The admiral snapped, 'That's enough, Commodore Stagg. This is a discussion, not a court martial!'

Blake felt the room closing in around him, the faces of the spectators merging into a blur with Stagg's at the centre.

He heard himself say, 'I'll stick by my opinion, sir. In wartime you have to put up with a lot. Putting up with an insult like Commodore Stagg's doesn't happen to be one of them!'

The admiral rose lightly to his feet, like a cat. It was over. For the present.

To the room at large he said severely, 'We will destroy the raider, and any other which comes our way. I will tolerate no interservice recriminations.' His eyes flitted between Stagg and Blake. 'From anyone!'

The officers moved obediently to the door, but Stagg said abruptly, 'A word, Blake.'

They stood a few feet apart by one of the broad windows.

Stagg said calmly, 'Sorry I had to do that. But I'll not beat about the bush. I'm straight, always am. In a matter of weeks you'll be sent out of here. Probably to a plushy appointment, somewhere where your background will be useful. An Australian officer will command *Andromeda*, and things will be as our masters intended. But in the meantime you and I have got to get along, see? The war is beginning to go our way, and neither the Yanks nor the Brits are going to take over from me. You start to throw rumours about and some desk admiral in Washington or Whitehall will get in a panic. We'll have flotillas and squadrons out here we'll never need, and *not one* will be under Australian control!'

Blake nodded. 'And that's what you care about?'

Stagg grinned. 'That, and getting the German raider. So think about it. You'll be sitting pretty, it won't be your problem any more.'

As he made to leave, Blake called after him, 'Suppose we don't win the war?'

Stagg looked at him coldly. 'Then neither of us will have to worry, will we?'

Alone in the big room, Blake walked to the glass case which contained the bone model. Carved with such care, such accuracy.

Even in those days there had been such men who put personal advancement before all else. He felt the anger burning his insides like acid. Did Stagg really see him as the glory-seeking hero? A man so full of conceit that he needed to invent an enemy?

The door opened and she stood there watching him.

'Thought you'd be coming out with the others?'

He walked across the polished floor and faced her. 'It was good of you to wait.'

She tossed her head, the movement drawing Blake from his anger like a balm.

'They were rough on you,' she said. 'But the admiral's no fool. He'll be thinking about it. He's right.'

In the corridor Blake felt as if they were both invisible. Sailors and civilians bustled from door to door with pieces of paper, files of signals, while they stood unmoving amongst them.

She asked, 'Are you staying?'

He thought of Fairfax, the much-needed repairs which Weir intended to complete before leaving again.

She added slowly, 'If you are, maybe you'd like to meet my family? Like you said.' She looked away, withdrawing, like a stranger. 'I'll quite understand if you've better things to do.'

He reached out and took her elbow, turning her towards him.

'I've not, and I'd like to very much.'

She nodded and said, 'That's settled. I'll get a car.'

She removed the dark glasses and suddenly it was all there. The dinghy, the sea rising around them like a restless range of hills, his arm around her as the plane had come looking for them, the shark.

She said, 'By the way, the name's Claire, in case you'd forgotten.' But she could not keep it up. 'I'll be ready as soon as you've telephoned the ship.' She watched his expression

118

and said simply, 'You've been through it. Now I think I can understand what it's like.'

Then she turned on her heel and walked swiftly through the door of her office.

Commander Victor Fairfax sat at his desk in the ship's office, his feet up and his shirt unbuttoned while he drank a cup of black coffee and held the telephone to his ear at the same time.

Even being alongside again felt different, he thought. Feet clattered overhead, and through an open scuttle he saw the wooden piles of the pier, some dockyard workers dragging equipment towards the brow. In a few moments it would all be confusion once more. People came and went from the office, speaking to the writers or leaving forms for him to sign.

The telephone line buzzed and crackled in his ear. But he was lucky to have got one direct to the shore, he thought.

Suddenly he heard her voice, as if she was in the ship with him. Sharing her.

'Hello, Sarah!'

'Oh, Vic, it's *you*!' She was laughing and crying together. 'Can I see you?'

Fairfax said, 'Is the car okay? If not, borrow one and drive down here. I'll fix a dockyard pass for you. I've missed you so much, Sarah!'

He knew that all the writers had stopped work and were listening intently but he did not care.

She said, 'I've been so worried about you.' She sniffed. 'God, I do love you!'

The line clicked and a weary voice interrupted, 'Call coming in from HQ, sir.'

Fairfax snapped, 'Get off the line!' In a calmer tone, 'Soon as you can, Sarah.' He replaced the telephone carefully, as if it were made of crystal.

Gross, the paymaster commander, peered through the door. 'We should have a party. How about it?'

Fairfax grinned. 'A great idea.' He thought of Blake and added, 'I wonder what the hell is going on in Melbourne?'

Gross shrugged his plump shoulders. 'The skipper will come through. He always does.'

'You like him a lot, don't you?'

The paymaster commander thought about it. 'He'll do me.'

He turned as the chief telegraphist entered the office, a signal pad in his hand.

119

Fairfax frowned. It was not like the chief petty officer to bother himself running errands.

'What is it, Pots?'

Lougher, from Fairfax's home town, almost the same street, said bluntly, 'From the Admiralty. For the cap'n.' He glanced at the paymaster commander. 'His father's dead. Tough, ain't it, sir?'

Fairfax stood up, pictures of an old man he had never seen crowding in on him.

The paymaster commander asked. 'Will you tell him at once?'

Fairfax took the pad and glanced at the brief signal. One bloody thing after another.

'We'd better forget the party.'

Gross lifted one foot over the coaming. 'Don't do that. He'd not wish it. You asked me just now if I liked him. Don't you see? We've all got him up there on the bridge, somebody to rely on. Now *he's* got nobody. That's why I say don't duck the party. It wouldn't help.'

Fairfax nodded very slowly. 'I'll see to it.'

He picked up his cap and walked out into the passageway where Macallan, the master-at-arms, and therefore the most unpopular man aboard, was waiting.

'You takin' defaulters in lieu of this mornin', so to speak, sir?' His eyes flickered over Fairfax's unbuttoned shirt as he added coldly, 'I can 'old 'em back for a while if you like, sir.'

Fairfax shook his head. At times like these he was heartily grateful for the humourless Macallan. He would expect his officers to be perfectly turned out if they were walking the plank.

'I'll be up in three minutes, Master.' He touched the man's arm. 'Thanks for telling me.'

Macallan watched him hurry aft to his cabin. Bloody Aussies, he thought savagely. No respect, that was their trouble.

On the upper deck a young American sailor paused beside the Catalina's small yellow dinghy and looked at it for a long while.

The gangway sentry said, 'A car's come for you, Billy. So long, chum. Take care of yerself.'

The youth nodded and walked blindly down the brow.

Seeing the little dinghy had brought it all back. Now he could never forget.

120

● ● ●

The car with the naval markings swung off the main road and slowed to take a sharp bend. Blake kept a firm grip on the door, conscious of the girl beside him, the fierce way she drove, as if every minute counted.

Melbourne had fallen a long way behind, and the country-side into which the car was heading was empty, with sunburned scrub, timeless hills, with the sea showing itself every so often. Sometimes they passed near a deep cove, or saw the sea only far-away like the high water of a dam. It all helped to give a hint of the country's size, that they were merely on a foothold of it.

She said, 'Something's wrong, isn't it?' She glanced side-ways at him, her hair, free of the tricorn hat, whipping in the hot breeze.

Blake thought of Fairfax's voice on the ship's telephone, shared his difficulties as he had told him of the signal from that other world.

He replied, 'My father died last week. I just heard.'

The car slewed off the road, its wheels embedded in rubble, as she swung round in her seat to look at him.

'I'm sorry. I really am.'

It was suddenly very quiet as she cut the engine, and the dust settled across the bonnet and the two occupants.

He said, 'He's been ill for years.'

She nodded. 'I know.' Her hands moved in her lap. 'I—I'm sorry. I heard a lot about you at HQ.'

Blake looked past her, at a strange bird on the hillside. Another world, and in the twinkling of an eye it had all changed. He had been expecting it for a long time, but that did not help. He could see his father in the garden as if it were yesterday, or this morning. In his old panama hat, his pockets full of twine and oddments he used for his roses. He clenched his jaw, suddenly unable to bear it. For it was still bleak and cold in the old garden on the Surrey-Hampshire border. Maybe it was just as well. No roses to leave behind.

He said quietly, 'I never really knew if he understood what was happening. But he was always *there*, somehow.'

He looked down as she put her hand on his.

She said, 'What about your wife?'

He watched her hand, the tiny golden hairs on her wrist.

121

'She never cared for him.'

Another quick picture. Diana on that first night of his leave. Tossing her head with anger as she had brushed her hair in front of the mirror, her eyes watching him in the bedroom.

'I promised we'd go out! Life doesn't just revolve round the Navy, you know!'

Blake said, 'Sorry to let you in for all this. I knew he couldn't last. My aunt will write about it when she can.' He looked away. 'The Admiralty doesn't have much skill at sending this sort of signal. Usually they're going the other way.'

'Do you still want to meet my people?' She watched him gravely. 'Or do you just want to be quiet?'

He tried to smile. 'You drive. I'll talk about it, but stop me if you get fed up with it.'

And so, as the car bumped back on to the narrow road and headed south-east towards the coastline of the Bass Strait, Blake talked. About his father, and of the *Andromeda*. Sometimes he had to pause to collect his thoughts, as if, like a painter, he had to capture an exact moment. Perhaps for the first time in his life he was able to share that side of himself he had kept hidden. His fear, and his fear of showing it before others. The moments in harbour when he should have been resting, when the telephone by his bunk had shrilled in the night. The dreadful, ice-cold terror which never completely left. The following minutes while he got over it. Until the next time.

On a headland high above the blue water she stopped by the roadside and pulled a thermos of coffee from a canvas grip. They stood looking down at a tiny beach, listening to the boom of surf, the noisy arguments of sea-birds.

She said, 'Remember when you made us stay alive with your quiz games and damned questions about sea-birds? I almost hated you. I wanted to die, even though I needed to live.'

He put his arm through hers and felt her tense momentarily.

'I'm not likely to forget.'

She disengaged his arm and looked at her wrist-watch.

'Time to move on.'

Blake sank down on his seat and watched the landscape pass. He must not be a fool, or be such a bastard as to use her for his passing relief. Escape.

He glanced at her, at her well-shaped legs as she jammed on the brakes while the car rattled round a bend. Her white uniform shirt left little to the imagination and he could see small freckles on her skin where she had bared it to the sun.

The land lifted like a shoulder and the sea disappeared. The car began to descend, and Blake saw some houses in the distance, and on a far hillside some sheep clustered together like an untidy patch of scrub.

'Home sweet home.'

The car slowed while she pointed out the individual houses, a store, a sturdy little church and a war memorial with some parched flowers at its base.

The car rolled to a halt and she switched off the engine.

'This is it. Not exactly Melbourne or Sydney, but the people here like it.'

Blake got down and stretched his legs. He felt hot and sweaty and there was grit between his teeth. But in a strange way he felt unwound, able to accept what had happened.

He saw a tall, lean man in a flapping white jacket and a pipe jutting from his jaw striding down the path from the church.

He said, 'You'd better move the car. This looks like the vicar!'

She picked up her hat and bag from the seat and pushed the hair from her eyes.

'Yes, it's the minister, so mind your language, please.'

Then, as Blake watched with astonishment, she ran across the road and threw her arms round the minister's neck and kissed him.

'Hello, Claire! This really is a nice surprise!' He looked past her at Blake. 'And who have you brought with you?'

She turned, her hand in the minister's arm, her eyes suddenly bright.

'Dad, I want you to meet Captain Richard Blake. He's a sort of friend.'

Blake took a firm handshake with a grin. 'I'm glad to meet you, sir.'

The girl stood back to watch them, trying as before to hold up her aloof guard.

'He's quite nice. For a Pom.'

It was a beautiful evening for a party, everyone agreed who stepped aboard *Andromeda*'s quarterdeck with its awnings and colourful bunting, and with the perspiring stewards bustling to meet each arrival with a well-loaded tray of glasses.

From Y turret some of Captain Farleigh's marines were playing a selection of what they considered to be popular music, and with the officers in their best 'ice cream suits' and the women guests with bared shoulders and bright dresses, it could almost have been a peacetime affair.

Fairfax stood with his wife where he could watch the new arrivals, assess their rank or importance and ensure they were received accordingly.

Sarah, her long fair hair hanging across her shoulders, in a gown which she had warned him had taken a month's housekeeping money, stared around at the bustle and excitement with disbelief.

'After reading in the papers about that raider, I thought you'd all be in a state of shock.' She looked at him warmly. 'God, you've changed, Vic. In so short a time, you've got something new, I can't explain it.'

He grinned. 'Some of me is the same, as I think I showed you.'

She dug him in the ribs. 'Is that all you think about?'

He said suddenly, 'You know that Stagg's coming?'

'I heard. I think you're mad. He'll probably get fighting drunk. After what he's said to your captain, I'd have thought you would keep him at the end of a barge-pole!'

Fairfax shook hands with a major of marines with a girl hanging to his arm. He said softly, 'It's not that easy, Sarah. There are several captains here, even two admirals. It's impossible to leave out your own commodore!'

'Where is your captain, by the way?' She studied the jostling throng with new interest. 'I only met him once. I liked the look of him. He seems too young to command this great pile of armour!'

'He'll be up in a minute. There were some signals for him to see.'

'Pity he hasn't got someone nice to be with. What with his wife on the loose and now his poor father dying suddenly, he could do with some cheering up.'

Fairfax replied, 'You remember Second Officer Grenfell?'

His wife stared at him. 'Claire Grenfell, the minister's daughter? God, not her surely? Your captain'll get frost-bite if he gets too close to that one!'

Fairfax shifted awkwardly. 'Perhaps you've got the wrong idea. Maybe we all did. And she had a bad time after the plane was shot down. It was only luck we found her.'

124

'You mean, *you* found her. I was so proud when I heard about it. You are a bit of a goer when you get the urge.' She became serious. 'Do you think it's over, the raider, I mean? You've been back here for four days and nothing's happened. Perhaps the Germans have left, gone home.'

Fairfax smiled. 'Let's hope so.' He looked around the quarterdeck and up towards the guns. 'I wonder what sort the next skipper will be. Not like Richard Blake, that's for sure.'

He stiffened as Blake appeared on deck and moved towards them. He said, 'Party's getting going. Big mess bills in the wardroom after this.'

Blake said, 'You look very lovely, Mrs Fairfax.' He took her hand. 'Too good for him.'

'It's what I keep telling him.' She flushed with pleasure. 'But I can't compete with *Andromeda*!'

Moon eased his way through the throng, avoiding out-thrust hands and demands for attention.

He saw Blake and raised his small silver tray on which stood a solitary glass.

'For you, sir. Special.'

'With you, it always is.'

Blake raised the glass to his lips, saw the way the people nearest to him had stopped their chatter to watch. As if it really was a special occasion.

Sarah Fairfax asked, 'Can we share the secret, Captain?'

Blake looked over at Moon. 'It's his way of helping. He's like a prop to me.' He downed the drink and held back a cough.

Moon beamed. 'Thought you'd like it, sir. Learned about it when I was in the old *Bombay Queen* runnin' out of Shang'ai in the thirties.'

Lieutenant-Commander Scovell strode aft from the gangway and said, 'Your guests have arrived, sir.'

Blake walked with him while Moon retreated with the empty glass, satisfied with his gesture.

Fairfax saw the two figures stepping abroad, a tall man with a clerical collar, the girl, in uniform, beside him. He heard his wife murmur, 'She keeps the uniform on as a barrier.'

Blake shook the minister's hand. He had already instructed Weir and the paymaster commander to keep him away from Beveridge, the chaplain. Old Horlicks, with his God enlisted on the side of the Allies, and particularly so with the Royal Navy, would seem a world away from that quiet little church where she had taken him.

He put his hand through the girl's arm. She was very tense, but was looking around at the other curious faces with a kind of defiance.

'I'm so glad you could come, Claire.'

She looked at him. 'Mother would not join us. Ships, the Navy, you know. She still feels it badly about David. But Dad's been looking forward to it, bless him.'

Fairfax saw their exchange of glances and said quietly, 'Sarah, for just once in your life I think you've miscalculated badly. I really do.'

She put out her tongue. 'Pull the other one. Now get me another drink, *Commander*, and let's have a party!'

10

Making a Start

Blake sat at his desk, half-heartedly reading the various papers which the new chief writer, Brazier, was methodically laying before him. Brazier was another Australian, one of the latest draft which had come aboard as replacements.

It took some getting used to. Each time Blake left his quarters he heard new voices, different dialects and saw the lost expressions of men exploring fresh surroundings.

It had been touching when the latest batch of old Andromedas had left the ship. They had gathered in an embarrassed, shuffling group while he had said a few words to them. But how did trite phrases and emotional handshakes sum up what he felt, what they all must have felt?

Those men in their best uniforms, starting back along the passage to Britain. New ships, courses, promotions, adjustments in every way.

Now he was back in his day cabin he could recall each man as he had once fitted into their élite company. A sun-reddened face yelling defiance as the Stukas had come screaming down. Another murmuring encouragement to a messmate pinned beneath twisted steel. Sailors wading ashore to lift wounded troops from Tobruk, Farleigh's marines firing a volley over a line of graves.

He thought suddenly of a wardroom party. A great success, everyone had said. But even though it had been two days ago, it was already hard to hold it in perspective.

He knew why, but would not admit it. He had seen very little of her during the party because of Stagg's arrival. Booming voice, a kind of fierce confidence which seemed out of place.

Now the girl was in Sydney. Whether she had been ordered there or had volunteered to get away from him he did not know.

Blake recalled exactly when things had gone wrong. He had taken her to the deserted upper bridge, leaving Stagg with two admirals.

Under the stars, the bridge, usually a place of movement and decision, had seemed strangely ghostlike.

She had asked him about England again, what he would do after the war. They had stood side by side on the gratings, looking aft where the quarterdeck awnings glowed from the little lights which were hung like garlands along the guardrails and stanchions.

He had said, 'The Navy will be cut back to the minimum. As it was in my father's day. I'll probably be politely put on the shelf, until the next blow-up.'

She had laid her hand on his. 'Why not come out here? It may seem a bit quiet to you, but it'll be different one day.'

She had not resisted as he had turned her on his arm so that her spine had been against the bridge screen. But he had immediately felt the change, the passive resistance, when seconds before he had felt hope and longing.

A messenger had arrived panting on the bridge and had saved the situation, if only by preventing him making a complete fool of himself.

Chief Writer Brazier said, 'That's the lot, sir.' He patted the signed papers into a tidy pile.

Blake smiled at him. Soon there would be none of the old company left. *Andromeda* would begin again, moulding a new one to suit her own ways.

He tried to keep his thoughts in order but his short visit to the girl's home kept coming back. The little church could have been in England, and when he had said as much she had laughed at him.

'You've got that English look again! All green fields and thatched cottages. Even if we win the war it may not be like that any more.'

He had shared her mood. 'There's that!'

He switched his mind with an effort to Stagg as he had last seen him, here in this cabin. Serious and overpowering as he had laid his beliefs about the raider on the line. The two admirals had been present, one politely interested, the other too far gone to care.

But there had been no doubting Stagg's sincerity, nor his obsession with the raider. Perhaps it was as important for him to aim all his hate an the one German as it was for Blake to accept there might be two raiders on the rampage.

The interested admiral had remarked, 'You've given it a lot of thought.'

Stagg had leaned on a table, his face glistening in the lights. 'I had plenty of time to think. Lying in a sweat-box, reeking in my own filth and waiting for the door to be opened, to be half-blinded by sunlight before the little bastards got going with their torture, their 'amusement' for the day!'

Later, as Blake had seen him over the side, Stagg had turned and had muttered thickly, 'Good party. Don't go much on them these days.' He had had some difficulty in making up his mind before he had ended with, 'I still mean what I said. You ride with me and you're welcome. Go against me and I'll not be too happy, see?' He had given Blake a punch on the shoulder. 'We'll show 'em!'

The door opened and Fairfax entered. He looked relaxed but tired. Blake thought of the beautiful Sarah and then pushed his envy aside. Fairfax was just lucky. It was to be hoped he appreciated it.

Fairfax waited for Brazier to leave then said, 'Signal from HQ, sir. Two days' readiness as of noon today. The last of the supplies will be aboard by the end of the first dog watch. After that, it's anyone's guess, I suppose.'

Blake waved him to a chair. He really wanted to be alone but once again he knew the reason and despised his own pettiness.

More new men, changing methods, fresh routines. Only outwardly would she be the same ship. Soon he would not even have her to himself. Stagg was probably right about his future. A nice soft job in the Admiralty or lecturing young hopefuls on the merits of command. He sighed.

'Something wrong, sir?'

'I keep thinking about the lack of news. No more sinkings, so where the hell is or are the enemy?' He smiled ruefully. 'See? Even I'm doubting my own ideas.'

Fairfax watched him thoughtfully. He had been with Sarah all night. In the darkness she had pressed her nakedness against him and had whispered, 'Ask Richard Blake to dinner. I'll get a girlfriend for him. Remember Jane what's-her-name?'

He had groaned. 'Jane? I thought just about the whole fleet had been with her!'

'That's horrible of you!' She had nestled closer, stroking him and driving away any chance of rest. 'It was just an idea.'

Fairfax said, 'You ought to get away for a day. There's some great country round Melbourne. I could give you a name or two.'

'No, but thanks.'

Blake thought about his father and the note he had received from the Navy Office that morning. As 'things' were quiet again it would not be impossible for Blake to be flown home. His father was an only relative, and with Blake's record and unbroken combat service there would be no opposition.

It sounded as if Stagg had had a word somewhere. They were trying to get shot of *Andromeda*'s captain, too. He could hardly blame them.

Fairfax added, 'I see that they are allowing individual sailings as of this week. That may bring out the wolves.'

Blake said, 'Apparently Jerry was making a big thing of it on the radio. Convoys wiped out, us looking like bloody fools, all the usual stuff.' He did not mention the propaganda from Berlin which had laid full stress on his own Victoria Cross. *Britain's best meets his match.* There was no need to. It was doubtless all over the ship.

It was just as if the high commands of both sides were trying to inflame the two antagonists into some explosive action, like knights at a joust.

Or maybe the raider really had slipped away. To be interned in Argentina or to brave the patrols and sneak home to Germany.

Fairfax fiddled with his cap. 'It's none of my business, sir, but I think we've become pretty close during the past weeks. If there's anything I can do. . . .'

Blake looked at him. So it was that obvious. 'I'm a mess, Victor. When you face up to it, you have to admit that war is all I understand. I can't cope with my wife, and I keep thinking about my father, dying as he did, penned up in his mind.'

Without realizing it he was on his feet, pacing about the cabin while Fairfax watched him.

'Maybe I've been in combat so long I'm out of my depth on this sort of mission. In the Atlantic or the Med every wave was a potential threat, each floating stick a periscope. I can't just settle and accept it. I know in my heart that the enemy is out there. Watching our every move like a tiger. It would make no difference if we had another cruiser or half the home fleet. One carrier would be enough, but the minds of people who plan these things are way, way back in the Kaiser's war. It's always the same. Ship to ship, honour before all else, never mind the bloody losses!' He grimaced. 'It must be this heat, Victor, I'm too steamed up.'

'We're getting on for our winter, sir. When you get home your summer will be waiting.'

Blake looked through a scuttle, her words easing through his guard. *All green fields and thatched cottages*.

What the hell was the matter with him? He had come through when many better men had died or been made into wrecks. He had been given the country's highest decoration. *For Valour*. It said so on the cross. Yet, just because he was being moved on, because his personal affairs were in a muddle, he was acting like a lovesick midshipman.

But it was not like that. He wanted the strange, enigmatic girl with the sun-bleached hair and the rare smile. But, like Diana, he had driven her away, destroyed their brief association.

The telephone buzzed and Fairfax whipped it to his ear. Then he said, 'Dock office, sir. The commodore's on his way.' He stood up. 'That'll make everything just perfect.'

Later, as Stagg stood with his large feet well apart on the quarterdeck and regarded the activity along the jetty, the litter of crates and bundles which were waiting to be checked aboard, Blake sensed his new glow of urgency and confidence. That seemed to be Stagg's way. Up one minute, rock-bottom the next. *I'm a fine one to talk*.

Stagg said, 'Still loading, eh? *Fremantle* was finished yesterday.'

As Blake led the way to his cabin Fairfax remained by the gangway. *So there*, Stagg's words seemed to imply.

Stagg got down to it right away. 'This is the toppest secret you've ever handled, believe me. But I've at last convinced the right people that we need to take the initiative. Thank God old Jack Quintin is still laid up, otherwise I'd get another bloody argument!'

Blake waited, watching the big man's latent power, the way he moved about the cabin. He recalled what Stagg had let out about his captivity and felt a sudden pity for him. A man so large, tortured, humiliated, made to grovel by the Japanese, it could not have been easy to overcome.

Stagg said calmly, 'The Germans monitor all our broadcasts, right? They have some good agents in the field, and probably get their hands on most of the local codes, too.'

He broke off as his mind switched to something else. 'They're letting individual ships sail on the safer routes, by the way.'

'Yes, I know.'

131

Stagg grinned without warmth. 'On the ball. What I like to hear.'

He continued. 'We're going to provide some bait. The admiral's given it the go-ahead. The rest will be up to us.'

He leaned forward, the buttons of his white tunic protesting violently. 'The one thing you and I really agree on is the area where the raider works. A big one, but with a common factor. I intend to 'create' an unescorted merchantman, preferably neutral, and lay it on the table for our German friends. Rather like a Q-ship from the Great War.' His mood changed again and he added fiercely, 'But this time there'll be no harbour nice and easy to run for. With *Fremantle* and *Andromeda* working together, and using what air coverage we can put up ourselves, I think we shall flush him out.' He sat back and asked, '*Well?*'

Blake nodded. 'It could work.'

Stagg lifted his hands. 'God preserve us, the man agrees!'

Blake smiled. 'It's worth a try anyway. It's so dated an idea that the German command might just swallow it.'

Stagg stood up. 'Settled then. We shall put to sea day after tomorrow. If the raider stays quiet, we'll work into position. If not, we'll go after him as before. But this is to be treated with absolute secrecy. Not even Fairfax is to be told.'

'What d'you mean, sir? *Even* Fairfax?'

Stagg grinned hugely. ''Cause he is to command the bait!' He searched Blake's face for opposition and added, 'Your first lieutenant did Fairfax's job before he found his feet, right? Well then, he can do it again. He's due for a command of his own anyway. Good experience for him.'

Blake followed Stagg on deck. It was like travelling in the wake of a whirlwind.

'What shall I tell him, sir?'

Stagg regarded him calmly. 'Send him to Sydney. I'll lay it on for you. He can liaise with the boys there while Quintin gets his sea-legs again in the hospital. Tell him he can take his wife.' He dropped his voice as Fairfax appeared. 'I wouldn't mind bedding *her* down myself!'

Fairfax saluted. 'Are you leaving, sir?'

Stagg nodded curtly. 'It looks like it.'

Surgeon Lieutenant-Commander Bruce was on his way aft to make his sick report to Fairfax and watched as the commodore was duly piped over the side.

He remarked quietly, 'He looks as if he means business.

I shouldn't be surprised if he ends up running your Navy after the war.'

Fairfax grinned bitterly. 'The Navy, Doc? He'd like his head on a coin as the first king of Australia!'

Blake walked past them without a word. Now that Stagg had gone his plan of action had already lost some of its steam. He had been on the point of saying that Fairfax could take command of *Andromeda* while he took over the so-called bait. Perhaps that was what Stagg had been expecting, waiting for. Blake's desire for more glory coming into the open.

He turned by the companion and looked back at Fairfax. It would all probably blow over. Schemes like this one usually ended where they had begun, in some Admiralty filing cabinet.

Moon was waiting for him in the cabin.

'Second Officer Grenfell just called, sir. I told 'er you was with the commodore but she wouldn't wait. A bit on edge, I thought, sir.'

Blake sat down and seized the telephone.

Moon said helpfully, 'She was at the Navy Office, sir.'

It seemed to take an age before Blake's call forced its way through the complex of shore lines, priority ratings and then eventually to the intelligence department's office.

'I want to speak with Second Officer Grenfell.'

There was another maddening pause and Blake expected the line to be broken for another call.

He heard her voice and said quickly, 'It's me. I was on deck when you rang, is something wrong?'

'It, it's nothing, I'm sorry. I just got back from Sydney. Your steward shouldn't have bothered you. You must have a lot to do. I—I—' She broke off.

Blake spoke carefully and deliberately. 'Listen, Claire, I *want* to see you.' When she did not speak he added, 'Please, don't hang up. I'm not going to be a nuisance or anything. I just want to see you. Be with you.' He could imagine the Wrens in her office, his own men on the switchboard. Nothing seemed to matter more than this.

'I know.' She sounded a hundred miles away. 'I was going to explain. To apologize. I treated you so badly. After what you did, I behaved like a stupid schoolgirl. Because of what we went through I actually imagined I knew it all. But I didn't. And just now, when I called, I knew I could not make it seem clear so that you would understand.'

Blake said, 'Can we go somewhere?'

There was a pause and he thought he heard her speaking to someone.

Then she said, 'I'll fix it. Give me time. But don't say you want to meet me because you're sorry for me. I couldn't bear that.'

The line went dead. Whether she had hung up or they had been disconnected, Blake had no idea.

Fairfax entered the cabin. 'Any orders about leave for tonight, sir?'

'What?' Blake shook himself. 'Er, the usual. Just the duty part of the watch to remain aboard. All-night leave for natives.' He tried not to think about Stagg's plan. 'That includes you. You're to go to Sydney tomorrow. Stagg told me. You can take Sarah, "on the firm".'

Fairfax stared at him. 'For what reason, sir?'

'They'll tell you. It's just for a few days, but I imagine it is important, so no careless talk. Number One will have to manage until you rejoin the ship. I shall be ashore myself, so he'll have to get used to the idea!'

Fairfax was dazed by the swiftness of events. 'Whatever you say, sir.'

Blake faced him and said bluntly, 'Second Officer Grenfell. Her brother was killed in *Paradox*. What else do you know about her?'

Fairfax shifted under Blake's gaze. 'She went to the same school as Sarah, although they didn't mix much. When she was commissioned she was at Sydney for a time. She had quite a thing going for a Kiwi lieutenant who was on attachment there. But nothing came of it, and she transferred to Melbourne, to Captain Quintin's staff.'

Blake nodded. 'Thank you.' It was not even half the story, but he should not have asked Fairfax anyway.

Fairfax said, 'I've always liked her, sir. Quite apart from being damned nice looking, she's different.'

'Yes.' Blake filled his pipe slowly. 'Carry on, Victor. I'll see you before you go.'

The telephone buzzed again and Blake had it in his hand in two seconds.

She said quickly, 'I can't get away yet. Could you, I mean, would you come into Melbourne?'

'I'm practically there.' He tried to sound relaxed, at ease.

'It's nothing really. I thought you might like to come to my home again. I know about your orders. When you'll be leaving.

134

Tomorrow I can get time off, if you like we could do the tourist thing, Captain Cook's cottage, take some pictures.'

Despite her equally matter of fact tone he knew his reply was important.

'I'd like that a lot, Claire. It will do us both good. I'll get some civvies and—'

'No. Come as you are. For me.'

Blake replaced the telephone and pressed Moon's bell.

'I'm going ashore, Moon. You've been in Melbourne lots of times, I suppose?'

'Me, sir? I should jolly well think so. Indeed, when I was in the old *Renown* we come 'ere once with royalty.'

'I should have guessed. Well, there's a shop I want to know about. . . .'

The two men stood in the garden of the white-painted house beside the little church, their pipes glowing like fire-flies in the twilight.

Blake could hear the late breeze hissing through the sun-scorched grass, the click . . . click . . . click of some kind of insect beyond the fence.

'When did you first decide to make the church your life?'

It was amazing how easy it was to speak with the tall, lean minister after so short an acquaintance. Now, as they lounged companionably by the back porch waiting to go inside for supper, Blake felt he had known the man for years.

Hugh Grenfell sounded far-away. Perhaps he often tried to pinpoint the exact moment.

'I was in the infantry in the last lot, the PBI. I went through most of it, the Dardanelles, France. Lice, mud and corpses. I expect it was around that time. I never really thought I'd come through. So many didn't. In just one morning, between dawn and eleven o'clock, we lost twenty thousand. Not all Aussies, of course, but enough to have left a real gap in most of our small towns to this day. When it was finally over I suppose I felt I should give something back. For being given a chance.'

Blake nodded, thinking of his own father. 'I was sorry about your son.'

'Yeh. Dave was the apple of his mother's eye. Mine, too, in some ways.' He turned the matter aside and asked, 'What about our Claire? You seem to get along just fine.'

Blake stared straight in front of him. 'I expect she's told

135

you about me. That I'm married?'

'No, but the fact you told *her* makes a difference.' He waved his pipe in the air. 'Easy, Richard, I'm not canvassing for marriages!' He chuckled. 'But I'd be a liar if I said I wasn't interested!'

Blake said, 'My marriage is finished. I'm not blaming Diana entirely. She's a product of our times, live while you can, to hell with tomorrow. I've tried not to believe most of it, to tell myself it was only a passing thing. But I was naïve, I can see it now.'

Hugh Grenfell glanced at Blake's profile. 'I'd have guessed differently. From her view-point, that is. A nice looking chap, a hero, you can't do better than that?'

Blake had thought along the same lines. Often. Now that he had the VC, the splash of publicity which had followed *Andromeda*'s spectacular victory, maybe she would try to erase the past, to come back to him. He had asked himself many times, what would he do, how would he react? Until he had met Claire.

'Perhaps.'

'Of course, some people misunderstand Claire, you know.' It was casually put. 'But she's not a big city girl, and despite the fancy uniform and the trust she's been given by her boss, Captain Quintin, she's unsure, vulnerable. Then there was this New Zealander she met in Sydney. He's gone now. Just as well.' He turned and added mildly. 'Otherwise I'd probably have forgotten my cloth and beaten the hell out of him.' He tapped out his pipe and ground away the red ashes with his heel. 'She loved him, or thought she did, and that's what counts, isn't it? But he only wanted one thing from her, and then he turned out to be spliced to a nice girl back home.'

Blake listened to the hurt in the man's voice and guessed he was unused to talking so freely about it. It explained a lot. The girl's aloofness when he had first arrived, her remarks about Diana. It was more than likely that the unknown New Zealander had accused her of being frigid just to break down her guard.

The minister cocked his head. 'Time to eat, by the sound of it.' He touched Blake's arm. 'I'm glad we talked. You saved Claire's life, and if there's anything you need from me, just ask.'

They walked into the room with its table groaning under the weight of food.

Two of the Grenfell's neighbours had come across to eat with them, but as far as Blake was concerned the girl stood completely alone from all of them.

There was as much food on the table as would be given in rations to a whole family for a week at home, he thought.

They soon got the topic of conversation round to Britain, to the war, how long it would last.

Once he found himself thinking of the German captain, Rietz, and wondered if he nursed the hope for an early peace.

Throughout the meal the girl said very little, unless it was to answer a direct question. She sat opposite Blake, and he was very conscious of her nearness, the way she watched his hands, or his face when he was speaking. Comparing him with the New Zealander? Wondering if he, like the other man, had the motives of a fraud?

The telephone jangled, and with a chuckle Hugh Grenfell stood up and said, 'One of my flock, I expect. Needing to borrow a quart of this home-made brew until next week.'

But it was not. The call was from Melbourne and the message for Blake was brief.

He re-entered the room, seeing their faces turned towards him, the way the girl had screwed up a napkin in one hand without apparently noticing it.

He said, 'I have to go back.' He looked at her, their glance excluding the others. 'They want you, too.' He felt suddenly deflated, embittered by the interruption.

She said quietly, 'I'd have driven you anyway. Those HQ drivers are crook.'

Her mother said reprovingly, 'I don't know, Claire, you're as bad as your father!'

As the girl went for the car her mother took Blake to one side, her face grave as she said, 'I hope you can come again, Captain Blake.'

'Please. Call me Richard.'

She smiled. 'When you come again.' She glanced round to see if the others were out of earshot. 'Don't hurt my girl. She's been through enough. You're a fine young man, but war changes things.' She stretched up and kissed his cheek. 'Take care of yourself, and God bless you.'

After shaking hands with the others, Blake went over to the car, strangely moved.

She asked, 'All set?'

'Yes.'

He gasped as she let in the clutch and sent the car bouncing back up the hill, the headlights cutting through the dusk like sword-blades.

They did not speak much on the way back to the city, but as the car made the last turn towards the sea, the horizon glittering in the moonlight in an unbroken line, Blake said abruptly, 'Stop the car, will you?'

She obediently pulled off the road and turned to look at him through the darkness. 'What's wrong?' She sounded on edge, guarded.

'I have to say something.' He reached out and took her hand from the wheel. It felt hot, as if she had fever. 'I want you to like me so much I'll probably make a mess of this. But if I do, *please*, Claire, don't shut me out, give me sea-room to manoeuvre for an approach which you will recognize as genuine.'

He pulled her hand towards him, feeling her resisting, knowing that in seconds he could smash everything.

'I went shopping in Melbourne before I met you at the Navy Office.' He lifted the ring from his pocket where it had been burning a hole all evening. Gently he slipped it over her finger, hearing her startled intake of breath. Then he said, 'I'm in love with you and there's nothing I can do about it, even if I wanted to. Later, if you can feel something towards me, put the ring on your left hand. Then I'll know.' He waited, his heart pounding painfully. 'It can be our secret.'

She gripped her hands together and he thought she was trying to drag the ring from her finger.

Then she said huskily, 'We'd better get going if it's urgent.'

She put her hand on the wheel and Blake suddenly saw that she had moved the ring to her left hand.

Almost defiantly she said, 'They can all think what the hell they like.'

She leaned over and kissed his cheek and he thought he could taste salt from a tear.

'As far as *I'm* concerned, we're engaged!'

The rest of the journey was like a dream sequence, and had he thought about it Blake would have been thankful there was so little traffic on the road as she drove the car like a speedboat.

Before they entered the Navy Office, which was in almost total darkness, she said, 'You can kiss me, if you like.'

He held her carefully and then more firmly as she came

138

against him. She kissed him like a child, but with such tenderness that Blake could barely contain his longing for her.

Then she stood back from him and straightened her tricorn hat.

She said shakily, 'That's settled then.'

The map room was glaring bright and some noisy insects were banging against the lampshades like pellets. The overhead fans had stopped for some reason and the faces of the officers around the big table were glistening with sweat.

Blake hated the way she was hemmed in by these people who were unknown to him. She nodded to each of them as she sat at a small desk and studied herself in a mirror from her bag.

It was hard to believe it was the same girl. Then as she glanced over the rim of the mirror and looked directly at him he saw the quick thrust of her breasts against her white shirt and he knew her defence was barely holding.

The double doors swung inwards and Blake saw Captain Quintin being wheeled into the map room by an orderly. He was strained and pale beneath his suntan, but his face was set with determination.

'Evening, all!' He saw Blake and grinned. 'Hello, Dick, sorry about this, but I had no choice.' He glanced at the girl. 'You're here, too, Claire. Fine.' His eyes swivelled back to Blake, half questioning, partly amused. '*Fine.*'

The lieutenant-commander who had received the worst end of Stagg's anger said, 'You should be in a hospital, sir. I can manage—'

Quintin gave him a cheerful grin. 'They want the dog for this work, Bill, not his bloody breakfast!'

To the room at large he said, 'An oil tanker was sunk yesterday. She was sailing alone as the area was supposed to be clear. Fortunately, she got her Mayday off in time and most of her lads were picked up this morning.'

Blake leaned over the table with its bright counters and flags. Allied ships, convoys, sinkings, hostile sightings, the panorama of war.

Names jumped out at him, places he had visited in the past, in peacetime. A million years ago. Seychelles, Mauritius, Dar es Salaam. A black cross marked with the name ss *Kawar Shell* showed where the latest sinking had been.

Then he glanced at the other officers around him. Mostly

lieutenant-commanders, and he guessed they were escort commanders and from the local patrol services.

Quintin said, 'I've not got the whole gen yet, but the signal I received from NOIC Aden leaves no doubt, the tanker was put down by a mine, and the M/S boys have discoverd another 'drifter' in the same area and landed it. It was German, so it must have been dropped by the raider.' He seemed to be getting weary. 'Anyway, gentlemen, this is to keep you in the picture. I suggest you return to your commands and be ready to reinforce the convoy escorts.' His eyes settled on Blake, 'Except you, that is.'

He waited for the anxious-looking orderly to wheel him to a table with some decanters upon it and said, 'You can shove off, son. I'll call when I need a tow.'

He looked at the girl. 'You pour the drinks, Claire. Just like old times.'

To Blake he said, '*Fremantle's* weighed. She's on her way north-east to make a sweep of the area. Too late of course, but we have to go through the motions.'

Blake wondered if Quintin had been back long enough to hear about Stagg's bait. He doubted it, but it would not take long.

'Fact is, Dick,' Quintin held his glass to the light, 'that area *was* clean. Nothing but a mouse could have penetrated the patrols.' He looked at Blake and added. 'There was a ship reported heading north, the Swedish *Patricia*. She was vetted by *Fremantle* and ordered to join a convoy. The one which was blown to hell.' He waited, his face creased against the pain in his leg. 'Are you thinking what I'm thinking, by any chance?'

Blake looked across at the big map table. It would destroy Stagg if it came out. That he had been hoodwinked by the raider in broad daylight and had even opened the door for him to blast the convoy into scrap.

He suddenly recalled his own words, the ones he used to new and junior officers joining his command. What his previous captain had once said to him. You must not see something merely because you expect to see it. Because you *want* to see it.

He said, 'It's possible. *Barely* possible. But if it's true then the German must have guts of steel and the ingenuity of ten men!'

'Anyway, it means Commodore Stagg is well and truly in trouble.'

Quintin sat back and waited, while from another chair the girl watched Blake with equal curiosity.

Blake said slowly, 'I think it's best left alone. The raider will feel more secure, think we have taken the hook, line and sinker. And if the admiral was to blame Stagg, I feel the friction might do us real harm.'

Quintin nodded, as if he had already known. 'And that means you would decline to take over the command? Stagg would act differently in your shoes. Well, it's not up to me, but still—' He did not finish.

Instead, he groped in his pocket and dragged out a small package. 'Here, Claire, unwrap it while our gallant captain wheels the old relic to the table again.'

As she stooped over the chair Quintin seized her wrist and held it like a vice.

The ring was hand-made, fashioned in the design of a shell, with a solitary pearl set inside it. In the overhead lights it shone from her finger like a tiny star.

Quintin nodded slowly. 'Very nice.' He pulled her down and kissed her cheek. 'I'll say nothing, Claire. But I'm sure it will turn out just fine for you both.'

Blake watched her, seeing the confusion and indecision crossing her face. But she was pleased too, excited by the old captain's acceptance.

Quintin barked, 'Well, don't stand there, girl, open the package.'

She unfolded the wrapping and held out something shiny. Quintin passed it to Blake. 'Take a look.'

It was an ordinary boatswain's call, the kind which was rarely absent from any messdeck throughout the Navy.

Blake turned it over and saw a scratched inscription on the keel, *Tasmanian Devil*.

Quintin grabbed a pointer and tapped it on the chart. 'A whale-catcher on her way to the Cape from the ice put a party ashore *here*.' The pointer touched some tiny scattered islands, specks on the Indian Ocean, some three and a half thousand miles west-south-west of this very room. 'They were looking for some fresh water for their tanks. There are plenty of islands scattered around there, most of them unpopulated, for obvious reasons. Anyway, one of the whalers found this bosun's call jammed in a rock.' He looked up, his eyes grim. '*Tasmanian Devil* was HMAS *Devonport*'s nickname.'

Blake stared at the map. Tiny, meaningless islets, south of the forty-fifth parallel and off all the sea routes. It was just possible.

Quintin said, 'I've got top approval. You'll sail today. Round up your people or leave without them if necessary. I want you to search those islands, and that one in particular. It may be nothing. But that bosun's call didn't get there on its own. I can't send half a dozen destroyers, even if I had them to spare. This must be kept "in the family".' He tapped his nose. 'There have been enough cock-ups without adding to the list!'

Blake looked at the wall clock. It was two in the morning.

'Sorry to hear about your father.' Quintin looked at him sadly. 'Fine man. But it seems to me that something good has happened, too.' He glanced at the girl. 'Off with you and get some sleep. I'm back now, and intend to stay until this lot's sorted out, and no damn arguments!'

She followed Blake into the empty corridor and said, 'I'll be thinking of you.'

A night-worker from the code room paused and looked down the corridor. A naval officer with a Wren in his arms. Just like the movies. All right for some, he thought.

Alone by the map table, Captain Jack Quintin wheeled himself towards the decanters and poured another, larger drink. Then he sat back and thought about the girl with the ring on her finger, the young captain who would be her lover, and what his own wife would have to say when she heard he had discharged himself from the hospital.

He was still sleeping with the empty glass in his fist when the early morning cleaners arrived.

11

'It Happens—'

Blake ran the last few steps of the ladder to the upper bridge and saw the watchkeepers stiffen as they always did when their captain was about. After the sticky humidity of his sea cabin it was almost a relief to be on the bridge again, even though he had left it barely two hours earlier as dawn had tried to force an appearance.

This was the morning of the seventh day out of Williamstown after Quintin's dramatic announcement about the whaler's discovery. And now, here were the islets, sprawled untidily across the starboard bow, colourless in the strange light. For as *Andromeda* had ploughed her way steadily towards the west the sea had risen, and for the past three days they had battered through ranks of angry rollers while the ship had been washed with heavy rain and incoming waves until there was barely a dry set of clothing to be had.

Blake touched his cap to Lieutenant Friar, the Australian torpedo officer, who was in charge of the watch.

'All quiet?' He had to shout above the rumbling din of water as it surged aft from the plunging stem and crashed around A turret like a fast tideway.

'Aye, sir. Revolutions for twenty-one knots, course two-five-two.'

Blake gripped his chair and climbed to the fore-gratings. Like the change of weather, it was strange to see all the tanned faces around him, eyes squinting against needles of spray, while each man was made even more uncomfortable by a heavy, glistening oilskin.

Blake slid on to the seat and watched the islets. Still a good way off. Bleak, wet, inhospitable. Many a good ship had ended her days there.

For a week they had pushed through a vast, empty ocean, with depths falling away to nearly three thousand fathoms to a dark unknown world. Then with the startling suddenness of cathedral spires the sea-bed had showed itself in tiny groups of scattered islands, boundaries of the Mid-Oceanic Ridge, the submarine mountain range which made man's knowledge a mockery. As if to remind him of this, Blake heard the muffled bleep of the echo-sounder, seemingly ineffectual when set against the world beneath the cruiser's keel.

He would have liked to fly off the Seafox for a quick recce around the islands. It would have saved time. But the sea was rising and falling in an impressive swell, and it would be pointless to lose their one aircraft for no good purpose.

Blake smiled to himself. Had he suggested it to Masters he would have taken off from the catapult without even a murmur.

He said, 'Reduce to twelve knots and bring her up two points to starboard. One watch is at breakfast, remember? It might stop some of the plates from flying if we head into it a bit more.'

He left it to Friar, who had already proved himself a good officer, and returned his gaze to the islands. Uninhabited except for the hardy sea-birds, but Scovell, who had once served down here in a survey ship just before the outbreak of war, had painted a grim picture. The islets were littered with driftwood, discarded fireplaces where survivors from wrecked vessels had clung to a hope of rescue until they had died. Scratches on rocks to mark the passing days perhaps, or to measure the issue of dwindling rations.

Cocoa was being passed around the gun positions, and he saw a seaman pause by a guard-rail, legs braced, a fanny of 'kye' steaming in his spare hand while he watched the bows begin to rise free of the sea before he made his next dash for safety.

Blake had had a lot of time to think during the restless, uncomfortable week. He missed Fairfax, and often wondered what he was doing, and if anyone had explained about Stagg's proposed big game hunt. Scovell had withdrawn into his haughty shell even more than usual. Maybe he was thinking how short-lived his position of acting-commander would be, or was cursing the wasted days searching for the raider when he could have been in England on his commanding officer's course. Either way, Blake had been left much to himself. It was good for him, he thought. For the ship also. The rough edges between the old hands and the new 'owners', as Moon called them, were fast smoothing away. Palliser, the gunnery officer, had remarked loudly, 'We're down to those who know it all and those who only think they know it all!' But by and large they were getting on well.

Harry Buck, the chief yeoman of signals, had been less charitable to one of his young Australian signalmen.

'Listen, Bunts, of *course* you're gettin' used to it all! You've bugger all else to do on this billet, *right*?'

Blake had not heard the signalman's reply. The Toby Jug was too formidable to accept any sort of argument from anyone, except possibly his captain.

Blake felt the deck sidle more comfortably into an oncoming sea and pictured the grateful faces in the engine and boiler rooms as the telegraphs signalled a reduction of speed.

He raised his glasses and levelled them on the nearest islet. Like a basking sea-monster, ugly with spray-soaked bushes and brown grass. A few hillocks but no trees.

Behind him he heard the navigating officer unclipping the canvas hood above his ready-use chart table, and someone asking, 'Do you think we will get any closer to that lot, sir?'

Then the South African's harsh reply, 'Why not, eh? According to my little book of words there is *only* an average of sixty-eight cyclones a month in this part of the Indian Ocean around this time of the year, so why worry?'

Blake knew Villar was on edge about something. A letter from home or, like most good navigating officers, he was probably worried at the ship's nearness to the islets. No anchorage, no bottom at all until the last mile or so, it would not need a cyclone to make things hazardous.

Scovell appeared on the bridge, his eyes cold as he surveyed the humps of land.

Blake said, 'We'll do it as planned. One island at a time. Take the best motor-boat and hand-pick your landing party. See that they're armed. Just in case.'

Scovell shrugged. 'There's nothing there, sir. I think we're clutching at straws. Wasting time.'

'Perhaps.'

Blake felt suddenly irritated by Scovell's attitude. He had been getting steadily worse since their arrival in Australia. He wanted to go, pick up the threads, and for that Blake could not blame him. But in his heart Blake felt a nagging certainty that sooner or later they would meet the raider, and fight. For that he was saving his strength without conscious thought. Like his reluctance to fly off the Seafox. No lives were at risk, no battle undecided, so, like her sister *Ajax* at the River Plate, *Andromeda* would hold her resources until the precise moment.

He said, 'The sea's eased a bit since dawn and the sky's clearer. Be ready to hoist out the boat in about an hour.' He met Scovell's flat stare. 'Carry on.'

Blake thought about the girl he had left in Melbourne. Taut, eager and frightened all at the same time. He wondered if she was still wearing the ring, defying the curious stares and subtle questions. Why she was prepared to accept the embarrassment which his gesture must be costing her. Unless of course she had put the ring in a drawer in an effort to change things back again.

Villar called, 'Nearest islet has a landing place, sir. Protected from the breakers for the last fifty yards or so.'

Blake could hear him tapping his teeth with his pencil as he always did.

'Good. Pass the word to Number One, will you? Then close the shore for another half mile. We will stand off but retain contact with the landing party. Make certain there's a good signalman with the boat, Yeoman.'

The Toby Jug's red nostrils flared. 'Already done, sir.'

Villar grinned. 'Never doubted it, Yeo.'

The seaplane's crane was already swinging above the boat tier, and small oilskinned figures scrambled amongst the tangle of blocks and wires like marooned seals.

'Slow ahead together.' A pause. 'Steer two-seven-one.'

Blake watched the horizon, a blurred mess of green and blue. A water-colour left out in the rain, ths shapes and distances smeared into nothing.

When he got back to Williamstown there would be more mail for the ship. A letter from his aunt, most likely.

'Course two-seven-one, sir. Both engines slow ahead.'

Behind and below Blake's chair the ship and her people moved like an oiled machine.

A speaker crackled into life. 'Sick-berth attendant to the boat tier on the double. Able Seaman Robbins has broken his leg.'

A lookout chuckled. 'Poor old Terry. Pity he didn't fall on his head. He'd not even notice that!'

Blake thought about the house. What should he do? Sell it or give it to his aunt? Share the sale price? Though it was unlikely to raise much interest with the invasion of Europe still only a dream to most people.

'Standing by, sir.'

Blake slid off his chair, his chest and thighs were running with sweat under the oilskin, and he had a mad desire to rip everything off and stand naked in the pattering spray. That would really give Stagg something to moan about.

He watched the motor boat swinging outboard while the cruiser's side made a lee against the heavy swell.

'Stop engines. Lower away.'

He saw Scovell standing by the motor boat's canopy, a webbing belt and revolver round his waist. His men were huddled together, some gripping Lanchester sub-machine-guns, the rest clinging to the gunwales as the boat's keel dug into the water and the screw frothed into action.

Blake watched the boat's progress as Villar ordered the wheelhouse to alter course and increase speed again. Bumping and lurching, like a speed-boat at the seaside. Beach balls, ice cream, all the fun of the fair.

What had she said? That it would not be the same again.

He looked at the endless stretch of empty sea, the desolate islands which appeared to be attached to the starboard anchor as they probed across the water as if they and not the ship were moving.

Then he thought of how she had felt in his arms, how much he wanted her. Needed her. Maybe Scovell had the right idea and he was the only odd man out. Let's get it over with and get on with living.

Lieutenant-Commander Francis Scovell leaned against a high rock which had somehow been split in halves like a giant egg. He was tired, dirty and knew his temper was worsening with each dragging hour.

It was past noon and his stomach felt raw with hunger. He looked around the litter of fallen rocks, dead bushes and weed with distaste. The fourth island so far. His men, equally tired and irritable, were wandering about, their first interest having gone two hours back.

There had been some jokes to begin with, mostly because *Andromeda*'s chief boatswain's mate was the senior rating in the party. His name was Flint, and more than one wag had suggested they were only here to find his lost treasure.

But even Chief Petty Officer Flint's usual rough humour had gone. Like the rest, he was filthy from clambering over rocks and man-handling the motor boat safely past the rocks. He looked across at Sub-Lieutenant Walker and asked, 'Can't we shove off, sir? I'm missing me tot badly an' so are the lads.'

The young New Zealander peered at his watch. 'What about it, sir?'

Their combined fatigue gave Scovell strength. 'Take half

the men up to the ridge, Sub. I want a line right across the island. We're not leaving here until we're satisfied, *I'm* satisfied!'

Under his breath Walker murmured, 'That's never, then.' To the chief boatswain's mate he called, 'One more sweep, Buffer. Come on, chop, chop!'

And so it went on, made no easier by the occasional glimpses of their floating home as she moved slowly and protectively past the island.

Leading Seaman Jack Musgrave, the bearded captain of *Andromeda*'s forecastle party, plodded away from Flint's group with his own smaller squad. Musgrave was two different people. In his responsible position in charge of the forecastle, with all its attendant clutter of anchor cables, mooring wires and capstans, he was a tower of strength. Ashore, he was a menace, and had dipped the leading seaman's anchor from his arm at the defaulters table more times than he could remember. He would steal almost anything, a skill which had earned him the nickname of Hydraulic Jack, because there was nothing too big for him to lift.

Now, neither afloat nor in truth ashore, he was prepared to amble along, wait for the snotty-nosed Jimmy the One to give up and then get back to the ship. A tot of neaters, and another from his secret bottle, and then head down in his mess for the seven days back to Aussie.

He saw the ordinary seaman called Digby sitting dejectedly on a stone. He looked as if he would burst into tears.

Poor little Digby. A CW candidate, as they called them. In the Service just for the war, ear-marked for a temporary commission after a few weeks' sea-time, and then able to yell and rant, make any poor jack's life a misery.

Except that Digby's expected return to the officers' selection and training depot had been violently interrupted. By the battle with the three bloody great cruisers.

Musgrave eyed him sadly. Poor little sod. He was frightened of his own shadow. If he got a bit of gold on his sleeve after his performance in *Andromeda*, Leading Seaman Musgrave would definitely sign the pledge.

He passed his water bottle to the pinched faced seaman. ''Ere, 'ave a wet, Diggers.' Strange that he felt sorry for a CW candidate, really. Musgrave had been fifteen years in the Andrew and now had to take orders from fresh-faced kids just out of school.

The youth peered at him timidly. 'Water, is it?'

'Well, it bloody would be with old high an' mighty Scovell runnin' things, wouldn't it?'

He glanced round. They were out of sight of the others, the ship, everything. Musgrave sank down and stretched his legs on the wet sand.

'What the *'ell* did you do before the war, Diggers?'

Digby searched his face, expecting sarcasm or an insult. He had never accepted the lower deck's brutal kindness, nor had it accepted him.

'I—I worked for a museum. I was hoping to get a degree.' He waved his hands vaguely. 'Old buildings, Roman fortifications, and that kind of thing.'

Musgrave, whose home had originally been in an East London slum, studied him with amazement.

'What, *you*?'

The other two seamen in the party grinned and moved nearer.

'Well, yes.' Aware for the first time that the big, bearded leading hand who ruled his mess with an iron fist and language which could sear the paintwork was genuinely interested, Digby launched into his brief career before he had joined the Navy.

He stood up, ignoring the grins from his companions, and pointed at the barren island.

'I—I could tell you about the layers, the styles and substances of this place. How it has been changed, the pattern influenced over the years.'

Musgrave scowled. 'That's a load of balls. Nobody's been 'ere.' He wondered why he had even bothered with him.

Seeing his slender life-line already slipping from his grasp, Digby plunged past the seamen and seized a spade. 'Here! I'll show you!' He was gasping, almost sobbing, as he dug frantically at a fallen bank of sand and small stones. "Perhaps... gasp... once upon a time... gasp... some fishermen came here and—' He reeled back against Musgrave who had been about to thump him into sanity.

Musgrave snapped, '*You*, Adams! Take 'old of Diggers! 'Old 'im, you poxy-faced bastard!' With surprising tenderness he took him by the arm and turned him away from his small, pathetic hole. 'Easy, lad, *easy* now.'

Then, as the other man gripped the youth, still unaware what was happening, Musgrave knelt down, his stomach mus-

149

cles in hard knots as he reached into the hole and wiped the wet sand from what Digby had seen. Two clenched hands, bound together with cord, and below them the naked spine of a corpse.

Musgrave said quietly, 'Fetch Jimmy th' One. Tell 'im to get up 'ere fast.' He turned his face from the stench. 'There's more than one buried 'ere, if you ask me.'

He walked across to the retching, sobbing Digby and said, 'You get to the boat an' tell Mr Walker I said so,' He raised Digby's chin with his great fist, the one with the flying swallow tattooed on it. 'You done all right, see? But for you, an' me listenin', of course, we'd still be at square one.'

Scovell came stamping up the slope. Normally he was in charge of the forecastle for entering or leaving harbour. He knew all about Musgrave and his funny ways.

'If this is some bloody joke!' He looked at the hole and said tonelessly, 'I shall inform the ship at once.' He made himself stoop over it. 'I've heard about this sort of thing.' He broke off, perhaps because he had momentarily forgotten himself enough to confide in a mere rating.

Musgrave said firmly, 'It was Diggers what found it, sir. All by 'isself.'

Scovell nodded, needing to throw up, but afraid of doing so in front of his men.

'I see. Good. I'll tell the captain.'

He beckoned to the signalman, bent almost double with his equipment and swaying aerial.

'Call up *Andromeda*. Make, *have discovered a dead body, maybe more. Request instructions*.'

Musgrave nudged the white-faced Digby and whispered, 'An' don't forget the rum!'

Digby did not know why he had not gone back to the boat and Sub-Lieutenant Walker, whom he liked. Nor did he know how he had stopped himself from running away until he had fallen into the sea.

What he did understand was that something hideous had changed everything for him, and life would never be quite as bad again.

Blake stood apart from the rest of his men, his shoes covered by wet sand and tiny stones which had been churned up by heavy overnight rain.

It was unreal, a scene from some macabre painting. The

150

shallow trench, one side of which had already collapsed under the rainfall, the double line of canvas bundles. Thirty-three bodies. They had once been men like the stiff-faced marine bugler, or the surgeon who with his assistants had worked all through the previous afternoon on an improvised examination of the corpses.

Beyond a low hillock he saw *Andromeda* shining in the morning light which filtered through the cloud to play on her pale dazzle-paint. In the distance she looked clean and remote from all this horror.

It was still raining, but the heavy drops tasted of salt spray. Like tears.

Thirty-three bodies. It was impossible to tell exactly who they had once been, except for their common bond as sailors. Every identity disc or scrap of clothing, which might have left a clue for the sake of humanity, had been torn from them.

The other thing which was common to them all, as Surgeon Lieutenant-Commander Bruce had explained, was that they had all been injured or wounded much earlier, probably in one of the actions against the raider.

But why this? Surely the Germans had a doctor, or some means of getting their wounded captives to safety? Instead they had been dragged or carried ashore to this miserable scrap of land in the middle of an ocean, stripped naked with their hands pinioned behind them, then shot, one by one, in the back of the skull, to fall into a hastily dug grave.

Blake felt the hatred coursing through him, the revulsion he had felt with each terrible discovery. And but for a frightened ordinary seaman named Digby the secret might have remained.

Most of the murdered men were from the Australian cruiser *Devonport*. Their youth, their uniform haircuts and the occasional tattoos marked them apart from the others. Which, he wondered, was the man who had managed to drive a boatswain's call into some rocks so that one day someone might discover it and he with his companions might be avenged?

He could almost hear the limping procession to the edge of the pit. The bark of orders, the slamming crack of a machine-pistol. *It happens,* they said. Why then did you always expect it to happen to others and not to your own kind?

Captain Farleigh, his helmet dripping with water, saluted smartly. 'Ready, sir.'

Blake nodded and walked slowly through his men, aware

151

of the sadness and the hate, the way they gripped their spades like foot soldiers at Agincourt.

The chaplain stood very upright by the grave, his surplice blowing in the wet breeze, his wispy hair plastered across his forehead while he waited to begin.

What was he thinking? Blake wondered. Sickened by all of it, like Hugh Grenfell had been after the Dardanelles disaster, or still holding on, believing and hoping? They had been through a lot together. Death came in all shapes and guises. But this was different. This was part of hell.

Beveridge's thin voice cut through the swishing rain. 'They that go down to the sea in ships, that do business in great waters—'

One of the firing party was swaying slightly against his rifle, his boots squeaking in the sand. Most of the original landing party were present, even young Digby, red-eyed but strangely determined as the chaplain's voice droned on.

Chief Petty Officer Flint looked across at his ship as she moved so very slowly past the island yet again. There was home. Mates. Something he understood. He sighed and glanced at the chaplain, poor old Horlicks, as he struggled on with the service. It would soon be over now.

'We commend unto Thy hands of mercy, most merciful Father, the souls of these our brothers—'

Flint felt the rain running down his neck and chest. Did God really care? he wondered. Did anyone?

Somewhere a man was sobbing quietly, as if he had known one of those graceless bundles.

Farleigh snapped, 'Royal Marines, *ready! Present!*'

The rifles rose towards the bleak sky.

Blake saw Flint's expression across the grave and guessed what he was thinking. He had known him quite a long time. Had seen him promoted, had watched him enjoying himself as well as when he had been fighting mad. Now he was watching the marines' rifles and probably wishing they were a firing squad for the men who had done this bloody murder.

'*Fire!*'

The volley crashed out and sent a cloud of screaming sea-birds wheeling from their hiding places.

Blake saluted and turned his back as Flint's burial party moved in with their spades.

In the Mediterranean and the Atlantic he had always known exactly what he had been fighting, what to expect. Until he had stepped ashore here he had not found it easy to understand his involvement with the German raider. Now he knew.

He saw the boats rising and falling on the swell while they idled near the tiny beach to lift off the burial party. They shone with blown spray like glass.

Blake quickened his pace down the slippery sand and would have fallen but for the surgeon's hand on his elbow.

He looked at him. 'Thanks, Doc. I almost broke the rules and showed my true feelings.'

The surgeon nodded. 'You'll forget, sir.'

Blake turned and looked up the beach. A small file of marines coming down to the boats, the slap of spades on sand as the seamen tamped down the grave. Old Horlicks standing above it all like a spectre. The last to leave.

'Not this time, Doc. Not until I've put that bastard down.'

He was shocked by the tone of his own voice. More so that he meant each word.

The motion of the dinghy was getting worse, and try as he might he could not rouse the girl or make her aware of the mounting danger, the insane clatter of machine-guns.

Blake awoke gasping and fighting in the gloom of his sea cabin, his mind reeling from the fantasy while he grappled with reality. He gave a violent start as the telephone buzzed above his bunk, and as he struggled to drag it from its rack he realized it must have been ringing earlier and the sound had filtered into his nightmare.

'Captain speaking!' He made himself control his voice. 'What is it?'

'Officer of the watch, sir.' It was Palliser. 'Radar reports a ship, almost dead ahead. Range about eight miles.' He sounded wary, as if astonished by the captain's tone.

'I'll come up.'

Blake rolled off the bunk and lost precious seconds while he adjusted to the steep roll and plunge of the deck. The islands lay two days astern, and after making a brief signal of their findings there, Blake had turned his ship towards Australia once more, the worsening weather doing much to keep his men too busy to brood on what they had discovered.

He peered at the bulkhead clock. Four o'clock in the afternoon. It would be early dark in the foul visibility. What was a ship doing out here, miles from anywhere?

He hurried to the bridge, feeling the wind sweeping over

the glass screen as he crossed to the chart table. Warm and wet, a sickening motion and the pungent smell of funnel smoke as a quarter wind forced it down over the sodden watchkeepers.

Palliser said, 'Radar say that they are getting a poor reading, sir. The conditions are bad and—'

Villar emerged dripping from beneath the chart table's hood.

'Ready to turn on to new course, sir.' He saw Blake's expression and added, 'Unless you intend to chase after that ship.'

'Who have you got on radar?' Blake was thinking aloud, seeing the ocean, two ships moving on an invisible thread.

Villar said, 'Gibbons, sir. He's good.'

Blake crossed to the rack of telephones and lifted one from its case.

'Gibbons? This is the captain. What do you make of it?'

'The range is about the same, sir, but I'm almost certain she had altered course. We're getting a lot of interference.' He sounded apologetic. As if it was his fault. 'But I'm pretty sure she was steering south-east. Now we're on the same track.'

'Good work, Gibbons.' He put down the handset. 'Sound off action stations, if you please. Tell the engineroom to increase revolutions for twenty knots.'

Villar glanced at the surging crests alongside as if to say, *in this?*

Seconds later the alarm bells jangled throughout the ship and men surged towards their stations, their movements automatic, even if their minds were still below in their messes.

Palliser left to go to his director control tower, and Blake said to Villar, 'Muster your plotting team, Pilot. I want every move, every *thought* put on paper!'

'Ship at action stations, sir.'

'Very well.'

Blake jammed his cap in the signal locker to allow the spray to soak his hair and face until his mind was clear again.

'Alter course. Steer zero-eight-zero. Tell radar to keep watching for any change of course by the other ship.' He had almost said *enemy.*

'Aye-aye, sir.'

The bridge groaned and rocked as the mounting revolutions reached up through the glistening steel.

Blake heard the gunnery speaker click on and then Palliser's voice from the director.

'Ship bears Green oh-five. Range one-five-five.'

The right gun of B turret rose a few degrees and then dipped again, as if it, not the contents of the turret, was coming to life.

Villar came back banging his wet hands together. 'Hell, look at it!' He glared through the screen at the low, angry clouds. The sea was violent and in disorder as it mounted under the cruiser's stern and then smashed over the side in solid sheets.

Sub-Lieutenant Walker staggered to Villar's side. 'Will we make a signal to base, sir?'

Villar grinned through the falling spray. 'Why, Sub? There's nothing between us and the nearest land but sixteen hundred miles of bloody ocean and that ship!'

'The ship is still on course, sir.'

Blake moved restlessly about the bridge, his shoes slipping on the wooden gratings. The other vessel was not equipped with radar, otherwise they would have detected it by now. She must have been keeping a damn good lookout to spot *Andromeda*'s upper works in this visibility, even with the sun behind her. That was unusual for the run-of-the-mill merchantman, especially in these waters.

He thrust his hands into his pockets and examined his reactions like a surgeon at the operating table.

Was he over-reacting because of what had happened?

He said, 'Yeoman, write this down and pass it to the W/T office. *Am investigating strange ship in position so and so.*' He heard the Toby Jug's pencil pause over his pad, then added, '*I will transmit my amended ETA when satisfied.*'

He strode to the chart, beckoning Villar to follow. Beneath the canvas hood they peered at the stained chart, their own pencilled track, the neat procession of crosses where Villar had recorded the other ship's positions.

Blake said, 'Give the yeoman a position about *here*.' He pointed to the north of their intended course. 'A nice easy one, about a hundred miles away. If that other ship is an enemy, he'll think we're in company and our consort has made a contact further north. We'll see what he does about it.'

They ducked out into the wind and Villar handed his scribbled latitude and longitude of the mythical sighting report to the yeoman of signals before asking. 'What then, sir?'

'He'll get the hell out of it, thankful that we were stupid enough to go after the wrong ship. If he's on the level, he'll not only fail to comprehend our signal, but will remain thankfully on his lawful occasions.'

The yeoman said thickly, 'W/T informed, sir.'

'Alter course. Steer due north. Tell radar and DCT what we're doing.'

Beam on to the big rollers, *Andromeda* heaved and swayed to a sickening angle. Her lee side was buried several times beneath tons of water, and Blake pitied the damage control parties throughout the hull who were trying to keep equipment and vital machinery from tearing itself adrift.

The minutes ticked past, and Blake could sense the disappointment around him. Wrong again. A waste of time, as Scovell would soon be saying.

'Radar . . . bridge!'

Villar had the telephone to his ear in a second. *'Forebridge!'*

'The ship *is* altering course, sir. Turning to starboard.'

To confirm this, Palliser's voice came through the speaker again. 'Ship now bears one-three-zero. Range one-six-oh.'

Villar exclaimed, 'The bastard's heading away, sir. He swallowed it, the whole bloody bit!'

Blake stared at him, his mind like ice. 'Bring her round, Pilot. Course to overhaul and intercept. Twenty-five knots.'

A boatswain's mate looked at his friend and grinned. 'Tally-bloody-ho!'

Like an avenging beast, *Andromeda* swung steeply to starboard, her guard-rails buried in spray as she pointed her stem towards her invisible quarry.

Down in his brightly lit corridor of roaring machinery, Weir looked at his subordinate and then shook a gloved fist at the telegraphs.

He mouthed the words through the din. 'They're going bloody mad up top!'

The second engineer nodded agreement and then turned back to his gauges.

Weir stared at his stokers and ERAs bowing and lurching through the oily mist like phantoms. One slip and you were mincemeat. He wished Blake would ease up. But from what he had heard, the skipper had his reasons.

The second engineer patted his shoulder. 'You okay, Chief?'

'An' why shouldn't I be, man?'

Weir swung away before the lieutenant could see his face. It often hit him like that. Remembering his wife and two children, buried in a common grave after the air raid.

He thought of the islands they had left astern, what the returning landing party had said. He ran his hand along the

156

polished rail of his catwalk and said softly, 'Come on, my lass, let's be having you, an' none of your tricks now!'

The second engineer glanced at him curiously. It was as if the Chief was speaking to the ship.

12

No Proof

While *Andromeda* pounded after the unknown ship, low cloud and a heavy downpour reduced visibility to less than a mile. Only the radar's invisible eye and the gunnery control's blurred glimpses of the other ship told them they were not alone or charging after a phantom.

'The ship is resuming course, sir. Range now down to five miles.'

Blake wiped his mouth with the back of his hand. It was hard to think with the rain sweeping across the bridge like pellets, the ship lifting and surging forward in great sickening swoops.

'Warn Guns. Be ready to open fire instantly.'

He tried to picture the other ship. She had seen them at last. Or had already picked up *Andromeda*'s radar on a detector. Only another warship would turn and fight. A merchantman would stand no chance against the cruiser's speed, which at this moment was over twenty-five knots, with a few more in hand if required.

The stranger would appear on *Andromeda*'s starboard bow, unless she made some last effort to wriggle away as darkness closed in for the night.

Blake thrust an empty pipe into his mouth and bit on the stem. There was no sense in prolonging it.

'Five star-shell. Yeoman, use your big light and signal her to heave to. You know the drill.'

As if the signalmen had been waiting for the order, the biggest searchlight clattered into life, the glacier beam probing through the oncoming rain with quick, irregular flashes.

Stop instantly. This is a British warship. Do not attempt to scuttle.

Someone gave a yelp of pain as a four-inch gun crashed out, and seconds later the low cloud exploded into life from the star-shell.

It was all there. The other ship, almost end on, her high

158

stern glistening in spray and the glare from the drifting flare.

Villar said, 'Christ, he's switched on his navigation lights, the crafty bastard!'

More lights appeared through the rain, and Blake saw the Spanish colours painted on the vessel's side, the urgent flash of a morse lamp from her bridge.

The Toby Jug growled, 'Says she's the *Jacinto Verdaguer*, sir.' Even his clumsy pronunciation failed to disguise his contempt, his anger.

'She's not stopping, sir.'

Blake picked up a handset but kept his eyes on the fading shape of the other ship as the flare began to die.

'Guns? One round. Close as you like.'

The violent crash and recoil of B turret's right gun made the bridge jump as if kicked.

Blake watched for the fall of shot, saw the blurred flash of the explosion and a leaping column of water, which had it been any nearer would have exploded inside her hull.

'She's stopping, sir.' A seaman strapped in his Oerlikon gun gave an ironic cheer.

Like a chanting monk, one of Palliser's gunnery ratings was repeating, 'B gun reload, semi-armour-piercing.'

Sub-Lieutenant Walker shouted, 'From W/T, sir! That ship's transmitting!' He sounded confused. 'Says she's being fired on by British warship, it's an SOS, sir!'

Scovell appeared on the bridge, his boots skidding in the slopping water.

'Shall I send off a boarding party, sir?'

Blake levelled his glasses again. He was not mistaken. One of the other ship's boats was beginning to jerk down the falls towards the waves alongside as the ship began to drift downwind.

He said, 'Signal her again! *Do not scuttle! Do not abandon! Stand by to receive my boarding party!*'

He heard Palliser's voice again, calm and detached, as he trained the two forward turrets on the drifting ship.

It might be a ruse, a last attempt to lure *Andromeda* near enough to loose off torpedoes or open fire with some concealed guns.

The swift change of events, the other ship's sudden call for help seemed totally at odds with her previous movements.

Scovell said, 'We'll have to get closer if we're to send a boat across, sir.'

159

Blake glanced at him. 'If we don't put some hands aboard, every scrap of evidence will go over the side before dawn, you can bank on that!'

Walker yelled, 'That was an explosion, sir!'

A dull, metallic thud rolled against *Andromeda*'s hull, as if she had charged across a submerged wreck.

Smoke belched through the other ship's forward deck, to be driven instantly downwind.

Scovell rasped, 'Bloody hell! They've fired a scuttling charge!'

Blake looked across at the ship. In his imagination he could already detect a list.

'Make to her once more. *Do not abandon.*'

Villar staggered across the gratings. 'Tell 'em we'll leave every mother's son to drown if they do!' He looked helplessly at Blake. 'Why not, sir? They'd do it to us.'

The lamp clattered and the yeoman said, 'No acknowledgement, sir, *and* they're lowering another boat.'

The ship had begun to list. She was obviously well loaded, and her cargo was lending its weight to her execution.

'Slow ahead together. Pilot, alter course to make a lee for those boats.' He could not disguise his bitterness as he added, 'Maybe *they* would, Pilot. But they obviously know us better than we do ourselves.'

Villar strode to the compass platform muttering, 'If it was my decision I'd—'

Scovell snapped, 'Well, it's not, so stop bloody well moaning about it!'

Another bang echoed across the water, a scuttling charge or some internal explosion, it was impossible to tell.

'She's settling down.'

Able Seaman 'Shiner' Wright, the navigator's yeoman, peered through the rain.

'I've checked her on the list, sir. The name's genuine anyway. Spanish ship under charter to a company in South America, Buenos Aires, to be exact.'

He withdrew hurriedly as Villar glared at him.

Scovell said softly, 'Well, there's a thing.'

The tannoy bellowed, 'Stand by to take on survivors. Scrambling nets, lower away!'

Lieutenant Trevett, Villar's assistant, said savagely, 'Survivors my ass!'

Blake looked at him. A newcomer to the ship, and an Australian from another way of life. But already he was sharing it. Could feel the same bitterness as himself.

He said, 'Number One, I want every man from that ship put under guard. Nobody is to converse, nothing is to be discarded.'

Scovell's eyes were in shadow. 'You still believe it was an enemy—' He broke off as the ship heeled over and plunged beneath the surface in a welter of boiling foam and steam. 'A supply vessel of sorts?' Without waiting for an answer he left the bridge, calling for some armed marines to receive the floundering boats alongside.

Blake said, 'Fall out action stations. Lay off a new course for base, Pilot.'

Villar looked across the ticking gyro-compass. 'Well, *I* think she was a bandit, sir.'

The speaker intoned, 'Fall out action stations. Port watch to defence stations. Hands to supper.'

Blake climbed on to his seat again, going over the fast-moving chain of events. Villar shared his views. Why had the ship displayed no lights nor an indication of her neutrality? How had an ordinary merchantman under charter managed to detect *Andromeda*'s approach and her sudden alteration of course?

But suppose he was wrong. Palliser would be the first to deny that a single shell from one of his guns could have sunk the merchant ship. But the evidence now lay on the sea-bed, and at a court of enquiry the facts of the present moment would be flimsy to say the least.

'Course to steer is zero-seven-zero, sir.'

'Very well. Revolutions for fifteen knots until the Chief says otherwise. When you've done all that, have a signal coded up for our correct ETA.'

Villar watched him as he walked aft to the ladder which would lead him to his sea cabin, his prison.

To Lieutenant Trevett he said, 'Command? You can have it, man! The way the top brass make the rules for skippers you'd think we were on the wrong side!'

In his sea cabin, the sides of which were running with condensation despite the fans, Blake threw his oilskin on the deck and lay on the bunk.

It was no longer a matter of luck. You had to be right, and to go on believing you were right, no matter what. The Spanish merchantman had been a supply ship for the raider. No other explanation fitted. Her captain had obeyed his masters very well. No evidence, but more than that, he had used attack as the best form of defence.

The German high command had chosen its people with extreme care. They knew how to drag a red-herring, how to make every Allied warship so troubled about sinking an innocent vessel that he would have to think twice before attacking. Except it was unlikely he would get a second chance.

He thought, too, about the tiny island and the hastily dug grave. Thirty-three dead men. Even one would have been too many under those conditions.

He rolled on to his side hoping the dream would return. But, like the sleep he so badly needed, it stayed away.

Commander (E) Robert Weir stood on the opposite side of Blake's littered desk and said firmly, 'I understand all that you're doing and trying to do. Lord, we've been in each other's pockets long enough for me to know that. But the engines are my responsibility, and I'll not be able to answer for them if we go on like we have been of late.'

Blake stared past him, his eyes sore from strain and lack of sleep, and from long hours on the upper bridge. And yet it was as if nothing had happened. He recalled the girl, right here in the cabin, when she had first come aboard. Her surprise, which he could have taken for doubt, at the stillness and order so soon after a savage battle.

Through an open scuttle he could see a tall gantry, drifting smoke from some dockyard machinery. Williamstown again, their new refuge.

They had docked in the early morning, to be met by a fully armed escort for the crew of the merchantman, some blank-faced intelligence officers and then the usual horde of officials and workers.

Blake said, 'I was right. I *know* it.'

He thought of the *Jacinto Verdaguer*'s captain when he had had him brought to the bridge. Angry to the point of hysteria, but behind all the bluster Blake had detected a defiance too, a sort of wild triumph. As if by sacrificing his ship the man had done his best to crucify Blake.

Now, alongside once more, Blake's orders were brief. Take on fuel and stores. Local leave only to be allowed, but no loose talk. One hint about what had happened, and as a cheerful

162

Australian naval officer had said, leave would become something as unknown as a good cup of coffee.

Fremantle was due in this afternoon, her patrol having passed without incident. Stagg would send him packing when he heard what had happened. Once he might not have cared. But now it mattered. Because of the girl, and for a lot of other reasons, too.

The telephone buzzed and he lifted it to his ear, hoping a shore line was already connected.

But it was Friar, the torpedo officer, who was OOD.

'Sorry to bother you, sir.' Through the telephone his Australian accent seemed far more pronounced. 'But there's a commander come aboard to see you.' His voice faded as he turned from the telephone and Blake heard him ask, 'What was the name again?'

Weir muttered, 'Another bloody "expert", no doubt!'

Friar continued amiably, 'Commander Wilfred Livesay, sir.'

Blake stared hard at the bulkhead, a face emerging like one at a séance. Wilfred Livesay, a slightly-built youth, with dark plastered-down hair, like a survivor from the Great War, a face which laughed too readily, and often on the defensive.

They had been in the same training cruiser as cadets. Straight out of Dartmouth with the world at their feet. He had met up with Livesay several times in his career. He never seemed to change much in spite of the war, and yet Blake felt he had never really got to know him.

'Show him down, please.'

Weir grunted, 'I'm away then. Before those thieves from the dockyard rob us blind!'

Blake stood up and looked at himself in the bulkhead mirror. There were deep lines at the corners of his mouth. His hair was untidy and thick with salt. He looked like an unmade bed, he thought wearily. What was Livesay doing in Australia? he wondered. A command perhaps. He was the same age and seniority as himself, but *Andromeda* and a VC had put Blake far above him.

The door opened and Livesay stepped over the coaming. Just like all the other times. Neat and careful.

He was perfectly turned-out, and his face shone as if he had just walked out of a shower.

He held his cap with its gold-leafed peak under one arm,

as if unsure whether or not he would be invited to stay.

They shook hands, and Livesay said, 'You look a bit worn out, sir.'

'For God's sake, Wilfred, not now!'

Livesay seemed pleased. 'Sorry. I find it a bit hard to call you Dick.' He sat down and looked round the cabin. 'Quite a ship.' He was wrestling with something, which was nothing new either. 'They say it will soon be winter here. It will suit me. They don't know what a real winter is. I was just saying—'

Blake said gently, 'Look, Wilfred, it's me, remember? You don't have to waste time with the coming-shortly bit. You're here for a reason, right?'

Livesay sat back and stared up at the fan. With his eyes screwed up he looked like the nervous midshipman again.

He said, 'Fact is, er, Dick, I've just arrived, so to speak. I'm attached to the Navy Office on behalf of our High Commission. Sort of staff job. Getting ready for the time when our Pacific fleet is formed again, for a crack at the Nips.'

A staff job. That would be right up his street.

Blake tried again. 'Have you had breakfast yet? We've only been alongside for an hour or so.'

'Yes. Look, the fact is, I've been sent.' He stood up, his cap rolling unheeded on the carpet. 'It's a bit beyond me. But I was summoned by their lordships before I was flown out.'

Blake tensed. *Flown out.* It had to be important.

Livesay turned to peer through a scuttle. 'I think they chose me because we've known each other for a long time.' He swung round, his eyes troubled. 'You don't mind, Dick? But I've always looked up to you, envied you, I suppose. Then along comes the war and everything's different. Even the worst officer stands out like a genius against some poor devil who has been commissioned after a few weeks' training. And I'll not deceive myself, I was never much good in peacetime. The fact is—'

Blake waved him back to the chair. 'If you say "the fact is" once more, Wilfred, I shall probably go berserk. We've had rather a bad time lately, and I'm too bushed to guess why you're here, so let's be having you.'

Livesay wriggled in his chair. 'You know the Navy, Dick. It's a family. People talk. News gets round. Everybody in the UK is too keyed up about the coming invasion to bother much about what's going on here, but in the Service, *they* know.'

'Know what, for God's sake? If you mean that I'm trying to help catch a raider, all I can say is—'

Livesay seemed to relax for the first time. 'Oh, *that*! No, Dick, it's about, well, you know, your personal life.'

'I see.' He felt for his pipe but had left it in the sea cabin. 'Diana's been on to you, has she?'

'Well, yes and no. You remember Vice-Admiral Tasker? Well, he's at the Admiralty, and I was on his staff before I was sent out here. He's a big noise now, and after the war he's the obvious choice for planning the new structures for employment and appointments. He told me as much.'

'I feel I should tell you to leave, Wilfred, *old friend* or not. I don't think I'm going to like this at all.'

Livesay stared at him as if mesmerized, 'Please don't do that! It's because of our friendship, and the fact they know you would not even discuss your private affairs with a senior officer, that they sent *me*!' He looked as if he might burst into tears. 'Like it or not, Dick, when they gave you the Victoria Cross they did more than you realized. After the war, and even during the next critical phase of it, you are the kind of officer they'll be marking down for higher command. You know what it was like in our fathers' time. Good chaps thrown on the beach, selling their medals and begging for work. I'd not want that to happen to us, to me.'

Tomorrow, next week or next month we may all be killed. But an admiral in Whitehall, poor old Wilfred and God alone knows how many others were concerned for him and his postwar prospects. Blake did not know whether to laugh or weep.

Livesay said tightly, 'Your wife wants to come back to you.' He flinched as Blake stood up, as if he expected to be thrown bodily through the door. 'The fellow she's been going with, well, he's pretty senior and a friend of sorts of Admiral Tasker.' He took a deep breath. 'I feel terrible being here like this.'

Blake looked at him gravely. 'I think it was *terrible* of them to ask you.'

So that was it. It did not matter who had got tired of whom first. Maybe the man she had 'been going with', as Livesay had so delicately put it, was also married and wanted to clear his yard-arm. Or perhaps the VC had changed things for her after all.

He looked at Livesay, suddenly sorry for him. He had never been much use in the Navy. He tried too hard, wanted to succeed so much that others often saw him as a crawler. In fact, he was completely insecure, and any threat of being dropped from the Navy List after the war would be all it needed to bring him here.

Blake said, 'So this is a sort of warning. Either be a good boy, a hero for the people to cheer, or I'm in the cart, eh? Everybody surfaces looking nice and clean, and discipline will prevail!'

In the adjoining cabin flat Blake could hear the murmur of voices and the occasional buzz of a telephone. His writer would have a whole list of people for him to see, forms to initial, letters to sign.

He said, 'Well, thanks, Wilfred. You did your best.'

Livesay stood up slowly and then stooped to retrieve his cap.

In a small voice he said, 'I've a letter here. It tells you to report to our office in Sydney while the ship has three days to overhaul. *Andromeda*'s duties will be partially covered by an armed merchant cruiser which is coming from Bombay.' He tried to smile but nothing came. 'We're doing all we can.'

'What's the purpose of my visit?' Blake glanced at the sideboard and suddenly needed a long drink.

'Well, our people in Sydney will want to go over the matter of the Spanish ship, of course. There's one hell of a hullabaloo coming from their consul and also the Argentinian authorities. But then, I imagine you anticipated that?'

He looked at the door and then blurted out, 'The fact is, Dick, your wife is here, too. She flew in the same plane.' He recoiled as Blake faced him and said, 'I had nothing to do with it, I swear!'

Blake saw him place the sealed envelope on the desk but was conscious only of Livesay's words. She was in Australia. It was no longer something vague and out of focus, lost over the thousands of miles and which you could choose to ignore.

Livesay said, 'You're to go as soon as you've instructed your second in command.'

He made for the door, but stopped dead as Blake called after him, 'Before you leave, Wilfred.' Blake moved towards him, seeing the man's apprehension, even fear. 'You and I shared a lot . . . once. But that was a different world, another sort of Navy. Some of us have been lucky, have stayed alive long enough to see that peacetime minds are no match for wartime conditions. I used to think much as you do about these 'wartime wonders', like most of the officers in this wardroom are. Now I know differently. They have minds uncluttered by peacetime prospects, seniority and promotion. They just want to win and get home in one piece afterwards. Like my navigator. Dreaming of the day when he gets back to the Union Castle, or the paymaster commander who'll use his war to entertain the ladies around his table aboard some P & O liner. And if I've influenced them in some ways, they've certainly done the same to me. I don't care a damn about who gets what later on. I want us to *win*, but to win our way, not in the fashion I've just witnessed!' He smiled grimly. 'Sorry about the lecture, Wilfred, but try and learn from my mistakes. And the next time some "gentleman" offers you a reward for doing something you inwardly hate, tell him to drop dead! Now, if you don't mind, I've a ship to run.'

When he turned round again the cabin was empty.

Scovell was the first visitor. He entered the cabin just as Blake was putting down the telephone. There was no shore line yet, because of another priority, they said. It was more likely that someone had been told to keep *Andromeda* and her captain as isolated as possible.

'Well, Number One?'

'There will be some defaulters shortly, sir.'

'What, already? Can't you cope?'

Scovell eyed him dispassionately. 'Three of our ABs threw a dockyard worker off the pier, sir. He apparently shouted something they disapproved of.'

Blake frowned. He could well imagine what it had been. That the cruiser had sunk a helpless neutral. Too quick on the trigger. Too eager by half.

He pressed Moon's bell and when the steward appeared he said, 'Pack a bag, Moon. For a couple of days. I shall be in Sydney.' He looked at Scovell. That had obviously shaken him inside his shell.

'So *you* deal with the defaulters, Number One. In fact, you take charge of everything until I return.' He looked slowly around the cabin. If they let me return.

The telephone buzzed and the switchboard said, 'Shore line's been connected, sir.'

Blake nodded. 'Thank you, but I don't need it now.'

He put down the telephone and looked at it for a long moment. What could he tell her anyway? Don't worry, I'm going to see my wife. But we can still be friends, can't we?

167

He felt the anger surging around his head like a fever.

But I love you, Claire. I want you so much. I really do.

Scovell excused himself and left. Probably imagines I'm halfway round the bend, Blake thought.

Moon called, 'I'm runnin' a bath now, sir.' He hovered by the door, his gloomy face troubled even more than usual. He said, 'The shop in Melbourne, sir, was it all right? You've bin too busy for me to ask before.'

'Yes.' He thought of the defiance as she had put the ring on her finger and what it would cost her after this. 'It was just right.'

Moon watched him dubiously. 'The lads is all be'ind you, sir. Never did like the bloody Spaniards anyway. They're a sort of Nazi bunch themselves. 'S'fact, sir, *Andromeda* won't stand for no nonsense, Jerries, Eyeties *or* Spaniolas!' He shuffled off shaking his head angrily.

Blake stared after him. Moon believed he had made a mistake and had forced the neutral ship to do something stupid. But to Moon, like the three seamen who had pitched the unfortunate dockyard worker into the water, it hardly mattered. Now, as always, the ship, and that included her captain, came first.

Blake waited for the hotel porter to lay his small travelling bag by the bed and close the door behind him before he could bring himself to move.

He strode to the window and opened it, the smell of the sea and the sounds of traffic rising to greet him like old friends.

Sydney. Much as he had imagined it. The great bridge, the 'coat-hanger', the pale buildings, and beyond the harbour the open promise of the Tasman Sea.

But for the low cloud and a hint of rain, the sea might have been blue. But it was dull, like pewter. *Suitable for the way I feel.*

Blake thought about the short flight from Melbourne, the first time he had been in an aircraft since the crash. He had gone over it several times, more perhaps than previously. He had found himself listening to the engines with a different ear, had watched the passing banks of clouds as if expecting to see that seaplane again with its stabbing machine-guns.

He had been bustled straight from the airport to Garden Island, where he had found himself confronted by an imposing table full of senior officers and some men in plain clothes who could have been anyone.

He had not seen any more of Livesay, nor had he flown to Sydney in the same aircraft. Maybe he was afraid Blake would change his mind about coming, or involve him in some new trouble. Perhaps he did not even want to risk being seen with him, in case Blake was about to be reprimanded, or worse.

Blake felt the returning anger and crossed to his bag. As he tore open the straps and felt inside for the bottle which Moon had packed he recalled the line of bland faces. Their curiosity, their doubt.

A British rear-admiral had been in overall charge, and had laid it on well and truly, as if to prove to his Australian colleagues that there was going to be no favouritism.

'You say that the *Jacinto Verdaguer* had altered course after your original contact. But you admit that conditions were bad and that even your most experienced radar operator was unsure. You have stated that the ship was not sunk by the one shell fired by your main armament. But there is no proof. Nor is there any proof that she was a supply ship for the enemy, or that she carried some advanced radar detection equipment. The Spanish master has admitted he was steaming without lights. But that was his own risk, and he had good cause to doubt our protection if there had been a raider nearby. The only *fact* you have laid before us is the discovery of thirty-three murdered men. Men, already wounded, and killed before they became an inconvenience.'

Blake had said, 'Spain and Argentina have helped the Germans often enough, sir. They are bound to make a strong protest. The Spanish captain was well briefed. He knew he could not escape my ship, but was determined to make the most of his own loss by screaming to the world that we were attacking him.'

'Be that as it may, Captain Blake, I have ordered the release of the *Jacinto Verdaguer*'s company, and no doubt His Majesty's Government will eventually be faced with a heavy bill as the result of this, er, escapade.'

There had been more. A whole lot more. Blake unbuttoned his jacket and sat down heavily, the bottle still unopened in his hand.

The rear-admiral had skirted around what would happen next, but Blake had no doubt that he would be replaced as soon

169

as possible and sent home to an appointment much as Livesay had described. Untarnished. The hero with clean hands.

He opened the bottle and poured a large measure of whisky into a glass.

The bedside telephone jangled loudly and made him start. He must have been dozing, he thought.

'Hello?' Who was he expecting. Half-hoping for, partly dreading.

'That you, Blake?' The voice was so loud he had to move the telephone away from his ear.

'Yes.'

'Christ, you're a bloody hard man to find. Those half-wits at the base know as much about their commandeered rooms and buildings as my backside knows about dominoes!'

Blake relaxed slowly. It was Stagg. Fierce, angry and out for a quick kill.

'What can I do for you, sir?'

There was a gurgling sound and Blake guessed Stagg was also drinking.

'I've heard *all* about it! Every white-livered, pansy-minded load of crap which you had to face up to. Man, if I'd been there I'd have told them a thing or two! What the bloody hell do they know? Don't they understand it takes guts to land a VC and fight three cruisers single-handed?' He was shouting, his thick voice filling the room. 'I've just been with the First Member to put in my pipeful. I told him, and I told him straight. If you want to interfere with one of my captains *you will do it through me*!'

Blake swallowed hard. At a loss for words. 'Thank you, sir.'

Stagg laughed. 'Thank me when we've caught those krauts.' In a strangely controlled tone he added, 'I saw that old fool Jack Quintin, too. I suppose he means well.' He was dragging it out, finding it hard to say something. Then he said, 'He told me about the *Patricia*. I've had a sneaking suspicion in my own mind since I let the ship join that convoy without a closer inspection. To think that it was very likely that cunning bastard Rietz. I'll bet he was laughing all over his bloody face. I keep thinking of the convoy. Wiped out because of me.'

Blake thought of the smooth-talking rear-admiral. *There's no proof.*

'Anyway, I just wanted to thank you. For saying what you did to Jack Quintin. There's many an eager-beaver who'd have used it to knock me down, I can tell you. Can't say any more. Someone might be tapping the line.'

Blake had to smile in spite of his feelings. Stagg had already revealed enough to fill a front page.

Stagg said vaguely, 'See you when you get back here. I'll tell you how we're going to catch that cold-blooded pirate, in spite of our superiors in London and Sydney, certainly not because of them!' He guffawed, the old Stagg slowly emerging again. 'I was wrong about you. In fact, I've been wrong about quite a few things.' He chuckled. 'But don't rely on that. I'll still be a pig if need be!' The line went dead.

Blake walked to the window and stared hard at the harbour and its slow-moving craft. It must have cost Stagg a lot to admit he had made a mistake and to lay his own head on the block again when he had no way of knowing if Blake was in the right or not.

All at once Blake needed to get out of the room, to walk about, to see some real people living normal lives.

Claire would be on duty in Melbourne. He would telephone her later at her quarters. He had to see her before he went back to the ship.

He reached the hotel lobby and was about to hand in his key when he heard Fairfax's voice.

'Hello, sir! I'd heard you were in Sydney.'

Blake turned and faced him. 'Yes. We made quite a splash, one way and the other.'

Fairfax did not smile, in fact, he seemed unusually strained.

He said urgently, 'I found out where you were staying. Sarah's with me.'

Blake waited. They wanted to cheer him up when all he needed was to walk, to think about the girl in Melbourne.

Fairfax dropped his voice. 'Your wife is with us, sir.' He watched Blake's eyes and added, 'I had no part in it. I wanted to tell you that before you see her. *I told her nothing.*'

Blake replied, 'Maybe I won't see her.'

'I think you should, sir.' Fairfax was pleading. 'For your sake, and for Claire Grenfell's.'

Blake took time to think about it. He had got to know Fairfax very well, and what he knew he liked. He was not the kind of man to panic or to shrink from responsibility like Livesay.

'If you say so, Victor. Although I don't see why you and Sarah should get dragged into this mess, too.'

Fairfax walked with him to a wide lounge. 'In the ship you've got your responsibilities, sir. I wanted you to know that here you've got at least two good friends.'

A waiter with a loaded tray stepped to one side and there she was. Diana.

She was watching him, her mouth moist as she smiled in the way he remembered so clearly.

'Why, there you are, Richard. At last.'

13

Secrets

It was late afternoon, and although the wind had fallen away and the rain gone completely there was the suggestion of a storm in the air.

The thin, dark line of a tiny islet appeared to be almost covered at times by the long, booming ocean rollers, but it was enough to act as a breakwater, to provide a brief resting place for the three ships. They lay at their various angles, the sea rolling along their worn sides, while their engines attempted to hold them motionless.

The two raiders were so much alike that it was no wonder they could baffle even a skilled observer. And although one had begun her life in Kiel and the other in Hamburg, with a year's difference in their age, their roles had become united.

The third vessel, a heavy freighter named the ss *Waipawa*, which was the sole survivor from *Salamander*'s attack on the convoy, was much closer to the islet, anchored while Rietz's prize crew examined her cargo and equipment, although it had taken nearly every shackle of her cable, so deep was the sea hereabouts.

Rietz stood on the *Salamander*'s flying bridge, hatless, his face damp from the salt air and the low, humid breeze. There was a storm about. He felt his ship's uneven motion and was conscious of his anxiety for her sake.

He watched a motor boat moving clear of the other raider's shadow. *Wölfchen*'s captain was coming aboard as Rietz had requested. In his heart Rietz felt that their time was almost up. It would soon be the moment to leave, to find their separate ways back to Germany, or to an internment camp somewhere. He had known most of the risks, even if the grand admiral had not. But circumstances ruled the game, and the wounded and sick men in *Salamander's* hull were beginning to pose a real problem. Without a surgeon, and only the barest facilities for looking after his mounting list of captives, Rietz knew he was going to have to do something. Release them, or put them aboard a neutral ship, and the hunt would be on fiercer than ever. The news of their ruse would be out, and two raiders instead of a single ship would double the forces searching for them. Land them on a deserted piece of coastline and the risk would be greater still. Shore-based aircraft would soon discover them and shoot down his Arado seaplanes.

Rietz turned his head casually to watch one of the *Wölfchen's* seaplanes, like a motionless insect against the silver-bellied clouds. They had four Arados between them. In spite of fuel shortages they had to keep one airborne while they met at this arranged dot on the ocean for their first meeting in months.

He heard the boat coming alongside, the hoarse command of a petty officer who was evidently still trying to cling to the ways of the real Navy.

I had better go and meet him. Why did he dislike Vogel so much? He scarcely knew him, except from his image which was fashioned by the propaganda agency.

He saw the navigating officer watching him from the wheelhouse.

'Yes, Schoningen, what is it?'

The lieutenant had a weighted signal file in his hand. It would go over the side the very moment they were engaged by superior forces.

'It is our bulletin, sir.' He looked sick. 'From Berlin.'

Rietz eyed him calmly. 'The Tommies have landed in France, right?'

Schoningen shook his head and then handed his secret file to Rietz without another word.

Rietz tried to accept the decoded information as if he was reading about something else or another time.

Storch ran up a bridge ladder, his sea-boots jarring through Rietz's mind like hammers of hell.

The first lieutenant opened his mouth to speak, saw Schoningen's expression and shut it again.

Rietz said eventually, 'It seems I have been worrying for nothing, Rudi. Our most gallant and courageous comrade has solved the problem of wounded men in his charge.' Almost blindly he thrust the file at his subordinate. '*Read this*, Rudi, read about thirty-three men who died in the name of Germany!'

For a long moment there was complete silence on the open flying bridge. Across the water from the captured freighter came the occasional clatter of a winch, but all other sounds were muffled, as if each man had been stricken by some terrible disease.

Lieutenant Busch, the gunnery officer, appeared on the ladder, stiff-backed and empty-eyed as usual. He saluted with a flourish.

'*Wölfchen*'s captain is here, sir.'

Rietz took the file and handed it back to the navigating officer.

'You will tell no one about this.' He looked at Storch. 'That bulletin would have been decoded aboard Vogel's ship while he was on his way here.' He did not explain what he meant but added, 'I will be in my state-room. Show the good captain there also.'

Fregattenkapitän Konrad Vogel was junior to Rietz but walked with the springy step of a conqueror. There was something theatrical about him . . . his cap set at a rakish angle, the jutting beard beloved by the photographers, the Tiger.

Rietz waited for his visitor to sit down, then rang for his steward.

Tiger? He looked more like a jackal.

'I have taken the unusual step of arranging this rendezvous so that we can prepare for the immediate future.' He nodded as his steward, trained originally for the Hamburg-Amerika Line, padded in with his tray. 'Schnapps.'

Vogel relaxed in his chair and regarded his superior blandly. 'My command is in better shape than your own. As we fitted out originally in Japan we had to steam shorter distances. My fuel and machinery are thus able to serve me longer. I notice from the scars that you were hit by that convoy's escorts. Nothing serious, I trust?'

Rietz swallowed the schnapps and realized he had emptied the glass. He never drank at sea except in moderation, and only rarely. But he knew he would be on his feet shouting abuse at the fish-eyed man opposite him, cursing him for what he had done, the dishonour he had brought on their flag.

'*Another!*' He made himself speak slowly. 'I have some wounded, and my surgeon was killed. I am filled to capacity with prisoners and neutral seamen. As to fuel, I am not altogether satisfied. With *Bremse* gone and our Spanish supply ship also on the bottom, things are bad, although not critical. *Yet*. Berlin has informed us that a further supply vessel was intercepted in the Atlantic and sunk by a submarine when she refused to stop.'

Rietz ticked off the points on his fingers. He had to do it like this to keep from seeing those helpless, murdered sailors. Whatever Vogel had done would not change his own responsibilities, and he had always accepted this. But to be seen in the same light, to be known as a murderer and a coward, was abhorrent to him.

He said, 'Food and ammunition are in good supply. Fuel and machine spares are not. I have only three mines left, the others were to be carried in *Bremse* to your rendezvous and then we could have shared them later. The high command saw fit to equip us with a totally unsuitable mine, and the chance of a ship hitting one in this vast ocean poses a doubt on their sanity.'

Vogel's glass froze halfway to his mouth. '*What?* Do you criticize our command? I personally believe we have been well guided, and our intelligence sources could not have done more.'

Rietz shrugged. 'So you say. But the end is near. Time to discontinue the attacks and return to base.'

Vogel stared at him with amazement. 'But that is fine for you to say! You with nine merchantmen sunk, one captured and two warships destroyed. It will look splendid when you enter Kiel with all the house-flags flying!'

Rietz said, 'You destroyed a heavy cruiser, as well as two merchantmen. That is surely enough? Between us we have made our mark, caused havoc with the supply routes and convoy sailings. To prolong it further is to invite our own destruction.'

Vogel flailed about with his empty glass. 'That prize which you have at anchor? Can you use her?'

'Perhaps. But I would have valued a better cargo. Of all the ships in that convoy, I would have to capture intact the one loaded with mining machinery and railway track. Not a lot of use in mid-ocean.' He took a grip of himself. The schnapps was getting a hold. He snapped, 'But I will decide, and when I am ready I will signal my instructions.'

Then Rietz stood up and walked across to one of the scuttles, feeling the faint tremble of the engines through the worn carpet as the watch on the bridge held the ship in position.

'When you return to your command, Vogel, you will discover a bulletin waiting for you. It is mostly information obtained from enemy newspapers and radio broadcasts. About those men you murdered and buried like beasts. You, a hero of the Reich, the long arm of Germany's might who can still stoop to such filthy degradation, you, Vogel, *make me sick*!'

Vogel, too, was on his feet, his face working furiously. 'I acted as I thought fit, my duty to my own men as I saw it!' When Rietz remained silent his voice grew louder and more stubborn. 'There can be no half-measures in war. The old values cost us the last one, and your kind of sentiment can endanger our fight today! I am proud of what—'

Rietz turned on his heels and said harshly, *'Proud?* You have no pride, Vogel, only conceit. By your vicious, contemptible action, and probably many more besides, you have brought the world down about our ears! You have defiled the name of Germany and drowned honour at the same time! Now get back to your ship and write a full report for me. The names of those dead men, and the officer you ordered to execute them. I will hand that report to the grand admiral if we ever get home again. Now get out of my sight! But one more act like that and I will ensure that you at least never reach Germany alive!'

Vogel drew himself to his full height and exclaimed thickly, 'I shall not forget. After the war things will be different. Then we shall see who was right, *sir.*'

As he made to leave Rietz called, 'All your prisoners are to be ferried across to *Salamander* now. I want every boat in the water right away. And I am taking your surgeon from you also.' He watched Vogel's defiance begin to wilt. 'See to it.'

After Vogel had gone, Storch entered the state-room and saw his captain sitting at the table, his head in his hands.

'Can I do anything, Captain?'

Rietz did not look up. 'My father served in the High Seas Fleet, Rudi. He died without means, broken-hearted at what had happened to his Germany. But he kept his pride!' Rietz stood up violently and swept Vogel's empty glass smashing in fragments against the bulkhead. 'How dare that bloody swine talk of *pride* to me!'

Storch watched him, disturbed and yet strangely moved. It was like sharing something special, something fine, which he could not describe.

Rietz walked across to him and laid one hand on his shoulder.

'To work, Rudi. Lower the boats and bring the prisoners and wounded from *Wölfchen.* Her surgeon, too. I have to make plans, to think and prepare.' He shook the lieutenant's shoulder very gently. 'You are a good fellow. I hope to God there are many more of you when we need them.'

Storch went out to the boat deck and looked at the slow procession of clouds.

When we need them. Did the captain mean, when they met with the cruisers, or at some later time, after the war, perhaps?

He strode on down the deck, his eyes searching for the boatswain.

No matter what he had meant, Storch knew he would be proud to be a part of it when the time came.

Fairfax got to his feet and said, 'We'd better go now if we're to meet the others on time.' He stared hard at his wife who, after several drinks, showed no intention of leaving Blake alone with his wife. 'Come *on*, Sarah.'

She tossed her head defiantly. 'If we must.'

Blake said, 'I'll give you a ring later.' He looked at Fairfax. 'I've got to discuss something with you anway.' He forced a smile but felt like death. 'You two go and enjoy yourselves. It may be some time before it's possible again.'

Only when they had left did he say, 'Well, whatever you've come to do, Diana, let's have it out in the open.'

She sat back in the deep chair, one leg crossed over the other, an amused smile on her lips.

'Thank God they've gone. They really are a pair.' She leaned forward and touched his knee. 'Can't you say something nice? It's been a long time.'

Blake looked at her. She was elegantly dressed in a bronze-coloured costume which had certainly not come from a book of clothing coupons. Her dark hair had been washed and set that day, and there was no sign of fatigue from the long flight, putting down at all the various airfields, nor was there any hint of uncertainty or guilt.

But beautiful she certainly was. Desirable, passionate, he felt his mouth go dry as he wondered how many others had made that discovery.

He said, 'You shouldn't have come. How you fixed it I'll never know. I suppose it was your father, as usual.'

'Don't speak of him like that. You make him sound like a tyrant.' She lifted her chin with sudden impatience. 'Let's not argue. You can blame me for what happened, but you were so involved with your work I'm surprised you even noticed.'

Two young American officers paused across the room and stared at her with open admiration.

178

Blake saw her eyes settle on them, without warmth or encouragement. If there was anything at all it was contempt. The two young men hurried away in confusion.

She said, 'Children, the lot of them.'

Blake tried again. 'It won't work, Diana. It's over, finished. You'll have to sort it out with your lover, whoever he is.'

'I see.'

'You don't. You never have. It's a game to you. It will happen again if you have your way. But as I said, I've had enough. A divorce is the only thing left.'

'Really?' She leaned back, entirely relaxed. 'You do surprise me.'

Blake was caught off balance. He had expected anger, scathing words which could sting a man out of his wits.

He said, 'Your father will fix it. You seem to have a lot of very important people on your side.'

She smiled. 'Don't be bitter. It sounds petty. I've come to make up, to forget the past and try again.' She reached out and gripped his hand, pulling it to her side beneath her breast while she said softly, 'You know you want me. I can make you forget. Bring us closer than we've ever been.' She looked at the door. 'We'll go to your room. I'm sick of being stared at.'

Blake withdrew his hand, astonished that it had been so easy.

He said, 'You think I'm joking? In a minute I'm going to walk through that door. Things are quite bad enough at the moment without you making them worse.'

She stood up and smoothed her skirt. 'Divorce then. But we'll do it my way.' She looked at him and added quietly, 'But when your poor little Wren gets her name dragged through the courts, and her father, a *reverend* gentlemen, I believe, is stared at by the yokels in his village or whatever it is, *don't come crawling to me*!'

Blake clenched his fists to his sides. It was like part of a nightmare.

'It's nothing like that, and you know it!'

'Perhaps I do, but try to ask yourself who will be believed?' She took a pace away from him. 'I'm still here. Waiting.'

Several people in the lounge were at last aware that something was wrong and were staring with unveiled curiosity. The dark, beautiful girl and the young captain with a crimson ribbon on his jacket.

She said, 'I'll tell you this, *dear* Richard, if you won't do as I ask, I'll not give you a divorce without a fight. When I've done with your little madam she'll loathe the ground you walk on!'

'You bitch!'

Blake felt the room closing in. She was mocking him, enjoying his torment and despair. And she meant every single word of it. As if in a flashback he saw the little church, the glow of pipes in the garden, the girl slamming on the car's brakes while he gave her the ring. His need of her would destroy them both.

She picked up her handbag. 'I am staying at a somewhat better hotel down the road from here. If you change your mind, call me. If not, don't say I didn't warn you.'

Blake was staring at the place where she had been standing for several seconds after she had gone.

He turned and walked from the lounge, the buzz of conversation welling up behind him as he knew it would.

All the way to his room her words kept coming back to him. It was pointless to wonder how she had discovered about Claire and her father. But she knew her weapons as well as her own strength. After losing their son in the *Paradox*, Claire's parents were in no position to withstand another hurt. In a small town like theirs the minister was important. How could he expect to protect his daughter and hold the people's respect whom he met each day of his life?

And it was all his own fault. He had come to do the job he was trained to do, the one which had first attracted Diana and then as quickly repelled her.

The room looked even smaller than before. Blake sat down on the bed and stared at the whisky bottle and at the telephone.

After a further hesitation he telephoned the base at Williamstown. It took an age to get connected with *Andromeda*, and when he finally got through to Scovell he barely knew why he had called. To kill time, to put off the moment when he would have to call Claire and tell her.

Scovell sounded clipped and formal. *Probably thinks I don't trust him in control.*

'Nothing to report, sir. The dockyard is still working on the radar and the starboard outer shaft. But everything's in hand.' He coughed politely, impatient to hang up. 'Was there something, sir?'

'No. Not really. I'll call you tomorrow.' He put down the receiver.

There was no point in delaying any further. Claire would be at her quarters now. He opened his pocket diary, the scribbled dates and numbers blurred as he gripped it with both hands.

Blake reached for the telephone and then gave a start as it began to ring.

A bored voice said, 'You're through, sir.'

For a moment Blake thought it was Stagg again, but this time it was Quintin.

He barked, 'Glad I found you. What with Commodore Stagg and the Navy Office, your Admiralty and the Spanish consul, I'm about ready to drop!'

Blake pictured Quintin as he had last seen him in his wheelchair.

'You shouldn't get involved, sir.'

'Don't talk such rot, and stop calling me sir. We're both the same rank, even if I am damn near old enough to be your father.' He broke off in a fit of coughing. In a more controlled voice he continued, 'Can't talk much over the phone, but things are moving at this end. You can forget about courts of enquiry, being sent home and all that stuff. You are going to be needed right here, and soon, if my information is correct. But enough of that. Walls have ears.'

Blake found he was holding the telephone with such force that it was a wonder it did not split in halves. The absurd contrast between his scene with Diana and Quintin's guarded comments about the immediate future were enough to push anyone over the edge, he thought.

Quintin said, 'I think we've become very close, what with that bloody air crash and what followed. I know a lot about war, what it costs, what it can take out of a man. I'm very fond of Claire, too, but then you know that.'

Blake sat very still, his heart suddenly pounding at his ribs.

Quintin said, 'She's been through a lot, and when I saw what was happening between you two I thought I should add my weight. There have been people asking questions, snooping about like spies, but being in charge of intelligence here gives *me* an advantage. I heard about your wife's arrival in Sydney, and what I could not guess about it I dragged out of that spineless halfwit Livesay.'

Blake heard him take a deep breath and then say, 'Now hold on to your hat and don't hang up on me. Your wife has tried to get you both together again, is that right?'

'Yes, but I don't see. . . .'

'You will, Dick, you *will*.' Quintin lowered his voice. 'The man she's been living with in London, and he outranks both of us pretty considerably, by the way, wants her to get a divorce from you then marry him, all very neat and dignified so far. He's an ambitious man and wants no scandal. It would not look too smart to take the wife of a VC, now would it? So she's to divorce you, after laying the blame firmly at Claire's doorstep, with all that involves. You know the idea, man away from home, service love-affair, mud-slinging all round.'

Blake's spirits sank. He did not know what he had been expecting, but he had held on to a hope that Quintin's blunt involvement might help in some way.

'I know. She told me she'll start proceedings unless I agree to her proposal. But she said nothing about the man, nor that she expected to marry *him*.'

Quintin spoke very slowly, so that Blake should not miss a word. 'She failed to allow for one small thing. She got herself pregnant. Whether it was by our senior officer or somebody else doesn't matter much. The man she wants to marry would run like a scalded cat if he thought there was a nice juicy scandal in the offing!'

Blake said, 'And her father would not help with this. It's about the only thing he would draw the line at, where she's concerned.'

'Yeh. I got that much out of Livesay. Did you ever meet such a creep?'

Blake felt light-headed, as if he was going to be sick.

'So Diana needed me just for one night. To provide her with a case.'

Quintin sounded suddenly cheerful. 'Right! Think about it. How you would have looked. Giving your wife a child even though you were having an affair with Claire. She would come out whiter than white, and you and Claire would be right in it up to your necks!'

Blake asked, 'How did you get all this out of Livesay? It's more than I've ever heard him say in his life.'

Quintin chuckled. 'I threatened to tell the admiral he was no good out here and to have him sent back to the UK with a duff report. Rank has its privileges, and boy I was happy to use 'em after what he tried to do to you.'

'Thanks for telling me. I don't know what to say. A few minutes ago I felt like jumping off the harbour bridge. I'm still a bit stunned by all of it. Sickened at being caught with my guard down again. I should have known. People don't change. Especially Diana.'

'I've got to go. I promised my wife.' Quintin added brightly, 'I feel a whole lot better myself!' He slammed down the telephone.

Blake sat for a long time just looking at the opposite wall. It had very nearly worked. It would have been easy for Diana, especially as she had discovered how much he cared for Claire Grenfell. To protect her he might have gone to bed with Diana. Just to get rid of her. To wait until she had got herself into a situation where she was in danger for once. He stared round the room. And she was out there somewhere, expecting him to call her. Unless Livesay had told her what had happened.

The telephone rang again and Blake picked it up. Diana or Jack Quintin, or perhaps Stagg with some crazy scheme for catching his German raider.

She sounded very close, as if she was standing beside him with her mouth to his ear.

'I hoped I'd catch you.' She sounded unsure. Out of breath.

'Claire! I was just going to ring you. To try and explain—'

'Please, don't talk. I want to tell you. What I've been thinking about. Everything.' She gave a quick gasp, like sob. 'You don't have to explain anything to me. I love you, Richard. It's so easy to say when you can't see my face or touch me. I know about your wife. . . .'

'Yes, but you don't know what's happened—'

'Please, you mustn't talk. Not yet. And I do know. She came here to see me. It was horrible to start with. I'm no good at that sort of thing. And then I thought of you. Us. In that terrible raft. With the shark always there. It was then I began to fight her, Richard. When she threatened me and my family I told her to go to hell.' She tried to laugh. 'Not like me at all.'

'Claire, I do love you.'

'I know. I think I knew from the beginning. Captain Quintin told me the rest. He must have seen I was worried. He's been pretty wonderful.'

Blake said, 'I must see you. I'm so sorry to get you mixed up with this. But I'll make it up to you. Nobody will hurt you any more, I promise.'

She was half laughing, partly crying, as she said, 'What's it like in Sydney?'

Blake looked at the window. It had begun to pour, the rain

like steel needles across the nearest rooftops.

'It's suddenly very beautiful!'

'Here, too!' There was a metallic click and she said huskily, 'Sorry. That was your ring. It hit the phone. It's still there, I've not taken it off since that night.'

He said suddenly, 'Can you come, Claire? Here, to Sydney. I'm not certain how long it will be before. . . .' No, he had to shut that from his mind. Nothing mattered now. 'I want to see you so much.'

She could not control the tears any more. 'Tomorrow. Captain Quintin will fix it. I love you.'

Blake lay back on the bed, his fingers interlaced behind his head. He was still lying there, staring at his own thoughts, when darkness closed over the city.

In another part of Sydney, Commander Victor Fairfax stood by a window looking out into the gloom, but seeing his wife's reflection in the glass as she finished packing his suitcase.

She turned and looked at him, her breasts half bare in the special nightdress which she had bought for the trip.

'I still don't see why you've got to leave so early tomorrow?'

He shrugged. 'You know the Navy, Sarah. Always at the crack of dawn.'

She crossed the room and put her arms round his neck and pressed herself against him.

'God, I shall miss you, Vic.'

He stroked her bare back and laid his chin in her hair. She was worried, and so was he. Neither wanted to hurt the other on the last night. It was always the same. Except this was worse.

He said, 'It will soon be over and done with, I expect. Or another false alarm. I wonder what the skipper's doing?'

She recognized his attempt to change the subject. 'I mean, why all the secrecy? Surely you can tell me? You're off tomorrow and I shall go back to Melbourne. It's not as if nothing has happened!'

He tilted her chin with his fingers. 'I can't tell you. It's top secret. You know the score.'

'You mean, it's *dangerous*?'

'Even crossing the road's that, my love.'

'Well, you be careful. I love you so.'

He pulled the ribbons on her shoulders and she stood back from him to let the nightdress fall to the floor. She did not take her eyes from his face as he lifted her breasts in his hands and ran his fingers over her body.

Then with great care he laid her on the bed and undressed while she watched him.

Then she said, 'You'd *better* come back to me! Otherwise. . . .'

The rest was lost as his mouth covered hers and with sudden urgency they joined together.

In Williamstown, a small, inoffensive man paused to watch some tipsy sailors lurching towards the heavily-guarded dockyard gates. He smiled at them, a gentle, amused smile, but the sailors were too far gone to notice. Beyond the wired gates the ships stood like unmoving blocks of steel, peaceful now that the rivet guns had stopped their din and the last of the workers had gone home.

The man was a clerk in the dockyard, too frail for military service, but very useful when it came to ledgers and lists of requirements for the ships under construction or repair.

He was on his way home, at exactly his usual time, pausing only at this one shop to buy some cigarettes and an evening paper. Then he would take his dog for a walk, and sit down for the evening meal with his wife and mother-in-law. All as usual.

The man behind the shop counter nodded to him and passed over a pack of cigarettes. The little clerk gave him in return a small envelope. Then he went on his way, knowing his dog would be at the gate, waiting impatiently for him.

The shopkeeper bolted the door and went into his back room, opening the envelope without haste and whistling quietly to himself.

In an hour the contents of the envelope would be flashed across the ocean, a thousand miles or more. To the German raiders.

14
Last Chance

Commodore Rodney Stagg took a heavy lighter from the desk and lit his cigar with great concentration.

Across the desk, his face lined with fatigue and pain, Captain Quintin watched him warily. He had been in his office for most of the night, in spite of his wife's protests, and Stagg's booming cheerfulness was getting on his nerves.

Through the windows he could just discern the early morning sounds of Melbourne coming to life for another day. But the office, and those adjoining it, were already busy, and had been for the past two days. The clatter of a teleprinter, the murmur of voices on telephones, the occasional clink of coffee cups, it was as near to a flagship as Quintin would ever get now.

Stagg asked, 'What time's Fairfax getting here?' He looked meaningly at a wall clock. 'In my day. . . .'

Quintin groaned. 'This *is* your day, sir. Or soon will be.'

Stagg grinned. 'Sure thing. It's all dropping into place, and I must admit we couldn't have had a hope in hell without your department's aid. Yours, too, of course.'

Quintin gave up. 'True.'

The commodore's massive shadow loomed over Quintin's map of the Indian Ocean and at the latest markers placed there by his staff.

'No more sinkings reported. Not from the raider anyway. It makes sense. The bastard's running out of fuel and supplies. I'll bet my pension that Blake was right about the Spaniard. That's two supply ships down and another prevented from reaching the area.'

Quintin smiled wryly. It was a change for Stagg to admit anything at all.

Stagg added, 'You've checked everything yourself?'

Quintin sighed, hating the smell of the cigar. 'Yes. I had a signal from NOIC Aden. A fleet oiler, the *Empire Prince*, is ready to sail. She's loaded with fuel, too. Any extra subterfuge like filling her with ballast instead of oil would only involve more people. We want security down to a minimum of personnel.'

Stagg nodded, his copse of hair shining in the bright overhead lights.

'Good thinking.'

Quintin said. 'The Second Naval Member was not slow to point out what would happen if we make a mistake. The raider will get his hands in enough fuel to last him for months, and we'll have egg on our faces.'

'*Worse*, if I know him!' Stagg moved back to the map. 'A small, hand-picked crew of volunteers, with Fairfax in command. I'm not sure about him though.'

'Hell, sir, he's a good man. His captain says so, and I agree.'

'Huh. Well, we shall see. What about the latest on the German agent?'

Quintin grinned. 'He'll be taking his dog for a walk about now, before he goes to work.'

'The bastard. I'd like to choke him to death with my own hands!'

Quintin said, 'Any other way would have been a risk. To lay a false trail to some useless Q-ship or the like would have been smelled a mile off. This way the Germans will know it's real and that the bait is worth the taking.'

A Wren looked through the door. 'Commander Fairfax, sir.'

Stagg growled, 'About bloody time.'

Fairfax entered, carrying a briefcase and looking surprisingly fresh after a flight with the Navy's mail.

It took Quintin about fifteen minutes to describe the mission and what was required. When he had finished he said, 'If you've any thoughts, I'd like to hear them.'

Fairfax glanced at Stagg, but there was no reaction.

'I'd say it was a good idea, sir. It could work.'

Stagg said shortly, 'Could? It bloody must!'

Quintin said, 'It was the dockyard office which gave my people the idea. There is no other place where so much information comes in about stores and equipment which will be needed by incoming ships, berths and slipways required for this or that type of vessel. The *Empire Prince* will make a signal when she's on her way to Williamstown. To say that she has suffered damage and needs immediate dockyard facilities on arrival. That way she will be able to point out the necessity of off-loading her fuel without delay. I imagine that our little spy will be only too eager to pass on that information.'

Fairfax asked, 'You said that he had already sent a message to his contact, sir?'

'Yeh. I had it spread around that I am preparing a decoy which will be sailing in a couple of days from Perth. I have even drafted a signal to that effect, repeated to *Fremantle* and *Andromeda*.'

Stagg had been watching Fairfax's profile with some irritation. 'Well?'

'If I was the German captain I'd think it about perfect, sir. The two cruisers away in another direction with their decoy, while a real, fat prize comes unexpectedly from Aden. I'd also know all about *Empire Prince*. She was captured by the Germans in Holland at the outbreak of the war and later used as a supply vessel for the *Bismarck*. The Brits retook her and learned a lot from her gear which the Germans had fitted. Having no bases, they had equipped the ship for oiling at sea.'

Stagg looked at Quintin and said grudgingly, 'He's done his homework.'

Fairfax said, 'We've had our differences, sir. But I still maintain I was right. I couldn't have saved your men without losing every passenger under my command.'

Stagg rolled the cigar in his thick fingers. 'Maybe. But if you'd been made to watch your boys lined up and slaughtered, and then had the little bastards going over you with their knives and bamboo needles, I guess you'd be a bit sour on the subject!'

It was as near to an agreement that they would ever reach, Fairfax thought.

He looked at the map and remembered Sarah's arms about his neck as he had left for the airfield. They had become closer than ever, and the Navy's casual acceptance of a marriage had given way to something stronger, something which, if he could stay alive, would last.

Stagg said slowly, 'I've given orders for both my ships to be ready to sail tomorrow afternoon. It won't do any harm for people to see us doing what we say we are going to do. It's got to work this time. There's a big troop convoy due at Cape Town shortly. The soldiers are needed for the Pacific. If we let the raider slip past us, the convoy will be delayed. The good old chain reaction which starts from the top.'

Quintin kept his face blank. 'Never mind, sir, when you are at the top you'll be able to change all that, eh?'

Stagg glared at him. Then his face split into a slow grin. 'Sonofabitch!' He made for the door. 'I'll be in touch. About Blake?' He raised an eyebrow.

Quintin replied coolly, 'I'll tell him.' As the door closed he looked at Fairfax and smiled. 'Later.'

A young Wren entered with a tray of coffee and toast. Quintin liked morning toast, a habit he had gathered with the Royal Navy.

He looked at the girl as she poured the coffee, wondering what Claire was doing, hating what he would have to do. But he would delay it as long as possible.

Fairfax seemed calm enough. What was he? A potential hero or a probable sacrifice?

He said, 'You'll have a very small crew for the auxiliary. Just enough to keep her moving. The cruisers will be shadowing you all the way, and the first hint you'll probably get will be a Jerry aircraft coming to take a look at you. If they order you to shut down your radio, do it. You'll be riding on real juice, and I don't want you blown up just to prove something. Besides, your lovely wife wouldn't like it.'

'About Captain Blake, sir.' Fairfax watched the older man for a reaction. 'I met his wife in Sydney. If there's anything I can do. . . .'

Quintin grinned. If Fairfax could worry about Blake and his bloody-minded wife when he was about to begin a mission, which to put it at its best was extremely hazardous, he was a good hand.

'It's being taken care of. The best I can do. And thanks for the offer.'

The door from the operations room opened and a tired looking lieutenant said, 'Transport's here for Commander Fairfax, sir.'

Quintin noticed that the officer did not look at Fairfax as he spoke. Perhaps he had seen too many leave the building on some hare-brained scheme, never to return.

Fairfax walked round the desk to prevent Quintin from struggling to his feet.

'So long, sir.' He hesitated. 'If anything happens, goes wrong, maybe you could see Sarah for me?'

'Will do.' Quintin shook his hand. 'Do the same for me if I fall out of this bloody chair, eh?' He forced a grin. 'Have a good flight.'

Once more Quintin was alone. He sipped his coffee and

went over the plan for the millionth time. If there was a flaw Rietz would see it. If circumstances changed in the next few days, a lot of men would die for nothing.

He thought of Blake again and the cruelty of life which might deny him the happiness when he almost had it in his grasp.

The telephone jangled on his desk. He picked it up, his thoughts automatically clicking into order again.

'Staff Officer Intelligence speaking.'

The car stood like a half-drowned rock at the roadside, the roof and bodywork streaming in the downpour.

The girl was sitting at the wheel, just as Blake had remembered her. Except for the one big difference. She was not wearing her uniform. Blake had never seen her in a dress before, and when he had waited at the airport to meet the plane from Melbourne he had been almost sick with disappointment as he had watched the hurrying passengers.

Then he had seen her. In the simple yellow dress she was wearing now, looking at him across the busy concourse, her eyes shining with pleasure, and yet somehow unsure of herself.

They had dropped off her case at the hotel, and then she had told him of a small restaurant on the city's outskirts, one she had discovered during her time in Sydney.

The restaurant was there now, separated from them by a pavement and the biggest, noisiest downpour Blake had ever encountered.

But it did not matter. Nothing did. He put his arm round her shoulder and touched her hair, seeing a small pulse move in her throat, the quick heart-beat under her dress.

She said, 'We can't sit here for ever. Shall we make a dash for it?' Then she turned and put her arms round his neck, her breath warm on his mouth as she said, 'I'm suddenly not hungry, are you?'

They sat quite still, the implication as strong as being shouted aloud.

'No.' He put his hand on her neck, feeling his longing, not wanting to spoil it, to repel her by his eagerness. 'I love you, Claire.'

She kissed him, gently at first, and then as he came closer she pressed her mouth against his, her lips parting as if she could no longer help herself.

Blake was dimly aware that the rain had stopped and that

190

the car was streaming with water. Two people had stopped on the pavement to peer into the car, and one of them gave a thumbs up sign and called, 'Good on yer, mate!'

She pulled away, but there was no longer the shy defensiveness, the uncertainty, as she said, 'I think we'd better go. If you're still sure about the meal?'

He nodded, hardly trusting himself to speak. 'I'm *certain*!'

The drive to the hotel was all like that, vague and indistinct, broken here and there by a quick word or the touch of hands. At the hotel they gave the keys of the hire car to the doorman and together they went straight to Blake's room.

It was like a delicious madness. Blake knew he should have taken a separate room for her, should have made certain his wife had already left Sydney to rejoin her lover, ought to have done so many things, but for these few, precious moments he could think of nothing but the girl.

A bottle of champagne stood glistening in a pail of ice, the hotel did not apparently run to a proper ice bucket. Nor to champagne either, for that matter. Blake had seen a Free French destroyer in the harbour, and with a vague recollection of meeting her in the Med and using the Navy's special Old Pals' Act, had obtained the bottle from her wardroom.

She said breathlessly, 'I feel wicked!'

She came against him and said, 'How long do we have?'

Blake felt her tense as he loosened the strap across her tanned shoulder. 'Only tonight, my darling.' She nestled against him, her resistance gone before it could hurt. 'Next time it will be what *we* want.'

She put her hand on his shoulder and gently pushed him away. For an instant longer Blake imagined it was because of his actions, his clumsiness. Then she said quietly, 'Let me.'

She stepped out of the dress and then turned momentarily away as she threw it on to a chair. She said, 'You do the rest. I'm shaking so much, I. . . .'

He kissed her shoulders, and saw the pale skin where her costume had covered her from the sun. Then he turned her, holding her away, taking in every detail of her perfect breasts, her skin, the nakedness which was her way of putting the seal on their love.

She sat on the edge of the bed and watched him, her eyes misty as he undressed and then struggled with the champagne cork.

Side by side on the bed they drank a glass of champagne

as if it was the most normal, the purest thing in the world. Then she lay back, her arms above her head as she said, 'No matter what happens, my darling, this is for ever.' Once more the almost childlike doubt crossed her face. 'Isn't it?'

He bent over her, his hand moving round her breasts, down over the smoothness of her body, until he could feel the fire which burned inside her.

'For ever.'

She closed her eyes tightly as he came down on to her, her strong legs encircling him, making him a prisoner and a victor.

Then, as he pulled her up to enfold him she opened her eyes and gave a quick gasp of pain. They were one.

Blake lay very still staring up at the ceiling, conscious of the girl's breath against his chest, the beat of her heart. She was lying very close to him, one leg across his, her arm around his waist.

He moved his eyes to the window and saw the edges of the curtains turning pale grey as the dawn opened up across the city.

He felt completely spent and yet elated at the same time. They had made love at first with tenderness and then with an almost desperate abandon which neither of them had ever experienced.

Blake moved his fingers down her spine, planting each memory of her in his mind, to hang on to, sustain him until. . . .

She stirred drowsily. 'Is it time?'

'Soon.'

He knew that the instant they were parted he would remember all the right words. Like so many desperate faces he had seen in this war. At railway stations, on a dockside. All the trite, usual sentences when a heart was bursting or a man or woman needed only to say *I love you*.

She ran her fingers over his chest, her breath suddenly unsteady. 'I never did take you to see Cook's cottage at Melbourne.' Her hand moved more slowly, as if it and not she was sensing his returning desire. 'Next time.'

'Yes.'

He pushed her gently on to her back and kissed her hard, their mouths opening as if to devour every precious moment. She writhed from side to side as he kissed her again, on her breasts, her stomach, everywhere, until they could hold nothing back.

Then they lay motionless, listening to each other's frantic breathing, not wishing to break the moment with words.

They were still lying together when the telephone rang beside the bed.

Blake put it to his ear. It was Quintin. How typical of the man to make it his own personal business.

'Time to make tracks, Dick.'

Blake pictured him in his wheel-chair, his littered office with its maps and lines of filing cabinets. It is men like him who should get the VC, he thought.

He said, 'I'm on my way.'

'Good. Transport's laid on. All you have to do is *be here*.' He seemed to hesitate and then said, 'Tell Claire that her desk is waiting for her.'

Blake raised himself on one elbow and looked down at her face. 'Did you hear that, Claire?'

'Yes. I'll be there.'

He kissed her again and then held her arms to her sides. 'If I don't leave now, I'm never likely to. There'll be a car coming for me. You stay and have breakfast in bed. One of those great Aussie affairs, you know, steak, eggs and chips!'

He slipped off the bed and dressed with feverish haste. He would not even stop to shave. Any second now and she would give way to the tears which had been lurking very near as soon as the telephone had rung. Perhaps for much longer.

As if reading his thoughts she said softly, 'I'm all right. Really.'

He tried to smile. 'I know. Like me.'

He opened the curtains and stared across the water. A fine day, the rain clouds gone in the night and neither of them had noticed. He turned and looked at her. Like a beautiful nymph, sprawled on the bed, her nakedness making her seem innocent. He saw the glint of the champagne bottle. Only one glass each, that was all they had allowed time for.

Blake bent over the bed and she sat upright instantly, her arm round his neck, her free hand feeling his unshaven face, his hair, his body.

He felt her touch the ribbon on his jacket as she said, 'No more like this, darling. Promise you'll take care?'

'It's a promise.' He kissed her lightly. 'I'm off.'

It was like a terrible and yet beautiful dream. One second he was there, looking at her body, her eyes wide as she tried to see him clearly through the early morning gloom. Now, he was standing on the well-used carpet, the door shut behind him.

He thought he heard her call out, or perhaps it was a cry for them both.

In the lobby he found a bleary-eyed driver waiting for him, some girls with brooms and cleaners waiting to begin a new day.

'Looks like a great day, Cap'n.' The man took his bag and fell in step beside him.

Blake paused on the pavement and stared up at the hotel, but with all the windows he was not certain which one was hers.

The driver slid behind the wheel and swung away from the pavement with a scowl. Another stuck-up Pom, he thought. And me just being friendly.

Lieutenant-Commander Scovell's eyes followed Blake around the *Andromeda*'s day cabin like needles.

'I must say, sir, I've been wondering what all the flap was about. So we're going after the enemy in earnest and the decoy ship was *just* a decoy after all?'

Blake had been back aboard for two hours, each minute of which had been crammed with making and answering signals, dealing with the dockyard manager and his men, as well as trying to keep Scovell's questions at arm's length until the ship was at sea.

Now it was almost that time. The brows had been hoisted away by the dockyard cranes, the last man had been checked aboard who might notice something different and shout his doubts to a chum on the pier.

The cabin shook steadily to the engines' pulsating beat as Weir and his men made their final tests.

He said, 'In earnest, Number One. If we make a mess of it, it'll be a long chase at best. At worst, the enemy will disappear into thin air.'

He tried not to think of Fairfax and his pretty wife. Now he was already in his strange command, probably going over all the things he would have to remember, just as he was doing.

Scovell shrugged. 'I'll not be sorry to get out of it.'

Blake regarded him thoughtfully. All Scovell could see was his own command, another step up the ladder while there still was one.

It made life simpler to be like Scovell, he thought.

He said, 'I shall speak with the ship's company later on.

I'll leave it to you to spell it out to the wardroom.' He eyed him gravely. 'But just the facts, Number One. I don't want them to think it's another useless patrol, right?'

Scovell gave a thin smile. Then he asked, 'Bad flight, was it, sir?'

'Average. Why?'

Scovell gathered up his file of defaulters, requestmen and his changes in the watch-bill with a kind of panache.

'I noticed you'd not had time to shave, sir?' His eyes were opaque, like the shark's.

'I'll attend to it right away. First things first. . . .'

Scovell glided to the door. 'Rather like Francis Drake, sir. Still time to beat the enemy afterwards, what?'

Blake stared at the door. It was the nearest thing to a joke he had ever heard the first lieutenant make.

He wondered if Claire was in her office yet. Quintin had had her flown back by a later aircraft. He was obviously taking no chances.

Around and above him the ship was becoming more restless, eager to leave. Machinery clattered from somewhere, and he heard wires and fenders being hauled along the deck overhead, the occasional sarcasm of an impatient leading hand.

'Come on then, Ginger! Wot do you think this is, a bleedin' pleasure cruise?'

The harsher note of a petty officer who had no doubt noticed that the skylight on the quarterdeck was open and unshuttered, which meant that the captain was just beneath their feet.

Blake walked to the adjoining bathroom and switched on a light above the mirror. He had almost expected to see a shadow staring at him, but the face looked younger, more relaxed than he could remember.

He frowned. That could be dangerous for what he had to do.

A shadow covered the scuttle and he saw the funnel of a tug gliding past, ready with a helping hand when needed.

Blake had the razor in his hands but the soap was drying on his face as his mind drifted away once more. When he touched his ribs he thought he could feel her, the way her hair had brushed over him like silk, had driven him to a frenzy.

He gave a great sigh. *The boy captain*. He was certainly acting like one.

'Signal from *Bouncer*, sir. *Are you ready?*'

Blake re-crossed the bridge, the watchkeepers and special

sea-dutymen parting to let him move freely.

Bouncer was the tug at the stern, puffing out smoke and looking as aggressive as her name as she idled under the port quarter.

Sub-Lieutenant Walker had a handset to his lips, and called, 'Singled up to head and stern ropes and back spring, sir.'

'Very well.'

Blake walked back over the scrubbed gratings. He had to put all else behind him. This steel tower, the bridge, was his domain. To it, and so to his brain, went every telephone line and voice-pipe. Others did the work, his was the responsibility of using it. And winning.

Some smoke was drifting from the cruiser's trunked funnel, but little enough.

As he peered over the screen and looked aft along the length of his command, Blake saw the disorder of getting under way already forming into patterns. The quarterdeck party under Lieutenant Friar, the torpedo officer, and squat Mr Donkin, the gunner.

Wires rose and fell from the jetty as *Andromeda* rocked slightly on another tug's wash.

A handful of dockyard workers had come from huts and sheds to watch, and Blake found himself wondering if the spy was looking, too, from his office somewhere at the end of the yard. What sort of a man would do it? He had seen Quintin just prior to being driven to the ship from Melbourne, and he had merely remarked, 'I'll let you know. When you've got rid of the raider.'

Blake could understand a man who spied for his country. But to pass information to an enemy who was intent on killing your own people was beyond him.

'Ring down stand by.'

He looked forward where Scovell, hands on hips as usual, was watching the forecastle party fighting with coils of mooring wire, as if uncertain which would win.

The telegraphs jangled, and in his mind's eye Blake moved through the bowels of his command. From Couzins, the burly coxswain, sealed in his steel wheelhouse with his quarter-masters, along to the boiler rooms, to the engines, the gearing and the rudder controls. Noise, the sweet smell of oil, and furnace heat which defied every fan when the revolutions mounted.

Andromeda would go out stern-first. Once clear of the jetty and moored vessels she would make a fine sight, he thought.

If he ever saw it, it would be when he left her for the last time.

He stepped on to the port gratings. 'Let go aft. Tell *Bouncer* to take the strain.'

He saw the Toby Jug waddle to the special flags he kept for the rare occasions they needed tugs.

'All clear aft, sir.' Walker sounded keyed up.

From his compass platform Lieutenant Villar took a couple of test fixes, his gaze lingering on the ancient tower in the dockyard, the device which in the old days had signalled the exact time to every ship in harbour so that their chronometers would be reasonably accurate. After this commission Villar intended to request a transfer to the South African Navy. A 'friend' had written to him about his wife. They had only been married for three months when Villar had been sent to join *Andromeda*, and she was 'getting around' already. Villar had considered it as calmly as he knew how. If it was the man he suspected, he would need crutches before long.

'I've got the charts you asked for, sir.'

Wright, his young yeoman, was looking up at him with something like awe. Theirs was a strange relationship. Charts and notebooks, fleet orders about the removal of a buoy here, a wreck in a channel there.

Villar gave his wolfish grin. 'Well done, Shiner. I'll make a navigator of you yet.'

The stern was already moving slightly from the jetty, the dripping rope fenders being hauled inboard and rushed further forward as the well-bruised piles edged dangerously near to the paintwork.

'Slow ahead port.'

Blake waved his arm to Scovell and saw his men slack off the spring which, as the ship nudged forward, lifted until it was bar taut. Slowly but surely, using the pull of the tug and the springing action of the wire, the cruiser angled away from the jetty, the oily water bobbing alongside, waiting to be filled by another hull.

'Stop port. Let go forrard.'

Blake raised his binoculars and looked towards the town. Some of his men leapt into view as the lenses passed across them. A serious-faced signalman folding up the Union Jack which had been hauled down at the instant *Andromeda* had got under way. Scovell, watching his men, one foot tapping with impatience. And the captain of the forecastle, the bearded Musgrave, 'Hydraulic Jack,' pushing an inexperienced seaman aside as the head-rope came snaking dangerously past his ankles.

Blake wondered if Musgrave still remembered the dead men on the island, or if his face would be appearing across the table again as a defaulter, full of all the old excuses. *It was like this, y'see, sir. Me an' my oppo was set on by a bunch of squaddies, etc., etc.* Set on? Blake had known him lay out three military policemen single-handed in Alexandria.

'All clear forrard, sir.'

Blake turned and looked at the anchorage. A few ships in the distance, nothing dangerously close.

'Slow astern together. Tell the other tug to stay in company.'

The tannoy bleated, 'Fall in for leaving harbour!'

Wires were finally being vanquished by gloved seamen and were slowly vanishing into lockers and stores until the next time. On forecastle and quarterdeck the men were falling into line, their caps like white flowers, moving slightly to the ship's stern-first thrust.

'Stop engines.' Blake looked at Walker's youthful eagerness. 'Here we go, Sub.'

The land was swinging past as the cruiser continued to drift with her way and current, until the long jetty, seemingly filled with warships, lay across the bows, with a tiny gap between a destroyer and a partly repaired minesweeper. It did not seem possible that *Andromeda* had fitted into so small a space.

Apart from the men required on deck, everyone else was out of sight until the ship was clear of the harbour. There was a smell of new bread coming up from the galley funnels, and Blake guessed that the paymaster commander had made allowances for a few extra delicacies during the brief stay in port.

Villar said, 'Ready, sir.'

Blake looked at him. It had been a good team. The best. Now it was almost over.

'Starboard twenty. Slow ahead port. Starboard engines slow astern.'

Froth surged along the side, and a young Australian seaman, very new, paused in his cleaning of the bridge screen to exclaim, 'Gee, isn't this *something*?'

Villar groaned, and the Toby Jug muttered, 'Gawd'elp us!'

The land was swinging more swiftly now, the tugs turning on their tails to keep pace with the lean cruiser.

'Stop starboard.' Blake ran his eye over a harbour launch, but it was staying well clear. 'Wheel amidships. Slow ahead together. Tell the tugs, *thank you*.'

The *Bouncer* turned away, her seamen hauling in the towline while her skipper gave a shrill toot on his siren.

'Take over the con, Pilot.'

Blake climbed on to his chair, her words in the night coming at him without warning. *If only I could be with you and your ship*.

'All secure forrard and aft, sir.'

Walker was watching him with obvious interest. Even without turning his head Blake could feel it in his tone. Was I that bad? Has she changed me so soon?

'Good. In fifteen minutes you can tell the hands to fall out from harbour stations—'

He broke off as a man yelled, 'Hell, sir, look at *that*!'

Even as Lieutenant Trevett began to blast the rating who had made such a startled report, Blake saw what 'that' was.

A Walrus flying boat was hurtling past a slow-moving freighter and was in danger of colliding with two corvettes which were about to leave the harbour.

The flying boat hit the water, bounced off again with its pusher engine spluttering madly, before landing once more within feet of the freighter's side.

Scovell appeared on the bridge, his usual calm gone as he shouted, 'What is that bloody madman doing?'

The Toby Jug lowered his long telescope and sucked his teeth. Then he said, 'I think it's the commodore, sir.' He coughed politely. 'I gather 'e wants to come aboard.'

'Away sea-boat's crew!' Blake's voice brought the astonished bridge party to movement again. 'Lively with it!'

'Tell the Chief, Sub. Dead slow. We don't want to hit anything now.'

There was chaos enough. The two corvettes were almost overlapping as they tried to recover their proper station, while from the freighter's high bridge there came a stream of obscenity and abuse, magnified for all the harbour to hear by a loud hailer as the master's first fear for his ship gave way to fury.

Blake watched the *Andromeda*'s bows in case she should lose way in the current. He had no need to use his glasses to recognize Stagg's towering shape. Why was he here? Perhaps the mission had been aborted, or the Germans had attacked elsewhere.

He did not have long to wait.

Beaming to all and sundry, Stagg arrived on the bridge even as the dripping whaler was run up to her davits again. Nobody, it seemed, gave a damn about the luckless Walrus.

Stagg shook hands and boomed, 'Fast as you like, Captain Blake. I'm sailing with you.'

As normality returned, and the watch below vanished from the upper deck, Stagg added, 'As that fool Livesay would put it, *the fact is,* we had a bit of bother.'

Blake watched him, seeing the effort it was taking to make the man sound so untroubled and calm.

'We had just cleared the bay and we met with an incoming destroyer. An American, naturally.'

'*Met* with, sir?'

Stagg eyed him coldly. 'Yeh, she ran into *Fremantle.* Right down the bloody side of the fo'c'sle. You'll see the pair of 'em in a moment. I've sent for tugs. The destroyer got the worst of it, and I'll see her skipper in bloody irons when we get to the court martial!'

Stagg looked at his hands. 'All right if I use your quarters aft? Good. I wasn't going to be left behind, not now, by God. I'd have crippled that Walrus pilot if he'd missed you.' He grinned. 'I had a feeling it would turn out this way. Just you and me against the bloody world.' He went off, tossing casual salutes to all and sundry as if it was one great joke.

Blake sat for a long time in his tall chair. *I had a feeling it would turn out this way,* Stagg had said. But to Blake it meant something else. Ever since it had all begun he had had the strange, unnerving feeling that he had no choice, no control over what was happening. Fate had already decided. Claire had been his one moment of reward and true happiness. Now he was going to be made to pay.

'*Fremantle* on starboard bow, sir.'

Another voice said, 'Gawd, what a mess. A real dockyard job, that one!'

The American destroyer was so low by the bows she might even have to be beached. But none of it meant a thing any more to Stagg. *Fremantle*'s own captain would have to cope. *He* had more important things to do.

Villar said, 'Alter course to two-three-zero.'

Blake slid off the chair and laid his cap below the screen. Was it only this morning? Another place, where the world had been the four walls of a small hotel room.

He looked at his watch. She would be at her desk now, neat

and cool in her uniform. Her Wrens would have seen the ring on her finger, and they would probably be wondering.

Blake turned and saw Villar watching him. *As these men do about me,* he thought.

Surprisingly, the thought helped to steady him, and he said to Scovell, 'I'm going round the ship, Number One. We shall exercise action stations at dusk. Just to blow away the cobwebs.'

As he left the bridge Villar said quietly, 'He seems as bright as a new button.'

Walker smiled. *They don't understand, any of them. But I do. Good luck to him. If anyone deserves it, he does.*

Scovell's voice scattered the sub-lieutenant's thoughts like a shotgun.

'Come along, *Kiwi*, we have *work* to do!'

When darkness fell the land was well astern, and *Andromeda* had the ocean to herself.

15

Dirty Weather

After making her rendezvous west of Perth with the original decoy ship, *Andromeda* turned her stem towards the Indian Ocean once again. The five days it had taken to complete the passage to Perth had been an almost leisurely affair. Despite regular drills with main and secondary armament, damage control exercises and fire-fighting, the ship's company seemed relaxed by their solitary cruise, and as Moon had gloomily predicted, it would be the calm before the storm.

Blake had been surprised at how Stagg had managed to vanish for long periods at a time, appearing only for important exercises or the traditional ceremonial of Sunday divisions.

Even the weather was strange. Long hours of bright sunlight, but already lacking the warmth which had welcomed them from the Mediterranean.

The sky was harsh and difficult for the lookouts to scan without using coloured glasses. Sometimes when he went on to the upper bridge Blake thought it was like sharing it with a crowd of blind men.

The secret signals arranged by Stagg and Quintin came at regular intervals. Fairfax's *Empire Prince* had cleared Aden and was heading on a south-easterly course and, like *Andromeda*, would be paying heed to every signal whilst maintaining complete radio silence.

Blake had gone over it with Stagg several times in the chart room, where Villar's plotting team kept an hourly record of ship movements.

It was almost unnerving to compare the vastness of the ocean with their own puny resources. The latter had been halved when *Fremantle* had been involved in the totally unexpected collision.

Eight days out of Williamstown and steering west along the thirtieth parallel, Villar entered the wardroom where most of the officers were still lingering over their breakfast.

The British amused Villar greatly, and the Australians were

getting just like them, he thought. Their need to read a paper at breakfast, for instance. Each propped on a little stand in front of every munching officer. As if they were studying music. The fact that most of the papers were weeks old seemed to make no difference.

He sat down resignedly and waited for a steward to notice him. A typical breakfast, he decided. Powdered eggs, strips of crinkly bacon and some toast. And, of course, tea.

'Coffee,' he snapped. It always gave him some pleasure to arouse a little disapproval.

Palliser looked over his paper and smiled. 'All quiet up top, Pilot?'

Villar sipped the coffee, he was going to enoy the next part.

'Actually, Guns, we're in for some dirty weather. Could be a cyclone.'

Cups and cutlery clattered down and faces turned towards the wiry lieutenant.

Surgeon Lieutenant Renyard, never a good sailor at the best of times, exclaimed, 'But won't that make a difference? Will we return to harbour—' his voice trailed away as several of them chuckled, '—or something?'

Villar munched his toast with relish. 'Ask him.' He jerked his head towards the after bulkhead. 'The commodore will be delighted to tell you, eh?'

Captain Farleigh of the Royal Marines said quietly, 'The difference could affect our rendezvous surely?'

Up until that moment Farleigh had not really been thinking much about the prospect of battle. He would be going home soon, and all this would be lost. Here he was his own master, but back at barracks again, ordered about by men who had held their soft billets throughout the war, everything would be different. *Andromeda*'s marines were still wearing their white sun-helmets, when orders clearly stated that caps or berets would be worn for the duration. It was Farleigh's way of declaring independence.

Villar looked at him. 'It could. Our job is to work into position about two hundred and fifty miles from the *Empire Prince,* never more at any given time. At full revs it would take us about eight hours to run down on her, to be in range anyway.'

He looked at the scuttle opposite him. The sea's edge rose slowly, as if the scuttle was filling with water. Then it steadied, motionless, before falling back again. A nice easy roll, at an economical cruising speed. But Villar knew from hard experience how these seas could change. It was funny, he thought, that only the marine had seen the danger.

Beveridge, the gaunt chaplain, seemed to rise from his brooding.

'I was in a storm once.'

Palliser murmured, 'I can imagine.'

Lieutenant Steele, the second engineer, glanced at the wardroom clock. The engines' steady throb felt just fine. But it was time for his rounds again, and it did not do to have Weir getting there first.

Beveridge said, 'It was in the North Atlantic. A convoy. The U-boats attacked in groups even in those early days. It was a massacre.' He stared emptily at his plate. 'And the weather was getting worse all the time.'

Bruce, the surgeon, sighed. *Here we go again*. He had heard it before but had never had the heart to shut him up.

The chaplain continued, 'I was in a life-boat after the ship capsized. There was a party of civilians aboard. Refugees, I think. They all died eventually. There was just the one little boy. I kept talking to him and praying someone would find us.'

Steele lurched to his feet. 'Oh, for God's sake, Padre! Do you have to swing the lamp at a time like this? I've just about had a bellyful of so-called religion.'

There was silence in the wardroom now, and even the stewards were staring at the second engineer. Steele was like most of his trade and rarely seemed to mess with his fellow officers at the usual times. His sudden outburst had put him in a different light.

Beveridge said, 'There is no call for that! I was merely telling how—'

Steele stood opposite him, his eyes feverishly bright. 'I *know* what you were saying! And I think it's a load of rubbish! I'll bet that Jerry raider said a prayer after he'd shot those prisoners, and I'd like a prayer said for all the other poor devils who've lost someone in this bloody war! Like my chief, for instance, have you seen the way he clams up when some thoughtless bastard starts going on about his wife or family?'

The surgeon, who was the senior officer present, said, 'Easy now. The padre didn't mean to make light of it. Quite the opposite.'

Steele swallowed hard. 'I'm sorry, sir. But I lost a brother in Crete, and I think I can understand what I feel about *that*!'

The curtain across the door swished aside and Commander Weir, dressed as usual in his white boiler-suit, said calmly, 'Time to get on with our rounds, I think.' Nobody knew how long he had been standing there. 'Are you coming, Trevor?'

Steele nodded blindly and followed him from the wardroom.

Villar reached for the last piece of toast and asked softly, 'Well, Padre, did the little lad live?'

Old Horlicks sank back in his chair. 'No. I'm afraid he did not.'

Villar stood up. 'Then there's not much point to it, is there?'

Commander Bruce glanced around the table. How could he ever go back to a passenger line after this? He had seen this little drama often here and in other ships. You thought you were safe from the war as you moved across the sea, carrying your home with you like a turtle. Then, as now, it came out of hiding, the tension, the latent fear which had always been there.

He gave a great sigh. It was time to visit the sick-bay to see his handful of 'cases', the genuine and the shammers.

Bruce glanced at the nearest scuttle and frowned. In the space of a few minutes the sea had altered its colour and the horizon seemed blurred. Villar was probably right about the weather. He usually was. Bruce hoped that before the ship paid off and was handed to her new owners he would find something to like about Villar.

On the upper bridge the sea-change was even more apparent, and when *Andromeda* shipped water over her forecastle the spray looked like yellow lace.

Blake stretched his legs around the bridge, a mug of coffee in his hand. Up, down, roll. He felt the ship sliding into a trough, sensed the urgent race of her screws as the stern lifted towards the surface.

Villar appeared on the central ladder, some crumbs on his shirt.

'It's worse already, sir.'

'Are you all right, Pilot? You sound a bit down.'

Villar grimaced. 'Bit of an argument aft. Nothing which won't wash clean. The usual, sir. Too long at the same job. Nowhere to escape.'

Blake let it rest. Before he had met Claire he had been feeling it himself. Not wanting to leave his ship, not wanting to stay.

Stagg loomed up the ladder, his shirt soaked with spray,

a doused cigar jutting from his jaw.

'Morning.' He nodded to the watch and then moved to Blake's side. 'Looks bad. What d'you think?'

Blake glanced abeam at the glass-sided rollers, their crests as yet unbroken.

'I believe we'll cross the edge of it, sir. Once we're on station it won't be so difficult. If we get a hint of the enemy we can close with him and use our speed to good advantage.'

Stagg rubbed his chin. 'Fairfax might get cold feet.'

'I think it's unlikely, sir.'

So the old antagonism was still there, like a canker.

'We'll see.' He squinted his eyes as the spindrift floated over the bridge and splashed against the fire-control tower. 'Bloody weather. Without *Fremantle*'s two planes it's bad enough. Your little kite could never get airborne in this mess!'

Blake turned away. Masters would take-off if he asked him. He would just as certainly never be able to land-on again. In a big sea his Seafox would break up in seconds.

Blake wanted Stagg to go aft again to his cabin, to leave him with his thoughts. The fact that the commodore was obviously getting rattled did not help at all.

Scovell stamped his feet on the gratings and glared as Palliser appeared on the bridge.

'Are you supposed to be my relief, Guns? Or is yours the watch *after* this one?'

Palliser grinned. 'Sorry, Number One. I was delayed.'

Scovell slammed from the bridge muttering to himself.

Palliser checked the chart and spoke with the wheelhouse, then he walked forward and peered down at the two turrets below the bridge.

Blake looked away. No matter what they all said, they knew there was a raider out there somewhere. Somewhere.

Rietz opened his eyes and looked at Storch's face for several seconds without recognition. He had been trying to sleep in the hutchlike cabin at the rear of *Salamander*'s charthouse, but the dank air, and his own restlessness, had done him more harm than good.

'Sorry to rouse you, Captain.' Storch waited as Rietz threw his legs over the side of the bunk. 'We have received a signal.'

Rietz fought to bring his mind back under control. He had been dozing and waking, more often than not thinking about his wife. Was she managing to keep healthy on her rations, to stay safe from the raids?

'About the decoy, Rudi?'

Storch shook his head. 'No, sir. She sailed just as our agents reported. This is another. A naval oiler, outward bound from Aden.' He watched the understanding pushing some of Rietz's lines aside. 'A full cargo. She is in trouble and requires instant attention when she berths at Williamstown. Our man there has done well.'

Rietz got to his feet, his ears picking out the noisy clatter of loose gear, the hull's groan as she swayed in a steep swell. The glass was steady enough, but that meant nothing. There was a big storm coming. But it was no cause for idiotic action.

'Is the *Waipawa* still anchored?'

'Yes, Captain. But Lieutenant Ruesch requests permission to weigh and stand offshore. The anchor is dragging. If the swell gets worse we will have to steam well away from the island.'

Rietz felt the deck pitching heavily. Even her eight thousand tons could not act as substitute for her falling fuel gauges.

Rietz stared at himself in the cabin mirror, hating how he felt, the smell of damp and unwashed clothing. He had ordered rationing for all essential stores, from fresh water to soap.

Gunfire, the grinding anxieties of being hunted by enemy warships, all these things they had managed to accept. But in war a sense of defeat showed itself in other guises. In what they found aboard their prizes, for instance. After four and a half years of war the enemy still had good woollen clothing and warm garments for their watchkeepers. Fine soap and real coffee, Virginia cigarettes and nourishing tinned meats, which most of Rietz's men had long forgotten.

'Very well, Rudi. Signal the group to get under way. Then we will steer north while we examine the enemy's intentions and the exact position of this oiler—' he smiled '—from heaven.'

In the brightly lit chart and plotting room, shuttered and concealed from the outside world by its dull-painted steel, Rietz went over the chart and his navigator's calculations, item by item.

He was still unsure, in spite of Storch's youthful confidence and the past reliability of the secret agents in Australia. Where better to have a special spy? His brief but powerful transmissions were virtually undetectable amid the mass of radio traffic which came and went from Williamstown and from up the bay in Melbourne. But they had been cruising for too long, and too soon after the previous raider's downfall. Stagg, he knew, would give anything to run him to ground. He glanced at Blake's newspaper picture on the bulkhead. He would be a hard one to beat, too. He was young, not a lot older than Storch, and well used to the harsh demands of battle.

There was talk of another troop convoy en route to the Pacific. To be able to scatter that, even destroy some of its overcrowded ships, would offer a suitable moment to retire from the area. But to do it they had to have fuel, and be certain that the cruiser force was nowhere within possible contact.

He looked at Blake's face again. Suppose the decoy ship had been a deliberate hoax, to give the raiders the impression they were safe to move at will? It would be just like Stagg to think of that. The cruisers might even now be making another sweep, in the hopes that Rietz would go for the troopships.

Rietz considered it from every angle. His chief engineer was getting really worried. On the other hand, Vogel might see his caution as an unwillingness to sacrifice his own ship and thus be unable to take his report to Berlin on the *Wölfchen*'s atrocities.

The lights went out and came on again as Petty Officer Fackler lurched through the door from the bridge.

'Captain!' He could barely stop himself from grinning. 'Another signal. The Australian cruiser *Fremantle* has been seen in Williamstown with her bows stove in!'

Storch exclaimed, 'You are certain, man?'

Fackler nodded excitedly. 'She hit a Yankee destroyer!'

Rietz turned back to the chart. In his heart he knew he would have avoided contact with the oiler. He had never risked his ship or men without a good chance of success.

Vogel was said to have powerful friends in Germany, but even that would not have deterred Rietz. This made everything different. With *Fremantle* out of the game, the odds had shifted considerably, decoy or not.

'Tell Schoningen I want him to lay off a course to intercept this, er, gift from heaven. Advise *Wölfchen* of what I intend and prepare the Arados for take-off.'

He rubbed his chin thoughtfully, 'Then find out all you can about the oiler and plan accordingly. We may have to go alongside in a heavy swell, so I want every hammock, fender, spare cordage and canvas on deck ready to be slung between the two hulls. If we strike, I want to bounce off again in one piece!'

Storch strode away to fetch the navigating officer, his mind dwelling on the captain's complete confidence. Minutes before there had been doubt, anxiety. Now the news had changed all that. Even the prospect of finding the damaged oiler and taking her intact in worsening weather seemed to have been brushed aside as trivial.

When he got home . . . Storch paused and gripped the rust-streaked guard-rail hard to steady himself. His girl was dead, and yet he kept thinking of her as being there, waiting for his return. There *was* no home.

With the captured freighter *Waipawa* trailing astern, the two raiders steered away from their tiny islet, which in a mounting swell had all but vanished.

Rietz left the charthouse and walked on to the flying bridge. Sticky and humid, and there was more rain about somewhere.

If they could fill the bunkers, even half fill them, there was a good chance for their survival. They had done what they had set out to do, and his men deserved far more than the misery of a prisoner of war cage with the additional smear of Vogel's cruelty on their heads.

He raised his powerful glasses and sought out the captured freighter. It was early evening, but the visibility was so poor it could have been night.

All the same, he would take no chances. A wild animal was caught usually because of hunger and a deadly moment of carelessness. The gun or the trap did the rest.

He thought of Stagg and wondered what he would say when he heard the news. If hunger often put paid to the wild beast, then hate surely killed many a hunter.

It was almost midnight, and in her office in Melbourne Claire Grenfell sat at her desk, her chin resting on one hand as she stared at the last of the signals which had been checked in.

The letters and figures seemed to blur, both from strain and from emotion. She had been working doubly hard since the *Andromeda* had sailed and *Fremantle* had made her own ignominious return under tow.

The building was so quiet it seemed to be holding its breath. She loosened her shirt and plucked it away from her damp skin. As she did so her fingers touched her breast, and like a pain it all came back again. The room, Richard holding her, loving her, making her react as she had never believed possible.

She knew she should go to her quarters, and yet could not face it. The friendly smiles, but the eyes which asked, what was it like? What did you do?

She had even seen it on her mother's face when she had

gone home for a few hours' break. Her father had understood, even though it had not been mentioned. It was as if he had always known. That, and his trust, had helped a bit.

The door opened with a crash and Quintin stood looking at her, his face aflame with triumph.

'*Ta-ra!* See the mighty have risen again!' He was balanced precariously on two sticks. 'I did it, all the way from the car!'

She ran to help him into a chair. 'You're beat!'

Quintin grinned at her. 'Too right. But who cares? Any coffee about?'

He watched her as she walked to the table. A lovely girl. Funny, when she had first come to his department he had merely thought of her as a reliable, highly trained officer. But she was a girl. It seemed that the neat uniform could no longer hide or protect the fact.

Quintin said, 'The Met Office think there's a storm blowing up in mid-ocean.' He saw her arm stiffen.

She said, 'I heard. But they might miss it.'

'Yeh.' Quintin went around what he had in his mind and decided to go straight to the point. 'You're in love with him, aren't you?'

She turned, lightly, warily, like a cat.

Quintin shook his head. 'I'm not interfering. I just want to help.'

She placed the coffee cup carefully by his elbow, and Quintin could see the strain in her eyes, the way her chin lifted as she said, 'Yes, I love him. I'd do anything, *anything* for him. He told me a lot about himself, his father, the house in England. I could have killed his wife for what she did.' She looked directly at Quintin, her breasts moving quickly as she added, 'That woman may try to make trouble for us, but we'll be ready!'

Quintin smiled. 'I'm sure. But I don't feel you'll get any bother from her now. She's beaten at her own game. I've no doubt it will all be done by some nice, trustworthy lawyer with a quick settlement at the end of it. But that's not what you're telling me, is it, Claire?'

'No, not really.' She tossed the hair from her eyes. 'He's been through so much. Even you and I when we were with him in that dinghy saw what he was like. And for him, it's been going on for years.' She shook her head slowly. 'No, I don't reckon anyone will hurt either of us after that.'

Quintin watched her cross to the shuttered window, seeing

all the familiar movements and gestures he had taken for granted before and which now seemed new, like someone else.

She said, 'When I asked him to meet me, d'you know what he said? Should he come in uniform. As if he was making an apology for what he was, for what he'd done. When I think of some of the drifters, the glory-boys who want to send everyone else off to fight but themselves, I get steamed up. I did then. I wanted him to know I was proud of him, to be seen *with* him.'

Quintin waited. It was coming, like the storm which was soon to break out there in the ocean. He was disturbed, but moved that he was the one to share it with her.

'Before he left,' she groped in her jacket which was draped on the back of a chair, 'he gave me this. I didn't know until he'd gone. He wanted me to have it.'

Quintin saw her hand shake as she held it out to him, the cross with the crimson ribbon.

'Don't you see? He thinks he's going to be killed, and this is all he's got to give me.'

She seemed to realize he was trying to get on his feet and said brokenly, 'I'm all right. Don't send me away, *please*. I want to be here.'

She sat down at her desk, the bronze cross gleaming dully in the office lights.

Blake put down a half-eaten sandwich and looked at Villar as he stepped into the sea cabin.

The motion was still very uncomfortable, although less violent, but Blake knew the signs, and the most recently intercepted signals had confirmed a storm of unknown intensity approaching from the south-west. With luck they might pass through the fringe, but with no luck at all they might never find the *Empire Prince*.

Villar grinned at him. 'Provided the *Empire Prince* is on station, sir, we should pick her up tomorrow morning.' He gripped the hand-basin as the deck slid away once more. 'Though radar isn't too hopeful. This sea is not helping it much.'

Blake stretched his arms. Another day, and now another night. The ships blundering towards each other like helpless drunks. One signal would be enough, but if Rietz was anywhere nearby it would be all that was needed to smash everything.

The weather was the one enemy they had not allowed for.

Fairfax was to make another signal when he was in contact with the enemy. An ordinary follow-up to his original one about damage. A signal would be flashed instantly to *Andromeda*, the rest was mostly up to Weir. But they had to be certain where Fairfax was. An auxiliary oiler was not the most manoeuvrable of vessels. She could have drifted in the swell, been forced miles off course.

Villar said quietly, 'You could send Masters at first light, sir. He's done it before.'

Blake pictured the Seafox dipping and circling the yellow dinghy, the sense of gratitude and pride he had felt for its pilot. But Villar was right. The sea might ease tomorrow. Already he knew he was finding an excuse from sending two men to do the impossible.

'I'll think about it, Pilot.'

Andromeda's bows lifted and then smashed through a steep roller like a giant plough, the impact making the bridge shiver, the guns rattle on their mountings.

Down on the forward messdeck there was a chorus of shouts and curses from the off-watch hands who were still grouped round the wooden tables. A few unguarded plates and mugs scattered in fragments amongst a growing pile of sea-boots and oilskins.

Leading Seaman Musgrave had been attempting to darn a hole in his sock and threw it down with disgust.

'Roll on my bleedin' twelve! I've just about *had* this!'

Another yell broke out as the ship seemed to reel over to the thrust of the sea, and they heard it thundering along the deck overhead and cascading over the side like a waterfall.

The tannoy came on. 'Aircraft handling party and catapult crew will be required at oh-six-thirty tomorrow.'

A seaman said, 'Skipper must be gettin' eager. I wouldn't fancy flyin' in this lot!'

The tannoy again. 'Cooks and sweepers clear up messdecks and flats for rounds. Ordinary Seaman Corker muster at the master-at-arms' office.'

They began to tidy up their mess, a table set in a line amongst many, where they lived, slept, slung their hammocks and endured.

'Poor old Dicky Corker's been up to his tricks. Up before the jaunty, eh?' There were several unsympathetic chuckles. 'Shouldn't have joined if he can't take a joke!'

Musgrave looked round his domain with approval. 'Fair enough, lads.'

He listened to the boom of the sea against the cruiser's hull, the way the nearest scuttle was weeping sea-water each time they shipped it green. And that was in spite of a steel deadlight well screwed down over its glass.

He thought about the double line of corpses, the rain and old Horlicks rabbitting on about God and forgiveness. It made him feel uneasy. After this he would ask for a transfer to small ships, a frigate maybe, or spin it out for a bit ashore on a petty officer's course. He grinned. Provided, of course, he didn't go and get busted before they got home again.

Someone asked, 'Who's doin' rounds tonight, Hookey?'

Musgrave frowned. 'Lieutenant Blair, "our Micky".'

He was the Australian quarters officer of B turret. He was quite popular with the lower deck, but they still thought him a bit odd.

Musgrave explained, 'You know, the one 'o comes in an' says, "'Owarewealldoin' then?"'

A marine's bugle shattered the calm and a petty officer bellowed, 'Attention for rounds!'

Lieutenant Blair came through the watertight door, swaying unsteadily as the ship took another plunge.

He gave a cheerful smile and asked politely, 'How are we all doing then?'

Commander Victor Fairfax pressed his face against the bridge windows and stared towards the oiler's blunt bows. The *Empire Prince* appeared to be swinging to starboard, but he knew it was an illusion. The rollers had eased away into a long running sea, with great streaks of foam writhing across the ship's path. It should still be daylight, but it was barely possible to make out the forecastle from the oiler's high bridge. For several hours there had been a strange, peach-coloured sky, like an artist's impression, without reality.

He walked to the rear of the bridge which, compared to a man-of-war's, was spacious. The quartermaster stood on his grating behind the polished wheel, his eyes lifted to the gyro-repeater. There was a lookout on either side of the wheelhouse, a petty officer making notes in the deck-log.

The *Empire Prince* was so well loaded she seemed almost indifferent to the angry water around her. A rich prize for any raider.

He glanced at the faces of the men on watch and tried to memorize the others around the ship. It was strange to be serving with men he did not know. Few of them knew each other, and he guessed it was the usual arrangement for a special mission, or an 'early suicide' as Lieutenant Williams, his temporary second in command, had described it. Williams was the real expert, an RNR officer, he had served most of his peacetime life in oil tankers. He was a laconic, nuggety Welshman from Cardiff with few illusions left about the reliability of the top brass.

Williams entered the bridge, banging his sodden cap against his thigh, his eyes nevertheless taking in the compass, the ship's head and the general alertness of the watchkeepers.

He nodded to Fairfax. 'I suggest you get your head down, sir. You'll be busy in the morning, I shouldn't wonder.'

Fairfax replied, 'I feel okay.'

'Mebbee.' Williams jammed the battered cap on his head and took out his pipe and pouch. 'But you know I'm right, all the same.' He glanced at the interwoven gold lace on his sleeve. 'I understand ships, sir, but I'm not much of a man of action. I'm a survivor, if you like.'

Fairfax watched him as the blue tobacco smoke went jerkily upwards into the fans.

'Why did you volunteer for *this*, then?'

Williams grinned. 'Perhaps I misunderstood the question, sir.'

'Well, I'm glad you are here.' He peered aft towards the squat funnel and the remaining superstructure. Between it and the bridge the masts and derricks with their complicated array of rubber fuel hoses looked like some kind of obscene creeper. 'I'm more used to being able to shoot back!'

Williams smiled. Fairfax seemed all right. Not one of those hell for leather madmen who were usually the first to crack wide open when they were most needed.

He said, 'What d'you reckon our chances, sir?'

Fairfax walked to the chart table. '*Andromeda* will be about here.' He tapped the pencilled lines. 'Pity about *Fremantle*. We could do with a bit more muscle.'

Williams shrugged as if it was no concern of his at all. 'Well, we have our orders. No heroics, no matter what. Surely a cruiser can cope with a bloody armed merchantman, sir?'

Fairfax looked at him grimly. What was the point in telling him what Blake had suggested, that there were two raiders, not one? They were committed, and any more anxiety was pointless. He saw the stubborn lines around Williams' mouth. Any more than there was a point in Williams' remark about

214

no heroics. They both knew that if it came to the crunch they would have a go at the bastard.

He said, 'I think *Andromeda* will cope.' He looked at the camp-bed by the chart space. 'I'll do as you say. Call me if. . . .'

Williams nodded. 'I know, sir, *if.*'

Fairfax lay down and turned on his side, his back to the wheelhouse. He listened to the muted beat of engines, the occasional flurry of blown spray across the windows.

Tomorrow. Nothing might happen at all. He thought of Sarah, could almost feel her pressed against him.

Fairfax had had quite a few girls before he had settled down with Sarah. Even after their marriage he had played around once or twice when his ship had been away from her home port. It had been a part of his life, something everyone treated as normal.

He closed his eyes tightly. *Not any more.* They both knew that now.

He slipped suddenly into a deep sleep, one arm out-thrust and moving in time with the ship's motion.

Hours later, Lieutenant Williams was refilling his pipe and thinking of sending for his relief. The sea was calmer but some rain had begun to fall. It was drumming over the wheelhouse like busy fingers, insistent and somehow menacing.

Williams was unperturbed. He knew about the storm, and he had a good idea that the rain was in its path. If it was, it would get worse before long, and so would the sea. But the *Empire Prince* was a well-found ship. Pity they couldn't be bothered to build them in peacetime, he thought.

The starboard door slammed back and an oilskinned figure lurched into the wheelhouse, streaming with rain and spray as if he had come from the sea itself.

A petty officer yelled, 'Shut that door, you half-wit! You'll light up the whole ruddy ocean!'

Williams regarded the intruder coldly. It was a lookout from the bridge wing.

'Well? This had better be good!'

The seaman gulped air and wiped his reddened face. 'I— I'm not sure, sir.'

Fairfax hurried across the bridge, his hair tangled over his forehead.

'What's happened?'

The seaman was beginning to regret his impulse. He said,

'I thought I heard an aircraft, sir.'

Fairfax said sharply, *'All lights out!'*

The wheelhouse was suddenly pitch black, except for the luminous glow of the gyro-compass and the helmsman's eyes, like two white marbles.

'Open the door.'

Fairfax groped out on to the slippery plating, his ears useless against the roar and hiss of the sea, the jubilant sluice of water along the oiler's fat flank.

Williams said dryly, 'Aircraft, you say? We're nowhere near any air cover and out of range of everything but the bloody birds!'

Fairfax gripped his arm. 'Listen! *Now!*'

There it was. A faint, indistinct drone, lost almost at once in the ocean's noises.

Williams stared at him in the darkness. 'By God, they've found us.'

They strained their ears for a few more moments but there was nothing.

In silence they re-entered the wheelhouse and snapped on the lights.

Fairfax said slowly, 'I think a drink all round is indicated, and one for the lookout.'

16

'Am Engaging!'

Lieutenant Jeremy Masters groped his way cautiously across the upper bridge, each hand seeking a firm hold before letting go with the other. Water surged everywhere, gurgling noisily through the scuppers or splashing over the huddled Oerlikon gunners on either wing.

It was dawn, but when he peered over the screen all he could see was the foam boiling along the side or rising over the guard-rails as if to knock some unwary seaman from his feet. Beyond the tossing spray the sea was as black as a boot.

He saw Blake's shape in the familiar bridge chair, shining faintly as the rain and spray bounced across his oilskin. Masters measured the distance, took a deep breath and hurled himself towards the forward gratings.

The Toby Jug, massively black and unusually cheerful, called, 'That's right, sir, one 'and for the King but keep one for yerself!'

Blake half turned and said, 'Look at it. You can't fly in this.'

Masters sensed his anxiety, his frustration, as the ship plunged and reared over the dark water.

'I could have a go, sir.'

'No.'

What was the point in discussing it? The Seafox's range of four hundred odd miles left no room for error. Masters and his observer could fly on and on into oblivion and discover nothing.

A small figure hovered by the chair, trying to guard a steaming jug from the mixture of salt and rain.

'Cocoa, sir?'

Blake nodded. He felt stretched out like piano wire. Almost at breaking point. Damn the weather. Where was the change of luck they needed so desperately?

He noticed that the slightly-built seaman was Digby, the one who had discovered the grisly remains on the islet.

Blake sipped the cocoa, it was scalding, in spite of the long

217

haul from the galley. It seemed to cling to his stomach lining like an extra skin.

He asked, 'All right, Digby?'

The youth stared at him, astonished that anyone remembered his name, especially the captain, and at a time like this.

'Y-yes, I mean, aye, aye, sir.'

He took a quick glance past the captain, knowing he would always remember the moment. When he had shared this high, unprotected place with Blake. Out there, beyond the streaming arrow-head of the forecastle, was the whole ocean. Unlike some of his tough and seasoned messmates, Digby knew there was no land within safe distance. The nearest was straight down, twelve thousand fathoms beneath *Andromeda*'s keel.

Masters was saying, 'You're certain it'll be today, sir?'

Blake turned angrily. 'I'm not bloody sure of anything!' He touched the airman's jacket impetuously. 'Sorry. Unforgivable.'

Masters grinned. 'We all take you for granted, sir. That's the best of being a "temporary gentleman"!' He ducked as more spray came inboard. 'Nobody expects *anything* of me!'

Villar clawed his way across the bridge. 'Signal, sir! From Naval Operations, immediate. *Empire Prince* has made her arranged signal. My team is plotting the position now, but as far as I can gather she's about two hundred and seventy-five miles south-south-west of us.'

Masters said under his breath, 'Just as well I didn't fly-off.'

Blake thrust past him and lifted the hood above the chart table. *Empire Prince* in the original plan would have done well. But in this mounting sea things could change.

He said, 'Alter course to intercept, Pilot. Warn the engineroom.'

He felt the lieutenant duck from under the hood. He was alone with the stained chart, the small glowing lamp above it.

Fairfax could not possibly have sighted anything at that time. His situation would be like *Andromeda*'s. Desperate the Germans might be, but to risk seizing an oiler in pitch darkness was inviting failure. He thought of Masters. Rietz must have launched an aircraft. An Arado was bigger and far more powerful than Masters' Seafox. The German pilots would be the best available, professionals well-used to tracking surface vessels under all conditions. So they were there. More to the point, the lure of fuel had pushed caution aside.

Blake stood up, waiting for his eyes to get accustomed to

218

the darkness again. What would he do in Rietz's place, with the only chance of survival a tempting cargo of fuel with the means to bunker at sea? He did not need to answer his own question.

He felt the bridge shaking more insistently as the revolutions mounted.

'Course two-one-zero, sir. Revolutions for twenty-five knots.'

Blake walked past a petty officer who was holding his handset like a talisman.

'Tell the engineroom I need more revs right now.'

Palliser came from the shadows, his collar turned up as more spray burst over the bridge in a solid sheet.

'Up she rises!'

But nobody laughed.

Palliser glanced at Blair, who was sharing his watch.

'Bloody hell. I feel like a leper all of a sudden!'

The Australian grinned. 'Nothing new, Guns.'

Blake moved restlessly across the slippery gratings, listening to the various reports from radar, from the W/T office, even from the sick-bay. The last one was to announce that a steward had broken his wrist after being hurled down a ladder when the ship had made an impressive plunge.

Scovell appeared to tell Blake he had been right round the ship as instructed. There had been no point in rousing the whole ship's company just for that. There might be long delays, with the tension building up in each man until he would be unable to see or think clearly.

Scovell said, 'All checked, sir.'

He sounded out of breath. Lack of exercise or fear, it was hard to tell.

'Good, Number One. Pity we don't know where the enemy is, or from which bearing she'll put in an appearance.'

He thought of Villar's neat calculations, tide and current, the wind's direction and drift. Rietz was probably shadowing the oiler from the south-west. Keeping well back until he was ready. The captain of any fully loaded tanker would not risk a clash. Fairfax would have to tread warily. To act otherwise would make the enemy suspicious and invite disaster.

Scovell peered at the watchkeepers as if to sniff out a man dozing on his feet.

'Rain's getting heavier. Lull soon. Then *wham*.'

Blake turned away. Scovell's pessimism did not help. A

storm and a battle did not go hand in hand or leave room for manoeuvre.

Blake listened to the screws' steady beat, felt the ship's violent motion as she hurled herself into the weather as if she hated it and what they were all doing to her.

He said, 'Call the hands half an hour earlier, Number One. I want them fed and ready to go to action stations as soon as we've got some daylight.' He added, 'Tell Paymaster Commander Gross to get his department on top line. Sandwiches and tea to all the gun positions. Chocolate, too, if he can spare it. Then make sure the commodore's been roused.'

Blake heard Scovell's boots clattering down a ladder. Probably thinks it's unnecessary. A waste of time. Sentiment, when all they needed was a firm hand.

He saw Digby creeping round the after part of the bridge gathering up empty mugs. Scovell should try to see it like Digby. A helpless feeling made worse by the darkness, the empty desert which had already taken care of the *Devonport* and a few others besides. You needed more than cold armour-plate at times like these.

In the sick-bay Surgeon Lieutenant-Commander Bruce scrubbed his hands and tried not to look at his assistant's green face. The motion was terrible down here, with every jar and bottle clattering on shelves and in cupboards like dancing skeletons. Bruce glanced at the sick-berth attendants in the adjoining flat, laying out the instruments, checking the stretchers. He sighed. He was getting too old for it. Past it.

The ship's company was wide awake now, and there were many who had been unable to sleep anyway. Plates were left untouched by some, others ate with a kind of desperation, as if it was the last meal on earth.

Cooks and stewards piled small mountains of sandwiches on trays, while stokers of the damage control party went round the ship looking at life-rafts and Carley floats, timber for shoring up bulkheads, all the odds and ends of survival.

Both the boiler rooms and the engineroom were fully manned, with overalled figures scrambling through the steamy haze while they tried to stay on their feet. Weir watched from his catwalk, his face set in a grim mask. Steele was moving towards him, his mouth speaking silent words to the chief stoker while the din roared and rattled around them.

On the thick watertight doors the clips were greased and ready to be slammed shut. In action men would pause to look

220

at these doors. Safety for some, death by fire or drowning for others.

On the long messdeck in *Andromeda*'s forecastle Leading Seaman Musgrave ran his eye quickly over the bare neatness. The messdeck, like the others below his feet or aft from where he was standing, was prepared for battle. The clutter of half-written letters, repair-jobs on uniforms, ship-modelling and the like were stowed away. Only here and there were signs of habitation, the garish pin-ups displaying their teeth and their breasts. A pair of sea-boot stockings hung to dry on a deckhead pipe. But otherwise it was empty, the long, scrubbed tables and benches adding to a sense of loneliness.

Musgrave rapped the nearest table with his torch. 'All done 'ere, sir.' He looked at the officer who had been sent to check the messdecks with him. To get him from puking up his guts most likely, he thought.

Midshipman Steven Thorne nodded stiffly. He was so frightened that his eyes felt too big for their sockets. He wanted to say something, to assert himself, to discover the kind of strength which the leading seaman seemed to take for granted.

He asked huskily, 'You were aboard when you fought the three cruisers, Musgrave?'

'S'right.' Musgrave felt both sorry and irritated by Thorne's misery. If he got through this lot, Thorne would probably be throwing his bloody weight about in no time. You never knew how they would turn out. He added, 'Any reason for askin'?' He dropped the sir. It was Musgrave's special way of finding out how far he could go.

Thorne seized a fire-hose as the ship swayed noisily over a solid bank of water.

'I—I just wondered what it was like.'

He sounded so wretched that even Musgrave felt a twinge of pity. He looked along the broad messdeck, remembering the savage gashes in the side, the sea streaming past as *Andromeda* pressed on with her attack. A lot of good blokes had bought it that day, and before. He could see them now. On or off watch, up in front of the jaunty or Jimmy the One. Runs ashore in Alex and Gib, booze-ups and fights with the police and the civvies. Now they were gone.

He said, 'It was rough. But this one will be a piece of cake. I think the skipper's 'ad just about a gutful of the Jerry. I wouldn't give much for *'is* chances!'

There was a metallic squeak and Musgrave saw the young

midshipman jump with alarm. He followed his gaze to the great circular steel trunk which passed through the mess from the deck below and the one beneath that. It supported the crushing weight of A turret on the forecastle, whilst through it passed the ammunition hoists between the magazines and the breeches of the guns.

Thorne said in a whisper, 'Oh God. I think I'm going to be sick.'

' 'Ere, grab this fire-bucket.'

Musgrave pushed the youth over until the sand was within a foot of his face. *Poor little sod. Don't even shave yet.*

But Thorne was not sick. He stammered, 'Thanks, Musgrave. Close thing.'

Above the door to the messdeck was a red-painted gong.

Musgrave said quietly, 'Listen. In a moment or two that bloody thing is goin' to sound off like the clappers.'

Thorne said, 'I know. Action stations.'

Musgrave swung the door behind them. 'More to it than that. We're goin' to *fight* today. I feels it. When that 'appens you can forget all that swill they teaches you at the officer's school.'

'I—I don't understand?'

'You will.' Musgrave stuck out his beard. 'There's blokes up top 'o'll be lookin' to you, God 'elp them. 'Cause you're an officer. The fact that you're just off your mother's apron strings an' 'ave never been in a scrap like this one'll be never comes into it. So when the shit starts to fly, *sir*, just remember not to let 'em down.'

Thorne nodded, his fists clenched to his sides. 'Yes, I see.'

Musgrave looked up. The rain was easing off a bit and so was the motion.

Thorne said, 'Thank you.' He straightened his cap. 'Let's get on with it, shall we?'

Musgrave grinned. *I'll bet nobody's spoken to him like that since he was caught pinching apples.*

It was at that precise moment the alarm began its insane clamour.

'Action stations! Action stations!'

Musgrave glanced at the midshipman and started to run for the nearest ladder. Just before he scrambled through the hatch to the deck above, Musgrave paused and looked back. It was then that it struck him. Like a fist. He was never going to see that messdeck again.

Scovell saluted. 'Ship at action stations, sir.'

Blake peered at the sky. The cloud was breaking up, with patches of steely blue showing occasionally to light up the set faces around him and give substance to the sea.

He half listened to the chatter of reports and checks as each department went through the drill. A and B turrets were moving, their paired barrels glistening in the dull light where the salt had formed a crusty surface.

He had to know what was happening. *Had to*.

'What do you think, Pilot?'

Villar came back instantly. 'Another six hours, sir. It's my guess that the Germans will have stopped the *Empire Prince* by now and are probably taking on fuel. Commander Fairfax's last signal to base might have made them jumpy, but I doubt it.'

Blake peered at his watch. Six hours. It was too long. He looked at the sky again, hating it, dreading what might happen to Fairfax and his men.

He glanced round as Sub-Lieutenant Walker said, 'Here comes more rain!'

Rain . . . it looked more like a solid wall as it advanced towards the cruiser's surging bow wave. Then it hit the ship, driving out thought and understanding with its drenching intensity.

A seaman thrust a telephone towards Blake and shouted, 'Engineroom, sir!'

Blake jammed it to his ear. *'Captain!'*

Weir called, 'I can give you another two knots now, sir.'

Blake stared at the telephone while the rain roared through the bridge, battering his cap and oilskin like a flail. Yet through it all he heard Weir's quiet confidence, the prop he needed more than Weir would ever know.

'Everyone seems good and busy, Captain.'

Commodore Stagg's rich voice tore his mind from the complex equation of speed, time and distance.

Stagg walked to the bridge chair, oblivious to the downpour. 'Got bored aft.' He shot Blake a questioning glance as he joined him by the screen. 'Something bothering you?'

Blake could smell bacon and eggs on his breath, fresh coffee, too. Stagg's massive confidence helped to settle his mind.

He replied, 'It's going to take longer than planned.'

Stagg growled, 'Rietz will need a whole lot longer to get his fuel across in this swell, damn him.' He rubbed his wet hands. 'He's lost his safety margin. *Andromeda* will have him by the guts long before that. He'll know he can't outpace us.'

Blake pulled his pipe from his pocket and put it between his teeth. There was nothing more he could do. If they were closer he could get the Seafox airborne, if only to give Fairfax confidence, to show him help was near.

Stagg had to shout above the drumming downpour. 'You worry too much! Don't you see? We've got him cold!'

They both turned as the gunnery speaker barked, 'Ship, bearing Green two-oh, range one-four-oh!'

Stagg stared at Villar accusingly and shouted, 'You said six hours!' Then, surprisingly, he grinned and said to Blake, 'So Rietz was suspicious after all, damn his bloody eyes! Fairfax must have got the wind up! But it doesn't matter now!' He gripped Blake's wrist. 'D'you hear? Go *get him!*'

The speaker's metallic tones pierced the rain like a lance. 'Two ships, repeat *two* ships at Green two-oh, range one-four-oh.'

Blake lowered his glasses, the misty picture fixed in his mind. The rain passing on and over, the sea riding in long, undulating rollers to meet them, and then, just off the starboard bow, two blurred, oncoming shapes.

He shouted, 'I was right! There *are* two of them!'

Stagg stared back at him, his jaw hanging open.

Blake turned away, barely trusting himself to speak.

'Ships altering course. Now steering zero-four-zero. Rate two hundred, closing.'

Blake looked at the men around him, his eyes settling on Villar.

'Tell W/T to make the signal. *In contact with two German raiders. Am engaging!*' He watched Villar move swiftly to a voice-pipe. 'Fast as you like, Pilot.'

Scovell asked, 'Shall I stay here or go aft to damage control, sir?'

'Carry on, Number One. Tell Masters to be ready to fly-off immediately and to make sure his plane is fully armed. He'll understand.'

Scovell hesitated, his eyes moving from Blake to Stagg and back again. 'Good luck, sir.'

Blake nodded and then looked at the Toby Jug. 'Very well, Yeo. Hoist battle ensigns.'

'All guns with semi-armour-piercing, *load, load, load*! Follow director!'

Blake wiped his binoculars with his handkerchief. He was sweating under the oilskin and his hands felt as if they were shaking uncontrollably. But when he looked at them they were quite steady. A faint shadow moved over the bridge, and when he glanced up he saw one of the big ensigns running up to the yard, the white like snow against the dull clouds, the red cross like fresh blood.

Stagg said loudly, 'One or twenty-one, what's the bloody difference, eh?' He was speaking to the bridge at large but it sounded like an appeal.

'Open fire on leading ship!'

The gong rattled faintly below the bridge's protection and both forward turrets fired together.

Blake jammed himself in a corner of the bridge and tried to cushion his body against the crash and recoil of the four guns, the shuddering of the steel superstructure as *Andromeda* continued her onward charge.

Crump...crump. Crump...crump. Blake levelled his glasses and watched the fall of shot. It was like firing into steam, but he saw the vivid red flashes, the pale waterspouts which shot skyward to mark the neat array of explosions.

'Up two hundred. *Shoot!*'

Blake looked at Villar as his face lit up in the flames. 'Alter course two points to port. That'll give the marines a chance.'

More shellbursts blinked through the rain and spray. Like someone opening furnace doors. Far away and without danger.

He felt the deck tilt to the pressure of rudders and screws as Villar said tersely, 'Course one-nine-zero, sir.'

'*Shoot!*'

Muffled voices crackled over the intercom. 'A *hit*! We hit the bastard!'

Blake saw the glow of flames, like tongues, changing shape and spreading as he watched. The leading ship was hit, probably badly. Just one of *Andromeda*'s hundred-pound shells would blast through an unarmoured hull with terrible effect.

There was a lot of smoke about, billowing low across the sea, lifting and swirling as it was caught in a freak gust of wind. Beyond it, at a range reduced to about six miles, the flames were adding to the confusion.

Stagg bellowed, 'That's taken the wind out of him, by God!' He was standing on tiptoe, his face streaming with blown spray, his cap cover smeared with gunsmoke. 'Hit him, my lads!'

X and Y turrets opened fire at an extreme angle, the shells ripping past the cruiser like express trains.

'*Captain, sir!*' Sub-Lieutenant Walker waited for Blake to look at him. 'W/T report that the first ship has made contact with us! She's the *Waipawa*, captured in that convoy!'

Blake snatched up a handset below the screen, his mind compressed into a tight, desperate ball. Rietz had fooled them after all. He had kept the merchantman for this sole purpose, to draw their fire while he worked into an attacking position where he would be unhampered by extreme range.

'Guns! Shift target! The leading ship is—'

The bridge seemed to rise under his feet so that the pain lanced through him from his heels to the nape of his neck. He heard no explosion but was momentarily rendered speechless by concussion, by the terrible lurch which threw men about like rag dolls.

Then he heard Palliser's voice and realized the handset had been blasted from his fingers and was swinging on its flex.

'Captain! Direct hit!' There was something screaming in the background. It was too terrible to be human. 'Can't cope here. . . .' his voice was getting fainter, more slurred. 'All dead up here. . . .'

Blake peered aft, aware of the fumes, the stench of burned paint. He saw the director control tower rising above the streaming trail of smoke like a knight's helmet. A knight who had been cut down in combat. Blood was running down the sides and there were several holes punched through the plates, which in turn were pouring out smoke. There were eight men inside there. Or had been.

'Shift to local control.' Blake strode back to the compass. 'Hard a-port.'

'Thirty of port wheel on, sir.'

Stagg was yelling, 'What are you doing?'

Blake stared past him, his eyes stinging with smoke. 'He's got his sights on us now. We must close the range.' He waited, trying to shut out the sound of the screams. He was not sure if it had stopped and was only in his mind.

'Midships. *Steady.*'

Loose equipment clattered across the bridge and was trampled unheeded by the crouching lookouts and messengers.

Someone was calling for a stretcher-bearer, and through the tannoy a voice shouted, 'Damage control party port side forrard, at the double!'

Walker called, 'First lieutenant, sir!'

Blake took the telephone. 'Yes?'

'That shell passed through the starboard flag deck and exploded on the port side. Couple of boats are gone and an AA gun has been flung overboard.'

'Casualties?'

Blake winced as the hull bucked violently and he saw two great columns of water rise over the bridge before roaring down on the forecastle in a solid mass.

'The DCT is knocked out, sir. Guns is dead. About ten men in all. The doc's got some splinter cases aft.'

The phone went dead.

Blake said, 'Alter course again. Hard a-starboard!'

Men fell and slipped from their feet as the helm went over once more. The four turrets were already swinging across as the bearing changed, their muzzles crashing back as they fired again.

Without the control tower and main range-finder each turret had to fend for itself. Blake recalled Palliser's comments about the new men in the forward turrets. Now he was dead and his subordinate was down there in charge of B turret. It was history repeating itself.

'Midships. Steady!'

Blake raised his glasses. If only the sky would clear. It was like fighting shadows.

Crash. A shell exploded right alongside, shaking the hull from stem to stern with such force that a seaman fell to the deck.

Blake ran to the side, and when he glanced at the receding pattern of hissing foam he saw the flag deck directly below him. It was hanging down towards the water alongside like buckled cardboard, its signalmen and Oerlikon crew flung into the sea and already far astern if they had managed to avoid the racing screws. Either way they were lost.

'Shoot!'

That was Lieutenant Blair in B turret, his voice unemotional over the speaker as if he was at target practice.

'Over. Down one hundred. *On! Shoot!*'

Blake's ears were cringing from the jerking crash of the forward guns.

Stagg was sitting in the chair, his eyes unblinking as he peered through his glasses.

'Target's altered course, sir. Steering due north.'

Stagg shouted hoarsely, 'Probably going to launch his tin

fish at us! Some hopes in this sea!'

Blake climbed to the opposite side and wedged his elbows on the wet metal. Strange they had forgotten about the storm. That was for real people, not for lost madmen like themselves.

He said, 'Pass the word aft to Masters. Stand by to fly-off the instant I reduce speed.' He lowered the glasses, able to ignore the urgent voices repeating orders. 'The German is turning to get his seaplanes airborne.' He saw Stagg's disbelief. 'He's nothing to lose, has he?'

'All ready aft, sir!'

Blake hurried past the rating, his eyes everywhere until he was in the after part of the bridge. Something fell on the shattered glass by his side. It was blood, black in the filtered light. Palliser and his men. Up there above it all. They would still be there when the ship went down.

Blake wanted to tell Masters and his observer. But what? That he was sorry they had to die? That to be able to keep attacking, *Andromeda* needed to have her engines moving at full power. The Arado seaplane carried bombs. Not big ones, but enough.

'Stop engines!'

Andromeda seemed to lean forward as the way went off her shafts. A few moments later two shells exploded directly ahead. Where she would have been but for Masters.

Blake's heart sank as the little Seafox shot along the catapult and tilted drunkenly to the driving wind and rain.

Then he said, 'Full ahead together!'

The freighter which had been deliberately used to draw *Andromeda*'s opening salvoes was already moving closer, her hull down by the bows and one anchor cable dangling in the sea as evidence to the damage below decks. There were several fires raging, and tiny figures were racing about with hoses and other equipment like demented beings. Someone had run up a white flag, and Blake saw a few of the crew pausing to stare towards the cruiser, as with her battle ensigns streaming brightly above the smoke and pain she charged to the attack.

The *Waipawa* with her German prize crew would have to fend for herself. It was a race. Who would get to her first? The storm or the victor of the fight?

'Aircraft bearing Green four-five! Angle of sight three-zero!'

Like angry dogs the short-range weapons jerked skywards, pom-poms and Oerlikons, machine-guns and anything which would bear.

228

Blake saw the aircraft coming straight for the starboard bow. There were two of them, the second slightly lower and buffeted about by the wind.

It was all there, fixed in his mind. The seaplane racing over the shattered Catalina, cutting the survivors down, then returning across the limp corpses just to make sure. It was probably one of these pilots.

'Barrage! Commence . . . commence . . . commence!'

Tracer lifted from the sponsons to join the small, vicious shellbursts from the anti-aircraft guns. The noise, blanketed every so often by the main armament, was shattering.

The first seaplane flew directly for the ship, turned at the last minute, its cannon ripping across the bridge structure like a steel whip.

A bomb hit *Andromeda*'s forecastle and skidded over the side without exploding. Another burst in the water, fragments clashing against the armour-plate, while others cut through some signal halliards high above the bridge.

One of the ensigns tugged away on its severed halliard and the Toby Jug shouted, 'Another flag, Bunts! Don't stand there gawping!' He turned away, angry with himself and with the destruction of his department. The young signalman was sliding very slowly down the side of the bridge, a red smear marking where he had been cut down by a splinter.

'A hit!' Someone was cheering like a maniac. 'Got him!'

Blake swung round in time to see the sparks and smoke spreading away from the other ship like signal rockets, but had to duck as the second aircraft roared overhead, guns hammering, a bomb already on its way down.

The deck shook under his feet and metal shrieked past him, punching through steel and slapping hideously into solid flesh. Two men were down, another was trying to drag himself towards the bridge gate, his agony making him try to reach the darkness below decks. But the other darkness mercifully found him first. As he rolled over to lie staring at the sky, Blake saw that he had a hole in his chest as big as his fist.

'Stretcher-bearers to the bridge!'

The second aircraft was swinging away, trying to gain height as the tracers followed it with merciless concentration. Fire rippled along its wing and belly like droplets of molten liquid, then it exploded and threw fragments as far as the ship.

The first attacker was standing well away, waiting for a chance to cut through the smoke and perhaps rake the open bridge, just as sharpshooters had once marked down the officers of a ship of the line at Trafalgar.

Lieutenant Masters peered at the terrible panorama below him. The sea seemed brighter from up here, so that the ship with her bow wave and wake zigzagging away through broken rollers like plough marks appeared out of control. Great patches of white froth drifted nearby where enemy shells had exploded, while from *Andromeda*, with her wounds made small by distance, came the regular flash of gunfire, the mounting smoke from her funnel as Weir turned his back on the red danger markers.

Provided *Andromeda* could avoid a fatal hit in a magazine or shell room, and keep away from those drifting patches of white foam, it would soon be over, Masters thought.

The listing freighter had stopped altogether and was in a bad way, her hull sliding into each successive trough and finding it more difficult to rise up again.

Masters looked towards the enemy. The raider was badly hit, too, with fire and smoke trailing astern as she continued to shoot from her hidden mountings.

Masters' earphones crackled and he heard the observer say calmly, 'Sorry to disturb you, Skipper.' When Masters craned round to look at him, Duncan was actually grinning. 'But there's a ruddy great bird coming just underneath us!'

The Seafox was a midget by comparison, and with reconnaissance in view when it had been designed it had only been fitted with a single Lewis gun. But the two Germans in the Arado's crew had other things on their minds and were not even aware of Masters' presence as they overtook the Seafox about two hundred feet below its floats.

Masters said quietly, 'If they spot us, Jim, we're done for. What about it?'

Duncan was still grinning. 'Ready when you are!' He cocked the outdated Lewis and swung it over the side of the cockpit as if he had been doing it all his life. To the gun he shouted, 'Just don't jam on me, that's all I ask!'

Masters dragged the stick over and saw the Arado right beneath him, and far beyond its perspex cockpit he could even see the cruiser. A last-second warning made both Germans look up together. They were still staring, unable to believe what they saw, as a stream of tracer smashed through the cockpit and turned it into a torch.

Masters watched the blazing plane reel away in a tight spiral, a greasy plume of smoke marking its fall, until with a silent explosion it hit the side of a long, crested roller and vanished.

He heard Duncan whooping in his cockpit and wondered if any of them would ever be the same after this, if they survived.

It was nearly over. Two German ships run to ground. As the thought touched his mind he saw a great mushroom of fire burst through the raider's well-deck, tiny feathers of spray darting from the sea around her as wreckage was scattered in confusion.

Duncan was saying, '*Andromeda*'s ceased fire! God, she looks knocked about, Skipper!'

Masters steadied the aircraft. 'She looks just fine to me, you misery! Look at the kraut! Slowing down and taking on a list, if I'm not mistaken!' The recklessness held him like a vice. 'Let's go and take a closer look.'

Duncan nodded, sharing the mood. 'Not too bloody near though!'

Lifting and falling on the unruly air currents, the little sea-plane flew towards the enemy ship. Several explosions hurled wreckage into the air and there was a lot of smoke. Through his binoculars Masters could see the damage and knew this was no bluff, no last-chance attempt to lure the enemy under the guns.

'She's stopped. God, I think they're trying to lower boats!'

He swore and dropped the glasses as he brought the plane back under command. When he looked again the raider was easier to see, and as he watched he saw the sky clearing far beyond her, the rain passing away and the sea changing again into those great, smooth rollers.

He stopped breathing, the glasses pressed against his eyes until they watered with pain.

Far away on the brightening horizon was a single ship. She was bows-on, and even at such a distance Masters could see the rising moustache at her stem which left no time for doubt, no room for conjecture.

He spoke into his microphone with deliberate care.

'Jim, old son, the captain was right. We were celebrating too soon.' He put the Seafox into a banking turn. 'We have company!'

17

Just a Man

Like two wallowing juggernauts the *Salamander* and the *Empire Prince* headed into sea and wind while the work of pumping oil got under way.

On the port wing of his bridge Rietz watched carefully, ready to use helm or engines if the two vessels swung too close together or veered apart before the rubber hoses could be slacked off.

It was all going remarkably well, in spite of the deep swell. The oiler's crew had not put up any real resistance, and after the *Salamander* had followed up her signal to heave-to with a shot across the other ship's bows, there had been no trouble. Rietz had sent sixty of his own men to help with the complicated derricks and guys which were used for swaying the hoses over the strip of surging water. He could see his chief engineer, old Hans Leichner, bobbing and peering at the pulsating hoses, while deep below his boots the bunkers continued to suck greedily on the fuel.

Rietz had been surprised to learn that the oiler's master was a naval commander, but the *Empire Prince* was a fleet auxiliary, an important vessel by any standards. He had been the only casualty when he had been clubbed down by one of the boarding party as he had tried to reach the radio room.

Rietz glanced outboard at the way the sea was smoothing in the wake of the rainstorm. They might miss the full brunt of the storm. He no longer cared much, with full bunkers he would be free again, able to move as he chose.

He thought briefly of Vogel in the *Wölfchen*, miles away to the north-east, making certain *Salamander* could replenish her empty bunkers without interruption.

Vogel was probably planning a way to escape the aftermath of Rietz's report when they reached Germany again. That was, if anyone would care at this stage of the war. They said a million men had died in Russia, and many more beside in North Africa and Italy. No wonder the grand admiral had put such stress on his raiders' importance. Germany was faced with probable invasion across the English Channel. When it came, each side would know there was no second chance. They were too worn down by war, its cost in men and suffering.

He heard a door slam back inside the wheelhouse and steeled himself. It was instinct, like a waking animal who senses danger near at hand.

It was Schoningen, the navigating officer.

He exclaimed, 'Captain, we have just received a signal from *Wölfchen*!'

Rietz watched him coldly. 'Am I to be told, Lieutenant, or must I guess?'

The lieutenant pulled himself together with an effort.

'*Wölfchen* is engaging a British cruiser, Captain. The prize ship is badly hit, but Captain Vogel has reported severe damage to the enemy. He is confident of victory.'

Rietz looked away, sickened. Vogel had broken the unwritten rules to serve his own ends. Another victory over a warship would clear his name and leave his own testimony in the dust.

He snapped, 'Call up Lieutenant Storch. We will discontinue oiling at once. See that all our prisoners and neutral seamen are sent across to the *Empire Prince* without delay.'

He was still on the bridge wing as Storch came hurrying up the ladder.

'Is it true, Captain?'

Rietz watched the first of the prisoners emerging uncertainly on deck to stare at the big oiler alongside.

'It is, Rudi. Vogel has sprung a trap and is taking full advantage of it.'

Storch stared from him to the growing lines of figures being herded on deck.

'What are you doing, Captain?' His face looked stricken as he asked, 'Are you going to fight?' When Rietz did not answer Storch said, 'Leave him, Captain. He has betrayed you, as well as the name of Germany. *Leave him,* as he would you!'

Rietz smiled gravely. 'You know it is not possible. It is a matter of convenience as well as honour, my young friend. That ship will be the cruiser *Andromeda*. There is none other in these waters. I think I knew it would be like this.' He became suddenly brisk. 'Now get those people passed across to the oiler and cast off the hoses. Have you dealt with her radio?'

Storch nodded, still only half understanding. 'Yes. The captain tried to stop my men. He had no chance.'

Some of the prisoners were staring up at the rust-streaked bridge as if they still expected a trick, a betrayal.

With a sudden impulse Rietz said, 'Bring the oiler's captain to me.'

By the time Fairfax had been ferried across in a wildly pitching motor boat most of the prisoners had already been transferred.

Rietz watched the young naval commander as he was led to the bridge and wondered if anyone would ever know or care.

Fairfax glanced around the bridge, the hurrying seamen in their worn leather coats and scuffed sea-boots. The prisoners were being sent over for a reason. So that the *Empire Prince* could be sent to the bottom with the last of the evidence. But before that terrible act of murder it was to be his turn. He sensed the guard beside him, fidgeting impatiently with his Schmeisser sub-machine-gun.

Fairfax felt very calm, almost empty of any emotion at all. All he could see in his mind was Sarah.

Rietz stepped forward and nodded curtly. 'You are Commander Fairfax of the Royal Australian Navy, yes?' He gestured towards the swaying oiler. 'In a moment you will be free to go. I regret that your radio must be destroyed, but it is a small price to pay.'

Fairfax stared at him. He had never seen a real enemy before. Not close to, as a human being. Perhaps that was almost as unnerving as the German's words.

Rietz said, 'You will know soon enough, there are two raiders. I suspect some of your people have always thought as much. It is no longer important. What is important is that you should know my ship was in no way responsible for the murder of helpless seamen. In war we have to do many cruel things, not least to ourselves.'

Rietz could hear the shouts from the petty officers on deck, the clatter of wires and tackles. They would all be waiting for him to act, would be needing his hand to guide them.

Fairfax said slowly, 'It is just your word, Captain.'

Storch thrust forward, his features flushed and angry. 'How dare you speak to my captain like that! Because of the prisoners we have wasted valuable time when we could be many miles away and you left to drown!'

Rietz snapped, 'That is enough, Lieutenant!'

But Storch could not stop himself. 'And because my captain is not the man you think he is, we are going to fight *your* ship!'

Rietz watched Fairfax's face and asked quietly, 'She *is* your ship, am I correct? At this moment our consort is attacking her. It is my duty to assist, just as it was yours to lure me here.'

He turned on his heel. 'Take him back to his ship.'

A seaman seized Fairfax's arm but he shook it off.

'Captain Rietz.' He waited until the man had turned towards him. 'Thank you for telling me and for giving your prisoners a chance to live again.'

He saluted and then followed the armed seaman down the bridge ladder.

Storch said bitterly, 'Arrogant dog!'

Rietz patted his arm. 'Not like us at all, eh, Rudi?'

The lieutenant smiled wearily. 'I'm sorry.'

Rietz watched the last boat being run up to its davits.

'Ring down for full speed. We will steer north-east.'

He trained his binoculars on the oiler and the men who crowded her decks to watch as *Salamander*'s screws began to beat the sea into a powerful froth beneath her stern.

Almost to himself he said, 'It will feel cleaner to fight under our true colours for once, Rudi, and may do more good than a thousand prizes.'

But when he looked round the lieutenant had gone.

Commodore Rodney Stagg sat on the bridge chair, a cigar glowing from his great jaw as he watched the busy figures around him. The dead and wounded had been taken away, and only the blood and blasted clothing were left to remind them of the battle and the cost.

Blake was on one of the telephones, and Villar was examining his compass to ensure there was no damage. Most of the smoke had cleared, like the sky, and Stagg found it hard to look up at the battered control tower with its bright punctures and long red stains.

Andromeda had reduced to half speed and Stagg knew it was because she had taken on a slight list to starboard. But the underwater damage was reported to be in hand, and Weir had managed to keep all the pumps going.

Sub-Lieutenant Walker took a long breath then lifted his glasses to look at the blazing raider. All her main armament had fallen silent, but *Andromeda*'s guns were still moving slowly on their mountings, watching for any sign of defiance.

Blake put down the telephone. 'W/T office report on the

storm, sir. We may give it a miss. Once I'm sure of the raider we'll signal her to abandon and take to the boats. But her list is much worse.' He wiped his face as if to clean away the sights and smells of battle. 'Close thing though.'

Stagg boomed, 'Nonsense! Chap like you should have more bloody faith!'

'Seafox in sight, sir. Fine on the port bow.'

'Warn the handling party.'

Blake listened to the engines' beat, the distant shouts of some of the damage control party as they cut their way to a trapped man. Masters had survived, had even brought down an enemy aircraft. It was impossible, they said. Well, once again, *they* were wrong.

A dull explosion deep inside the German ship flung more glowing sparks high in the air, and some giant bubbles, like obscene under-sea vehicles, nudged along the ship's side.

Was Rietz dead? Blake wondered. Or was he over there now, watching his executioner, as so many had watched him in the past?

'Seafox is signallin', sir.' The yeoman's brass telescope swivelled towards the wafer-thin silhouette like a cannon.

It was flying so close to the surface that the stabbing morse light was reflected across each long roller.

'German raider approaching from the south-west.' As the Toby Jug spelled out each word it fell into the bridge like a sledge-hammer.

Stagg said hoarsely, 'Can't be! Bloody fool's wrong!'

Blake turned to look at the blazing ship with its attendant clutter of splintered woodwork and rigging.

He had been proved right, but too late. He looked along his ship, at the scars and blackened holes. It was cruel, unbelievably so.

He heard himself say, 'Pass the word to all positions, Pilot, then warn the Chief.'

Stagg swallowed hard then threw his cigar over the side.

'We'll fight, eh?'

Blake answered, 'Of course.'

He looked up at the curling ensigns and remembered Claire. She was so clear in his mind that he thought he spoke her name aloud.

Sub-Lieutenant Walker, his face unusually pale, said, 'W/T have contact with Seafox, sir. Their short-range radio is working now.'

Somebody said, 'That makes a change.' But his voice was dull, like a man who has just witnessed something terrible.

Blake nodded. 'Tell Lieutenant Masters to continue spotting for us.'

Villar looked down from the compass platform. 'What about his fuel, sir?'

Blake did not reply. There was no point. Masters would understand.

Stagg lurched to his feet. 'Give me the microphone. I'd better speak to the ship's company.' He saw Blake's face and said quietly, 'No. It's for you to do. The ship *knows* you.'

Blake took it in his hand and stared at the strange, ragged clouds. He pressed the button as he had a million times.

'This is the captain speaking. We shall be engaging another German raider very soon. Some of us thought we had finished work for the day.'

He saw the Toby Jug nudge a boatswain's mate and grin. It was that easy to make them smile when he felt like crying for them.

'After that, most of us will be going home.' He gripped the microphone until his hand ached. 'I just want you to know how proud I am of you—'

He thrust the instrument into Walker's hand, unable to continue.

Stagg muttered, 'Well done. Not easy.'

Blake watched the little Seafox turning away and climbing slowly towards the clouds.

Not easy. 'There's that.' He had said as much to Claire when they had spoken about England.

Blake threw off the heavy oilskin and said, 'Tell Moon to bring me a clean shirt.' He looked questioningly at their lined faces. 'All right, lads?'

Several of them nodded, a few tried to grin.

Blake studied each one in turn. Ordinary, everyday faces. You would never notice them in a crowded street or a barracks.

But here, in the middle of the ocean, they were special.

Moon appeared with a carefully folded shirt, the shoulder straps strangely bright and alien amongst the dirt of battle.

He said mildly, 'I'll fetch some sandwiches later on, sir.'

Blake did not know whether to laugh or crack wide open.

He gripped the steward's shoulder and shook him gently. 'You do that thing, Moon. I shall look forward to it.'

'From Seafox, sir. *Enemy in sight!*'

237

Lieutenant Trevett, who was bringing some notes to Villar, said quickly, 'I'll say something for that galah. He's bloody punctual!'

Stagg looked at Blake and spread his big hands. 'Ready?'

Blake nodded. 'Ring down for maximum revolutions. Stand by to engage!'

Stagg was on his feet, restless and grim-faced, as the *Andromeda*'s bow wave peeled away on either side in steep banks of white foam.

'What d'you reckon he'll do?'

Blake raised his glasses and stared at the horizon. It had misted over slightly, and was made worse by the sun's harsh glare reflected from the sea.

'He'll make a diagonal attack, sir. These converted merchantmen usually have their armament in halves, one full battery on either beam. Torpedoes, too, but he'll not reduce speed to use those.'

He felt the deck lift slowly and then surge forward and down again, a long roller breaking past the ship's sides and flinging water over the deserted decks.

The raider probably had the latest range-finder, whereas *Andromeda* was almost blind. Blake turned his smarting eyes from the sun and knew the only chance was to get as close as possible and beat down the enemy's fire-power. If they waited until night the German could pick them off at leisure.

Walker said in a hushed voice, 'Engineroom, sir.'

Blake tried to keep his face expressionless as the men watched him stride to the telephone.

'Chief? Captain here.'

Weir said, 'I'll need to reduce speed, sir. Starboard outer is giving me trouble. Must have taken a bad knock from a bomb or shell splinter. If we cut the revs on the port screws it will give you a better chance.'

Blake stared past the telephone at one of the splinter holes where a man had died. Weir knew what he was doing. *Andromeda* would need all her manoeuvrability. She could not manage on helm alone, and with unequal thrust on her screws it would take longer to alter course, to avoid those first deadly salvoes.

'How long, Chief?'

Weir did not answer directly. He said, 'We're losing fuel, too.'

'I know,' Blake did not have to peer over the screen to

remind himself of the long silver-blue trail they were leaving astern. 'Do your best.'

Weir gave a short laugh. 'Aye, sir. I've no wish to swim home.'

Stagg asked, 'What did *he* want?'

Villar snapped, 'Enemy's opened fire, sir!'

There was a thin, abbreviated whistle, and seconds later a column of water shot from the sea barely half a cable from the port beam.

The two forward turrets began to whirr round, their guns lifting to their maximum sixty degrees elevation.

The quarters officers would find it more difficult at the reduced speed, Blake thought. The swell was noticeably heavier and the hull was corkscrewing back and forth in long, sickening swoops.

'Open fire!'

The gong gave its tinny warning below the bridge and A turret, followed closely by B turret, belched fire towards the horizon.

Over the speaker Blake heard the Australian lieutenant, Blair, call, 'Range one-double-oh. Inclination one-one-oh right!'

Blake blinded rapidly to clear his vision and tried again. Then as some of the mist parted below the horizon he saw the enemy for the first time. A solid dark shape, guns flashing from her hull even as he adjusted his glasses.

The four six-inch guns were moving very slightly now, the smoke from their opening shots still fanning abeam like hot breath.

'Sights moving, sir! Sights *set!*'

Whoosh . . . crash! The raider's shells exploded close alongside like twin thunder-claps. The hull shook and reeled to the force of the detonations, and splinters clashed against steel or whined away over the glittering water. Two more heavy shells arrived seconds later, bracketing the cruiser in shining waterspouts and filling the air with the shriek and crash of white-hot metal.

Blair's voice came through the din. *Shoot!*'

The four guns recoiled together, and Blake saw the shell-bursts to the right of the target, the white columns seeming to stand like pillars for ages before they cascaded into the sea.

Walker yelled 'X turret is jammed, sir! Seven marines wounded!'

A boatswain's mate stood back from his voice-pipe, his

eyes wild. 'Two pumps have carried away, sir! Damage control need more men aft!'

Blake snatched up a handset, his ears cringing to the crash of gunfire as the two ships continued to close the range. *Andromeda* had been badly hit and it was too soon after her punishment in the Mediterranean.

A frightened voice called, 'D-damage control, sir!'

'Get me the first lieutenant, *quickly*!'

The voice broke off in a sob. 'He's dead, sir! He's here, looking at me! All cut about!' He was close to hysteria.

Blake asked, 'Who is that?'

'Thorne, sir.'

A face swam through the smoke and despair. A replacement midshipman. Straight from the training school. A boy.

'Well, listen, Mr Thorne. Send a petty officer and some stokers aft to help your party there. Can you do that?'

There was a long pause, and in his mind Blake could see it all. The splinter holes, the blood and upended switchboard and damage control panel. Scovell, who had wanted his own command so much, lying dead with his men, staring at a terrified midshipman.

Thorne said in a whisper, 'Yes, sir. I'll do it now.'

Blake ducked his head as a great explosion smashed against the bridge, buckling steel plate and hurling broken glass and fittings amongst the crouching figures like missiles.

Two men were down, kicking out their life-blood, and Commodore Stagg was gripping his shoulder and staring at the spreading stain which ran down his side and on to the gratings at his feet.

Blake yelled, 'Starboard twenty!'

He strode past the bodies and a signalman who was dabbing his cheek with a bloodied flag.

'Midships! *Steady!*'

More steel hammered into the ship, and for an instant Blake imagined she was already going down. But *Andromeda* had dipped her stem deep into a breaking crest so that the sea surged aft along the forecastle before spilling over the sides as the bows began to rise again.

'*Shoot!*'

The four forward guns, their muzzles stained black from firing without a break, recoiled together, but through the distant bank of haze the raider continued to draw nearer, apparently unmarked.

The ragged clouds, impartial spectators to the savagery below, lit up suddenly to reflected tracer, neat lines of fiery balls, as the raider's short-range weapons opened up. A solitary star seemed to detach itself from the other bursts and fall slowly towards the sea. Just before it touched the water it exploded to leave a dirty smudge against the sky.

Blake watched the wind drive it away. Masters had got too close and had paid with his life.

Several of *Andromeda*'s company who were working on the exposed upper decks saw the Seafox fall like a comet. One of them was Ordinary Seaman Digby who, with a handful of assorted ratings, was rushing to hack some blazing canvas from a search-light mounting and throw it overboard before it spread to something more vital.

He paused, sobbing for breath, his mouth hanging open while he stared at the sea as it rushed below the guard-rail. Occasionally it would surge over the deck, sweeping broken fragments of boats and rafts away like litter, and once Digby saw a seaman he had spoken to several times being rolled bodily over the side. Before the next wave sluiced across the wet metal he saw the man's blood.

A petty officer bellowed, 'Over here, lads! Lively now, there's two blokes trapped under this lot!'

One seaman raised an axe, another took a firm grip on some twisted metal.

Digby saw it all like a still life or an old photograph. Then the shell burst somewhere below, probably on one of the mess-decks, and the world seemed to erupt in smoke and flying metal.

The seamen were hurled down and scattered like butchered meat, and the petty officer who had been calling to some men pinned beneath the collapsed flag deck dropped to his knees and remained there.

Digby vomited helplessly, stricken and unable to take his eyes from the horror. The petty officer, kneeling to listen for sounds of life, had no head.

A voice rasped through the smoke, ''Ere, lend a 'and, someone!'

It was Leading Seaman Musgrave. He was badly cut about the face and there was more blood shining beneath his life-jacket.

The sight of Musgrave seemed to give Digby a kind of strength, and wheezing like an old man he seized his arm and

241

began to drag him beneath the shelter of the trunked funnel.

Musgrave took his hand gratefully and asked, ''O's that then?'

He was moving his head from side to side, and it was then Digby realized he was blind.

'It's me, Hookey! Diggers!'

He could barely stop himself from weeping. At their frailty and their loneliness. Most of all at seeing the man he had come to admire so much cut down and so utterly dependent.

'Diggers?' Musgrave grimaced as the pain grew worse. 'Good lad. 'Ow bad is it?'

Men were shouting, and smoke billowed through a gaping hole by the boat tier as if the whole ship was ablaze.

Digby said, 'I'll get help. You'll be all right.'

Musgrave gripped his wrist, but was so weak that Digby could easily have prized his hand away.

The bearded leading seaman whispered, 'No, Diggers. You stay along of me. Just for a bit, eh? Feel dicky. Real rough.'

Digby sat down beside him, oblivious to the sprawled corpses of men he had scarcely known and conscious only of the one he now knew was dying.

'I'm here.'

Musgrave tried to touch his eyes and said, 'You'll make a good officer, Diggers. Just remember wot I said. . . .' His head lolled and he was dead.

Some sick-berth attendants, their steel helmets awry, the heavy red cross bouncing against them as they ran, paused and looked at the solitary, crouching seaman.

'You all right, mate?'

Digby stood up slowly. 'Yes, thank you.'

One SBA said, 'Right then. Up to the bridge. Chop, chop!'

Digby walked after them. He did not even duck as a splinter slammed through the funnel and ricocheted over his head.

He might be going mad, but he was no longer afraid. It was as if the strength of that coarse, violent seaman had somehow drained itself into him.

Blake felt someone tugging at his arm. It was Sub-Lieutenant Walker, his hat gone, and some tiny flecks of blood on his forehead. He was tying a crude dressing round Blake's arm.

'Might help, sir!'

Blake looked past him, seeing the smoke pouring from the ship's wounds. He had not even felt the blow on his arm.

242

Stagg was roaring like a bull, and Blake turned towards him, almost afraid of what he would see.

Stagg shouted, 'The bugger's turning away! He's going to fire a full broadside at us!'

Blake levelled his glasses, his teeth grating on the dust and chipped paint which seemed to fill the air.

There was the raider, angled away across the starboard bow, smoking from several hits now, but moving as firmly as before.

The sea was rising more and more, and the smoke seemed to mix with the blown spray as if trying to save the ships from mutual destruction.

But Blake could see the flashing guns, the rectangular openings in the raider's side where the massive shutters had been dropped.

Two more shells exploded off the port beam, and he guessed the German gunnery officer was preparing for a final straddle before he closed in to use his torpedoes.

It would not take much longer. *Andromeda* was barely answering the helm as with her pumps unable to cope against the racing screws she was listing more and more to starboard.

Blake looked at the angry sea and knew there would be few left who would be able to tell of their fight and their sacrifice.

Forward of the bridge, and sitting on his little steel seat at the rear of B turret, his eyes glued to the sights, Lieutenant Blair, who came from Queensland, studied the blurred target with something like despair.

He knew that forward of his turret the other two guns were silent, most of their crew killed by a direct hit. Down aft, X turret was still jammed solid, and Y was unable to train on the enemy.

Blair heard the hissing sounds of the shells being guided into the smoking breeches, the hoarse bark of orders and then the slamming click of the locking mechanism.

'Both guns loaded, sir!'

Blair adjusted his sights with elaborate care. The enemy was moving on a different angle now, but what was more interesting was that she was heeling over steeply whenever her stern lifted above the crested rollers.

Sweat ran down the side of his nose, and he tried not to flinch as the sea boiled to the impact of another big shell from the raider. He felt the little steel seat shiver but, like the rest of the fight, it was remote, sealed off by the inch-thick armour-plate. Only when it burst in on you did it have real meaning.

He watched the magnified picture of the raider's bridge, a tiny pale sliver as it rolled once again towards him.

'Sights moving! Sights *set*!' He held his breath. *'Shoot!'*

Blake had been knocked aside as a seaman fell from a voice-pipe clutching at his chest and screwing his uniform into a bright red ball. As he lurched to his feet he saw a single explosion directly on top of the enemy's bridge.

It was a brief orange flash, and then as the armour-piercing shell plunged down through the decks, aided by the *Salamander*'s steep turn, it exploded against one of the magazines.

Two more vivid flashes cut through the drifting spray, and then as some of *Andromeda*'s men jumped up from behind their gun-shields the sky seemed to dim to one tremendous explosion.

Stagg shouted hoarsely, 'What's *that*, for Christ's sake?'

He was streaming blood, and had twice punched a sick-berth attendant who had tried to fix a dressing.

Blake stared, mesmerized, at the pale line beyond the ship which was reeling to more internal destruction which must be leaping from point to point like one giant fuse.

The line was a bank of rollers, built up into a single, massive force over hundreds of miles of ocean with nothing in its path but the stricken raider.

Blake shouted, 'The fringe of the storm!' He tore his eyes from the oncoming mass and shouted down the voice-pipe, 'Slow ahead together! Wheel amidships!'

He swung round, trying to keep his mind from the fact that he had destroyed Rietz and his ship and deal with the safety of his own.

'Pilot, have it piped round the ship!'

He stared at Villar's body below the compass platform, the small red stain just below his heart.

Lieutenant Trevett said, 'I've taken the con, sir.' He glanced at the dead South African. 'Reckon I had a good teacher.'

Blake nodded. 'Warn all hands.'

The unending bank of water seemed to roll against the *Salamander*'s side without any sort of urgency. As if it was almost spent.

Then, as the ship began to turn turtle, the pressure mounted against her bilge keel, thrusting her over and down, and making a lie of the deceptive slowness.

One final explosion blasted the *Salamander*'s hull wide open, and as the sea surged over her shattered plates the side of the wave was lit up from within so that it looked like a solid sheet of bloody glass.

Blake heard the raider breaking up, machinery tearing loose to add to the destruction within the hull. Exploding ammunition and fuel and, as she took the last plunge, the booming roar of her boilers. Then nothing.

Perhaps the fringe of the storm had really spent its fury, or maybe it had done enough even for the ocean's greed. But as it reached the *Andromeda*'s stem and lifted her effortlessly towards the smoky sunlight it was already passing astern before anyone could really accept that it was over.

Sub-Lieutenant Walker had a telephone in his hand and said huskily, 'It's the Chief, sir.'

Blake took it but kept his eyes on his ship, the men around him and the tattered flag which had remained overhead throughout both actions.

Weir sounded tired. 'Thought you should know. I can give you more revs now.' He gave what might have been a chuckle. 'The old girl was playing me up, nothing worse.'

'Thank you, Chief.'

Blake handed the telephone to Walker and rejoined Stagg by the broken screen.

'Fall out action stations. Post extra lookouts in case there are any survivors in the water.'

Stagg was staring at the sea where his old enemy had been just moments earlier.

He said dully, 'I thought it would mean something.' He sighed and allowed the Toby Jug to fold a shell-dressing over his torn shoulder. 'But Rietz was nothing special after all. Just a man.' He looked at Blake. 'Like the rest of us.'

He pulled a silver flask from his hip pocket and took a long swallow. Then he wiped it on his sleeve and passed it to Blake.

Blake drank without knowing if it was brandy or champagne. A lot of good men had died, and much had to be done for the ship before they reached safety again.

But he needed this moment. Just for himself. To accept he had survived one more time.

Stagg eyed him thoughtfully. 'After this I'll be needing an assistant in Melbourne. How would it suit you?' He grinned suddenly. 'I can see it would!'

Blake thought of what he would say when he saw Claire again. What words he could use to tell her how much he needed her.

Stagg watched Moon's doleful features as he crept nervously on to the bridge with a flask and some sandwiches.

'Of course, the new commanding officer will take over from you soon, so that's no real problem.'

'You already know who it will be, sir?'

Stagg picked up a sandwich. It looked like a postage stamp in his great fist.

'Fairfax, of course. If he's still in one piece, that is.'

Blake stared at him. 'I thought you said. . . .'

Stagg grunted. 'Never mind what I said. It doesn't do to tell people too much, y'know.' He seemed uncomfortable in his new role. 'You'd better make a signal. Tell the people in Melbourne that we did it.' He gave a quick grin. 'Together, eh?'

The Toby Jug had his pencil poised. 'I'll tell W/T, sir.'

Blake looked at Villar's face, screwed up at the moment of impact. He thought of the others he could not see, the disdainful Scovell, a frightened youth named Thorne, the ordinary seaman who was bringing more bandages to the bridge, Digby.

Andromeda had been made to leave so many behind over the months and years of combat.

And now I am leaving her.

Blake thought of Fairfax and was suddenly glad for him, and for the ship.

He said quietly, 'Make this signal to the Navy Office, repeated Admiralty. *Two German raiders destroyed. With help from on high, HMS* Andromeda *is returning to harbour.*'

Quintin would see that and show it to Claire. She would know that he was safe.

There were no survivors from the German raiders, and with her own wounded to be considered, *Andromeda* turned slowly and headed towards the eastern horizon. Once again she had the ocean to herself.